SWEET MEMORIES OF YOU

It's 1943 and Peggy Reilly is at her best when the troubles of war come knocking at the door of Beach View Boarding House – especially when it concerns her younger sister, Doreen. Doreen is divorced from Eddie, but his letters have taken on a more threatening tone of late. When Doreen barely survives a traumatic disaster whilst on leave in London, she returns home to Peggy and Cliffehaven in the hope that the love and comfort she will find there can help her recover. However, Eddie continues to be an unsettling reminder of her past – and Doreen's life is about to change dramatically.

SWEET MEMORIES OF YOU

SWEET MEMORIES OF YOU

by

Ellie Dean

Magna Large Print Books
Long Preston, North Yorkshire,
BD23 4ND, England.

British Library Cataloguing in Publication Data.

Dean, Ellie
  Sweet memories of you.

  A catalogue record of this book is
  available from the British Library

  ISBN   978-0-7505-4339-2

First published in Great Britain by Arrow Books in 2016

Copyright © Ellie Dean 2016

Cover illustration © Jill Hyland/Arcangel by arrangement with
Arcangel Images Ltd.

Published in Large Print 2016 by arrangement with
Random House Group Limited

Magna Large Print is an imprint of Library Magna Books Ltd.

Printed and bound in Great Britain by
T.J. (International) Ltd., Cornwall, PL28 8RW

SWEET MEMORIES OF YOU is dedicated to the East End and the marvellous people who fought the war in their own inimitable way, and in particular to those who lost their lives on 3rd March, 1943.

Acknowledgements

I would like to thank Jenny Geras and Francesca Pathak, and also my agent Teresa Chris for her support and encouragement.

Thanks also go to the many people I've spoken to who have lived through the war and been so generous with their personal memories to help me really get the sense of place and time. The stoicism, and the almost off-hand acceptance that sleeves had to be rolled up, privations had to be borne and that bravery had very little to do with it all, is quite humbling. I salute all of you – especially Joyce Florence Williams. You were an absolute delight to talk to, and I promise that your story will be told during this series.

Prologue

London, February 1943

Doreen Grey felt a flutter of excitement as she adjusted her little felt hat, gathered up her overnight bag and gas-mask box and left the train she'd boarded at Knockholt station that morning. She knew some might think it ridiculous for a woman of her age to feel like this – after all, she was thirty-five, the divorced mother of two little girls, and held a position of great trust in the MOD. Yet here she was, as giddy and smitten as a schoolgirl, dressed up to the nines in her best slacks, sweater and overcoat, unable to contain herself at the thrill of seeing Archie again.

She could only imagine what her snooty sister Doris would have to say about such things – yet she didn't really care. Life was for living, and it was important to live it to the full, for no one knew what tomorrow might bring.

As she sat on the bus that would take her to the London docks, she caught sight of her reflection in the grimy window and was quite taken aback at how love and excitement had enhanced her appearance. Her freshly washed dark wavy hair shone beneath the rather fetching hat, her brown eyes were bright, and her clear skin radiated with her happiness. Archie was coming home for a whole week's leave while his ship was being

11

refitted for its next trip with the convoy across the Atlantic, and they had made so many plans to fill each and every moment together that she could only pray nothing would happen to spoil it.

She felt the blush rise in her cheeks at the thought of being with him in that small hotel room she'd booked, and the intimacy they would share once they were truly alone. It had been too long since his last leave – too many nights when she'd lain awake, terrified that he might be killed or injured during those perilous weeks at sea – and over the three years since they'd met there had been only brief encounters when he was ashore. In between, she'd had only his letters and sweet memories to sustain her.

She drew his latest letter from her handbag and looked fondly at the photograph he'd enclosed with it. Archie Blake was the Chief Engineer on a destroyer which escorted the convoys of merchant ships back and forth between England and America. He was a great bear of a man who'd escaped the poverty of the East End at fifteen through a naval apprenticeship and a career at sea. With thick black hair and beard and dark blue eyes, he was blessed with the sort of unrestrained laughter and joy in life that she found irresistible.

Doreen couldn't help but smile as she remembered how he towered beside her as they walked along; his seaman's kitbag slung over one broad shoulder, his gait as rolling as the ocean. And how the other girls would shoot him the glad eye, for he was an imposing figure in his naval uniform. Yet for all his size he was a gentle man – an unselfish and skilled lover who wrote beautiful letters and could hold her close with such tenderness it made her misty-eyed.

Doreen blinked rapidly and hastily stowed the letter and snapshot carefully back in her handbag. The bus had turned the last corner, and she could see the funnels and anti-aircraft guns of his ship above the roofs of the many warehouses lining the docks. She shot the clippie a grin as she waited for the bus to stop, unable to contain her excitement.

'Lucky old you,' the girl said with a knowing wink. 'You be sure to give 'im a kiss from me. All the girls love a sailor, eh?'

'They certainly do,' she replied before jumping down.

She walked quickly past the high fence that was topped with great thick rolls of barbed wire towards the heavily barricaded entrance gate where two armed marines stood guard. Pulling her identification papers and MOD pass from her coat pocket, she had to wait impatiently while they were checked minutely before she was free to enter the dockyards.

There was hustle and bustle everywhere, with stevedores loading and unloading the enormous grey ships, cranes lifting vast crates into holds, sailors and marines running to and fro on important missions, and warehousemen shouting orders to porters and the young boys who were employed as runners. Tugs chugged busily through the choppy waters as gulls screeched and mewled overhead amongst the barrage balloons, and barges laden with wood and coal slowly made

13

their majestic way, the great dray horses patiently plodding along the towpaths.

Doreen walked confidently through the melee. She was used to being outnumbered by men, for she was one of only a handful of women who worked amongst the boffins and engineers at Fort Halstead Projectile Development Establishment. She was private secretary to one of the scientists who, alongside the brilliant Barnes Wallis, was testing ground-breaking weapons to defeat the enemy. Her work was exciting and fulfilling, but now her thoughts were only for Archie.

'Doreen!'

She turned at the sound of his booming voice, her smile broad, her heart giving a little extra beat of pleasure at the sight of him. She dropped her holdall and ran towards him as he opened his arms – and within moments was engulfed in his embrace and lifted off her feet.

There were no words to say; their joyful, loving kiss was enough. Together at last, they could forget the war, their work and everything else and just be themselves.

1

Cliffehaven

Beach View Boarding House stood in one of the many lines of terraced Victorian houses which climbed the hill away from the Cliffehaven sea-front. The only view of the sea it afforded was from one of the top-floor windows, but that hadn't deterred the many holidaymakers who'd come to stay before the war. It had been Peggy Dawson's childhood home, and after her marriage to Jim Reilly, they'd returned to take over from her parents on their retirement and raise their children there.

It was still dark outside and Peggy Reilly lay in bed and wondered how her sister Doreen was getting on in London with her Archie. Their week together was coming to an end and soon he'd be back at sea. She didn't blame Doreen in the least for spending intimate time with him. After all, she was divorced and he was single. At times like this, it was little wonder that people disregarded the strict codes that had once stifled their natural instincts, for life was uncertain, and it was important to snatch every moment of happiness.

Peggy nestled deeper into the bedclothes as the rain splattered against the taped glass in the window and the wind howled up from the Channel to buffet the walls and rattle the loose drainpipe. This old house had seen many changes over the years. Once war had been declared and the holiday trade dwindled to nothing, Peggy had gone to the billeting office to offer a home from home for girls who, for one reason or another, needed shelter. Their arrival brought youthful life back into the echoing rooms left empty by her older children, and although there were only four girls lodging with her at the moment and Jim had been called up, Peggy still had her baby Daisy, the elderly and rather deaf Cordelia Finch, and her father-in-law, Ron, to look after.

The once rather sleepy little seaside town of Cliffehaven had also seen many changes during the past four years, for the chalk cliffs that sheltered the horseshoe bay now resounded with the roar of Spitfires, Wellingtons and Lancaster bombers taking off and landing at Cliffe aerodrome. The heavily forested Cliffe estate rang with the sounds of saws and axes as the women of the Timber Corps chopped down trees to provide railway sleepers, heavy beams to prop up mine shafts, and timber for emergency housing. The girls of the Land Army worked in the fields, sowing and harvesting much-needed crops to feed everyone now that the Atlantic convoys were constantly under attack, and the gracious old manor house was home to a regiment of American soldiers.

Beneath the towering chalk cliff at the eastern side of the bay, and stretching all the way to the rolling hills that tumbled towards the sea at the west, the promenade was heavily fortified with huge coils of barbed wire and several gun emplacements. The shingle beach had been mined, and vast concrete shipping traps were strung across the bay to deter enemy landings. The pier which had provided entertainment only a few years before was now cut adrift from the promenade, its blackened, rusting skeleton embedded with the remains of a German fighter plane. The elegant Victorian shelters bore the scars of bullets, and the line of rather grand hotels and guest houses that lined the promenade had been shattered by bombs to leave ugly, rubble-filled gaps that were already sprouting weeds and thistles.

The town itself bore little resemblance to how it once had been, for the cinema had fallen victim to a direct hit, the recreation ground was dug over to provide not only a vast public shelter but a vegetable allotment, and every iron railing had been removed to provide the metal needed to build planes. The large area of tenement housing behind the station had been wiped out by a firebomb attack at the beginning of the war – the station itself had lost its waiting room and ticket office – and where there had once been only a scattering of small industrial units to the north of the town there was now a vast complex of factories situated behind a heavily guarded wire fence in the shadows of huge barrage balloons.

And yet amidst all this devastation and change, Peggy was aware of the continuing sense of close community amongst the residents of Cliffehaven. The knowledge that they were fighting a common enemy on the home front while their men were away and their children had mostly been evacuated, meant they embraced the Allied troops, farm girls and factory workers who poured into town to drink at the pubs and attend the dances laid on in the church halls, rolled up their sleeves and got on with digging for victory, making do and mending, and providing endless tea and sympathy as well as practical help to those who needed it.

Beach View Boarding House might not be alone in providing shelter from the storms of war, but Peggy knew that few offered the same care and homely warmth that she was determined to give to her evacuees and lodgers. There had been terrible stories of neglect and abuse over the years, and it was a matter of pride to Peggy that her girls would always be regarded as family. After all, she reasoned, it was what she expected for her own children who were now far from home.

Girls had come and gone over the past four years, and following the departure of Suzy after her marriage to Anthony, there were spare beds to be had at Beach View which she should really address once she'd got through today and had more time to think clearly.

Peggy snuggled under the blankets as Daisy snuffled in her cot at the foot of the bed. Her smile was soft with affection as she turned her thoughts to the girls now sleeping under her roof. Fran had come to live here at the start of the war and was a theatre nurse at Cliffehaven General. With auburn curls and green eyes, she was blessed with an impish sense of humour as well as a mercurial temper, a touch of the Irish blarney, and a talent for playing the violin.

Tomboy Rita had come to Peggy's after her home had been firebombed, and was now an active member of the local firefighting team, and the driving force behind raising funds to build Cliffehaven's own Spitfire. And then there were Sarah and her younger sister Jane, who'd escaped from Singapore only hours before its fall to the Japanese, and had come to Cliffehaven in search of their great-aunt Cordelia Finch who had been boarding with Peggy for some years. Their mother and baby brother were safe in Australia, but agonisingly, there was still no news of their father or Sarah's fiancée, whom they'd last seen standing on the quayside in Singapore harbour.

Cordelia Finch was aptly named, for she was small and delicate and often twittered like a ruffled bird when she got overexcited. Her age was a closely guarded secret, but Peggy suspected she was approaching eighty. Cordelia was adored by all. The influx of young girls seemed to enliven her spirits, and she often had to be helped home after one too many glasses of sherry at the Anchor.

And then there was Ron. Peggy grinned into the pillow as she thought about her father-in-law. He was an old Irish scallywag who followed his own path through life without so much as a nod to convention, but with a great deal of charm and bluster. Yet Peggy knew that beneath those scruffy clothes beat the stout heart of a man who would defend his loved ones to his last breath. His dog, Harvey, was just as wilful and scruffy, and although he slept on Ron's bed, stole food from the table and generally made a nuisance of himself, he too had proved to be brave and faithful.

As Daisy shifted restlessly in her cot, Peggy tensed, waiting for her to cry out, but she quickly

19

settled again so Peggy relaxed. Daisy was fifteen months old now and teething; consequently the night had been a disturbed one, what with her crying and the RAF flying overhead and making enough noise to waken the dead. At least they'd been spared an enemy raid – the awful weather had seen to that – but the broken sleep had not been at all refreshing, and Peggy was feeling tired.

The sound of the rain and the wind began to seem oppressive as her thoughts turned to the rest of her family. They were scattered, and it might be years before they could all be together once more. It was an ongoing battle, fought every day along with rationing, restrictions, endless queues at the shops, and air raids. The sheer slog of making ends meet and keeping a smile on her face to hide her heartache was beginning to take its toll.

Anne, her eldest, was in Somerset on a friend's farm with her two small children and younger brothers, Bob and Charlie, while her husband Martin was flying with the RAF, and Peggy had yet to meet her new granddaughter, Emily. Cissy was in the WAAF, driving some bigwig about up at Cliffe aerodrome; her sister Doreen hadn't visited for years as she was heavily involved with the MOD and therefore rarely in one place for longer than a few weeks. She too must be suffering, thought Peggy sadly, for her two little girls Evelyn and Joyce were billeted down in Wales, and she hadn't seen them since the start of the war.

And then there was her own Jim, who was in India of all places!

At the thought of Jim being on the other side of

the world, Peggy sniffed back her tears and decided she couldn't lie here any longer feeling sorry for herself. Cordelia was suffering with a cold as well as her arthritis, and Ron had come in very late the worse for wear after a night out with his friends at the Fishermen's Club. She tossed back the blankets and sheet and slid out of bed to be greeted by the bitter draught coming from beneath the bedroom door and through the badly fitting windows that both Jim and Ron had made a hash of fixing over a year before.

With a sigh of stoic acceptance, she dug her feet into her slippers and pulled on Jim's thick, warm dressing gown. The day ahead promised to be yet another struggle, for Ron had to be made to look halfway decent before she got him to the Town Hall in time for the ceremony, and he'd made it abundantly clear that he wasn't going to co-operate. Judging by the racket he'd made last night, he'd be hung-over as well as grumpy – not that this would be unusual, he'd been grumpy ever since it was revealed that he'd been put forward for a bravery award. Most men would have been delighted, but not Ron, who saw the whole thing as nothing more than an opportunity for the Mayor to show off and therefore a waste of everyone's time.

She ran her fingers through her dark curls and scrubbed her face with her hands in an attempt to wipe away the weariness and instil a bit of enthusiasm for the day ahead. Doris, her older sister, had made it perfectly plain that she would hold Peggy responsible if Ron put a foot wrong at the Town Hall ceremony, and Peggy knew there

21

was every possibility that chaos would reign if she didn't take immediate charge of the situation.

Peggy tiptoed up the stairs to the bathroom. Beach View was still quiet at this early hour, although she'd heard Jane leave for the dairy about half an hour ago, and the other girls would soon be stirring. She smiled as she washed and dressed. Jane was turning into a real beauty, and now she'd just celebrated her nineteenth birthday, it seemed she'd grown in confidence and was as bright and lively as other girls her age.

Yet Peggy knew that Sarah had worried about her young sister ever since they'd arrived from Singapore, for Jane had been childlike and perhaps even a little backward then – the result of a nasty kick in the head from a horse – yet life here in Cliffehaven had given her the chance to blossom and mature. However, Peggy had the feeling Jane was becoming restless, that she was finding the work at the dairy a little tedious despite her love for the old shire horses she tended, and now Peggy wondered what was bothering her.

As she finished dressing and hurried back downstairs she fretted that perhaps Jane had become entangled with some young man – after all, there were enough servicemen in the town to turn any girl's head, and Jane was pretty enough to catch their all-too-roving eyes. She would have to have a quiet word with her when she returned, she decided. For now, she had to bath and dress Daisy, sort out breakfast and deal with Ron.

Ivy Tucker was thoroughly fed up, for it was her only day off from the munitions factory and

Doris had got her doing the housework in preparation for the arrival of her new lodger.

She was cross with herself for not standing up to the old cow, but now that Mary, her fellow evacuee and friend, had gone home to Sussex, she'd lost her nerve to answer back. She didn't usually have any problem with speaking her mind, but Doris Williams was a formidable woman, forever making her feel small and insignificant, and threatening to turf her out if she didn't toe the line – and Ivy knew she wouldn't find such a comfortable billet as this one if that happened.

She continued scrubbing the gas oven with some vigour, wanting to get the filthy job done so she could get out of here. Assessing that it was as clean as she could get it, she used scrunched-up newspaper to clear away the last of the grime and then wiped it all down with a damp cloth and fresh paper. Giving the oven door a good polish, she slammed it shut and threw the dirty paper in the waste bin. There was just the floor to mop now and then she could escape.

As she fetched the mop and bucket from the lean-to that served as a laundry room, she began to sing quietly to herself, calmer now that her work was almost over. As she filled the bucket and started to mop the linoleum, her thoughts drifted back to Hackney and the two small tenement rooms that had been her home for almost eighteen years. They might not have been the nicest place to live, and it had been a squash, what with her sharing a room with her three brothers and sister. Yet, despite the daily struggle to make ends meet, they'd been a tight-knit

23

family before the war had intervened and they'd been forced to go their separate ways.

Ivy had been in Cliffehaven for almost nine months now, and although the work at the munitions factory was dirty and dangerous, it paid extremely well. Her three brothers were ratings on the Atlantic convoys, and her sister was a typist working at Admiralty House. Her dad worked for the gas board, so he hadn't been called up, and her mum spent hours on her feet at the canning factory.

Their tenement block had been destroyed during an air raid in early 1942, and now her parents lived in one room above the Wellington Arms in Shoreditch. No doubt her dad was thrilled to bits to be living over a boozer – it had always been his dream – but her mum would have to keep a close eye on their money, for when he'd had a few too many, he'd insist upon buying rounds for his mates.

Ivy rinsed out the mop and regarded her handiwork. The floor was spotless now, but it would take time to dry, so she opened the back door and stepped outside to have a fag. It was cold but bright, the air smelling of the sea instead of the smoke and smog of those London streets, and Ivy sat on the doorstep, enjoying this brief moment of peace.

'This floor is still wet,' snapped Doris from the hall.

'That's why I've got the door open – to get it dry.'

'It's causing a draught, and all my lovely heating is being wasted. Close it immediately and run that drying towel over the floor.'

Ivy bit down on the sharp retort, took a last puff of her cigarette and pinched off the end before putting it into her cardigan's sagging pocket. She rummaged about in the laundry room for the old worn towel and had just got onto her hands and knees to dry the floor when the doorbell went.

'That'll be the new girl,' said Doris as she patted her immaculate hair and rushed off.

Ivy continued drying the floor, her hopes rising that this latest lodger would be as nice and friendly as Mary had been. She edged across the floor on her knees, ears pricked to try and catch what was being said in the hallway, but their murmur was indecipherable.

She'd almost reached the door into the hall when two pairs of neatly shod feet and slender legs appeared in front of her. Looking up, her spirits plummeted, for the new girl was about her age, but she was fair and elegant with a snooty look on her face. Her clothes were clearly of the best quality; her nails were long and manicured and she was as immaculately groomed and made-up as Doris.

'Caroline,' said Doris, 'this is Ivy Tucker.'

Feeling very much at a disadvantage, Ivy scrambled to her feet, hitched the strap of her dungarees back over her shoulder, and stuck out her hand. 'Pleased to meet yer, I'm sure,' she gabbled.

The blue eyes regarded her grubby hand coolly before ignoring it. 'Caroline Palmer-French,' she said in the plummy tones of someone who had probably never ventured far from the borders of

Kensington until today.

Ivy returned her cool gaze, decided she didn't like the look of her at all, and realised the feeling was mutual.

'Caroline will be the hospital administrator's private secretary,' said Doris gleefully, like a proud and pushy parent. She turned to Caroline. 'Ivy works at the munitions factory. It's a worthy post, but not one that requires much education, so she's well suited.'

Ivy fumed at this blatant piece of downright rudeness. 'I can read and write as good as anyone,' she snapped. She looked Caroline up and down. 'And the job I do keeps our boys in ammo to fight off Jerry – which is a damned sight more important than typing letters for some pompous prat in an office.'

'That is *quite* enough,' rasped Doris. 'I do apologise, Caroline. But these are difficult times and one cannot choose the sort of girl one has to billet.'

Caroline smirked. 'I do so admire you, Mrs Williams. It must indeed be frightfully inconvenient.'

'Please, you must call me Doris,' she simpered.

Ivy had had enough of this, so she threw the towel in the direction of the bucket and swiped away her bedraggled hair from her sweaty face. 'I'm off,' she said.

'Not until you've made us some coffee,' said Doris. 'I'm sure Caroline must be very thirsty after that long and tiring journey.'

Ivy looked at the pair of them, knowing there was trouble ahead. She couldn't help herself. 'Why, where did she come from, the moon?'

Caroline gave a tinkling laugh which set Ivy's teeth on edge. 'Chelsea, actually. And yes, I'd love a cup of coffee – but only if it's not that ghastly stuff out of a bottle.'

'We only have the best coffee in this house,' said Doris. 'Do come into the drawing room, Caroline. We can be more private in there.' She shot a glare at Ivy over her shoulder. 'You know where the percolator is, Ivy. And do be quick about it. I'm sure Caroline would like to unpack and get settled before she has to report in to her office.'

'She ain't sharing with me,' Ivy said quickly.

Doris and Caroline turned and looked at her with the same wide-eyed amazement. 'Well, of course she isn't,' said Doris. 'I wouldn't *dream* of asking her to do such a thing.'

As they went into the large drawing room which had magnificent views of the coastline, Ivy turned on her heel, grabbed her coat and gas-mask box from the lean-to and slammed the back door behind her. They could stick their coffee right up their posh jumpers.

The bright sunlight on the sea and the sight of the lovely white cliffs usually lifted her spirits, but there were tears of fury in her eyes as she walked along the promenade. Doris was a cow and that Caroline had all the makings of someone who thought she was better than most, and would no doubt be as snotty and horrible as Doris.

She blinked away the tears, irritated that she'd let the pair of them get to her. If only Mary was still here – at least then she wouldn't feel quite so isolated. But there was no point in wishing for the impossible; Mary was back home in Sussex, and although she'd written regularly, Ivy suspected she wouldn't see her again.

She plumped herself down on the bullet-scarred bench and watched the gulls swooping and hovering above the burnt-out wreckage of the enemy plane that was stuck fast in the remains of the pier. There was a glimmer of a chance that she could escape the house in Havelock Road, for Peggy Reilly had often said there was room for her and Mary at her place. But with Mary gone, would that offer still hold?

Mary was the sort of girl everyone took to, for she spoke nicely and was a vicar's daughter. But Ivy knew that these posh people down south were wary of a girl from the East End. They didn't understand her ways, or half of what she said for a start – and of course she was always getting into trouble by not keeping her mouth shut.

Ivy sighed. Peggy Reilly was lovely, but she lived in an even bigger house than Doris, with an indoor bathroom as well as a really swanky outside lav – and Fran, Jane, Sarah and little old Cordelia were ever so high-class. Rita was all right – liked a good laugh and a chat, and reminded her of some of her mates back in Hackney – but Ivy worried that Peggy might be already regretting her invitation and rather hoping Ivy had forgotten all about it.

'It looks like yer on yer own, gel,' she muttered as she headed for the café in Camden Road. 'Better make the best of it, I suppose.'

2

London

Still drowsy from the night's sleep, Doreen nestled against Archie's broad back as the rain hammered against the hotel window. The sound enhanced the feeling of intimacy and warmth, and as she rested her hand lightly on his chest, she could feel it rise and fall with each deep breath. These quiet moments were something to treasure, for the time they'd spent apart had made her realise just how much she loved him. She'd missed his masculinity, the feel of him lying next to her – the touch of his hands, his smell, his smile and the shared glances that spoke far more than any words could do. With Archie, she felt complete.

Doreen softly rested her cheek against his shoulder, breathing in the scent of his warm skin. It had never been like this with Eddie, not even in the early years of their marriage, for he'd never made her feel truly cherished, and had been a selfish lover.

At the thought of her ex-husband, she drew back from Archie and closed her eyes. She'd made sure Eddie had no idea of where she was billeted, but his letters had been forwarded on from her previous place, and she'd reluctantly replied to them without giving a hint as to where she was or what she was doing. At first, his letters had been harmless enough – usually full of self-pity and the struggles he was having to make a new life for himself and find work. But just lately they'd taken on a different tone which made her feel decidedly uneasy, and she'd consigned them to the fire and not replied to them.

Doreen moved restlessly against the pillows. His threats had been guarded, but the underlying message was that his visits to their daughters in Wales had proved far too expensive, and if she possessed a shred of decency she should send him some money on a regular basis so that their girls wouldn't feel totally abandoned by both parents. It was emotional blackmail – a talent that Eddie had perfected over the years, and as time had gone on, and the demands had become more in-sistent, she'd felt herself begin to weaken.

The guilt overwhelmed her, for she hadn't had the chance to see Evie and Joyce since they'd been evacuated from London, and she should be with them now, not lying in a London hotel bed with Archie. She tried to relax, to accept that a week simply wouldn't have been enough time to go all that way, but the guilt persisted. As for Eddie, it was all very well him going on about not finding work – of course there was plenty to be had if only he wanted it, but enlistment or a post in a factory was not something a man like him would even consider. Eddie preferred to spend his time gambling and womanising. As for send-ing him money...

'Dor? What's the matter?' Archie rolled over in the bed and reached for her.

'Nothing,' she said quickly.

'You can't fool me, gel,' he said softly. 'What is it?'

'I was just thinking about Evie and Joyce,' she replied. 'It's been so long since I've seen them.'

He stroked the hair back from her face and kissed her forehead. 'I've been selfish, wanting you to myself for this week,' he murmured. 'But on my next leave, we'll go straight down there.'

'That would be lovely,' she said on a sigh.

He reached across her and turned on the bedside light. His dark blue eyes regarded her thoughtfully. 'There's nothing else bothering you, is there? Eddie hasn't been causing trouble?'

She shook her head and determinedly pushed aside her worries over Eddie's letters. 'Absolutely nothing,' she assured him.

He smiled back at her as he drew her into his arms. 'In that case...'

Cliffehaven

Peggy had decided to leave Ron to snore a little longer while she got on with things, for that way, he wouldn't get under her feet. It seemed that Harvey, his large brindled lurcher, was similarly inclined to have a lie-in, for there had been no sign of him either.

The rain hadn't let up, but the wind seemed to have died down as the tide went out, and Peggy could only hope that the weather would clear in time for their walk to the Town Hall later in the morning. Having donned her wrap-round pinafore and tied a scarf over her freshly washed hair,

31

she riddled the fire to a blaze in the Kitchener range and heated up the porridge. Then she washed and fed a grizzling Daisy, who was in no mood to be coaxed into anything this morning, and put her in the playpen with her toys so she could get on with things.

Ron's only decent suit had been sponged and pressed last night and his shirt collar starched, and they were hanging on the back of the kitchen door. His shoes had been polished, but the matter of finding a clean tie was something she'd have to sort out later – just as she would have to deal with Ron's abhorrence to wearing one.

Peggy stirred the porridge with little enthusiasm as her thoughts skittered over all the things she had to do. Her larder was fairly well stocked with the jams and pickles she'd made the previous year, and Ron's garden at the back of the house provided her with fresh vegetables, but the cold weather seemed to have affected the chickens, for they weren't laying as well, and there wasn't an ounce of meat in the house. It would have to be vegetable stew again tonight, she thought wearily. There simply wasn't time to stand in an endless queue for the few scraps of scrag-end that Alf the butcher was able to sell her.

She glanced up at the clock on the mantelpiece, shifted the porridge off the hotplate and was about to go up to check on Cordelia and wake the girls when Sarah came into the kitchen, dressed and ready for her day's work in the office at Cliffe estate for the Women's Timber Corps.

Despite the rather mannish jodhpurs, stout shoes and unflattering green sweater, Sarah's elegant, fair beauty was not diminished. At just twenty-one, her blue eyes were bright, her figure slender, and her skin was fresh with dewy youth, making Peggy feel rather old and dowdy by contrast.

'Good morning, Aunt Peg,' she said as she grimaced at the rain slanting across the back garden. 'Not that it looks very inviting out there. I hope Jane remembered to wrap up properly. She'll get soaked through on her milk round.'

Peggy ladled the thin porridge into a bowl and set it on the table. 'Jane's sensible enough to dress properly, but I don't like the thought of you making that long walk across the hills in such dreadful weather,' she said. 'It's a great pity your Captain Hammond can't organise a lift for you through the winter months.'

Sarah dipped her chin, but couldn't hide the blush that coloured her cheeks. 'He's not *my* Captain Hammond, Auntie Peg, and it's not his responsibility to organise lifts for me. Besides, he has other more pressing things to concern him at the moment.'

Peggy had always been suspicious about Sarah's so-called friendship with the very handsome Texan, but as the girl had always strenuously denied any intimate attachment, she had to accept that Sarah was still in love with her fiancé, Philip, who she'd had to leave behind in Singapore. There was a complete blackout of any news coming from there since it had fallen to the Japanese, but Sarah seemed determined to remain hopeful that they would be together, again once this blasted war was over.

Peggy sat down and poured out the tea as Sarah ate her porridge. Due to the shortages, and the fact the leaves had been used at least three times, the tea was the colour of dishwater, but it was wet and warm and very welcome on this gloomy day. 'I don't see how Hammond can have anything pressing to worry about,' she said with a touch of asperity. 'After all, he and his men have been lounging about on the Cliffe estate doing nothing useful for months.'

'Oh, Auntie Peg, that's not fair. Troops come and go all the time, and he's in charge of their training, so of course he has to stay.' Sarah sipped some tea and the cup rattled in the saucer as she set it down.

'Anyway,' she said quietly, 'you can stop worrying about him and me. He's leaving tomorrow with his latest batch of GIs.'

Peggy eyed her sharply, for she'd heard the tremor in the girl's voice and noticed how she'd paled. 'Where's he going?'

Sarah shrugged and mindlessly stirred her spoon round and round in the remains of her porridge. 'I couldn't tell you even if I knew,' she murmured. 'But it won't be in England, that's for sure.'

Peggy reached for her hand and stilled the endless stirring of that spoon. 'You're going to really miss him, aren't you?' she said softly.

Sarah nodded, her eyes suspiciously bright as she refused to look at Peggy. 'Of course I will. He's been a good friend.'

Peggy squeezed her fingers in sympathy as all her suspicions clamoured and a teardrop escaped from Sarah's eyes to glisten on her lashes. 'He'll be all right, love, you'll see. And you can still be pen pals.'

The teardrop fell to be replaced by another. 'Maybe,' she murmured. 'But it won't be the same.'

'You're in love with him, aren't you?' The words were out before she could stop them, and she felt a pang of guilt for the distress in the girl's face.

Sarah took a deep breath, dashed away the tears and sat in silence, either unwilling or unable to answer her.

'It's hardly surprising,' Peggy continued softly. 'He's an attractive man, with winning ways. No one would blame you for falling for him.'

Sarah's fists clenched. 'But I blame myself,' she hissed. 'I knew how dangerous it was to encourage his friendship – and how vulnerable I am with Philip so far away and out of reach. I'm supposed to be engaged to him, Peggy, but here I am, shedding tears over a married man that I have no right to love.'

She buried her face in her hands. 'There,' she sobbed. 'I've finally admitted it, so you can congratulate yourself on being so damned clever.'

Peggy knew the girl was overwrought and so took no offence at her outburst, but moved to take her in her arms. 'Oh, Sarah, I can only imagine the sort of torment you must be going through, and I'm certainly not congratulating myself over the dilemma you've found yourself facing. But this will pass, believe me.'

Sarah lifted reddened eyes. 'But I feel so ashamed, Auntie Peg. Philip's more than likely in the hands of the Japanese, and probably clinging to the belief that I'll remain faithful and be waiting for him when the war is over. And yet I've let both of us down by–'

'You've let no one down,' Peggy interrupted hastily. 'And I won't have you berating yourself over it. This blessed war has everyone's emotions in turmoil. Not knowing if today is to be our last encourages people to do things they would never have dreamt of in peacetime. And you're far from home, separated from all those you hold dearest, of course you feel lonely and in need of love.'

Peggy paused, unsure whether to say more, and then decided it was time to get it all out in the open. 'Have you and he ... you know ... been...?'

Sarah gasped and her eyes widened in shock.

'Of course not. How could you think such a thing, Aunt Peg?'

Peggy was unfazed, her own experience with Jim during the last war lending her intimate knowledge of how easy it was to throw caution and sanity to the wind and be swept away in the turmoil of overwhelming emotions – just as Doreen was experiencing now with her Archie. 'It would only be natural when two people are in love during these uncertain times.'

'Well, we haven't,' Sarah retorted. 'In fact I've made sure he doesn't know I have feelings for him and even if he did, he'd probably be horribly embarrassed. He's not the sort of man to even countenance being unfaithful to his wife.'

Peggy was hugely relieved, but didn't dare show it. 'I'm sorry I had to ask, Sarah, and I apologise if I've upset you.'

Sarah flung her arms round Peggy and gave her

a hug. 'And I'm sorry for flying off the handle. I know you meant well, but I'm all at sixes and sevens at the moment.' She drew back from the embrace and kissed Peggy's cheek. 'It'll be easier once he's gone and life can get back on an even keel again.' She reached for her beret and heavy-duty raincoat. 'Now I must go, or I'll be late.'

Peggy watched her running down the garden path and through the gate until she disappeared from view along the twitten that led to the hills. If Sarah was in love with the American then she wouldn't find it easier once he'd left, but would be beset by regrets over what might have been, and guilt over her perceived betrayal of Philip. It would take time for her wounded heart to heal and to come to terms with it all – and Peggy could only hope that, with her love and guidance and the warmth of the people around her, it wouldn't be too traumatic.

Fran had left for the hospital and Rita for the fire station by the time Cordelia came downstairs, but there was still no sign of Ron, although even Cordelia could hear him snoring.

'I'm amazed he doesn't wake himself up,' Cordelia said crossly as she finished her breakfast and fiddled with her hearing aid. 'That's a terrible racket.'

'It's time I got him up, anyway,' replied Peggy, glancing at the clock. She tucked the blanket over Cordelia's knees and handed her the newspaper, noting how swollen and misshapen the old lady's hands were. 'Best you stay in the warm today,' she murmured. 'This damp weather isn't good for your arthritis, and you're still getting over your cold.'

Cordelia eyed her sharply over her half-moon spectacles. 'I'm not an invalid, Peggy,' she said firmly. 'And if you imagine that I'm staying here and missing out on all the fun, then you've got another think coming.' Her blue eyes twinkled. 'I've organised Bertram to drive us to the ceremony. There's no point in having a man about the place if he isn't put to good use.'

Peggy giggled. 'You are naughty, Cordelia. Are you sure he won't mind?'

Cordelia sniffed and rustled the newspaper. 'He'll have nothing better to do. The golf course will be closed today anyway.'

Peggy was still smiling as she went down the stone steps to the basement. The widowed Bertram Grantley-Adams, or 'Bertie Double-Barrelled,' as everyone called him, was a frequent visitor to Beach View since he and Cordelia had become friends. He didn't seem to mind Cordelia bossing him about, and was the epitome of the English gentleman, always ready to lend a helping hand and content to take Cordelia for little drives in his car. Where he got the petrol from was a mystery, for Peggy's car had been stored away in a garage since rationing began, and petrol coupons were as rare as hens' teeth.

The basement was chill and smelled damp after all the rain they'd had recently. It ran the length of the house, the only natural light coming from the narrow window which was half-shadowed by the steps leading up to the front door. The blast damage caused two years before had been skilfully repaired by good friends and neighbours who'd turned up without being asked and hadn't wanted any payment, but the floor was rough concrete as were the steps leading up to the kitchen, which chilled the feet even through slippers.

There was a copper boiler and stone sink with a mangle by the back door, and a wooden clothes dryer hung from the ceiling on ropes and pulleys. This was where Peggy spent most of every Monday doing the washing, and as she eyed the mangle and thought about the hard work involved in that weekly chore, she couldn't help but yearn for a proper washing machine like the one her older sister Doris owned.

Doris lived in the posh part of town in a detached house with a long back garden that looked over the promenade and the sea. She was the sort of woman who demanded the better things in life and saw their attainment as her right. She was still married to the long-suffering Ted Williams – but only just, as he'd left Havelock Road after confessing to a long-standing affair. The affair had come to an end, but it seemed Ted was enjoying his freedom from his wife's never-ending demands, and was now happily ensconced in a bachelor flat above the Home and Colonial store which he managed.

Peggy sighed as she studiously ignored the overflowing laundry basket. Doris might have a fine house, an expensive washing machine and smart clothes, but she wasn't a happy woman, and Peggy suspected she was lonely now that Ted had decamped and her son, Anthony, was married and living away from home. Perhaps, she thought, sh should show her a little kindness and pop round there to keep her company.

The idea was quickly dismissed. Doris wouldn't appreciate a visit, and would no doubt snipe and be catty about Jim and Ron, which would only wind Peggy up – and then they'd have a falling-out. With so many other things to worry about, she simply didn't have the will or the energy to place herself in Doris's firing line.

She pushed all these thoughts aside and went along the narrow passageway towards the sound of snoring. Ron had moved in here shortly after she and Jim had taken over from her parents. He'd been widowed by then and was still out most nights with his oldest son, Frank, in their fishing boat. But when he retired and handed over to Frank, he'd plunged wholeheartedly into family life and had proved to be a wonderful, caring grandfather to both his sons' children – which was about his only saving grace, she thought darkly as the snores reverberated through the closed door.

Peggy hesitated before knocking, for the basement evoked so many memories of how things had been before the war, and she could never come down here without thinking about her boys. Bob and Charlie had shared the second basement room until their school had been bombed and they'd been evacuated to Somerset, and there were times when she imagined she could hear their laughter and the sound of their feet scampering over the concrete floor.

She hadn't seen them for almost two years now, and although Anne was very good at sending photographs and letters, it wasn't the same as actually having them home to cuddle and fuss over. They'd left as little boys, but now Charlie was twelve and Bob was sixteen – a dangerous age in wartime when youthful blood could so easily be stirred by patriotism and stories of derring-do.

She swallowed the ever-present fear that if this war lasted much longer, Bob would be called up, and rapped sharply on the door. 'Ron, it's time to get up.'

The snoring came to an abrupt, snorting halt. 'Be off with you, woman, and leave a man in peace.'

'I'm not moving from here, Ronan Reilly, so you'd better stir yourself. If you're not out of bed and opening this door in the count of five, then I'm coming in.'

'Ye'll not be coming in here, Peggy Reilly,' he growled. 'I'm in no fit state for visitors.'

'You rarely are,' she replied, and began counting. She reached five and pressed her ear to the door. On hearing nothing, she flung it open, switched on the light, and was met by the sight of Ron and Harvey sprawled beneath the blankets as the ferrets scratched and mewled in their cage under the bed. She wrinkled her nose at the smell of second-hand beer and whisky which mingled with that of dirty socks, damp dog and muddy boots.

Harvey lifted his muzzle and eyed her warily as Ron turned over in bed and dragged the blankets with him.

Peggy's gaze swept the room in mounting horror. Clothes were strewn everywhere amidst a clutter of fishing tackle, stacked boxes, discarded

41

books and a collection of wellingtons and sturdy boots. Drawers gaped from the chest, disgorging underwear and sweaters that looked fit only for the rag-and-bone man, and the wardrobe door yawned to reveal a jumble of jackets and trousers which no self-respecting tramp would be seen dead in.

She stormed out of the room, opened the back door to let some fresh air in and then filled a large jug with cold water. Marching back into the room she held the jug aloft. 'You have two seconds to get out of that bed,' she warned. 'Or you'll get this over your head.'

Harvey whined, shot off the bed and headed for the safety of the garden. He'd witnessed this sort of behaviour before from Peggy and knew what was coming.

'Ach, woman, will you be still and stop your blathering,' grumbled Ron from the depths of his grubby bedding. 'To be sure 'tis still the middle of the night.'

'It's after nine, and you have to be at the Town Hall by midday.'

'I'll not be going to any Town Hall,' he muttered.

Peggy tipped the contents of the jug over him and he shot upright with a roar of disbelief and disgust as the icy water soaked his pillow, flattened his hair and ran down his neck. He looked at her with red-rimmed eyes as the water dripped from his shaggy brows. 'What did you do that for?'

'Because you've stretched my patience too far,' she snapped. 'You're a disgrace, Ronan Reilly –

and so is your room – and if you don't get out of that bed and sort yourself out, I'll blooming well soak you again.'

'You wouldn't dare,' he growled.

'Try me.'

His bright blue eyes were bloodshot beneath the bushy brows, but there was a hint of mischief lighting them as he plastered back his wet hair and rubbed his face dry with a corner of the grubby sheet. 'To be sure, Peggy girl, you're a wee fighter so y'are, and I don't doubt you'll attack me again. But if you want me out of this bed then you'll have to leave the room.'

'Not until I see you up and on your feet.'

Ron let the sheet slip down to reveal a broad, hairy chest and muscled arms. 'I'm thinking you'll see more than that if I do as you ask,' he said, gripping the sheet with menacing intent. 'But if you're so determined...'

Peggy went scarlet and shot out of the bedroom. 'You might have warned me you were naked under there,' she said as she slammed the door.

'Well, to be fair, Peggy, you didn't give me much chance,' he shouted back.

Peggy bit her lip to stifle her giggles and ran up the stairs to the kitchen, where Harvey was now steaming in front of the range, his head resting on Cordelia's slippered feet, his paws muddy from digging in the garden. She saw the tracks of dirt on her clean lino and, with a grunt of impatience, grabbed one of the old towels, cleaned his paws and rubbed him dry. It had been clear for years that Harvey and Ron were determined to run

43

rough-shod over her, and she'd just about had enough of it.

Harvey whined, his soulful amber eyes looking up at her as if he was suffering the greatest torture, and Peggy melted. 'You're as bad as Ron,' she muttered as she stroked his silky ears. 'You always know how to get round me.'

'They're both a couple of rogues,' said Cordelia.

'You can say that again,' muttered Peggy.

'I don't want to play in the rain,' Cordelia protested. 'Why on earth should I?'

'Cordelia, dear, please turn your hearing aid up.'

'There's no need to shout,' she replied with a sniff. 'I'm not that deaf, and neither am I daft. Playing in the rain, indeed. What nonsense.'

Peggy decided it was pointless to argue, and got on with hunting out the scraps and bonemeal for Harvey's breakfast. While he was gobbling this down, she lit a cigarette and plumped into a kitchen chair. She may have won the first round in the battle with Ron, but the war was far from over and she knew that the next two hours would prove to be a struggle.

Ten minutes later Ron stepped into the kitchen, dressed in his usual garb of faded shirt, baggy corduroy trousers tied at the waist with string, a sweater with more holes in it than a sieve, and his favourite stained and ratty cap squashed over his tousled hair. He dumped his long poacher's coat over the back of a chair and sat down. 'I'll have me cup of tea and then I'll be taking Harvey for his walk,' he muttered, avoiding Peggy's gaze.

44

'You'll be going upstairs for a bath, hair-wash and shave,' she replied. 'And then you will get changed into your suit.'

He glanced across at this offending item of clothing and then eyed her from beneath his brows. 'It's a lot of fuss about nothing,' he rumbled. 'And if Harvey isn't welcome, then I'm not going.'

'Dogs aren't allowed in the Town Hall,' she replied. 'And it's not a fuss about nothing. The Mayor is presenting you with a bravery award – and instead of being grumpy and rude about it, you should be proud to be honoured in such a way.'

Ron still wouldn't look at her as he fussed Harvey who, despite his size, was trying to climb into his lap and lick his face. 'If this auld fella hadn't heard that baby crying, we'd have lost her and her mother. It's Harvey who should be getting the damned medal, not me.'

'Well, they haven't got such a thing as medals for dogs, so you'll just have to accept it for both of you.' Peggy's patience had worn very thin. 'And it would be nice if you could do that with some grace.'

'Then it's time they did have awards for animals,' he countered.

Cordelia took off her glasses and glared at him. 'You silly old man. It's time you grew up and accepted how things are,' she said tartly. 'People have gone to a lot of trouble over today, and woe betide you if you let them down.'

Ron shifted his gaze back to Harvey, who had found some crumbs on the floor and was licking them up. 'I don't see why there has to be such a fuss. Why can't they just post it to me? They've got better things to do than make silly speeches.'

'I don't doubt it,' said Cordelia. 'But you won't be the only one there getting an award – and something like this is good for morale.'

Ron slurped tea from the cup Peggy had handed him and eyed them both over the rim as he drained it. 'Ach, I know when I'm beaten,' he sighed. 'I'll be off for me bath.'

As Ron grabbed his clothes from the back of the door and stomped out of the room, the two women looked at each other and stifled their giggles. They knew Ron had absolutely no idea of how elaborate the plans were for the award cere-mony – and if he had, then not even a ten-ton bomb would have got him out of bed this morn-ing.

Peggy had struggled into her girdle, found a pair of stockings that weren't too heavily darned, and changed into her best skirt and sweater for the occasion, dithering over whether or not to wear a hat. Deciding that she probably should, she pinned the rather shabby dark blue felt hat onto her curls and then set about preparing Daisy.

Once this was achieved, she carried her little daughter back into the kitchen and sat her in the playpen so she couldn't get hold of anything to dirty her knitted outfit – she'd got into the habit of chewing the anthracite from the coal scuttle – and then set about preparing Ron's breakfast of porridge and a stack of toast. He would need something warm and filling after all the drink

46

he'd consumed the night before, and perhaps then he might be in a more congenial mood.

As Ron seemed to be taking an inordinate amount of time in the bathroom, she hurried down into the basement and stripped his bed. Gathering the dirty clothes from the floor, she bundled everything into the laundry basket and quickly remade the bed. There was nothing she could do about the mess in here, but at least the ferrets, Flora and Dora, appeared to have a clean cage, which was a minor blessing.

She was about to go back upstairs when she remembered that Ron would need a tie. Scrabbling in the untidy drawers she discarded several before unearthing one from the bottom of the wardrobe that didn't appear to have any burn holes in it from his pipe, or the remainder of any food. It was dark blue and very crumpled, but a hot iron would soon sort that out.

She had just finished ironing the tie when Ron appeared in the kitchen. He was a changed man in his freshly pressed suit and pristine shirt, his hair tamed by a dab of Brylcreem and brushed back from his clean-shaven face. He was still a good-looking man, sturdy and strong, his thick black hair only lightly silvered with a few strands of grey, and Peggy could understand why her friend Rosie Braithwaite had fallen in love with him.

Ron sat down at the table and Peggy swiftly wrapped a tea towel round his neck to protect his shirt from spills as he tucked into the bowl of porridge and drank a second cup of tea. 'Rosie said she'd meet us there,' she said, 'and Bertie Double-

Barrelled will be driving us to the hall.'

He eyed her from beneath his brows. 'I suppose that sister of yours will be there?'

Peggy nodded reluctantly, knowing there was no love lost between him and Doris, and fearing he would use her presence as yet another excuse for not going. 'She helped to organise everything.'

She noted the belligerent glare this statement evoked, so she placed the tie carefully over the back of a chair, well away from the mess Ron was making with his toast and margarine, sat down and reached for his hands. 'Ron, please don't let the side down today. We're all so very proud of you and it would be such a pity after all the hard work that's been put in.'

He rolled his eyes and then gave a deep sigh. 'Ach, Peggy, you worry too much, girl. To be sure I'm not a child to be warned to be on me best behaviour, and if Rosie's coming, then of course I'll be the very soul of propriety.'

Peggy didn't believe that for a minute, and neither did Cordelia, for she gave a little snort of derision.

'Ach,' he growled. 'You can mock an old soldier who suffers terrible with the moving shrapnel. But you'll see I'm a man of me word, so I am.'

Cordelia and Peggy exchanged knowing glances and didn't even bother to reply to this blatant bit of self-delusion.

Bertram arrived promptly, looking as dapper as always in a tweed suit and belted gabardine mackintosh, the brown trilby tipped to just the right angle over his brow, a sprig of heather adorning his buttonhole. Cordelia let him help her on with her coat while Peggy knotted Ron's tie.

'Will you not be strangling me, woman,' he rasped. 'To be sure I have to breathe.'

Peggy loosened the knot fractionally. 'There, that's perfect. Just keep it on at least until after the ceremony.'

He glared at her from beneath his brows, then went grumbling down the steps to the basement with Harvey at his heels.

Peggy strongly doubted that tie would be in evidence within the hour, but at least she'd done her best to make him look presentable. She dressed Daisy in her warm coat and bonnet, tucking her little hands into mittens to keep out the cold, and once Ron had returned from the basement and shut the kitchen door on Harvey, they trooped outside under their umbrellas and were driven to the Town Hall.

As the little car drew up at the foot of the steps, they were greeted by the sight of Harvey shaking himself by the front door and looking very pleased with himself.

'How did he get here?' asked Peggy.

Ron shrugged and avoided further questioning by clambering out of the car and running up the steps to his dog.

Peggy should have been cross, but in fact she was finding it hard not to laugh at the shenanigans. Ron had clearly left the back door open and ordered Harvey to follow the car to the hall. The pair of them were wily old so-and-sos, and Ron was right – the medal he would receive today should have been awarded to both of them – but how would he manage to get round the strict rule of no dogs being allowed in the hall?

'Stay close, Harvey, and don't let them see the whites of your eyes,' Ron muttered as they headed for the carpeted stairs which would lead them to the banqueting hall on the first floor.

Harvey padded along beside him, his shaggy coat still damp from his gallop through the rain.

They were about to climb the final short flight when their progress was halted by the immovable force that was Doris Williams. She was resplendent in a brown hat, tweed suit and highly polished pumps and matching handbag, and Ron noticed that the pheasant feather in her hat was quivering with her pent-up indignation.

'Good morning,' he said cheerfully as he tried to get round her.

She stood firm. 'Dogs are not allowed in here,' she hissed. 'Get it out immediately.'

He'd faced the Hun in the trenches of the Somme, so Doris didn't faze him at all. He glared back. 'If Harvey goes, so do I.'

Doris's perfectly made-up face twitched with conflicting emotions – the uppermost being one of fury. 'You know the rules, Reilly. The Mayor is allergic to dogs.'

'I don't care what he's allergic to,' Ron retorted. 'Harvey comes in with me, or I leave.'

'You can't do that,' she squeaked in rising horror.

'I can and I will if you don't let us pass,' he rumbled. 'And the name's Ron, as you very well know, so don't come on with your airs and graces to me, Doris. You might think you're posher than most, but I know better.'

Doris reddened and shot a hasty glance over her shoulder to see if anyone had overheard. 'How *dare* you talk to me like that?' she hissed.

'I'll talk any way I want,' he retorted. 'Now, let us pass.'

Harvey growled in the back of his throat and sniffed at the hem of Doris's skirt, his cold, wet nose nudging her leg.

Doris slapped him away and Harvey's growl deepened.

'Hit my dog and I'll put you over me knee and tan your hide,' Ron promised.

Doris went puce. 'Then get it away from me this minute,' she demanded. 'Disgusting animal.'

Ron sidestepped her as she hastily wiped Harvey's dribble from her delicate stockings, and they continued up the stairs. 'I wish you wouldn't do that,' he said quietly to Harvey. 'You don't know what you might find, sticking your nose up there.'

Harvey sat at the top of the stairs, his tongue lolling as he wagged his tail and grinned up at Ron.

Ron looked round at the gathering outside the banqueting room doors, noting that most of them seemed to be members of the local council, with a smattering of snooty women who were the driving force of several charities and good works in the town – women whose little clique had been firmly closed against Doris following the scandal over her husband's affair with one of his shop girls.

51

Ron meandered over to the bar that had been set up with trays of glasses and plates of small, unidentifiable bits of food and discovered that only sherry and soft drinks were on offer. As he loathed watery cordial, he had no alternative but to choose the sherry. He swallowed the disgusting drink down in one and took another, which he despatched in the same manner. He needed the hair of the dog really, but any port in a storm was welcome if it would see him through this awful rigmarole.

As he edged a finger inside the stiff shirt collar that was threatening to cut his throat, he saw Doris hovering on the edge of the chattering group of women who were studiously ignoring her. He found that he actually felt rather sorry for her, which was a most unusual emotion when it came to Doris, for he disliked her intensely. Yet she really was her own worst enemy, for she talked down to everyone she considered beneath her – which was the majority of people living, in Cliffehaven – had never learned the art of tact, and was the most terrible social climber and snob. She might be his beloved Peggy's sister, but they were chalk and cheese, and Ron had never been able to understand how it was possible that they were related.

Ron finished the third glass of sherry, grimacing, he caught sight of the barman who usually worked at the Fishermen's Club and was an old friend. 'Have you not got anything proper to drink, Sam? I need something to take the taste of that sherry away.'

The man smiled and reached beneath the

counter. 'You should have said earlier, Ron. Rosie sent this over to keep you going.' He handed over a brandy flask. 'Don't wave it about too much, mate, there's a strict rule against any hard liquor.'

Gratefully, Ron swallowed some of the restorative brandy and surveyed the crowd again. Peggy and Doris seemed to be conducting a heated exchange, the topic of which was clear, for Doris kept jabbing a finger in his direction. 'Stay low, Harvey,' he murmured. 'Enemy at two o'clock.'

Harvey crept under the pristine white tablecloth covering the makeshift bar until only his nose and eyes were visible.

Ron drank his brandy, eased his neck once more against the restricting collar and tie, and wondered where his Rosie had got to. She was the light of his life and the girl of his heart, and the day would definitely go more smoothly with her at his side. He trawled the gathering for sight of her platinum curls, but she was nowhere to be seen, and his spirits plummeted. She must have had difficulty in finding someone to man the pumps at the Anchor, otherwise she would never have let him down.

As the crowd grew in number and the volume of chatter rose, the double doors at the far end were opened and people began to slowly filter into the large room which had once, before war and rationing, been the scene of lavish banquets. Not that Ron had ever attended such things, but he'd heard tell that, as the drinks flowed, those who considered themselves to be the social elite showed their true colours, and there had been many a scandal attached to the goings-on that ensued.

'Ron. I'm so sorry I'm late.'

Ron grinned, his spirits immediately soaring as Rosie kissed his cheek and gave him an approving once-over. She looked gorgeous in a neat skirt and jacket and high heels, her slender legs encased in the nylons he'd managed to get from an old army pal who had connections with the Yanks up at the Cliffe estate. He tucked her hand into the crook of his arm. 'Ach, to be sure you're a fine-looking woman, Rosie Braithwaite. And 'tis a lucky man I am to have you at me side.'

'Flattery will get you nowhere, but a drink might,' she teased, her blue eyes flashing.

Once she'd taken a sip of the sherry, she surveyed the crowd and Ron used the moment to further admire her. Rosie was in her early fifties, with an hourglass figure, heart-shaped face and mesmerising blue eyes which could quite often make him go weak at the knees. He'd pursued her from the moment she'd taken over the Anchor twenty years before, but it had only been in the past couple of years that she'd allowed him to kiss her and murmur sweet nothings in her ear. To his great regret and frustration, that was as far as she would permit him to go, for Rosie was still married – tied to a man doomed to spend the rest of his life in a mental asylum – and as a good Catholic girl she believed hell and damnation awaited her should she break her marriage vows.

'You're looking very serious,' she said. 'Don't tell me you're nervous.'

He shook off his gloomy thoughts and smiled back at her. 'Don't you fret, Rosie me darlin', this lot don't scare me.'

54

She glanced down as Harvey nudged the toe of her shoe with his nose and she grinned, her blue eyes gleaming with fun. 'Oh, Ron, you just can't help breaking the rules, can you?'

He grinned back. 'Life wouldn't be any fun otherwise.'

'Well, you won't be able to take him into the banqueting room.'

He raised a bushy brow, his grin still wide as he tapped the side of his nose.

'Oh, Ron,' she giggled. 'You are a caution.'

A commanding voice rose above the general hubbub. 'Ladies and gentlemen. The Worshipful the Mayor of Cliffehaven, Councillor Archibald Hammond, invites you to take your seats for the award ceremony. Those being honoured today are requested to proceed to the front row.'

'This is it,' whispered Rosie as she kissed his cheek. 'I'll see you after the ceremony.'

Ron patted her pert behind before she sashayed away from him to join the crush at the door. He waited until it had started to flow through and then clicked his fingers at Harvey, who was instantly alert. 'Stick close and stay low,' he ordered quietly before joining the melee.

With Harvey slinking beside him, they slipped through the door into the huge banqueting hall where three enormous crystal chandeliers hung from the high ceiling, casting light on the framed portraits of past mayors lining the panelled walls.

Rows of chairs had been placed to face the stage, where a long, cloth-covered table was almost hidden by a vast, overblown flower arrangement. Behind the table was an ornate, throne-like edifice embellished with the mayoral badge of office and the county shield. Flanking this prime example of bad taste were rather less grand red velvet-covered chairs – no doubt put there to provide for the wide, well-fed bottoms of the great and good of the Cliffehaven town council.

There were more flower arrangements placed artfully along the front of the stage, and bunting had been strung overhead. A rather elderly quartet provided a musical accompaniment, but no one seemed to be taking any notice as the chatter rose to drown them out.

Ron caught sight of Doris, organising the award winners in the front row, and before she had the chance to spot him, he clicked his fingers again and slid into a seat at the back.

Harvey silently slithered beneath it, and with a soft grunt flopped down, nose on paws, ears twitching at all the sounds around him.

Ron winked at the man sitting next to him who winked back, and as the whisper went down the line and curious eyes searched for sight of the hiding Harvey, the doors were closed and a fanfare of trumpets went up which made everyone jump.

Ron put his hand on Harvey to keep him quiet as the fearful racket echoed around the vast hall and the mayoral party rather grandly paraded in and took their seats on the stage. Ron grimaced at the pomposity of it all. The smug-faced Mayor was resplendent in a red cloak edged in ermine, the chain of office glinting on his chest, his tricorn hat with its white feathers looking preposterous on that fat, balding head. As for the rest of them, they fairly clanked with all the chains and medals they were wearing, and the women's hats were as overblown as the flower arrangements.

As the Mayor stood to address the audience and started to drone on about all the splendid things his council had achieved over the past year, Ron sighed deeply, crossed his arms over his chest and prepared to snatch forty winks. He still felt a bit worse for wear after last night, and the sound of the Mayor's voice was proving soporific.

He was startled awake by loud applause and sat up to see what was going on. It appeared he'd missed most of the ceremony, for there was a long line of people proudly displaying their awards for the press while the Mayor was handing over a medal to the leader of the Home Guard for services to the community.

Ron yawned and didn't join in with the applause. In his opinion, Jack Withershaw was a pompous ass who thought he knew it all, when in reality the only action he'd ever seen during the first shout was in the army kitchens well away from the fighting. Jack was also the Mayor's brother-in-law, which probably explained why he'd been given something in the first place.

He was about to settle back to his pleasant doze when the Mayor's voice rang out again and the audience stilled.

'And now we come to the special award which has been granted through public demand and our government's approval. It is an award for the extreme courage shown during the perilous rescue of a woman and her child.'

57

The Mayor's gaze swept over the front row and even from this far back, Ron could see the growing consternation in the man's flushed face. Yet he wasn't about to show himself – not until he was good and ready.

'Ronan Reilly,' the Mayor continued, his gaze now desperately searching the crowd before him, 'has been a citizen of Cliffehaven for many years. He was a stalwart member of our fishing fleet and a decorated hero of the Great War. Even now, he is an active and valuable member of the Home Guard, and we are proud to call him one of our own.'

He peered into the hall, the spotlight glistening on the beads of sweat that had broken out on his forehead. 'Ronan? Could you please step forward?'

Ron could see heads craning round and decided that as he was here, he might as well play the game and go and collect his award. Sliding out of his seat, he ambled down the long aisle towards the stage. He was aware that every eye was watching not only his progress, but that of Harvey, who was loping along beside him.

He caught sight of Doris's furious expression and felt a small glow of satisfaction. No one told him what to do, especially someone like bossy Doris Williams. As he came closer to the stage he could see the astonished looks on the faces of the council members, and hear the whispering amongst the gathering that was fast becoming a murmur interlaced with the occasional giggle and titter. He shot a wink at Rosie, who was clearly enjoying his moment of defiance as much as he was.

Ron climbed the few steps up onto the stage and approached the Mayor, his gaze steady as their eyes met. 'G'morning,' he said cheerfully.

Always aware of public scrutiny, the Mayor managed to plaster on a smile and shake hands with Ron before passing over the framed citation and small bronze medal hanging from a blue ribbon in a velvet presentation box. 'It's a great honour to award you with this, Mr Reilly,' he said with a rather sickly smile that didn't reach his furious eyes. 'Your bravery in the face of danger has saved many lives over the past four years, and in recognition of this, we of Cliffehaven salute you.'

As the thunderous applause rang out, Ron felt extremely silly standing there with his hand clasped damply in the Mayor's while flashbulbs from the press cameras threatened to blind him. He wasn't the sort to have his head turned by such goings-on – but at least he'd cut through all the nonsense and accepted the award in his own inimitable fashion instead of kowtowing to the Mayor and his cronies.

The Mayor's long, unpleasant handshake finally eased and he stepped away, indicating that Ron was now free to return to his seat.

That was not part of Ron's plan. Having wiped his hand down his hip to rid it of the clamminess left by the Mayor's grip, he turned to face the audience with Harvey sitting at his feet, grinning like a fool at all the fuss, his wagging tail thudding on the floorboards.

Ron waited until the noise had died down, then

59

adjusted the microphone, determined to have his say. 'I'm honoured to have been awarded this,' he said as he took the medal from its box and dangled it from its ribbon. 'But this medal and citation don't belong to me. To be sure I did no more than any man would have in the circumstances – and I wouldn't even have done that if it hadn't been for Harvey.'

The audience was so still one could have heard a pin drop.

Ron touched Harvey's head and the lurcher lifted his nose to nuzzle the palm of his hand. 'There are no medals awarded to animals, but they serve their country as faithfully as any citizen. They might not have a voice, or wear a uniform, but by their very actions, they have proved worthy of our praise and devotion and must not be forgotten.'

Ron could see he had them all engrossed, and as he stroked Harvey's head and gazed out over the audience, he continued. 'It was Harvey who heard those feeble cries under the rubble. Harvey who dug his way through the shifting, lethal debris of that fire-strewn bomb site to get to the girl and her baby. It was he who carried the baby in his mouth up to the surface before returning beneath that building – and his continuous barking which led us to her injured mother. So it is Harvey who should wear this medal.'

He slipped the ribbon over Harvey's head so the medallion gleamed against the brindled chest and the dog looked back at him with hazel eyes filled with love and trust.

The room erupted as the audience rose as one

60

to cheer and clap and stamp their feet – and Ron basked in the adulation for his beloved dog. It was worth wearing this awful collar and tie just to know there probably wasn't a dry eye in the house, and that Harvey's courage had finally been recognised.

Harvey gave a single loud bark, his tail windmilling as he fairly danced on his toes in delight. Unlike Ron, he loved the limelight, and before anyone could stop him, he'd bounded off the stage to mingle with his admirers and garner every pat and stroke coming his way.

Ron turned to wink at the Mayor, who'd gone puce in the face, then hurried down the steps to be with his Rosie and finally rid himself of his blasted tie.

3

Peggy's emotions were all over the place as they left the Town Hall in Bertie's little car and headed for Beach View. Ron was the absolute limit, hijacking the ceremony like that and flouting the rules. The poor Mayor had been sweating and sneezing for a long while after the applause had died and people began to drift away, for he was seriously allergic to animal hair, and Harvey had insisted upon licking his hand and pawing at his ceremonial robes.

As for Doris, she was incandescent, threatening to disassociate herself from Peggy's entire family;

not that such a thing would be entirely disagreeable – Doris was a complete pain in the neck at the best of times.

Yet despite all that, she couldn't have been more proud of Ron and Harvey, and it had certainly enlivened what had started out as a rather stuffy event. Her younger sister Doreen would have loved it, and Peggy could just imagine her being the first on her feet to congratulate him on not only defying Doris, but the entire town council. Peggy made a mental note to write to Doreen and tell her all about it.

Today's shenanigans would be the talk of the town for a while, and Ron would make the most of all the offers of free beer he'd no doubt get. As it was, he and Rosie had gone to the Anchor with an entourage of well-wishers, and she suspected he wouldn't return home until very late again.

As they arrived at Beach View and Bertie helped Cordelia up the steps to the front door, Peggy hoisted a fractious Daisy onto her hip and went to put the kettle on.

Once Bertie had helped Cordelia off with her coat, he'd left for the golf club where he'd arranged to play bridge with some of his fellow members. He would return on Wednesday to take Cordelia out to lunch at the Conservative Club, which she was looking forward to immensely and had already planned her outfit.

It was now almost six o'clock, so Peggy quickly put the vegetable stew in the oven, heated some of it for Daisy in a saucepan, and then fed her. A comforting bottle of milk and a teaspoon of malt extract soon soothed her and within the hour she was fast asleep in her cot.

Cordelia had made the tea and was sitting by the range fire with her knitting. It was in a tangle as usual, but she didn't seem to notice. 'Ron will make the most of all the fuss,' she said as Peggy sat opposite her with her own knitting. 'He might pretend not to like it, but I bet he's propping up the bar at the Anchor and regaling all and sundry with his adventures as the beer flows.'

'He'll be lucky if it is flowing,' said Peggy. 'Rosie told me only the other day that the stocks are getting shorter by the week.'

'There'll be even less after Ron's celebration.' Cordelia looked across at Peggy and smiled. 'Bless him. He's an utter scallywag, but you can't help but love him and Harvey, can you?'

'They're both a complete nightmare at times, but yes, life wouldn't be the same without them.'

They fell silent as the mantel clock ticked and their knitting needles clicked, and the aroma of vegetable stew began to permeate from the oven. Knitting had become a part of everyday life for the women of Cliffehaven, and the scarves, gloves, balaclavas and socks they produced from recycled wool were carefully packed and sent to the troops fighting abroad, along with little notes of encouragement, picture postcards and snippets of news.

'Have you noticed that Fran's out of sorts lately?' asked Cordelia sometime later. 'It looks to me as if we're in for a bumpy ride in the not too distant future.'

'I agree. She's certainly simmering over something, but I suspect it's nothing too serious, and will blow over as usual.'

'Let's hope so,' said Cordelia. 'But I've also been a bit concerned about Sarah and Jane.' She put dawn her knitting and took off her half-moon glasses. 'They both seem quieter than normal, and although I realise they must be enormously worried about their father and Philip, I get the feeling there's more to it than that.'

Peggy didn't want to break Sarah's confidences of this morning, and as the girl had given no hint of what had been worrying her to her great-aunt, it was clear she didn't want her to know. 'I expect they're just feeling low like the rest of us,' she said carefully. 'This war has dragged on for too long, and even though the Allies have made huge advances in Africa and Russia, we're still a long way from winning.'

Cordelia's gaze was steady as she regarded Peggy. 'If you say so,' she murmured, 'but I get the feeling they're both hiding something.'

'Well, I did wonder if Jane had found herself a young man,' Peggy admitted.

'That's highly likely. But if she has, then why doesn't she bring him home so we can give him the once-over?'

'You know how shy she is – and if its a very new romance, perhaps she's just wary of bringing him home so early in the relationship. We have to trust her, Cordelia. After all, she's nineteen and no longer a child.'

Cordelia gave a deep sigh. 'Things were very different in my day. If a young man wanted to court you, he'd ask your father's permission to call. Now it seems there are no rules and youngsters simply do as they please. I've even seen the girls walking out with the foreign servicemen, which can't be right.'

'It's a different world and a different time, Cordelia. We have to accept that boundaries between nationalities, colour and religion have broken down – and who knows, perhaps it will bring better understanding and make this world a more peaceful place.'

Cordelia fell silent and picked up her knitting again, and Peggy stared into the fire, wondering where it would all end. The sight of the black American GIs had come as quite a shock to the people of Cliffehaven, but it seemed they'd been accepted along with the dark-eyed, rather exotic-looking Indian soldiers in their turbans, and the fierce little Gurkhas who'd stayed in the town for a few days at the beginning of the year. And yet there was an undercurrent of mistrust and wariness that no amount of accord could dismiss, and Peggy didn't know how she would feel if one of her girls came home with such a man.

The slam of the back door and the heavy thud of boots on the concrete steps snapped her from her thoughts. Rita came stomping into the kitchen, and Peggy abandoned her knitting and put the potatoes on to finish boiling.

Rita pulled off her First World War flying helmet and goggles and dragged off her moth-eaten flying jacket to reveal her black fire service uniform jacket, tie and shirt. 'Whew,' she said as she ruffled her dark curls and plonked herself down in a chair to wrestle with the leather over-trousers she always wore when riding her motorbike. 'I'm glad today's over. I've had my head stuck under the bonnets of fire engines since eight this morning, because John Hicks decided they all needed a good service while it was quiet.'

Having divested herself of the bulky clothing, she kissed Cordelia's cheek and gave Peggy a hug. 'How was the ceremony?' she asked with an impish grin. 'I bet Ron did something outrageous – and that Harvey was involved as well.'

Peggy laughed and told her what had happened as she checked on the stew and handed plates and cutlery to Rita so she could set the table. 'I thought the poor Mayor would have an apoplexy,' she confessed, 'but because the press was there he didn't dare say anything.'

Rita giggled. 'I wish I'd been there, but no doubt I'll hear all about it later when I go to the Anchor.'

'Are you meeting Matthew there, or is he coming here first?'

Rita gave a great sigh. 'He's on ops again. I haven't seen him for days, and as long as they keep bombing Germany, I doubt he'll have any leave at all. Cissy's in the same situation now Randy's American squadron has been set up at Biggin Hill – but at least Matt is still local and I'll get a chance to see him sometime.'

Peggy said nothing as she tested the boiling potatoes to see if they were cooked through. Flight Lieutenant Randolph Stevens and Squadron Leader Matthew Campion were fine young men who risked their lives every day, just as her son-in-law Martin Black did – and she shared the girls' anxiety every time she heard the aircraft taking off from Cliffe.

She drained the potatoes, her thoughts with her

daughters. Anne might be far away, but that didn't lessen her worry over Martin, and she knew that Cissy counted the planes out on every raid and waited in an agony of apprehension to count them all back again. So many lives had been lost in this battle to defend Britain.

Rita shot off upstairs to get changed and moments later Sarah and Jane came up the basement steps. Peggy took one look at their wet hair and sodden clothes and ordered them both upstairs to dry off and change. As Sarah passed her she raised an eyebrow in question and Sarah gave a small nod, clearly keeping her emotions under tight control. It seemed that Captain Hammond had left the Cliffe estate, and now Sarah would have to find the inner strength to accept that her foolish heart had been misled and it was time to move on.

The front door slammed some minutes later and Fran came into the kitchen, shaking out her damp nursing cape. She kissed Cordelia almost distractedly, which was most unusual, and then pecked Peggy's cheek. 'Is Jane back yet?' she asked as she unpinned her riot of autumnal curls and shook them out to tumble over her shoulders and down her back.

Peggy frowned. Something had been eating at Fran for the past two weeks, and by the looks of her, she was about to blow. 'She and Sarah are upstairs getting out of their wet things.'

Fran's green eyes glinted. 'Right. Well, I'll be having a wee word with her, so I will.'

Peggy was all too familiar with the Irish girl's mercurial temper, and realised there could be

67

trouble ahead if she didn't put a stop to this now. 'If you've got something to say to Jane, then it can wait until after tea when you've calmed down,' she said evenly as she grabbed Fran's hand to stop her leaving the room.

'I'll not be putting up with it, Auntie Peg,' she retorted.

'Putting up with what, Fran? You're not making any sense.'

'She's been seeing Robert behind my back, that's what.' The green eyes flared as furious colour flooded her face.

Peggy blinked in astonishment. 'Jane isn't that sort of girl and Robert–'

'Jane might give the impression that she's sweet and innocent,' Fran snarled, 'but I know better.'

Peggy still had tight hold of Fran's arm to stop her from dashing off, but the girl's astonishing accusation was beginning to make an awful kind of sense. Jane had been preoccupied lately and coming in unusually late – and there was little doubt that she was keeping something secret. 'Fran, dear, you really shouldn't throw those sorts of accusations about without any proof.'

'I saw them together, Aunt Peg,' she snapped. 'Not just the once either, but tonight was the absolute limit. All cosy and very much involved, they were – to the point where they didn't even see me as they left the Lilac tearooms.'

'I'm sure it was all perfectly innocent, Fran,' said Peggy quickly. 'Are you certain you're not just jumping to conclusions?'

'I know what I saw.' Fran folded her arms and scowled.

'You've got it all wrong, Fran,' said Jane as she and Sarah came into the kitchen.

'Oh, yes?' stormed Fran. 'I see you and my man, heads together, smiling, laughing as if you hadn't a care. How the hell do you think that makes me feel? Eh? Eh?' She jabbed a finger at the younger girl, who stood her ground and kept her gaze steady as Peggy swiftly put herself between them.

'What on earth is going on down here?' asked Rita from the doorway.

'Fran's accusing my sister of stealing Robert,' snapped Sarah, 'and if she doesn't apologise immediately then she'll have me to deal with.'

'Girls, girls,' pleaded Cordelia. 'For goodness' sake, isn't there enough trouble in the world without you fighting in the home?' Her expression became stern, her blue eyes cold. 'Sit down,' she snapped. 'Sit down and be still, all of you.'

Everyone turned to stare at Cordelia, who'd never been heard to talk like that or look so fierce. As one, they sat down: Fran at one end of the table, Jane at the other, Sarah, Peggy and Rita acting as buffers between them.

'Right,' said Cordelia, who was clearly in no mood for nonsense. 'Fran, we've all heard what you have to say – now it's time to let Jane speak.' As Fran opened her mouth to protest, Cordelia raised an imperious hand. 'Silence! You'll get your turn later.'

Jane glanced first at her older sister and then at Peggy before shaking back her long fair hair and focusing on Cordelia. 'Robert and I have been meeting over the past few weeks to–'

'There, see!' shouted Fran as she shot to her feet. 'I told you!'

'Sit down, Fran.'

Cordelia's glare would have stopped a rampaging bull at fifty yards and Fran was no match for it, so, with poor grace, she did as she was told. Satisfied, Cordelia nodded to Jane. 'Continue,' she ordered.

'As you know, Aunt Peggy,' said Jane, with a nervous glance at Fran, 'I've always enjoyed doing puzzles and mathematical posers.' At Peggy's nod, she carried on. 'Well, it seems there is a very urgent need for people who can do such things, so Anthony suggested Robert should approach me to see if I'd be interested in doing something a little more complex.'

There was silence in the room but for the ticking clock. 'It's all very hush-hush, and I shouldn't be talking about it, even here. But as Fran has got such a bee in her bonnet about it, and I don't want there to be any misunderstandings between us, I'll have to trust you all not to breathe a word of what I'm going to say outside this kitchen.'

They stared at Jane in utter astonishment as they nodded.

Satisfied, Jane carried on. 'Robert brought something for me to work on that was a test, just to see what I could do. After I'd done several other things for him, he brought me something else.'

Jane's long fair hair drifted over her face as she looked down at her hands. 'It was very complex, and although I worked on it for hours, I just couldn't do it. It was upsetting, to be honest, because it just went to prove that I wasn't as clever as I thought I was, and I felt as though I'd let him down. I was actually at the point of giving up when I suddenly saw the links in the sequence and understood what they meant.'

'So you've not been having an affair with Robert?'

Jane looked across the table at Fran, her blue eyes innocent of guile. 'Of course not, Fran. Robert was just treating me to afternoon tea as a way of celebration.'

Fran blushed and looked rather shamefaced. 'Well, it's sorry I am, Jane. But it's hardly surprising I got the wrong end of things, is it? You've been very secretive lately.'

'Yes, I noticed that,' said Rita. 'And you've been coming in late.'

'I knew something was on your mind,' breathed Peggy, 'but I'd never have guessed...'

Jane's blue eyes widened. 'I didn't realise it was so obvious. Oh dear.'

Peggy laughed. 'And here's me worrying about you getting involved with some unsuitable GI.'

'But why didn't you say anything of this to me?' asked Sarah. 'You used to tell me everything.'

Jane reached for her hand. 'You've had other things on your mind, and there wasn't anything that I could tell you without breaking the Official Secrets Act that I've had to sign.'

Sarah blushed. 'You knew?'

'About Captain Hammond?' She smiled fondly. 'Of course, Sarah. I've known how you felt about him for ages, but it was obvious you didn't want to talk about it, so I decided to wait until you were ready to confide in me.' She squeezed her fingers.

'So you see we've both had our secrets.'

'I don't know what the pair of you are talking about,' said a ruffled Cordelia, 'but at least we seem to have cleared the air. A storm in a teacup as usual. Now perhaps we could have our supper?'

'There is something I have to tell you before we eat,' said Jane hesitantly.

Peggy regarded her warily, wondering what bombshell the girl was about to drop now.

'I've been offered a job and I've accepted it.'

'What sort of job?' Peggy asked swiftly.

'I can't really tell you. I'm sorry, Aunt Peggy.'

Peggy's thoughts whirled. Anthony and Robert worked for the MOD. Jane was clearly a natural at solving puzzles, so logically, there was only one kind of job they would have offered her: code-breaking.

'Are you sure about this, Jane? I thought you were happy and settled at the dairy?'

'Oh, I am. I love my shires, and really enjoy chatting to all my customers, but it's not really doing anything important, is it? There are lots of boys and girls who could easily do my job there, but I will miss Cliffehaven.'

There was a general gasp and Sarah grabbed her hand. 'What do you mean, miss Cliffehaven? Where are you going?'

Jane looked uncomfortable in the spotlight of everyone's attention. 'I'm sorry, Sarah, I can't tell you that, but it's quite a long way away.'

Sarah paled. 'Exactly how far is a long way?'

Jane shrugged. 'Again, I'm sorry, but I really can't say any more. I've already told you far too much.'

72

'But you're too young to be going off on your own like that,' Sarah retorted. 'What am I supposed to tell Mother?'

'You don't tell her anything,' said Jane firmly. 'One word of this in a letter could see me sent to prison – and you know how sharp-eyed the censors are.'

'But we can't just lie to her.'

'You don't need to lie. I'll still write to her and to you. We just won't let her know we're living apart.'

'I don't like any of this,' Sarah fretted tearfully. 'I promised Mother I'd look after you – but how can I do that if you're leaving Cliffehaven?'

'Oh, Sarah, I'm not a little girl. I don't need molly-coddling any more.' Jane gripped Sarah's hand. 'This is my chance to do something that might make a real difference. And surely we should all use what we do best to try and turn the tide of this war?'

'But you've never been away from me before, and the thought of you on your own, miles away... Are you absolutely sure, Jane? Have you really thought this through?'

Jane gave a sigh of frustration. 'Of course I have. Do give me some credit, Sarah.'

'I'm sorry. I don't mean to be so smothering, but you're my little sister, so of course I'm going to worry about you.'

'Well please don't. It's time I stood on my own feet and got on with things,' Jane said determinedly. 'And although it might be a bit scary, it's also very exciting, and I can't wait to get stuck in.'

As everyone bombarded Jane with questions, Peggy noted that the girl's eyes were shining and her face was aglow with happiness. Although she too had misgivings about her leaving, she realised they all had to accept that she was entitled to her own life and the freedom to do her bit for the war effort.

However, the thought of losing another of her precious chicks to the dangerous world outside the walls of Beach View made her feel tearful, and she had to clear her throat before she could speak. 'When are you leaving, Jane?' she managed as the hubbub of excited chatter died down.

'On Thursday.'

Peggy felt a jolt of shock 'But it's already Monday,' she gasped. 'Why so soon?'

'It is all a bit of a rush, I know. But with the way things are with the war and everything, Robert thought it best.' She looked round at their astonished faces then hurried on, 'I wanted to tell you sooner, but Robert didn't think it was wise until all the paperwork and travel arrangements were in place.'

Peggy nodded, unable to speak for the lump in her throat, and she saw that Cordelia was also trying very hard not to cry. It would be a wrench for her too, as she'd been so happy to have her nieces here after the long years of separation from the rest of her family, who were in Canada.

Jane looked round the table. 'I shall miss all of you dreadfully, and will no doubt be horribly homesick for Beach View at first. But I promise to write often and will telephone when I can.'

'I don't understand why you have to leave in

the first place, let alone rush off so quickly,' said Cordelia gruffly. 'Anthony and Robert work up at the Fort. Why can't you?'

Jane moved to crouch down by her elderly aunt, and, careful of her arthritic fingers, gently took her hands. 'It's because they do different jobs there, Aunt Cordelia, and I'm needed somewhere else. Please say you'll give me your blessing.'

Cordelia patted her cheek, her eyes misted with tears. 'Bless you, child, of course I will. Just you be careful, that's all.'

'I will,' she murmured, kissing her cheek. 'I promise.'

Once Peggy had settled Cordelia comfortably in bed with a hot water bottle and a cup of warm milk, she sat for a while and they talked about Jane's extraordinary announcement before Peggy went on to explain about Sarah and Captain Hammond.

Reassured that Cordelia wasn't too upset by all that had happened today, Peggy left her reading her book by the bedside light. Rita and Fran had gone to the Anchor, and as the sisters needed time to talk things over in their room, Peggy went downstairs.

The house was quiet but for the usual moans and groans of old timbers and pipes, and she sat by the range fire to have a last cigarette before bed. It had been quite an emotional day and her mind was so busy with it all, she doubted she'd sleep just yet. A glance at the clock told her it was almost ten, so the girls should be back soon. Whether Ron turned up was another thing, for no doubt he was now being the life and soul of the party at the Anchor.

These quiet moments were rare, and Peggy began to relax as her thoughts meandered through the events of the day. Poor Sarah was no doubt already feeling adrift following Captain Hammond's departure; now she had to contend with losing her young sister too. She would feel Jane's absence the most, for they'd rarely been apart and had relied on one another during their long journey from Singapore, bolstering each other when they were feeling low, and sharing their concerns over what might have happened to their father and Philip.

Peggy sighed. There had been so many departures because of this damned war, and there was hardly a person in Cliffehaven who hadn't been touched by them one way or another. However, if the war was to be won then these sacrifices were necessary, no matter how hard and distressing they might be.

She thought of Anne and her two little girls; of Charlie and Bob; of Doreen's Evelyn and Joyce – and all the girls who'd found shelter here before they'd left to make their own way in the world. She'd had letters from those girls, which warmed her, for it seemed she hadn't been forgotten, and it was lovely to know they were all doing well. Even Sally, her first evacuee from London who'd settled in Cliffehaven with marriage to the fire chief, John Hicks, had finally taken her two small children to safety in Somerset.

And then there was her beloved Jim, trying very hard to put a brave face on things in the unbelievable heat and squalor of what she'd guessed to be Bombay. He'd made light of his situation at the transit camp in his short airgraphs, but reading between the lines, Peggy suspected he'd found it tough going after all those weeks at sea.

She didn't need to read the airgraphs to remember what he'd written, for she knew them by heart. Jim and the other men had arrived in India just before Christmas, and they'd had to march through the city where they'd faced a certain amount of resentment from the locals, who clearly didn't want them there. The transit camp provided basic accommodation in brick huts, with shutters for windows and beds made out of rope, which he'd soon discovered were a breeding ground for bugs.

There had been little chance of sight-seeing, and as he was proving to be hopeless at speaking Urdu – and the natives didn't speak English – it was all a bit of a trial. Yet he and his friend Ernie had managed to have a swim in the sea, had discovered the delights of a leather market where they'd bought shoes for less than ten shillings, and eaten like kings back at the camp.

Jim had managed – as usual – to wheedle his way on to light duties, so instead of having to march the four miles to the station on the last day, he'd travelled with the baggage on a truck. The three-day train journey was sparsely described because of the censorship, but it seemed he was very taken with the sights, sounds and smells of India, but not so impressed by the number of beggars and the very strange food on offer.

Peggy smiled as she remembered his description of one dinner in which he'd been given bread, bully beef, a banana, raspberry jam, cheese, pickles and black dates, all rounded off by a bar of toffee. She'd served up some strange concoctions over the past four years, but none quite that odd. At least there seemed to be no shortage of fruit where he was, and she envied him that, for she hadn't seen a banana for years and the taste of an orange was a dim and distant memory.

Things were far more civilised at their base camp, for they had native servants who did everything for them, from shining shoes to doing their washing. There was a club with a dance floor and billiard room, three very square meals a day all served on posh china and real tablecloths, and their bed linen was of the highest quality. Jim was in seventh heaven, or would have been if it hadn't been so terribly hot during the day and freezing cold at night. It seemed India was a land of vast contrasts, and it would take him a while to get used to it.

Peggy finished her cigarette and damped down the fire for the night before going into her bedroom off the hall. Jim might be having the time of his life, but while servants waited on him hand and foot she still had to put food on the table – and that involved getting up early to join the inevitable endless queues outside the shops. One never knew what the queue was for, but you joined it in the hope it would be something nice – or at least useful.

4

Ivy's worst fears had been realised, for Caroline was as bad as Doris when it came to issuing orders and expecting her to skivvy, and she'd just about had enough of it. Deciding that it was time to either tell them what they could do with their orders, or swallow her pride and ask Peggy if she'd take her in, Ivy slammed the front door behind her and headed for the munitions factory.

It was almost eleven and the night was cold and dark, but she knew the way so well she could have done it in her sleep. Her heavy boots thudded on the pavement as she passed the shops and bomb sites in the High Street. She crossed the hump-backed bridge and paused for a moment to wave to Stan, who was outside his Nissen hut mending a wheel on a luggage trolley, before continuing on up the steep hill which led to the dairy and the ever-growing factory estate. The baggy legs of her dungarees swished against one another at every step – they were several sizes too large for her, and although she'd managed to cobble up the hem, she wasn't good enough with the needle to actually take them in or shorten the straps on the bib. That was the trouble with being short and skinny – nothing fitted well, and she usually ended up looking like some waif in her big sister's clothes. But at least the coat she and her friend Mabel had made out of Doris's discarded picnic blanket helped to keep out the cold, and she was glad of the thick shirt, vest and old cardigan as further protection from the wind that was whipping up from the sea.

Ivy paused to light a cigarette and prepare herself for the long night shift ahead of her. The work was well paid because it was dangerous, and the more bullets she could make, the more money she earned, but she'd had only one day off in the last month, and because she was always tired, there was little time for any real fun.

'Wotcha, gel. How come you're so early? It's not like you, Ivy.'

Ivy grinned at Mabel and then waved at her other East End friends, Dot, Glad and Freda, who were hurrying towards them. 'I 'ad to get out, didn't I?' she said with a grimace. 'Them two was driving me round the bleedin' bend.'

The other girls arrived slightly out of breath from their climb up the hill. 'You'd think we'd got used to that flamin' hill by now, wouldn't you?' panted Freda.

'Nothing gets easier these days,' Gladys moaned.

'I don't suppose any of you 'ave got room at your billets for a little one, 'ave yer?' Ivy asked hopefully.

There was a general shaking of heads and murmurs of regret. 'Never mind, Ivy,' said Mabel as she gave her a hug. 'We'll see you right the minute there's a spare room. Until then you got us to keep you cheerful.' She looked at the others. 'What you say?'

'Yeah, we canary gels 'ave to stick together,' said Dot, tying a scarf over her hair which had been streaked yellow by the sulphur she had to handle every day.

'That's the spirit, 'said Freda. 'Our skins and hair might be turning Chinese, but friendship is what really matters.' She looked round the group. 'Right, gels. Are you ready for this?'

They all nodded, stubbed out their fags and headed for the gate, where an armed guard was standing watch. They showed him their identification papers and passes and gave him a bit of banter. He was very young and clearly not used to girls chatting him up, so he quickly turned scarlet, which made it all the more fun. Giggling, they hurried across the vast concrete square to the furthermost point of the estate.

Ivy saw the two-storey factory looming ahead and could already smell the stink of sulphur drifting into the night. She took a last deep breath of fresh air and followed the others into the changing rooms. They took off their coats and checked their pockets for matches, lighters, torches and anything else that might cause an explosion in the highly rarefied atmosphere, then covered their hair with scarves and donned the white coats they all had to wear.

The factory was quite a lively place, for there was a great deal of chatter and someone was always starting a sing-song to help pass the time and lighten the spirits as they did their perilous job. None of them had been given any formal training, just a five-minute demonstration on how to work the heavy machinery, fill shells and bullets, lay trays of anti-tank mine fuses and insert the tubes into the bombs and grenades that would take them. It might have looked easy to the outsider, but it had to be pinpoint accurate to avoid accidents.

They were checked at the door by a supervisor and then they all trooped off to their work stations to be met by the regular thudding of the heavy machinery and the toxic stink of sulphur. The vast areas on both floors were divided into small workshops, each devoted to a particular munition. Ivy waved farewell to Mabel and Glad, who worked on filling landmines, and headed off upstairs to her own area with Freda and Dot, where they'd be filling anti-tank shells.

She set to work with a will, knowing that the harder she worked the more money she could make, and the quicker the night would pass. It was a matter of pride to Ivy that she could send her mum a good dollop of money each week and still manage to save a bit after she'd paid for essentials like new dungarees and shirts and decent underwear. The sum in her post office book was looking very healthy after nine months of this, and her aim was to save enough to be able to rent her own place and tell Doris where she could get off.

The job wasn't really that simple, for the rockets had to be filled up to a certain level from something resembling a large watering can. The mixture began to set almost immediately on contact with the shell, so the tube that would hold the detonator had to be quickly and accurately inserted. Then the whole thing had to be cleaned and scraped until it was at exactly the right depth inside the shell. It was, in fact, quite heavy work, for when her supply of TNT ran out she had to take her can over to a huge machine that looked like a cement mixer. This was filled with hot TNT, and the pong was so bad it turned her stomach and made her eyes water.

The night went on and Ivy had filled up her can several times. She was tired now and knew she had to be careful, for tiredness made people careless. She discovered that her can was empty yet again and so took it to the machine where Fred Ayling, who was in charge, could pour more of the revolting, stinking stuff into her can.

It weighed a ton and her arms were trembling as she carried it back towards her work bench, but when she tried to pass it from one hand to the other her boot skidded on something left on the floor and she went crashing down.

She cried out as the can's contents covered her legs and quickly spread around her.

'It's all right, ducks, I got you,' said Harry the foreman, and he picked her up and carried her at a run across the factory floor towards the medical room.

'Me legs,' she yelled. 'They're burning.'

'Lucky it weren't yer face, love,' he muttered, depositing her on an examination trolley.

Ivy struggled to get her dungarees off, but the doctor appeared and gently pushed her back onto the bed. 'You'll have to wait until it's set,' he said. 'Then it will all come off in one piece and we can save your dungarees.'

'I don't care about me flamin' dungarees,' she snapped. 'What about me legs?'

'They'll be fine,' he said. 'You'll just have to be

patient, and then you'll see. Nurse will see to you now, and once the gel has been removed you can go back to work.'

Ivy sat up and stared at her legs, praying that she wouldn't be scarred, and that the goo would set quickly so she could get it off. As the clock ticked away the time, the TNT began to set like a pale yellow jelly to mould the shape of her boots, legs and baggy trousers.

She began to pluck at the edges, but the nurse pushed her hand away and, after testing it, managed to get it all off. 'There,' she said. 'That wasn't too bad, was it?'

Ivy gingerly rolled up her slightly charred trousers to discover that all the hairs had been burnt away on her legs and the skin was red and tender to the touch. 'Blimey,' she breathed.

The nurse grinned. 'That'll save having to shave them for a while,' she said. 'Now, I'll put some salve on them to take away the redness, and then you can go back to work.'

'No chance of a cuppa first, I suppose?' Ivy asked cheekily. The nurse shook her head and Ivy sighed. 'Oh well, there was no 'arm in asking, were there?'

She slid off the table once the salve had been applied, and rolled down her trouser legs. With a glance at the clock on the wall she realised she'd wasted almost an hour of valuable earning time, so she hurried back into the factory, picked up a fresh can and got back to work.

The days had sped past and now it was Wednesday: tonight would be the last time Jane would sleep at Beach View. It was a sobering thought, and Peggy knew how much Sarah was dreading their separation. A party was planned for this evening at the Anchor, so that was something to look forward to, but otherwise the day would be like any other, filled with work and responsibilities. As if to emphasise the fact, the sirens went off just as Peggy was about to dole out the morning porridge.

There was a collective groan of frustration, and then everyone went into the routine that was almost second nature by now. As Harvey howled to the heavens and shot out of the back door, Ron carried the hot pot of porridge to the shelter along with bowls and spoons, while Rita helped Cordelia down the steps and along the garden path.

Jane had already left for her last session at the dairy and Fran for the hospital, so it was left to Sarah to grab everyone's overcoats and ease Daisy out of her high chair. Peggy threw the bread and margarine into the emergency box along with a sharp knife, spare box of matches and the little worn rug, and carried it out into the back garden.

The corrugated-iron Anderson shelter huddled malevolently at the bottom of the garden by the flint wall. It was covered in earth which now sprouted with Ron's spring vegetable seedlings, and was about as welcoming as a morgue. There were two steps down to the concrete floor from the narrow entrance and Ron had fixed wooden benches along the sides. A sturdy deckchair had been wedged into a corner beneath the arched roof so Cordelia could be comfortable during the long hours they'd had to spend in here, and if she fell asleep, which she often did, she was kept from sliding out of it with two fat pillows.

The overriding smell of the shelter was an earthy damp, and no matter what Ron did, he couldn't stop water from dripping down the metal walls onto the floor where it lay in dirty puddles. Peggy had done her best to make it cosy with a paraffin heater, a tilley lamp and gas ring, but sitting huddled in there for hour upon hour was not a favourite pastime for any of them.

There had been some discussion over whether they should invest in a Morrison shelter, which was a large, cage-like structure of steel, wood and wire that could be erected indoors. However, no one liked the idea of being trapped in such a thing should the house fall down around them, and once Ron had pointed out that, with so many people to accommodate, it was also impractical, they'd suppressed their dislike for the Anderson shelter, accepting it was better than nothing.

They crowded in and shut the door as the sirens wailed and Harvey howled piteously. There was very little room to manoeuvre, for the benches left only a narrow aisle in the middle, and the far end of the shelter was lined with shelves that were laden with tin mugs and plates, spare candles, old magazines, a large canister of fresh water, a kettle, and a can of paraffin to restock the heater.

Peggy put the box down on a bench as Ron mopped up the puddles on the floor and Rita settled Cordelia in her chair, pulling a blanket over her knees and hands to keep off the chill. Daisy wriggled and screamed in protest as Sarah tried to get her into the specially adapted cot that served as protection against any gas attack, and as the high-pitched noise rang through the metal shelter it even managed to drown out the sound of the sirens.

Peggy winced. 'Let her be, Sarah. It's too early in the morning for that sort of racket, and she's getting too big to put in it, really.' She pulled the worn rug out of the box and laid it on the floor.

Daisy was immediately all smiles, and she pulled herself up Ron's leg and beamed up at him before she lost her balance and bumped down on her bottom. Ron picked her up and she roared with laughter as she gave his wayward brows a hefty tug.

'Ach, to be sure you've a fair grip,' he muttered. 'I wish you wouldn't do that.'

'It's your own fault, Ron,' said Cordelia. 'If you trimmed those brows she wouldn't be able to get hold of them.'

Ron grimaced as he eased Daisy's little fist open and then bounced her on his knee to distract her. 'I'll not be trimming anything,' he grumbled.

'That's rather obvious,' she retorted with a sniff.

'To be sure, Cordelia Finch, 'tis too early to be at odds with anyone. Why don't you turn off that hearing aid so a man can get a wee bit of peace?'

'And to be sure, Ronan Reilly, it wouldn't make a bit of difference,' she replied waspishly. 'I'd still have to look at you – and I have to say, it's a particularly unattractive sight this morning after all the beer you obviously consumed last night.'

Ron rolled his eyes and looked to the others for a bit of sympathy, but there was clearly none forthcoming. He put Daisy down to crawl about the small rug Peggy had laid on the floor. ''Tis a terrible shame to mock the afflicted,' he grumbled. 'What with me moving shrapnel and me medal for bravery, one would have thought I'd earned at least a little respect.'

'Your headache is self-inflicted,' said Cordelia, 'so don't come the old soldier with me.'

Ron sighed deeply and then grinned at Daisy, who was looking up at him trustingly, and chucked her under the chin. 'At least one member of this family thinks I'm the bee's knees,' he said.

'Only because she's too young to understand what a liability you can be.' Cordelia's glare of disapproval was rather marred by the twinkle in her eyes.

Peggy and the others were used to these minor spats and took little notice of them, for they knew that for all their arguing, there was a deep affection between Ron and Cordelia. Peggy doled out the porridge and they all sat in their overcoats eating their breakfast as the sirens stopped wailing and the seagulls mewled and wailed overhead.

Harvey stopped howling and wedged himself beneath the bench with a sigh of contentment. He didn't mind the sound of the planes, or the thump and crump of bombs, he just hated that siren.

Peggy eyed the pair of them with affection. Ron was looking decidedly the worse for wear after yet another night of celebratory drinking, and Harvey didn't look much better. 'Have you been giving him beer again?' she asked as she fed Daisy.

'Aye. He likes a drop now and again.'

'It's not good for him, you know.'

'A little of what you fancy does no harm,' he rumbled as he finished his porridge. 'Are you going to put that kettle on, Peggy? A man could die of thirst, so he could.'

Peggy filled the tin kettle from the canister of water, lit the gas ring and hunted out tea and milk from the emergency box. 'I hope this doesn't go on for too long,' she muttered. 'I have to get to the shops this morning and then I've got my shift with the WVS at the Town Hall.'

'Bertie's taking me to lunch at the Conservative Club again,' said Cordelia for the umpteenth time that morning. 'I wonder what they'll be serving? Last time we had lamb cutlets.'

Peggy's mouth watered at the thought of lamb cutlets smothered in thick, rich gravy and lashings of buttery mash and mint sauce. Whoever was doing the catering at that club had to have connections with a black marketeer or a very obliging butcher, for she hadn't seen such a thing in months. She finished feeding Daisy and then smeared a bit of the regulation margarine on a slice of wheatmeal bread for her. It was foul-tasting stuff, made from fish oil of all things, but as Daisy had rarely tasted proper butter, she quite liked it.

The roar of fighter planes leaving Cliffe aerodrome reverberated through the shelter, and as Rita's gaze followed the sound, Peggy's heart went out to her. Matthew was her first love, so of course her emotions were heightened, and Peggy could understand how hard it must be for her to hear those planes and not know if he was up there – and if he was, whether he would return safely.

89

As wave after wave of Spitfires and Hurricanes thundered above them, Peggy's thoughts turned to Martin and all the pilots she'd been privileged to meet over the years. There had been tragic losses and close shaves, but it seemed this young generation was made of sterling stuff, and no matter what they had to face, they carried on determinedly. Kitty Makepeace was a prime example, for having lost a leg in the service of the Air Transport Auxiliary, she'd overcome the handicap, learned to walk on her prosthesis, got married to Roger, and climbed straight back into a plane again. Roger was still flying too, along with Kitty's brother, Freddy, in Martin's squadron, and all she could do was pray they would come through unscathed.

Ron poured some tea in a saucer for Harvey and then glared belligerently at the noise of the planes. He'd definitely had more than a drop too many the night before, for his head was pounding and the racket the RAF was making didn't help. Yet he realised they were heading west, so the enemy raid was probably going on further down the coast – in which case it wouldn't be long before the all-clear went.

He leaned back against the cold, damp wall of the shelter and quickly glanced across at Sarah before closing his eyes. She looked pale this morning, which was hardly surprising, for he'd come home well after midnight to find her alone and tearful in the kitchen. Immediately concerned, he'd made tea for them both and over the next hour or so, they'd discussed Jane's posting, and the very real fear she had that her young sister might find herself out of her depth amongst such august company.

Ron had been a bit befuddled with the drink, but he could empathise with the girl and allay her fears over her sister, who was clearly more than capable of standing on her own two feet. He also understood that Sarah's concerns were not just for Jane. She had a great deal to contend with, for not only was she far from home and family, but she'd been charged with her sister's care and now faced the prospect of being parted from her until the war ended, and having to keep all this from their mother.

On top of all that she'd confided in him about the American and her feelings for him, and the awful guilt she felt over what she saw as a betrayal of Philip. His heart had gone out to her as he struggled to find the right words that might help, for he'd been in a similar situation during the First World War and had wrestled for months with his own guilt. He knew he wasn't as good as Peggy with this sort of thing, and although he was flattered that the girl trusted him enough to confide in him, he'd found it a little awkward. But he'd done his best, and she'd seemed a little more positive by the time she'd finally gone back to bed.

He gave a sigh. There had been times over the past four years when he'd also felt adrift and helpless. Uncertainty over the future made him fret, for he'd already lost two grandsons – Frank's eldest boys – when their minesweeper blew up in the Atlantic. And now he had Jim and Frank to

91

worry over, as well as his surviving grandchildren and great-grandchildren who were scattered to the four winds, communication with them rare and unsatisfactory.

He gritted his teeth. This damned war had a lot to answer for, and if he'd been a younger man he'd have taken up arms and gone over there to knock Hitler's ruddy block off. Yet he knew his limitations and was content to do his bit for the Home Guard and shoulder the responsibility for Frank's wife, as well as Peggy and the rest of the household, until Jim and Frank came home and the family could be together again.

His thoughts drifted back to the conversation he'd had with Sarah, and to the girls who'd come and gone over the years. Peggy clucked over them like a mother hen, but these girls weren't helpless chicks, for every one of them had skills to play their part against Hitler's tyranny – and to Ron's mind, there was one in particular who would always stick out as very special.

Danuta had escaped from Poland early on in the war, and had come to Beach View in search of her brother who, sadly, had been shot down during an RAF raid over France. Ron had been very taken with her, for she was a fearless little thing, highly intelligent and burning with the desire to crush the enemy that had wiped out her entire family. Having survived the slaughter in Poland and made her way through enemy terri-tory to England, she was well qualified to fulfil that ambition, and had been frustrated that the only job she could get was in the hospital laundry or driving an ambulance.

Ron had understood her frustration and, through his many contacts, had arranged for her to meet some people who would hone her skills in covert attacks and sabotage as well as the more refined arts of spying and Morse code. He could only make an educated guess at what Danuta had been involved in since she'd left Beach View – and of course her irregular letters to Peggy revealed nothing – but he suspected she'd been parachuted in behind enemy lines to co-ordinate with the Resistance, and perhaps even to use her language skills to gather vital intelligence.

And now little Jane Fuller was following in her footsteps to Bletchley Park – not to spy or risk her life in occupied Europe, but to decode and decipher German signals.

He'd said nothing of this to Sarah, for he'd signed the Official Secrets Act many years ago and still adhered to it. And yet the years of covert action in the Special Forces during the first shout, and the contacts he'd made throughout this most secret of services, often meant that he knew a great deal about what was really going on – things deemed unsuitable for public consumption as morale had to be maintained.

He was roused from his thoughts as the all-clear sounded and Harvey started to scrabble at the door. He let the dog out, shooed the girls off to work, rolled up the rug, and helped Cordelia to her feet. Taking the heavy box of emergency rations from Peggy, he hurried indoors, and then grabbed his poaching coat. He needed fresh air and exercise after sitting in that shelter, and the hills above Cliffehaven were calling him – but first he'd make his weekly visit to the cemetery to place wild flowers on the graves of Danuta's brother, Aleksy, and her stillborn daughter Katarzyna. He'd promised Danuta he'd watch over them, and he intended to do so for as long as he lived.

Peggy had a great deal on her mind that morning as she stood in the slow-moving queue at the butcher's, so much so that, unusually, she was hardly aware of the gossip going on around her. There had been no airgraph from Jim in the morning post, which meant she hadn't heard from him for almost a month, which was more of a frustration than a worry, for she knew how delayed the mail could get – and yet it would have been nice to hear from him a little more regularly now he was actually settled at the mobile workshop on active service.

She edged forward with the queue as Daisy burbled in response to the attention from the other women, and gave scant notice to the speculation that there might be pork chops on sale this morning. Rumours were rife in every queue and rarely proved true, so there was little point in expecting anything remotely appetising.

Peggy's thoughts turned to Sarah and Jane. She'd heard someone go down to the kitchen very late and hadn't really given it much thought until she'd heard the sound of stifled sobs. She'd guessed it was Sarah, and had been on the point of going in to comfort her when she'd heard the rumble of Ron's voice. She'd lain awake until she heard Sarah return to her bedroom, and had hoped that her father-in-law had managed to quell the girl's concerns. Ron, of course, had said nothing this morning and shot off before she could pin him down and question him, but she suspected his wisdom and kind-heartedness had done the trick as usual.

Peggy inched forward again as a woman emerged from the butcher's clasping a small white package. 'What did you get?' she asked.

'Offal and a bit of mince,' she replied with a grimace.

Peggy nodded and sighed. She'd forget what proper meat tasted like at this rate, and Cordelia's remark about lamb cutlets still resonated, making the reality even harder to deal with.

She inched the pram forward and then turned up her coat collar and huddled within the long line of women to shelter from the icy wind that was tearing up from the sea. March was a depressing month at the best of times, but this year it felt as if spring would never come. What with the shortages and restrictions, the damp cold and the seemingly endless roar of RAF planes overhead, life was tougher than ever and her usual buoyant spirits had deserted her.

Her thoughts returned to the girls living at Beach View, and the empty rooms that could house someone in need. She really should do something about them – especially now that Jane was leaving tomorrow. Perhaps little Ivy might like to move in?

Stan, the stationmaster, had told her that Ivy wasn't very happy at Doris's now that Mary had returned home to Sussex. The new girl billeted there was from Chelsea or somewhere posh, and worked as a private secretary for the administrator at the hospital. According to Stan, who kept a close eye on everything that happened in Cliffehaven, this Caroline really thought a lot of herself, and to Ivy's dismay had toadied up to Doris something shocking. Now the pair of them had ganged up on her and made it clear she was only there under sufferance.

With the decision made to approach Ivy, Peggy felt a little better. She finally reached the counter. 'Good morning, Alf,' she said with determined cheerfulness. 'What delights are on offer today, then?'

His large, ruddy face looked doleful as his gaze swept down the waiting queue of housewives. 'Scrag end, offal, a bit of minced meat. Sorry, Peg.'

'I'll take as much as you can give me.' Peggy put her ration book on the counter and began to count out her money. Running the boarding house meant she received special food stamps – more than the average household – but even this largesse was barely enough to provide everyone with a decent plateful of food.

Alf weighed the unappetising-looking meat, and with sleight of hand that would have put a master magician to shame, conjured up three sausages which were wrapped in the blink of an eye with the rest. He winked as he took the stamps and money. 'Tell Ron the boys are meeting this Sunday,' he murmured, all too aware of those listening in the queue.

Peggy experienced a thrill of pleasure and nodded. Having stuffed the parcel at the foot of the pram, she pushed her way out of the shop, carefully avoiding the ever-watchful and suspicious gazes of the other women. Alf's cryptic message meant only one thing. A pig would be slaughtered early Sunday – one that hadn't been counted in by the food inspectors – and as Ron paid in each week to help feed and fatten the beast, he'd be in line for some of its meat.

With her spirits soaring at the thought of pork chops, Peggy's next stop was at the bakery where there was no queue. Bread wasn't rationed and as no one liked the wheatmeal loaf the government insisted they ate to conserve the stocks of white flour, people were in no hurry to buy it. With four loaves tucked into the basket beneath the pram, Peggy continued on to the hardware shop where she managed to get a light bulb, some candles, a can of paraffin and several boxes of matches. It seemed these too were in short supply and she came out with half of what she actually needed. Then it was on to the tobacconist's where she actually managed to get two packets of Park Drive, which was a real treat, and a couple of colouring books which she would send to Doreen's little girls, Joyce and Evie.

There were numerous stops on the way to the Home and Colonial stores, for Peggy knew so many people who, unlike her, seemed to have the time to chat. As each of them sang Ron's praises and asked after Harvey she felt even better, and by the time she'd parked the pram outside the large general store, she was back to her old cheerful self.

Doris's husband Ted was looking resplendent

in his pristine white coat as he stood behind the sadly depleted dairy counter and kept an eye on his staff. His decision to remain in the flat upstairs seemed to agree with him, for his usual, rather solemn expression had been replaced by a broad smile. 'Good morning, Peggy. And how are you?'

'Very well, considering,' she replied. 'And you look cheerful this morning too. How are things?'

He grinned back at her as he took her shopping list. 'I'm more content than I ever was. Master of all I survey and free to do as I like,' he replied. 'I should have left years ago.'

Peggy felt a twinge of pity for her sister, but it didn't last, for Doris had virtually forced him out of the house with her bossiness and lack of respect and care. 'So there's no chance of you going back to her then?'

He shook his head and carefully weighed out the few ounces of cheese she was permitted. 'Things would have to change radically, and I don't think that's likely, do you?'

Peggy didn't. 'Have you heard from Anthony and Suzy lately?'

'I saw Suzy the other day when she popped in for some shopping after her shift at the hospital, and Anthony has telephoned his mother. But they're still at the honeymoon stage, so I doubt we'll see much of them for a while.'

'It's not just their honeymoon keeping them occupied,' she said. 'They're both so busy with doing up that cottage and fulfilling their work commitments, I doubt they have time for anything else.'

Ted wrapped the cheese and placed it beside the pat of margarine and the tiny knob of real butter. 'I'm sorry I can't give you more, but you know what it's like,' he said ruefully.

She did indeed, but there was little point in moaning about it. Everyone was in the same boat.

Ted added the tins of Spam and corned beef, and with a wink, handed over a tin of peas. 'These came in yesterday, so I put one by for you.'

'Thanks, Ted, you're a diamond.' She hastily stowed everything away in her string bag and handed over the stamps and the money. 'And please come and visit whenever you want. You're still family, after all, and Ron could do with a bit of male company now the house is full of women.'

His smile was soft with affection. 'Thanks, Peg. I just might do that. But you're not to worry about me. I'm very content with my own company when I'm not playing golf, and I enjoy listening to my records and reading all the books I should have read long ago.'

'You play golf at the same club as Bertie Grantley-Adams, don't you?' At his nod, she continued, 'How do you find him?'

He looked rather puzzled by her question. 'He's a pleasant chap, and jolly good company.' He regarded her steadily. 'He's been escorting your Cordelia about lately, hasn't he?'

'Well, yes, and I've heard rumours that he's a bit of a ladies' man.'

'The women like him, certainly, and he's never made a secret of the fact. But I'm sure his intentions towards Cordelia are honourable.'

Peggy laughed. 'I should jolly well hope so at his age. Good heavens.'

'I didn't mean that sort of honourable,' he blustered. 'I meant that he's a well-set-up sort of chap, with a nice house and a good pension. He's not after Cordelia's money, if that's what's worrying you.'

It had rather, but she wasn't going to tell Ted that. She said goodbye and headed home. There was a lot to do before she had to get to the Town Hall for her afternoon shift with the WVS.

5

London

Doreen gripped Archie's sturdy arm and tried to keep up with him as they picked their way through the rubble in the blackout. Her mind was full of warm memories of the hours they'd spent in that hotel bedroom, and yet her bubble of happiness slowly deflated as they neared the station, for these would be the last few precious hours they would spend together until he was home on leave again. The week had passed so quickly; it didn't seem possible that before the night was out his ship would set sail and she would be heading back to Kent.

'I don't know about you, Doreen, but I'm starving,' he boomed as they came to an eel and pie shop. He looked down at her, his blue eyes

100

twinkling with merriment as he made no effort to lower his voice. 'It must be all that exercise we've had today.'

Doreen blushed and giggled as she swiftly glanced round to see if anyone had overheard him. 'Shh, you. I don't want half of London to hear what we've been up to.'

He dropped his kitbag and enfolded her in his arms, lifting her from the cracks and potholes in the pavement so he could plant a soft kiss on her lips. 'I don't care if the whole world knows how much I love you,' he murmured before gently setting her back on her feet and lightly smacking her bottom. 'Come on, girl, time you had a proper East End supper.'

Doreen reluctantly followed him into the empty café. Blackout covered the window and the glass in the door, but the light was bright inside. Jellied eels were laid out in dishes, pies were being kept warm above the fryer, a great pot of mushy peas was simmering on a gas ring, and the delicious smell of vinegar and fried potato made her mouth water. 'I'll just have chips,' she said.

He eyed her with amusement, his gaze travelling from her dark, curly hair, over her slender body and down to the sensible shoes, scuffed from walking the streets of the East End. 'I'll keep an eye on your figure, never you mind. At least have a pie and peas with the chips. You can't visit this neck of the woods without giving it a go.'

'What's in the pie?'

The woman behind the counter seemed to take offence at this and glared back at her. 'Spam and spud. There is a war, on yer know.'

Doreen stuck with chips while Archie ordered just about everything on offer, and the woman winked at him before fishing out a bottle of beer from under the counter. 'I always keep some by for our boys,' she said, plonking it on the counter. 'On the 'ouse, love.' She tapped the side of her nose with a grubby finger.

Doreen would have liked a beer, but it seemed she was not to be included in this generosity, so she asked for a cup of tea. When their food was ready, they carried the plates to a nearby table and sat down. She shuddered as she eyed the slimy jellied eel mounded on Archie's plate next to the suspiciously green mushy peas, the pie and the pile of fat, greasy chips. She honestly didn't know how he could eat such a very odd concoction.

He seemed oblivious to her sensibilities and ate his way methodically through his food while she nibbled on her rather soggy chips. He finally wiped the plate clean with a slab of unbuttered wheatmeal bread and sat back. 'That's better,' he sighed. 'We don't get food half as good on board ship.'

'We certainly don't get eel and pie in Halstead,' she replied, giving up on the unappetising chips.

'That's because they're all soft in Kent – don't have the stomach for decent food.'

She realised there was no point in arguing about it. Archie was a Cockney through and through, so nothing she could say would change his mind. She took a sip of tea and almost gagged. It was so stewed and strong it had the consistency of engine oil.

His laughter was loud and seemed to fill the tiny café. 'That's proper East End tea, my girl. Put hairs on your chest, that will.'

Doreen blushed and dipped her chin as she realised their exchange was being eagerly listened to by the woman behind the counter. 'It's all very well for you,' she hissed across the table. 'You're used to it.'

His expression became more serious as he reached across the table, his large hands engulfing her fingers. 'I'm sorry, Dor. I know it's not fair to tease you, but if you and me are going to have some sort of future together, you're going to have to learn to like eels and pie, and tea so strong you can stand a spoon up in it.'

Her heart began to thud as she looked into his tanned face and saw her reflection in his eyes. She loved him so much, and if the price of being with him for the rest of their lives was to eat eels every day, then she would make herself like them. And yet all this talk of being together wasn't exactly a proposal, so there was no point in getting ahead of herself. She decided it would be better to keep things on a lighter note.

'You can certainly take the boy out of the East End, but you can't take the East End out of the boy – no matter how big and grown-up he is,' she teased.

'It's who I am,' he said simply. 'This is where I was born and where I grew up. I might be all of a swagger in this uniform, but underneath beats the heart of a true Cockney.'

Doreen was well aware of the tough childhood he'd had growing up in this part of London, and

103

how hard he'd strived to escape the endless poverty and hardship through his naval apprenticeship, which had offered a good career. 'It wasn't all pie and eels, Archie,' she murmured, 'and things are even worse now the Luftwaffe has virtually flattened this part of London.'

He nodded solemnly then leaned back in his chair and drained the bottle of beer. 'I'm well aware of that, love. The old place is barely recognisable now.' He placed the bottle on the table and his smile was sad. 'But the spirit's still here, Doreen. Jerry will never destroy that, no matter what they do to us.'

Doreen realised that although his words were brave, he was still fretting over his parents' whereabouts. His search for them had come to nothing more than rumours and snatches of half-remembered sightings. It seemed they'd been bombed out twice in Shoreditch, and had managed to find temporary accommodation here in Bethnal Green. Yet that too had been so badly damaged in an air raid that it was deemed uninhabitable, and no one seemed to know where they'd gone after that – or even if they were still alive. It was an awful situation, and her heart went out to him.

'I'm sure the Red Cross or the Salvation Army people will track them down,' she said quietly. 'You mustn't give up hope.'

'I don't like leaving without knowing,' he rumbled. 'But I've no choice.'

'I've left my address with the different agencies, so if there is word, I can pass it on to you.' She rested her hand on his, wishing she could do more to help.

He took a deep breath and his mood lightened as he gently chucked her under the chin. 'No news is good news, as they say. If they were killed they'd be on some register somewhere. I expect they've gone to Wales to be with my sister and her brood.'

Doreen nodded but she wasn't convinced, for surely if they had gone to Wales, they would have written to him by now? She could see that he was thinking the same thing, but neither of them wanted to voice their doubts, for that would only make them seem more concrete.

He pushed back from the table and settled his peaked hat on his head before shooting her a beaming smile. 'Come on, girl. Let's take a stroll in Victoria Park. There's another half-hour before my train leaves and it would be a shame to waste it.'

Doreen smiled her thanks at the woman behind the counter and hurried outside, and Archie swiftly closed the door behind them: the ARP wardens were quick to spot a light in the black-out.

Archie hauled the kitbag over his shoulder and slipped his free arm about Doreen, holding her close to his side. They walked slowly down the street, guided only by a pale moon which appeared occasionally between the scudding clouds that promised yet more rain. It had been a gloomy day which they'd managed to escape by being tucked up snugly in bed together, and now, as the time for him to leave approached, it seemed to Doreen that the weather mirrored her mood exactly.

105

It was as if he sensed her thoughts, for he drew to a halt, pulled her closer and tipped up her chin so he could look into her eyes. 'It won't be long before I'm back again,' he said softly, 'so don't spoil this moment by thinking the worst.' He lightly kissed her brow. 'I've survived this long, and you know what they say about only the good dying young.' He shot her a wolfish grin 'Well, I'm a bad bad boy, and the Devil takes care of his own.'

Doreen wished she possessed the same faith, for she knew only too well how many brave men had been lost in the Atlantic over the past four years. She clung to him and breathed in his scent, safe for the moment in his strong arms, the sound of his steady heartbeat drumming in her ear.

They stood lost in each other as people scurried past them in the blackout. Life for Doreen was far more secure than for Archie, and she wished with all her heart that she could somehow cast a spell around him and keep him safe. Yet in reality he would remain in peril, while she would return to the house in Halstead that she shared with her colleagues, and continue her work in the knowledge that the government had seen to it that Fort Halstead's scientists and office staff were furnished with deep underground shelters and early warning systems.

'We can't change anything at the moment, Dor,' he murmured. 'But we can begin to make plans for when this war's over.'

She looked up at him, half afraid that if they made plans it would tempt fate.

He smiled. 'I know what you're thinking, girl, but if we don't make plans, then what's this war all about? It's important not to be bogged down in the present, but to look forward. You do understand that, don't you?'

She nodded and sniffed back the ready tears, determined not to spoil the moment. 'So what plans are you dreaming up, Archie?'

'You and me, girl, that's what,' he said gruffly. 'You and me and your girls in a little house by the sea; surrounded by our nippers.'

'Oh, Archie, that sounds wonderful,' she sighed. 'But what about your career? Won't you be staying in the Navy?'

He shook his head and grimaced. 'By the time this lot is over I'll have had enough of shipboard life,' he said. 'My plan is to start up my own business. England's going to need engineers to get her back on her feet again.'

'Then that's what we'll do,' she said softly.

He looked deeply into her eyes. 'I love you, Dor, and although I realise this is hardly the most romantic place to ask such a thing but... Will you marry me?'

Her heart seemed to swell as she reached up to cup his face in her hands. 'Of course I will, dear, dear Archie.'

He pulled her to him and kissed her passionately until she was quite breathless, then set her back on her feet and grinned down at her. 'You've made me the happiest man alive,' he said. 'And when I come home next we'll get a special licence. I'm not going to let you slip away from me ever again.'

107

Doreen gazed up into his eyes, overwhelmed by the depth of feeling she had for him.

Archie kissed her on the nose and then flung his arms wide and danced in a circle. 'I'm getting married!' he boomed out into the still night. 'My darling Doreen said yes!'

Doreen blushed furiously and tried to silence him as passers-by shouted their congratulations. 'Archie, stop it,' she pleaded, not knowing whether to laugh or cry with happiness.

He finally stopped prancing about and drew her snugly into his arms. 'I want the world to know what a lucky man I am,' he said.

'I think they got the message,' she replied through her laughter.

'Are you sure?'

She giggled. 'Absolutely certain. They could probably hear you in Cliffehaven, if not Carlisle.'

'That's all right then. And when I come back, we'll go down to Cliffehaven so your family can give me the once over.' He kept his hand round her waist and they wandered down the street towards the park gates, content with each other and the promise of a golden future.

The low moan of the siren slowly rose to an ear-splitting shriek as the searchlights fizzed into life and began to quarter the skies.

Archie grabbed her hand and started walking quickly away from the park.

She had to run to keep up with him. 'Where are we going?'

'To the new tube station,' he shouted back above the racket of the sirens.

'Can't we just go back to the café and sit it out?'

she begged.

'Don't be daft, Doreen. The tube's well underground. You'll be much safer there.'

She knew he was being sensible, but she had a morbid fear of dark, enclosed places, and even with Archie by her side, she knew she would have a terrible job keeping panic at bay. It was the same every time she had to go into the enormous shelters at the Fort – and they were light and airy compared to the fusty, gloomy tube stations.

Trying to be brave, she hurried along beside him. By now they were caught up in a stream of people coming out of the cinema and pubs and teeming from their homes, laden with night bundles and children. When Doreen saw where they were heading, her temporary courage deserted her and she pulled her hand from his grip and froze. The frontage of the tube station was covered in sheets of black-painted corrugated iron, and the entrance was so narrow that only one or two people could pass through it at the same time. It looked horribly dark down there, and the crush of people waiting to descend was growing by the minute. Cold sweat broke out on her spine. 'I can't, Archie. Really I can't.'

'I'll look after you,' he said, kissing her hair. 'Just hold my hand and stick close.'

Doreen knew she was being feeble and did her best not to show it, but the thought of going down into that black hole with so many people made her feel quite faint with terror. She closed her eyes, leaning against him in an effort to glean courage from his strength and solidity, but her heart was racing, the perspiration now running down her back.

Hand in hand they joined the orderly queue just as three buses screeched to a halt nearby and disgorged dozens of passengers who added to the line. The sirens were still shrieking, the search-lights still weaving across the scudding clouds and black sky, but there was no sign of the enemy. And yet everyone knew that now Jerry had lighter, swifter bombers there was less time to find shelter, and after the heavy bombing raids by the RAF two days ago on Berlin, it was odds-on that the Germans would retaliate.

They shuffled forward at a steady pace as those in front disappeared through the narrow entrance. Women were carrying babies and shopping bags, men and boys struggled with rolls of bedding, and the elderly were helped to move more quickly by willing hands. There seemed to be little fear.

Although Doreen had never witnessed it before, she'd heard about the stoic spirit of the East Enders, who'd borne the brunt of the Blitz and the terrible firestorm that had followed – and who, unlike her, now preferred to spend every night deep underground in the tube stations surrounded by other people.

Archie had to bend to get through the low opening and Doreen took a deep breath for courage as she followed him. A single light bulb, almost covered in black paint to meet the blackout regulations, barely alleviated the darkness, and panic was a living thing uncurling inside Doreen as she gripped Archie's hand and tried to find her way. Step by agonising step she shuffled down the unmarked stairs, using the wall to steady herself but unable to see anything beyond the moving shadows of the people in front of her.

'It's all right, love. I won't let you go. Just take it easy, there's no rush.'

She knew he was doing his best to keep her calm, but as she felt the press of people behind her and breathed in the stale, humid air of tightly packed humanity, she wondered how fast her heart could beat before it failed altogether.

She shuffled her foot forward to find the edge of the rain-soaked step, wishing there was a railing to cling to as well as Archie's hand. The narrow stairs meant she was pressed against the damp, unforgiving wall, and her overnight bag was heavy in her arm as she clutched it to her chest.

The explosion rocked the ground beneath her feet and trembled in the walls. The terrifying whoosh that followed it made her flinch and gasp in panic.

'It's a new kind of bomb,' someone cried out.

'Jerry's attacking. Quick, quick. The raid's started.'

The terror was infectious and the stumbling, steady pace was quickened as the cries of alarm echoed through the dark tunnel. And as those from above tried to push their way in, there was no choice but to be carried along in the great tide that was now moving quite swiftly into the bowels of the earth.

Doreen's fear was all-consuming as she was forced deeper and deeper into the unknown darkness, and it was becoming almost impossible to resist the desperate urge to turn and fight her way back to the open air. 'I have to get out,' she cried. 'Archie, help me get out.'

'Hold tight, darling, and just keep going,' he called above the surrounding noise. 'We're almost halfway there now.'

Only halfway? It felt as if they'd been going down these steps for hours. Was there to be no reprieve? Doreen could feel the darkness closing in on her as the press of bodies forced her downward. She stared blindly into the impenetrable blackness, realising that if she fainted now she'd fall and be trampled. It took every ounce of courage to keep going, Archie's strong hand the only thing keeping her from becoming mad with fear.

Her foot was on the very edge of the step when she felt the soft but determined press of bodies behind her, and as she was still trying to keep her balance, she was forced closer to the woman in front. As she knocked against her she heard someone below cry out and suddenly the gap widened in front of her.

She didn't have time to realise what was happening, or to take a breath, for the pressure behind had grown, ripping her hand from Archie's and sending her stumbling into the void. As she collided with someone ahead of her she felt a thud on her back which almost knocked the air from her lungs, and realised in horror that the line of people on the stairs were tumbling like dominoes and there was no way to stop it.

'Archie!' she screamed before her cry was cut short by the weight of those falling on her. She couldn't breathe, was crushed and buried, her

112

chest pinned to the wall. She had to get out – to find a way to reach air.

Terror and the desperate need to survive made her feral, and she began to push and claw and fight to free herself. Her lungs were burning now, her head was pounding, and there was so little room to manoeuvre, but she had to live – not only for Archie, but for her children.

At the thought of her two precious little girls she gave one last tremendous shove and finally, finally had her head above the crush. But there was no relief, for her neck was unbearably stretched and she was so tightly pressed between those around her and the wall that she could only snatch a tiny amount of air into her aching lungs.

Her heart was pounding as she struggled to keep her head above the press and breathe, and the darkness seemed to creep into her head as a terrible inertia came over her. It would be so easy to close her eyes and give up. To fall asleep...

Her eyes snapped open. Her children needed her. Archie needed her. To give up was to die, and she wasn't ready to die, not yet – and certainly not like this.

As she fought to breathe and keep her head above the crush, she could hear the feeble cry of a baby mingling with soft groans and desperate pleas for help. She could do nothing to help herself, let alone anyone else, for her arms were pinned to her sides and she didn't have enough breath to call out. But she could feel someone breathing close to her and could only pray that it was Archie, and that rescue would come before it was too late for any of them.

It was a living nightmare from which she feared she would never escape, for she was growing weaker by the minute. The cries for help were feebler now and the baby had stopped crying. There was a terrible silence permeating the stair-well, and a stillness that only increased her terror.

'Help,' she whispered on a frail breath. 'Help us, please.'

She had no idea of how long she'd been trapped there but it felt like a lifetime. Her head was swimming, her lungs burning as her heart began to struggle. The darkness was taking her, lulling her to sleep – a welcome sleep that promised relief from the pain and the terror – but a sleep strangely disturbed by the faint ringing of discordant bells and shouts.

Forcing her eyes open, she stared into the blackness as the bells and the shouts grew louder. And then it seemed the weight pressing on her was lightening and she was able to expand her lungs and breathe properly again. As she tried to understand what was happening a pair of strong arms lifted her up and carried her towards a shaft of pale light. She felt the cool mist of rain on her face and gratefully gulped down the wonderfully fresh, cold air. It was all right. She was alive and Archie had rescued her.

She looked up at the man who was carrying her. It wasn't Archie. 'You've got to find Archie,' she managed to gasp. 'He's big, with a beard and wearing naval uniform.'

'I expect he'll be with you soon, ducks,' he replied as he set her down beneath the railway arches and covered her with a rough blanket.

'You just sit tight and wait there so the medics can give you the once-over.'

Doreen, still numb and disorientated by her terrifying experience, watched him hurry away to join the other firemen. She couldn't think straight, her ribs felt crushed and every breath was like a knife as she tried to massage life back into her legs and arms and ease the awful crick in her neck. Yet that was nothing compared to the fear of not knowing what had happened to Archie, and as a first aider checked her over and declared her to be free of any broken bones, her gaze never left the rescuers who worked furiously to tear away the restrictive corrugated iron and bring up those trapped on the lethal stairs.

Some walked out without a scratch on them, bewildered and fearful for their loved ones; others had to be carried to the ambulances – while yet more were carried out in grim silence beneath blankets to be laid almost reverently on the pavement.

Doreen watched in growing disbelief and dread as the numbers of the dead increased and women screamed and sobbed over the pathetic remains of their children while men searched desperately for their loved ones, or simply slumped to the ground in shock, their faces blank and ashen with the sheer horror of it all. And through all this grim chaos, there was still no sign of Archie.

Still trembling with shock and sick with fear, she managed to get to her feet and stagger closer to the team of men working at the entrance to the tube. She stood aside while people emerged white-faced and shaken and children were handed up the line of willing rescuers to be scooped up by sobbing parents or the ladies from the WVS, who gave them tea and swaddled them in blankets.

Archie had to be helping the rescuers, she thought, otherwise she would have seen him by now. He was standing right next to her when she fell, so why wasn't he up here yet?

'Archie!' she yelled. 'Archie, are you down there?'

'Stand aside, miss,' said a grim-faced ARP warden. 'There ain't no one alive down there to hear you.'

She froze, unable to accept what he was saying. 'But he must be there,' she breathed. 'He's big and strong and probably helping get people out.'

A policeman came and took her arm. 'Now, now, miss, you come with me and have a nice cuppa. I'm sure you'll find him soon.'

She wrested her arm from his grip, wincing as the movement jarred her painful ribs. 'I don't want tea,' she retorted. 'I want Archie, and I'm not leaving here until I...'

Her eyes widened as two men emerged from the blackness carrying a stretcher. There was a blanket over the body, but the arm that hung down from beneath it was covered in Navy issue blue, there were gold bands at the cuff, and Archie's signet ring gleamed on his finger. 'No,' she breathed. 'No, no, no.'

As if wading through the morass of a hampering, clinging nightmare, she found she was following the stretcher bearers, and as he was gently lowered to the pavement she fell to her knees beside him. Numbed by pain and shock,

116

her hand trembled as she drew back the blanket that covered his face.

And there was Archie, his blue eyes staring through her to some far-off place, the laughter and life that had once shone from them now dulled and blank in death.

'Archie?' Doreen gently cradled his large head in her arms, her tears washing away the grime from his face – a face turned puce as he was smothered and crushed by the weight of all those who'd fallen on him. 'Archie,' she sobbed as she rocked back and forth, her fingers running through his thick black hair before cupping his face and covering it with kisses as if by sheer will she could breathe life back into him.

He lay heavy and still in her arms and she lifted her face to the skies and howled her anguish at the scudding clouds. How could he be dead when only minutes before they'd been talking about their future together? How could he be dead when he was so strong and sturdy – such a giant of a man who'd survived almost three years on the deadly Atlantic?

She bowed her head, resting her cheek against his, already feeling the first chill of death on his skin as her hot tears fell. How could fate have been so savage as to take this gentle, sweet man from her when all they'd wanted was to be together? And yet fate had shown no mercy, for it had snatched away their future in a moment, leaving her bereft and heartbroken.

Unaware of the turmoil around her, Doreen sat on the cold, damp pavement with Archie cradled to her heart as the unrelenting rain fell from an uncaring sky.

'Come on, love. We need to take him now.'

She looked up at the policeman and the warden, her thoughts shifting sluggishly, as she tightened her grip on Archie and shook her head.

'Come on, miss,' the policeman coaxed softly. 'We can't leave him here in the rain.'

'Where will you take him?' she asked as she continued to hold Archie to her heart.

'To the local morgue, miss. I'm sorry.'

She looked up at the men and a small part of her realised how difficult all this must be for them – and yet how could she let them take Archie from her? A morgue was cold and impersonal, and the final proof that Archie was gone. She tightened her grip on him, her thoughts in turmoil at all that she'd lost on this terrible night. Archie had been so full of life and energy; now she would never hear his laughter again or share an East End supper of eels and pies – or make love and see out their old age together surrounded by their children.

'Come on, love. I understand you don't want to let him go, but it's time. Really it is.'

She stared up at the policeman and saw from his expression that he really did understand the anguish she was going through – and that she had no option but to let them take Archie from her. She kissed his unresponsive lips for the last time and gently closed his eyes before allowing the warden to help her to her feet.

Once Archie's identification papers had been drawn from his pocket and placed on his chest, the blanket was drawn back over his face and two

ARP wardens carried the stretcher to a large army truck and deposited it in the flatbed alongside the other bodies.

'I want to go with him.'

'I'm sorry, miss, that won't be possible.' The policeman's face was lined and grey from the horrors he'd witnessed. 'But take this card. It's the address of the undertaker so you can make arrangements.'

Doreen took the card without reading it, her whole attention focused on the still figures beneath the blankets that would accompany her Archie to the morgue. As the truck's engine rumbled and the wheels began to turn she stood there in the rain unable to move – and as it disappeared around the corner and the sound of the engine faded, it was as if the living, breathing part of her had been carried away with it.

She slowly became aware of other trucks being loaded with the same tragic cargo – and as the sounds of sorrow finally penetrated her numbed senses, she realised she was not alone in her grief. 'How many lost their lives tonight?' she managed.

'We estimated there were about three hundred people trapped on those steps,' the warden said grimly. 'Sixty have been sent to hospital, and so far we've counted 173 dead.' He cleared his throat, his eyes bright with unshed tears. 'That includes sixty-two children.'

Doreen's tears fell down her cheeks to mingle with the rain. 'Something must be done to prevent this ever happening again,' she said fiercely.

'You can rely on that, miss.'

She looked up at him. 'It was a false alarm,

wasn't it? There was no raid?'

'It looks that way, miss,' he agreed with great reluctance. 'But I would advise you not to talk about what happened here this evening. Such a thing could be used as propaganda by the Nazis, and would be a terrible blow to British morale.'

Doreen nodded, mute with grief and still trembling with shock. The last thing she wanted to do was talk about it, for the horror of what had happened here would live with her for the rest of her life.

6

Peggy heard the pips going off and continued to prepare the evening meal in the hope that it was just a precaution and wouldn't turn into an all-out raid. They'd been going off half the damned day, and she was sick and tired of always being on edge.

Bertie Double-Barrelled had telephoned to say that he and Cordelia were staying on at the Conservative Club to play bridge and have a light supper before they joined the party at the Anchor. It was clear that someone was having a good time, and Peggy was just glad for Cordelia – although she'd have given almost anything for a slap-up lunch and supper there herself. Now it was very late and already quite dark outside, and the others would be home soon, as hungry as hunters to find that, because of all the day's delays, Peggy was well behind her usual schedule.

She had just placed the casserole dish into the slow oven of her Kitchener range when the sirens began to wail. She gave a groan of frustration and closed the door on the range fire, then scooped Daisy off the floor, plonked her in the pram which she'd left in the basement and hurried down the garden path. The pram just fitted through the entrance to the Anderson shelter, and she wheeled it in and firmly strapped a wriggling, protesting Daisy into it.

Running back to the house, she fetched her overcoat and the emergency box, then dashed back to the shelter where Daisy was now yelling fit to bust. Peggy got her out, shoved the pram into the garden and shut the door. Sinking onto the bench, she held on to Daisy as she fiddled in the darkness to light the lantern which swung from the roof, and once she could see what she was doing, she unfurled the small rug and placed it on the floor.

Daisy was all smiles now she was free, and Peggy gave her some toys to play with on the rug while the planes from Cliffe roared overhead towards the Channel.

Peggy watched her little daughter happily chewing on the ear of a teddy. Daisy had been born on the terrible night the Japanese had bombed Pearl Harbor and invaded Malaya. There had been no enemy raid on Cliffehaven that night, but within the first weeks of Daisy's life she'd become inured to the sound of sirens, bombs and planes – in fact, she'd even survived the blast that had taken out the cellar's back wall and put Peggy and Cordelia in hospital.

Peggy's smile was rueful. It wasn't the sort of life she'd wished for any of her children, and she could only thank God that Daisy didn't seem at all frightened by all the noise. Children were tough little beings, she mused. Those still living in Cliffehaven had learnt to recognise the planes and name them all, as well as make a game out of collecting bits of shrapnel and pretending to be Spitfire pilots engaged in dogfights.

To earn pocket money, some of them even scoured the bomb sites for scraps of metal and paper which they sold to the council to be made into something else, and there were a couple of very enterprising boys who came once a week with a wheelbarrow to collect old newspapers so they could be pulped and used again.

Peggy had little doubt that these budding entre-preneurs would one day run their own successful businesses – if the war ever came to an end. She sighed and put the kettle on the primus stove. At least she'd managed to get through most of her long list of things to do today despite the constant interruptions of the pips and the sirens – and the session in the Town Hall had been quite pleasant, as Doris hadn't shown up to stick her oar in and play the bossy WVS committee member. The only thing she hadn't achieved was a quiet word with Ivy, for the security surrounding the factories was strict, and she hadn't been allowed into the vast estate. Still, she mused, there was always tomor-row.

She gave Daisy a drink of her special orange juice from her bottle, then poured the boiling water over the much used tea leaves, added milk and a few grains of precious sugar and gave it a good stir. There would be ructions with Doris over Ivy coming to live here, for it would mean she'd have to take in a replacement to fulfil the demands of the billeting people, who were already questioning her about the second spare room now that Anthony had moved out permanently.

Her smile was mischievous as she bent down to rescue Daisy's bottle from rolling across the dirty floor. 'Your Auntie Doris is not going to be best pleased with your mummy, Daisy,' she murmured, 'but I'm sure Caroline hoity-toity must have a friend in need of a billet, and then the three of them can swan about feeling very pleased with themselves.'

Daisy clapped her hands and blew a raspberry.

'I couldn't have put it better myself,' said Peggy on a laugh as she gathered up her small daughter and gave her a cuddle.

Doreen remained standing there long after the trucks had disappeared, slowly becoming dimly aware of others around her who wandered lost and dazed, reluctant to leave in case a miracle happened and someone was brought out alive.

But no miracle was forthcoming, and as those who'd been on the platforms of the tube station began to emerge into the night, it was clear they'd been completely unaware of the tragedy that had happened only feet above them.

'Come on, ducks. Let's get you out of the rain.'

She regarded the woman in the WVS uniform, her mind slow to react. She hadn't realised it was still raining.

The woman's expression was kindly, but her hand was firm as she steered Doreen across the road and up the steps into what looked like a drill hall. 'Let's get them wet things off yer, and then you can warm up with a nice cup of tea.'

Her words seemed to be coming from a long way off and as her coat, hat and scarf were eased from her, Doreen could only stare at her in confusion. 'Archie's gone,' she mumbled. 'They took him away.'

There was a deep sigh and the grey eyes were sorrowful. 'There's a lot gorn this night, ducks, so you ain't alone – not that that will bring you no comfort.' She drew Doreen to some chairs that had been set close to a paraffin heater and gently pressed her down. 'I'll put these on the radiator to dry off a bit while I get you a blanket and some tea,' she said before bustling off.

Doreen sat as still as stone and watched the activity around her with glazed eyes. The ladies of the WVS had set up a canteen and were providing food, tea, blankets and towels to those who, like her, sat around in silence, too numb to cry or even talk. Even the children were silent, their wan, tear-streaked faces telling of the awful loss they'd endured on this tragic night. They looked so lost and bewildered as they waited for someone to come and claim them – and somewhere deep beneath the numbness of her own pain, her heart went out to them.

'There we are, ducks. Now you drink that tea.'

Doreen wasn't usually so biddable, but the soft, coaxing voice and the awful inertia that had taken her over made her do as she was told. She took a sip of the scalding stewed tea and as the sour taste hit the back of her throat, she burst into tears. 'Real East End tea,' she sobbed. 'Archie said it would ... would put...'

'Put hairs on yer chest, I expect,' said the woman as she rescued the cup and saucer from Doreen's shaking hands. 'From around 'ere, was he?'

'Shoreditch. But he joined the Navy as a boy, and he was trying to find his family – but they got bombed out – and he asked me to marry him – and...' Gentle arms pulled her close and held her against a soft bosom as she sobbed.

'There, there, ducks. Best to let it all out.'

Doreen had never felt so helpless. Ever since she'd turned sixteen she'd made her own decisions, carving her career path, determined to achieve something that would give her and her children respectability and a decent way of life. Yet now she felt as weak and vulnerable as a small child; unable to master the pain of her loss, or the tears that seemed to come from a bottomless well of grief.

And yet the tears did eventually stop flowing even though the pain remained raw, and she eased herself from the woman's embrace rather shame-facedly. 'I'm sorry,' she said as she used the borrowed handkerchief and tried to gather her wits.

'There ain't nothing to be sorry about, love,' the woman said comfortingly. 'It's been a terrible night for everyone.' She patted Doreen's knee. 'Would it help to talk about Archie?'

Doreen suddenly didn't want to share her

125

memories of Archie with anyone, even with this lovely kind woman, so she shook her head. 'That's very kind of you, but I'm sure you've got better things to do than listen to me.' She glanced across at the miserable huddle of children who were now being cared for by a group of nuns. 'What will happen to them?'

'They'll be looked after very well at the convent until relatives can be found to take them in.' The woman sighed deeply. 'Poor little mites. As if they 'aven't seen enough death and destruction without this.'

Doreen thought of her own two girls and sent up a silent prayer of thanks that they hadn't been orphaned tonight. It was hard enough being parted from them in the first place, and although Peggy would take them in and raise them as her own if anything happened to her, she couldn't bear the thought of not being here to watch them grow and make their own lives.

She realised then that although she was almost drowning in grief, she should count her blessings and do her very best to dredge up the courage to face the coming days. She drank the tea which was now even more sour, and then reached for her handbag to find her cigarettes.

'I've lost my bag,' she gasped, 'and it's got my identification papers in it, and money and my ration book, and...' She shivered as she remembered it also contained Archie's last letter, his photograph and those of her daughters.

'All the abandoned bags and bundles were brought in 'ere,' said the woman. 'They're in the other room under the watchful eye of Mrs Pendlebury – and believe me, she won't let no one take anything what ain't theirs.'

Doreen suddenly remembered her overnight bag, gas mask box and Archie's kitbag. 'I have to find them,' she said and got to her feet. Her head swam and nausea churned her stomach, and she sat back down heavily.

'You just put yer 'ead down to yer knees, ducks. After the shock you've 'ad it's no surprise you feel giddy.'

Doreen breathed deeply and evenly until the nausea subsided and her head cleared, then drank the glass of water the woman offered her. 'You're very kind, and I don't even know your name,' she murmured as the woman placed her coat, hat and scarf on the chair beside her.

'I'm Winnie,' she said and smiled.

'I'm Doreen.'

Winnie nodded. 'Feeling a bit better now?'

Doreen nodded. 'I'd better go and find those things,' she said, her gaze straying to the door at the end of the room where people were going in and out. She slipped on her coat, which was still unpleasantly damp, and stuffed her ruined hat and soggy scarf into the pockets.

'If you don't mind me saying, ducks, you ain't from round 'ere, are yer?' When Doreen shook her head, she continued. 'You got far to travel, love? Only you'd be better off staying the night now, 'cos most of the trains have stopped.'

Doreen hadn't thought as far ahead as to what she should do about getting home. 'I'm living near Sevenoaks, but I can't go back there, yet. I have to arrange ... arrange things for Archie.'

Winnie nodded. 'You got somewhere to stay? Only we got emergency shelter in the Pentecostal church hall. It's basic, but the linen's clean and you'll get a decent meal if nothing else.'

Doreen couldn't express her gratitude for this stranger's kindness, so she simply grasped her hand and kissed her cheek. 'Give me the address and I'll find it,' she managed through the gathering lump in her throat.

'Bless you, ducks, it's two doors down from 'ere. You can 'ardly get lost.' Winnie patted her knee and stood up. 'Now, do you want me to come with you to find yer things, or will you be all right on yer own?'

'I'll be fine, really I will,' she replied with rather more determination than she felt. 'Thank you for everything, Winnie. I won't forget your kindness.' She shot her a watery smile and headed for the other room before she disgraced herself again by bursting into tears.

The woman who stood guard over the piles of bedding, bags, shoes, coats and cases was a very different type to Winnie. Tall and ramrod straight in her severe dark green uniform, she possessed a formidable expression and suspicious eyes.

'What are you searching for exactly?' she asked without preamble.

'My handbag, overnight case, gas-mask box and my...' Doreen caught sight of Archie's kitbag lying at the end of the table. 'And Archie's Navy kitbag.'

'He'll have to collect that himself. I can't possibly allow a civilian to claim service property.'

Her tone snapped Doreen out of her debilitating lethargy. 'Archie died tonight, so he won't be able to collect his bag,' she retorted. 'I can tell you exactly what's in it, because I saw him pack it this morning.'

'My condolences.' The stiff nod and the cool gaze belied the grudging words. She walked to the end of the table and wrestled the heavy bag to the floor. 'What was the last thing he packed?'

Doreen could barely contain her anger at the sight of this awful woman mauling Archie's belongings. 'A brown leather case containing his hairbrushes; and another containing nail scissors, toothbrush, paste and a white flannel.'

The woman loosened the cord at the neck of the bag and peered inside, her hand dipping in to check that both items were there. 'Very well. Which handbag and overnight case are yours?'

Doreen pointed them out. 'You'll find my MOD identification card, ration book and a letter addressed to me in that,' she said as the damned woman picked up her bag and started rooting about in it. 'The holdall contains silk underwear, a cream satin nightdress edged with lace, cosmetics, a black dress, spare trousers, and a pair of high-heeled pumps.'

The woman did a cursory check and then eyed Doreen knowingly, for not many women carried such exotic lingerie and underwear about unless they were planning some mischief. She grudgingly handed over Doreen's property. 'I can't do anything about the gas mask, they all look the same.'

'Mine has my name on it and the insignia of the MOD.' Doreen snatched up the gas-mask box from the jumbled pile in the middle of the table and held it out. 'Do you want to search this too, or have you satisfied your curiosity by going through my underwear?'

'There's no need—'

'There's every bloody need,' snapped Doreen. 'I lost the man I love today, and it wouldn't have hurt you to wind that stiff neck of yours in, and at least try to be human.' Before the woman could respond, she'd grabbed Archie's kitbag and was dragging it out of the room, her anger once again lending her strength and the will to fight back.

'Blimey, love, you look madder than a scalded cat.'

'You need to get someone else to look after those things,' she replied to a puzzled Winnie. 'That woman's an unfeeling witch.' With that, she stormed out of the drill hall and went to find the emergency shelter.

She was welcomed with a warm smile and once she'd filled in the form detailing her reasons for being there, was shown the makeshift canteen, the washrooms and toilets before being led to one of the many beds that filled the crowded church hall.

The noise was quite deafening, even this late at night. Children ran about, babies cried and women gossiped. Bundles of bedding, clothes and sticks of furniture had been piled up everywhere and Doreen suspected they were the remnants of the lives these people had managed to rescue from their bombed-out homes. She also noted that those bundles were carefully guarded at all times, and so had to conclude that there must be a history of thieving in this sort of place – which, although it saddened her, didn't really surprise her.

She sank onto the thin mattress and heard the springs complain, but at least the bedding looked freshly laundered and the pillow felt soft and very tempting. She was deathly tired, aching with sorrow as well as the bruises she suspected darkened her battered body, and was still haunted by the terror of that black hellhole and the sight of Archie lying dead in her arms.

The woman sitting on the next bed eyed her speculatively, her gaze roaming over her good clothes and the kitbag. 'It ain't much, but it's home, ain't it?' she said as she lit a fag and stuck it in the corner of her mouth.

'It certainly is,' Doreen replied coolly as she hauled the kitbag onto the bed and began to stuff the contents of her holdall into it. She saw the woman's eyes flit over the now empty bag and knew that by morning it would probably have disappeared. She couldn't have cared less. Archie's kitbag was the precious one and she could sleep with her handbag under her pillow.

Leaving the empty case on her bed, she dragged the kitbag into the washroom, locked the stall and sank down onto the lavatory lid, head in hands, the tears so very close to falling again as exhaustion overwhelmed her. Then, determined to be brave and strong, she scrubbed her face with her hands, lit a cigarette and took her time to smoke it. She'd always had a bit of a temper and it had often got her into trouble, but tonight it had certainly helped her to focus again, and once she'd had a good night's sleep she would be more able to face the terrible task of making Archie's funeral arrangements.

Flushing the butt down the lavatory, she went to have a good wash. She wouldn't get undressed, she decided; the negligee was far too revealing, and despite the number of people crammed into the hall, it was cold and draughty.

Returning to her bed she was mildly surprised to see that her case was still there. Pulling back the blanket and sheet, she took off her shoes and just managed to stuff them into Archie's bag. She shook out her damp overcoat, draping the sodden scarf and hat over the bedhead, and then climbed into bed, tucked her handbag under her pillow and pulled Archie's kitbag alongside her. It was almost as if he was there with her as she draped her arm over it and caught a whisper of his cologne.

She closed her eyes, attempting to shut out the noise, the bright lights and the terrible images of being in that black tunnel. Tomorrow promised to be another harrowing day and she would have given anything to have Peggy by her side.

Darling Peggy had always been there to comfort and console when she'd scraped a knee or felt ill, or if Doris had been impossibly overbearing and bossy. She'd always been ready to quickly defend her little sister, even if it had been Doreen's mercurial temper that had led her into trouble in the first place. Doreen found a modicum of comfort from those childhood memories, and she clung to them like a lifeline.

As the youngest of the three Dawson girls by almost ten years, Doreen had been lucky to have Peggy as her little mother, for their own was always busy with running the boarding house while her father worked long hours on the fishing boats. Childhood was such a simple time, she thought sadly. She hadn't known then about wars and unfaithful, spendthrift husbands; the struggle involved in trying to raise two girls of her own while holding down a job – or experienced the death of someone so loved it was as if a part of her had been ripped out.

The yearning for her sister and the familiarity of her family home was almost too much to bear, and as the tears came and she buried her face in the pillow, she held Archie's kitbag close and wondered how she would survive this crippling sense of aloneness.

The party at the Anchor was in full swing, even though it had started much later than planned because of the raid. Peggy came downstairs once she'd made sure that Daisy was asleep in Rosie's spare bedroom, and stood for a while by the bar to watch the fun.

Harvey was stretched out in front of the inglenook fireplace with his pup, Monty, curled against his belly. Fran was playing the violin with her usual verve, while someone was bashing out a tune on the old piano and several servicemen were accompanying them with harmonicas, tin whistles and guitars. Sarah was looking very pale, but Jane's face was radiant with excitement as she and Rita linked arms and danced in a circle.

'It feels strange not having Mary here to play the piano,' said Rosie with a wistful sigh. 'That chap's not half as good, and I do miss her company and her lovely smile.'

Peggy understood Rosie's melancholy, for Mary had become an intrinsic part of Rosie's life – especially after the revelation that she'd been the child Rosie had planned to adopt eighteen years ago. 'She'll visit again when she can,' she soothed.

Rosie nodded and pushed back her platinum curls. 'I know, and we write regularly, so we won't lose touch.' She glanced across at her two middle-aged barmaids to make sure they were coping and then turned her attention back to Ron, who was enthusiastically playing the spoons. 'I couldn't have coped with any of it without Ron,' she said. 'He's been my rock over the past few months.'

Peggy's smile was wry, for she could think of a lot of ways to describe Ron – and although he could be a rock at times, he was more often than not a ruddy nuisance. 'Thanks for laying this on, Rosie. I simply couldn't have managed it.'

'You're welcome.' She grinned, her blue eyes flashing. 'And you know me, Peg. Any excuse for a party – especially on a Wednesday when it's usually quiet.'

Peggy laughed. 'Always the businesswoman, eh?' She noticed that Cordelia was on her third sherry. 'I'd better go and persuade Cordelia not to drink all of that,' she said, 'otherwise Ron will have to carry her home.'

Cordelia was jigging about in her chair in time to the music as she sang out of key and watched the girls dancing by the piano. 'Isn't this fun?' she shouted over the noise.

Peggy smiled back and surreptitiously moved the glass out of the older woman's reach. The music came to an end and the old walls of the Anchor shook as people stamped their feet, applauded and roared for more.

Fran carefully laid her violin on the table and sank down next to Peggy as the others joined them. 'Let someone else take over for a while,' she said after downing some of her glass of cider. 'To be sure, I'm exhausted.'

'You've done very well, dear,' said Cordelia. 'Jane's having a lovely send-off.' She frowned. 'Where's my glass of sherry gone?'

'I'll get you another in a minute,' said Peggy hurriedly. 'It's a bit busy at the bar.' She ignored Cordelia's baleful glare and admired the girls, who were all looking very pretty in their best skirts, blouses and sweaters. They'd made a real effort to give Jane a good party and she was so proud of them all – but she would miss quiet little Jane, and that was a fact.

As the music began again Peggy decided she would ask Rosie if it was all right to go up and make herself and Cordelia a cup of tea. If Cordelia drank any more sherry she'd slide out of her chair and end up under the table – and that would be most embarrassing for all concerned.

She'd just reached the bar when she heard someone call her name. Turning, she saw a large man approaching, dressed in the uniform of the Royal Engineers. 'Yes?'

He grinned and pulled off his beret. 'Hello,

Peggy. I tried the house and guessed you must all be in here.'

Peggy frowned, for although there was something about him that was vaguely familiar, she couldn't place him at all. 'I'm sorry,' she said hesitantly, 'but I don't...'

His smile widened and he stepped closer. 'I know I've been away a while, but I didn't think I'd changed that much,' he said wryly. 'It's Jack Smith.'

'Oh, my goodness,' she breathed. 'Of course it is.' She flung her arms round him to give him a hug before she stood back to look at him properly. Jack Smith had always been a sturdy sort of man, but he'd filled out in the three years since he'd left Cliffehaven. His light brown hair had been cut brutally short by the army barber, but there was still a twinkle in his nut-brown eyes and the ruddy glow of good health in his face. The Army had clearly been the making of him.

'Is she here?' he asked.

Peggy nodded in delight and pointed towards the table by the fireplace where the girls were in a giggling huddle with Cordelia and a rather bemused Bertram.

He put a finger to his lips and winked. 'Don't let on, Peg. I want it to be a surprise.'

Peggy nodded and followed him to the table.

'Hello, love. Remember me?' he said.

Everyone looked up and Rita gasped, shot out of her chair and flung herself into his arms. 'Dad! Oh, Dad,' she screeched.

Jack Smith roared with laughter, picked her up and swung her round as she clung to his neck and smothered his face in kisses. Then he set her back on her feet and looked down at her in amazement. 'You've grown,' he breathed.

She laughed and poked him in the stomach. 'So have you,' she teased. 'The Army has obviously been feeding you too well.' She hugged him again, the top of her head just reaching the insignia on his breast pocket. 'It's so good to see you, Dad,' she said as the tears welled up. 'But why didn't you tell me you were coming?'

'I didn't know myself until yesterday, so I thought I'd surprise you.' He looked down at her fondly. 'I'm sorry I haven't come before this, but with only a day off here and there, there hasn't been time to make the long journey south.'

'It's good to see you again, Jack,' said Ron as he shook his hand and placed a pint of beer on the table for him. 'And you've no need to worry about your wee girl. She's safe with us, so she is.'

'I can see that.' He regarded his daughter with pride. 'My Rita's grown into a beautiful young woman,' he murmured, 'and looks more like her mother than ever before.' He kissed the top of her head and drew her close. 'Although I'm glad to see she's no longer dressing like a boy.'

'Oh, Dad,' she replied with a nudge of her elbow. 'I'm dressed for a party. I can't swan about like this every day. Those boots and trousers are comfortable and practical.'

He laughed. 'Have you still got the Norton we built together?'

'Of course,' she replied. 'I've had to make one or two adjustments to her, but she's back at Beach View under a tarpaulin. Do you want to go

137

and see her?'

'Morning will be soon enough.'

Rita introduced him to everyone and explained the reason behind the party. 'How long are you staying, Dad?' Her tone was wistful.

'Only three days,' he replied regretfully. 'So you'll have to tell me everything you've been up to, show me the cycle racetrack you've rescued and perhaps even go and look at what Jerry has done to our old place.'

'There's nothing left of it, Dad. Which isn't a bad thing. Those houses weren't fit to live in anyway, you know that.'

He nodded. 'And what about the Minelli family? Have you heard from them lately?'

'Not since Roberto got married and Louise went north to be with him and his father. They're still interned and working on the farm, and I doubt that will change unless the Italians decide to change sides in the war.'

Peggy had little time for Louise Minelli after the way she'd treated Rita during those awful months when Roberto and Antonino had been interned, their home had been bombed and Rita had been at her wits' end to cope with the woman's histrionics. 'Where are you staying, Jack?'

'At the Crown, so I'm not far away.' He turned back to his daughter. 'Is there any chance you can take some leave from the fire station while I'm here?'

'I'll ask John – he's over there with the rest of the fire crew. I'm sure he'll agree – after all, it's been three years since you were last home, Dad.'

Peggy heard the gentle reprimand in Rita's

voice. As she looked from father to daughter, she realised they needed time together after such a long separation. 'Why don't you go back to the house where you can talk in private?'

'Thanks for the offer, Peg, but I'm quite happy here, and I've been looking forward to buying my daughter a drink now she's old enough to have one. In fact, it's drinks all round,' he said with a beaming smile.

'I'll have a sherry,' piped up Cordelia.

Rita was beaming with pleasure as she slipped her hand through the crook of his arm and grinned up at him. 'Lead on, Dad.'

Peggy watched them head for the bar, where Rosie was quick to serve them. It was lovely to see Jack again, and Peggy knew how much this surprise visit had meant to little Rita, so she wasn't about to spoil the evening by giving Jack Smith a good piece of her mind.

He'd been away for three whole years, in which time Rita had had more than her fair share of disasters, but his letters had been few and far between, and there hadn't been a single telephone call that she could remember. Peggy knew how deeply this had affected Rita, and although the girl had made light of it, and it was clear that he adored her, there really was no excuse for Jack's neglectful treatment of his daughter.

7

Mercifully, there had been no sirens during the night, but still Doreen's sleep was fractured and restless, her dreams full of the horrors of that tunnel and Archie's sightless eyes filling with rain. She'd woken several times, rearing up in bed, gasping for breath, heart hammering in the certainty that a crushing weight was bearing down on her chest. Sweat soaked through her clothing and dampened her hair, and by the time the first chinks of daylight began to show round the blackout curtains she was exhausted, and a terrible headache was lurking behind her eyes.

She looked round the room to discover that most people were still asleep, huddled beneath the blankets, their meagre belongings piled beside them. Slipping out of bed, she noted wryly that her overnight bag had indeed been filched. She fished her handbag from beneath the pillow and weaved her way round the beds and baggage, dragging Archie's heavy kitbag behind her. The washroom and lavatories were deserted, and once she'd had a good wash and changed her underwear, she felt marginally more ready to face what she knew would be an awful day.

She pushed through the heavy doors into the canteen to be greeted by the smell of burnt toast, reheated dried egg, and frying Spam. Leaving the kitbag at a nearby table, she eyed what was on offer and decided she wasn't hungry, but could murder a very large cup of tea. She dropped a few pennies into the donation jar and then sat down to savour the hot mug of strong tea and a morning cigarette.

As people started to drift in from the other room, Doreen fished in her coat pocket for the card the policeman had given her the previous night. The address of the undertaker's meant nothing to her, for she was unfamiliar with Bethnal Green, but someone was bound to be able to point her in the right direction. She just hoped it wasn't too far away, for Archie's kitbag was cumbersome and she'd damage it by dragging it everywhere.

After she'd finished the cigarette and tea, Doreen went back into the main hall to get directions from the woman in charge, then she signed out. Walker and Stroud's premises were about a mile away, so she'd have to put Archie's kitbag in left luggage at the station and pick it up later.

It was still early, and the weak sun was struggling to break through the thick layer of cloud that hung over London, but the air was cold and surprisingly fresh, which she hoped would dispel the band of pain in her head and help her to concentrate properly on what needed doing.

Passing Victoria Park, she determinedly looked away from the entrance to the underground station – but she'd already caught sight of the workmen who were widening the opening, erecting handrails and painting a white line on each step. It was a classic case of shutting the stable door after the horse had bolted. Just a glimpse of that awful place was enough to bring back the nightmares and make her heart and head pound.

Hurrying beneath the railway arches, she weaved her way around the rubble of collapsed buildings and the workmen dealing with a fractured water main until she came to the undertaker's.

Walker and Stroud was a dusty building with a high wooden fence and double gates to one side which were firmly secured with a rusting chain and heavy padlock. There was a bank on one side and a cobbler's on the other, in what proved to be a parade of little shops that hadn't entirely escaped the bombing. The frontage was painted black and the lettering above the door was in faded gold, while the windows were discreetly covered with net curtains and adorned with a rather depressing arrangement of faded paper flowers.

Doreen took a deep breath before she opened the door and stepped inside. As her eyes adjusted to the gloom she saw a man emerge through the brown velvet curtain hanging behind the large mahogany desk. He was past middle age, tall and very thin, with a long, pale face and sad brown eyes. She approached him warily and told him why she'd come.

His expression was suitably doleful, but he wasn't obsequious or cloying in his condolences, for which she was very grateful. In fact he seemed to understand it was better to be calm and efficient at times like these. He showed her to a nearby easy chair, and once they'd discussed the sort of service Doreen wanted, a date, time and venue was arranged. Archie would be buried in Bow Cemetery, just as many of the other victims would be, and as Doreen had no idea where that was or how to get to it, Mr Walker wrote down the names of the nearest stations and drew a small street map.

'I took it upon myself to inform the appropriate authorities of the Chief Engineer's passing,' he said in his deep voice. 'They will of course pay for the service and the interment, and as you have been listed as next of kin, they will be writing to you and sending on his personal effects.'

Doreen's head was thudding and she was finding it hard to breathe in this musty, dim room that seemed to smell of death and loss.

'I have taken the liberty of placing his personal effects in a small box,' he continued, 'if you wouldn't mind waiting while I fetch it. Only we don't like keeping valuables on the premises.'

She waited as he left the room, rubbing her eyes to try and get rid of the flashing lights that were threatening to blind her as the band of pain tightened. She felt simply awful, and wondered fleetingly if she was about to either faint or be sick.

'Are you all right, miss?'

'I've got a terrible headache,' she admitted. 'I don't suppose you have such a thing as an aspirin?'

'We have most things here,' he said with a smile and hurried back behind the curtain to appear moments later with two aspirin and a glass of water. 'You're very welcome to sit for a while until you feel a bit better.'

She took the tablets and drained the glass of cold water. 'That's very kind, but I'm sure I'll be fine now.' She took the box of Archie's possessions from the table and stood to shake his hand. 'Thank you again. I'll see you next week in Bow.'

She felt light-headed and nauseous as she followed him to the door and stepped outside. Breathing deeply of the cold air, she determinedly headed back towards the main-line station, the precious box tucked firmly under her arm. She would have liked to lie down and find sweet oblivion from the pain, but she had the journey back to Fort Halstead to contend with first – followed by an interview with her boss, who was no doubt furious that she was absent without leave.

Despite the very late night and the amount of alcohol that had been consumed, everyone but Jane was downstairs in time for an early breakfast and looking remarkably bright-eyed and bushy-tailed – except for Cordelia, who'd switched off her hearing aid in an attempt to nurse her headache, and Sarah, who was pale and tearful.

Peggy said nothing as Sarah helped her great-aunt to get comfortable at the table and poured her out a cup of tea, but she did place a couple of aspirin by Cordelia's plate. It was a bit worrying that Cordelia was drinking so much. Perhaps it would be better if she cut down on the socialising but then, at almost eighty, it didn't really matter. Life was for living to the full and Cordelia deserved a bit of fun – even if the consequences were a hangover.

She finished frying the slices of Spam and added them to the tomatoes she'd bottled last summer. There were even eggs this morning as the chickens had finally decided to co-operate, so it was quite a feast. 'Where's Jane?' she asked fretfully as she realised the time was slipping away.

'Here I am, Auntie Peg. Sorry if I'm a bit late.'

There was a gasp of surprise as everyone turned to greet her, for the long, heavy blonde plait was gone and now Jane sported a very fetching shoulder-length bob. 'Your hair,' breathed Sarah. 'Oh, Jane, your lovely hair. What have you done?'

Jane handed her the neatly plaited hank of hair which she'd tied at both ends with scarlet ribbons. 'Plaits are for little girls,' she said firmly. 'I thought it was time I looked my age.'

Sarah clutched the plait, too emotional to speak.

'It suits you like that,' said Rita.

'It makes you look much more mature,' said Cordelia. 'I like it.'

'So do I,' said Fran, 'but it needs a bit of tidying up at the back. I'll do it after we've eaten.'

Jane grinned her thanks and sat down. 'I feel quite light-headed now the weight of all that hair has gone,' she said happily. 'But I suspect I might feel the cold on my neck more.'

Peggy rather liked the shorter hair, for it suited the girl and was more appropriate for her new-found status. She glanced across at Sarah, who was battling to fight back the tears as she carefully placed the plait on her lap. The poor girl really was going to find it hard to accept all these changes.

Breakfast was soon over. After she'd helped to clear the table and wash the dishes, Rita hugged Jane and said a fond goodbye before she shot off to the fire station to ask for time off during her father's leave.

Fran tidied the ragged ends of Jane's haphazard haircut, and then gave her a kiss and hug. 'No hard feelings?' she murmured.

'Of course not, Fran.'

'Good luck then, and don't forget about us, will you?' she said warmly before she left for the hospital.

Cordelia drank three cups of tea before she felt able to switch on her hearing aid and join in any conversation, while Ron took himself off to feed the chickens and clean out his ferret cage.

Peggy took Daisy out of her high chair to let her crawl about the floor as Sarah and Jane sat close to Cordelia for the last few minutes of Jane's time at Beach View. Peggy was feeling very emotional, for another of her precious chicks was leaving, but at least it wouldn't involve that awful standing about on a station platform this time – Anthony had arranged for a car and driver to take Jane to wherever she was going.

As the clock struck nine there was a rap on the front door, which caused a flurry of barking from Harvey and a panic of last-minute goodbye kisses and promises to write. Ron went to answer the knock while Jane pulled on her coat and hat, and everyone trooped into the hall with Harvey close on their heels.

'Goodbye, Aunt Peggy,' Jane said as they embraced. 'Thank you for giving me such a lovely home – and look after Sarah, won't you? She'll find it hard being on her own.'

'Of course I will, dear.' Peggy held her close for a moment more and then let her go so she could

146

hug Ron and Cordelia and give Daisy a kiss. Tears blurred her sight as the two sisters embraced and murmured to one another, and then Ron was carrying Jane's cases down the front steps to the car.

The driver was a girl from the ATS, who organised the cases in the boot to her satisfaction and then opened the passenger door to wait for Jane.

Jane was clearly distressed as she tore herself away from Sarah and went down the steps and into the car. The girl slammed the door, climbed in behind the steering wheel and fired up the engine. As the highly polished car purred down the cul-de-sac, Peggy carried Daisy on her hip and joined the others on the top step to wave goodbye.

Jane looked back once and waved, and then the car was moving into the main road and out of sight.

Peggy saw that Ron was comforting a tearful Cordelia, so she put her arm around Sarah, who could now finally give in to the emotions she'd been holding back for so long. 'It's all right,' she crooned. 'She'll be back with us again before you know it.'

The aspirins had started to work by the time Doreen's train left Bethnal Green, and as she was lulled by the slow, rhythmic sound of the great iron wheels turning, she fell into a doze and only just woke in time to disembark at Knockholt station.

It was a bit of a scramble to get the kitbag down, but the obliging porter took charge of it and

147

carried it outside to where she'd left her bicycle. The bag was cumbersome and far too large for the wicker basket on the front, and she began to fret that she'd never get it home. The porter proved to be inventive, however, and lashed it firmly with sturdy garden twine to the flat metal parcel shelf on the back. Testing it thoroughly, he proclaimed it safe for her short journey.

Thanking him, she put her handbag and Archie's box in the basket, adjusted the gas-mask box strap across her chest, and slowly set off. The weight of the kitbag unbalanced her a bit, and made every small rise in the narrow country lane feel like a mountain, but her determination to make it back to her lodgings gave her the strength she needed, and before too long she caught glimpses of the house through the distant trees.

Halstead was a quaint village of white clapboard houses, grand mansions and thatched cottages set amongst sweeping farmland and dense woodland on the North Kent Downs. It was peaceful and very quiet on this early March morning, even though it was on the outer reaches of London and the airfield at Biggin Hill wasn't far away. Doreen had often thought she might like to settle here after the war, for it would be a perfect place to raise her girls.

Her legs were trembling from the effort of that long climb, and she almost fell off her bicycle as she reached the imposing entrance to her billet. Pausing a moment to catch her breath and steady herself, she pushed the bike past the brick pillars and over the gravel to the front step of the large Victorian house. With a sigh of relief, she leaned it against the wall, collected her things from the basket and went indoors to her downstairs room to find some scissors to cut the string and release the kitbag.

It was quiet indoors, for the other four girls were at work up at the Fort, and it seemed the elderly couple who owned the house hadn't heard her coming in – which was a blessing, for as kind as they were, their attention could sometimes be a little too much, and she simply wasn't in the frame of mind to be fussed over.

Catching sight of the letters waiting for her on the hall table, she sifted through them and her spirits tumbled further as she saw Eddie's familiar handwriting. She unlocked her bedroom door and stepped inside, her gaze going immediately to the soft and very tempting four-poster bed. She would have liked nothing better than to crawl beneath the covers, shut out the world and sleep, but she knew there were more important things to do before she could enjoy that luxury.

She tore Eddie's unopened letters into shreds, deposited them in the waste-paper basket and then opened the floral curtains that were lined with blackout material. Unnerved by the constant reminders of her ex-husband, she looked out through the heavily taped window to the large garden where pearly snowdrops beaded the grass, crocuses peeked from the flower beds, and the first few early daffodils bobbed their yellow heads beneath the trees. The orchard at the bottom of the garden would soon be a mass of pale pink blossom, and the rolling patchwork of fields that stretched away to the horizon would become a sea

149

of rippling wheat. The sight soothed her momentarily, and she knew she should count her blessings, for she'd fallen on her feet being billeted here and the tranquillity of this hidden paradise would surely help her to recover.

She turned from the window and surveyed her room. Unlike some of the lodgings she'd had over the past four years, this room gave her privacy as well as comfort. The furniture was old and sturdy, the carpet a little threadbare but of fine quality, and the four-poster bed was sumptuous with a downy quilt, soft blanket and good linen sheets and pillowcases. There was no doubt about it, she thought, with age comes a few privileges, and unlike the other girls in the house, she didn't have to share.

Doreen placed the box of Archie's belongings on the dressing table, her fingers drifting over it like a caress. She couldn't bear to open it, but just having it here seemed to bring him closer. Likewise with his kitbag, and once she'd released it from her bicycle, she laid it on the ottoman that stood at the bottom of the bed. She paused for a moment in deep thought, then, as the grandfather clock in the hall chimed midday, she realised she couldn't waste any more time. She needed a bath, not only to soak away the grime of the past twenty-four hours, but to ease the awful ache in her body.

The regulation two inches of water was piping hot and she stayed in it until the skin on her fingers wrinkled and it became unpleasantly cool. As she'd thought, she was covered in bruises, and her neck was still stiff, the headache threatening to return. She swallowed another two aspirin, dressed quickly in clean trousers, shirt and sweater, roughly dried her dark curls with a towel and then went back to her bedroom.

One glance in the dressing-table mirror told her that she looked ghastly – pale and drawn, her brown eyes dull with grief and pain – and she didn't have the energy to try to hide her anguish beneath a layer of powder and lipstick, so she simply grabbed her bag, overcoat and gas-mask box, locked her bedroom door and hurried outside.

The sun had broken through the cloud, its rays warming her face as she cycled out of the village and began the long, tortuous hill-climb up to the Fort which stood at the very top and overlooked the distant town of Sevenoaks.

Fort Halstead was polygonal in shape, surrounded by a deep ditch and high earthworks. It had been built late in the previous century to form part of a defensive ring of forts around London, and although most had fallen into disrepair, Fort Halstead had been used continuously as a scientific development site through the First World War and in the years following. Eighty new buildings, including cottages for caretakers and scientists, had been constructed in and around the Fort, and the laboratories at its heart were a hub of innovation and activity.

Doreen knew a great deal about what was being developed in those labs, for as a trusted private secretary to one of the scientists, she was privy to the many meetings he had to attend. She found the science fascinating, even though it was often bewildering and complex. The mathematics involved was way above her understanding, but she'd witnessed the development of the 7-inch rockets that were now used by the Royal Navy, and the 3-inch version used by the Army in hundreds of Z batteries which provided the air defence over Britain's towns and cities. With more rockets being developed and new ideas being tested daily, Doreen was rather proud of the fact that she was working at the forefront of Britain's highly inventive technology.

She got off the bicycle and pushed it up the last few yards to the footbridge that would take her into the Fort and past the heavily guarded and highly secretive laboratories in which, it was rumoured, the scientists were working on an atomic bomb. As her security rating didn't give her access to this part of the Fort she didn't know if the rumours were true or not – even so, she did find it disturbing to think she might be in such close proximity to such a weapon.

Hot and aching from her steep climb, she showed her identification papers to the guard and then rested for a moment to get her breath back. As she stood there, her heart pounding from the exertion, she saw Barnes Wallis hurrying across the quad. He was a frequent visitor, dashing between his various research labs, and Doreen had met him once when she and her boss, Dr Maynard, were invited to Wales to witness the first test of his bouncing bomb.

It had been a quite extraordinary experience to see that large, round bomb drop from the belly of a low-flying Lancaster and bounce across the water of the redundant dam to shatter its wall. The scientists had been jubilant, she remembered. Recently she'd learned that it was now being modified – something to do with the casing being too heavy – and would be tested again, offshore, sometime in the coming months.

Doreen blinked in the bright sunlight which was hurting her eyes and bringing back the pain in her head. Dipping her chin against the glare, she wheeled her bicycle across the quad to the cycle rack and then headed for her office. Dr Maynard would be in his laboratory at this time of day, and although it was doubtful he'd even noticed she'd been away, her supervisor and friend Veronica Parks would certainly be very aware of the fact that she was a day late.

Dr Maynard was the epitome of what everyone expected in a scientist: of average height and in his late fifties, with greying hair that was constantly standing on end – a result of him running his fingers through it in agitation, which Doreen found quite endearing. The lenses of his spectacles were as thick as the bottom of a bottle, and they slid down his nose to perch precariously on the tip.

He was a single man and often forgot to shave, to eat or to sleep – which could cause Doreen some inconvenience, for he would ask her to stay through the night to take copious notes, completely unaware of the time, or the fact that she'd be expected back in the office early the next morning. As he was so absent-minded, Doreen had taken it upon herself to look after him, to provide a clean shirt each day and deliver plates of food at regular intervals, and she hoped her temporary replacement had closely followed the list of instructions she'd left for her so that his routine would be undisturbed.

She stepped into her office and shrugged off her coat, immediately registering the mess of paperwork and drawings that littered her desk and almost buried the uncovered typewriter. Maynard was inclined to leave things everywhere, but the girl who'd come in to cover her work was clearly slipshod and not of the high standard the MOD expected from their administration staff. And as for leaving the office in a mess like this and forgetting to put the cover on her typewriter... Didn't the stupid girl realise how precious typewriter ribbon was, and how quickly it could dry out? Really, it was too much.

Doreen quickly put the cover over the trusty Royal, stacked the paperwork in a neat pile and slammed the desk drawers shut with a little more energy than was necessary. She'd deal with all this later, but for now she had to find Maynard. She pulled on the white coat she had to wear in the labs, snatched up a notebook and pencil and pushed through the door into the large, brightly lit laboratory that smelled of chemicals.

Maynard was leaning over a bank of test tubes at the far end, his glasses in danger of dropping from his nose into a jar of something he was heating over a Bunsen burner.

'Dr Maynard. I'm sorry I'm late back.'

He didn't answer for a moment, fully engrossed in what he was doing. Then he set aside the jar, pushed his spectacles up his nose and looked at her with a frown. 'I wondered where you were,' he said. 'But thank goodness you're back. That other girl was useless.' He shoved a pile of papers towards her. 'Could you type this lot out, Doreen? The powers that be want it before the end of the day.'

'Of course I will,' she murmured, not really surprised that he hadn't realised just how very late she was. 'Dr Maynard, I will need another day off next week,' she said hesitantly.

'But you've just had a day off, Doreen.' His myopic grey eyes stared at her through the thick lenses 'I can't let you go again so soon. There's work to do and things are taking an exciting turn.'

'I have to attend a funeral in London,' she said firmly. 'I'll only be gone for the day, and I'll ensure I have proper cover this time.'

He blinked owlishly. 'Oh. My condolences, Doreen. Yes, I can see that you're upset. Was it someone close?'

She nodded, unable to speak for the lump that was in her throat.

'Just make sure you don't leave that girl with me again,' he muttered before returning to his test tubes. 'She was completely hopeless.'

Doreen could see that his mind was already elsewhere, so she quietly left the lab and went back into her office. She would have to go and see Veronica, who was the chief administrator of the office staff, to tell her that Maynard had allowed her another day's leave.

Eyeing the telephone on the desk she thought of her children with longing, and wished it was possible to ring them so she could hear their voices and be reassured that they were still all right. But they were billeted in a tiny Welsh village that had yet to be connected to the outside world and it had been impossible to speak to them – let alone visit them – since war had begun. It was at moments like these that she really felt the distance between them, and would have given anything to just hold them.

The ready tears threatened again, so she turned from the telephone and opened the window to rid the small room of the smell of cheap perfume. Leaning out, she battled to overcome this awful sense of hopelessness, loss and isolation. Peggy would understand, and as she was on the telephone, it would be easy to talk to her. But what could she say? How to explain what had happened to her and Archie when she'd been warned not to breathe a word of it to anyone? And even if she did break the rules and make a private call on the office telephone, Peggy would know immediately that something was wrong – and it wouldn't be fair to worry her.

She left the window and began to tackle the mess on her desk. It soon became apparent that her temporary replacement didn't know how to file things, either. With a growing sense of frustration, Doreen spent the next hour going through everything until she was satisfied it was all correctly allocated. And then she dusted her desk, cleaned her typewriter and set to work on the latest batch of facts and figures Maynard needed by the end of the day. Work would get her through the coming hours and stop her from thinking, but she dreaded the night, for she knew there would be no escape from the dreams.

8

'Jane will miss the shires,' said Sarah. She and Fran were helping Peggy to prepare the evening meal of tiny meatballs seasoned with onion and peppery breadcrumbs, which would be served with macaroni and home-made spicy tomato sauce. 'She'll find it very strange not to feed and groom them every morning.'

'They'll still be here when she gets back,' said Peggy comfortably, 'and with things going so well in Russia and Africa, I'm sure this war won't last much longer.'

'They've certainly got Rommel on the run in Africa,' said Rita, 'but the rest of the world is still in chaos, especially in the Pacific. Let's hope you're right, Auntie Peg, and that all these bombing raids by the RAF will force Hitler to accept defeat. Poor Matt is exhausted from going out on so many sorties, and I'm terrified that he'll get careless.'

'It's a worry for us all, Rita,' sighed Peggy. 'When I think of Martin and the other brave young boys up there...'

'To be sure there's no point in getting maudlin about it,' rumbled Ron, looking up from lighting his pipe. 'Those boys know what they're doing.'

He sucked on his pipe until the match caught the tobacco and he had a good fug going. 'By the way, Rita, what have you done with your father this evening?'

'He's gone for a ride on the Norton to look at what's left of our old place before he eats at the Crown. I didn't fancy going back there – it's too depressing – so he's coming here after tea.'

'He could have shared with us,' said Peggy, even though there was little enough in the first place.

Rita shook her head and laughed. 'He's fine, Auntie Peg. The landlady at the Crown seems to have taken a shine to him, so he's being well fed, believe me.'

'Well, he needs to watch himself,' Peggy warned. 'Gloria Stevens has very few morals, and most of those are easily dispensed with at the sight of a good-looking chap with a fat wallet.'

Ron chuckled. 'Careful, Peg. You're in danger of sounding like Doris.'

'I speak as I find,' she retorted with a sniff. 'And there are many people in this town who would agree with me that Gloria runs a highly suspect establishment.'

Ron turned to Rita, clearly deciding it might be politic to change the subject. 'How did you get on with asking John Hicks for time off while your dad's here?'

'He was fine about it, but I'll have to stay on standby in case there's an emergency. It was lovely to see John enjoying himself last night, wasn't it? The poor man's really feeling a bit low now his Sally has taken the kids to her aunt in Somerset.'

'It was nice to see Sally and her little ones before she left,' said Peggy, who'd come down from her high horse and was feeling mellow again. 'Her

Aunt Vi is going to have a very full house, what with my lot, Sal's brother Ernie as well as her and the two kids. I have to say, I don't envy her.'

'Vi's a good woman who lives in a very large and rambling farmhouse,' said Ron around his pipe stem. 'And I'm sure Anne and Sal will roll up their sleeves, get all those boys organised in their chores, and make light work of everything.'

Peggy smiled fondly, for Sally and her little crippled brother had been her first evacuees from London at the beginning of the war. Sal had proved to be a wonderful dressmaker as well as a hard-working and caring little mother for Ernie, and Peggy had been thrilled when she'd married the fire chief – she did so love a good romance. She'd been even more delighted to hear that Ernie was walking again without the aid of callipers, which only went to prove that good country air, fresh milk, eggs and butter could heal most things, even the after-effects of polio.

She turned from her thoughts of Sally and the others and noticed that Sarah was sitting with her knitting in her lap, staring into the fire. Her little face was wan, her eyes still swollen from the tears she'd shed today. Poor Sarah, she was lost without Jane – just as Fran was lost now Suzy was gone – and John was feeling abandoned without his children and Sally. Peggy couldn't solve John's problems, no matter how much she might wish she could, but at least she might be able to put her own house in order.

She checked on the macaroni, waited until Fran had finished setting the table and then sat down. 'I was thinking of asking Ivy to come and live with us,' she said into the lull. 'She's not at all happy with Doris, and I don't like the thought of her feeling so isolated there.'

'That's a brilliant idea,' said Rita. 'Ivy must be missing Mary, and she'd fit right in here. But won't Doris take umbrage?'

'Of course she will, but I'm guessing it will only be a token objection,' said Peggy. 'Doris and Caroline Lah-di-dah have made it pretty clear they want nothing much to do with the poor girl except boss her about.'

'That Caroline is a snooty piece all right,' said Fran, shaking back her russet curls. 'She sits in the administrator's office at the hospital and looks down her nose at anyone who isn't a doctor or consultant. It's clear she's on the lookout for a rich husband, so I'd say she and Doris are perfectly suited. I certainly have no objection to Ivy coming here.'

'In that case,' said Peggy, 'I was wondering if we should have a change round in rooms. I could put Ivy in the single back room at the top of the house, and perhaps you two could share one of the big front doubles?'

She watched as Fran and Sarah looked at one another. Fran had certainly missed Suzy and although she'd said she rather liked having her own room, Peggy wasn't convinced. As for Sarah, she would need some company after sharing with Jane for the past year.

'What do you say, Sarah?' asked Fran. 'D'you think you can put up with me coming in all hours and making a mess?'

Sarah's smile was wan. 'I got used to Jane's

160

mess, so I expect I could cope.'

'Please say if you don't want to,' persisted Fran. 'I'll not take offence. But I'm thinking we're both feeling a wee bit lost, and it would be good to have someone to chat to at night.'

'Yes, I think that's a very good idea.' Then Sarah smiled. 'As long as you don't chatter all night – or snore.'

'That's settled then,' said Peggy before Fran could protest about her snoring – which at times was quite loud.

'I don't mind sharing with Ivy,' Rita piped up. 'She and I get on like a house on fire, and it will free up that single room as well as two of the doubles for someone else.'

'But you've never shared before,' said Peggy. 'Are you sure you wouldn't mind, Rita?'

'Of course I don't mind. It'll be fun.' Her brown eyes twinkled as she shook back her dark curls, the fetching dimple in her cheek enhancing her cheeky smile.

Peggy could just imagine the shenanigans with those two imps sharing. Neither of them was the tidiest of people, so she'd have her work cut out trying to keep them and their room in order. But then this old house needed livening up a bit. Things had become too gloomy of late.

She glanced up at the clock on the mantel. 'Cordelia should have been back from Bertie's dinner party by now,' she murmured. 'I do hope he isn't tiring her out.'

'To be sure it's probably the other way round,' said Ron with a glint in his eyes. 'That woman could try the patience of a saint, so she could.'

161

Everyone laughed and the mood was lightened as they sat in the heart of the home that was Beach View, feeling the closeness of the ties that bound them.

Doreen kept a close eye on the clock as she tried to decipher Maynard's scrawled writing and type the seemingly endless notes he needed before six. It was already dark outside, the blackout curtain was drawn, and the single low-watt bulb wasn't much help, for the words kept dancing before her eyes and her fingers were clumsy. Having rubbed out yet another typing error, she took two aspirin to ward off the ever-tightening band of pain at the back of her head and hoped they'd do the trick.

It was just past six by the time she'd typed the last few words and pulled the paper and carbon copies from the machine with a sigh of relief. The long day was finally over and now all she wanted was to sink into bed and hope that she'd fall asleep so deeply that she wouldn't dream. She didn't normally suffer from headaches and up until now her health had always been robust, so it was disconcerting to feel so poorly.

Deciding that she was simply low because of all that had happened, she placed the sheets in their separate folders and massaged her temples. She might have damaged something in her neck during that awful squash in the tunnel, for it was still tender and the muscles felt very tight.

'Hello, Doreen. I heard you were back.'

She looked round to see her supervisor and friend Veronica Parks standing in the doorway.

162

Ronnie was neatly dressed in a skirt, jacket and blouse, her fair hair curled back from her face in victory rolls and tethered in a dark green snood. Short and slender, she leaned heavily on an ivory-topped walking stick – a necessary aid since a childhood bout of polio.

'Yes, I'm sorry I was so late, but I got stuck in London,' Doreen explained.

'You're a whole day late, Doreen, and I've had the devil's own job to cover for you.'

'Again, I'm sorry, but I couldn't help it.'

Veronica's concerned gaze swept over her and she pulled out a chair and sat down. 'What happened, Doreen?'

Ronnie always did get straight to the point, and it was disconcerting, especially when there was something to hide. Doreen looked away from her and fiddled with the folders on her desk. 'I missed my train,' she hedged.

'Doreen, we've known each other for over four years and I can tell when you're holding something back. You look ghastly,' she said bluntly. 'You're not wearing make-up and certainly don't have the glow of a woman who's been away for a dirty few days with her man.'

She paused, but as Doreen made no attempt to answer her, she gave an exasperated sigh. 'Something happened to make you miss that train, Doreen, and I think you owe me an honest explanation.'

The images of that terrifying ordeal brought a lump to her throat and Doreen had to blink away the tears and battle to find some sort of composure. Ronnie deserved an answer, but to form the words – to say them out loud – was proving almost impossible. 'We ... Archie and I...' she began and then fell silent, the weight of memories too heavy.

Ronnie was immediately contrite and she reached across to take Doreen's hand. 'Oh, Doreen, don't say you've split up. But why? You seemed so happy.'

The touch of her friend's hand seemed to release something within Doreen, and the words came out in a rush. 'Archie died. He's dead.'

Veronica gasped as she gripped Doreen's fingers. 'Dead?' she breathed. 'But how? What happened? Oh, Doreen, I'm so, so sorry.'

The genuine sympathy was almost Doreen's undoing and for a moment she was unable to speak as the tears rolled down her face and she struggled to cope with the overwhelming grief.

Veronica put her arm about her shoulders. 'You don't have to talk about it if it's too painful, Dor,' she said softly. 'I'll understand, really I will.'

Doreen swallowed the lump in her throat and dug in her trouser pocket for a handkerchief to mop up her tears. Of course Ronnie would understand, for she'd been widowed only two years before, and with no children or any family to speak of, she'd relied on her friendship with Doreen to help see her through those dark days.

She looked back at her friend, realising that actually she did want to talk about what happened. She needed to purge herself of all the awful images that were going round and round in her head, and to come to terms with the consequences.

Veronica said nothing as Doreen stumbled

through her story, and when she'd come to the end, she gave her a heartfelt hug. 'Oh, Doreen,' she sighed. 'I can't begin to imagine what you've been through – and I wish I could find the words to bring you some comfort. But we both know that words are superfluous at times like these.'

Doreen nodded as she pulled and twisted the damp handkerchief in her lap. 'At least you understand,' she murmured. She lifted her chin, determined to put a brave face on things and not be a sobbing mess. 'I shouldn't really have told you any of it,' she confessed.

Ronnie's eyes widened. 'Why ever not? You can't keep something like that all bottled up inside you, Dor. You'd go mad with it.'

'We were all warned to say nothing because of the damage it might do to morale, and the fact that Hitler could use it as propaganda.' She gripped her friend's hand. 'So you've got to promise to keep this to yourself.'

Ronnie nodded thoughtfully. 'Of course I will, and I'm not at all surprised the authorities have put a lid on it. For such an appalling thing to happen to civilians without an enemy shot being fired would certainly cause a huge furore.' She patted her hand. 'But I'm glad you trusted me enough to confide in me, Doreen.'

Doreen discovered that she felt marginally better for having talked about it, but she was haunted by the images from that day, and suspected they would remain with her for as long as she lived.

'I really do think you should take some time off, Doreen,' said Ronnie. 'You need to rest and grieve and come to terms with things.'

Doreen shook her head. 'I'd rather not,' she said firmly. 'The thought of rattling about with only my thoughts for company makes me feel quite ill. Work will keep me occupied, and hopefully I'll be so tired every night I'll sleep well and not dream.'

Ronnie didn't look convinced. 'I remember how I was when Michael was shot down,' she said. 'I thought I could work my way through it and carry on as if nothing had changed, but look where I ended up – forced to rest in a cottage hospital for a month.'

'I know,' Doreen murmured, 'and I will take care of myself, Ronnie, I promise. I've already spoken to Dr Maynard about having a day off to attend Archie's funeral next week. Perhaps after that I'll think about taking a few more days' leave. But I can't afford not to work, Ronnie. There's rent to pay, food to buy, the girls are always needing new clothes and shoes and–'

'It's all right, I understand,' Ronnie soothed. 'And of course you can have all the time you need for the funeral. I'll sort out someone to take over here.' Her smile was wry. 'And I'll make sure it's someone who knows their way around an office. That other girl was so useless I've had to demote her to the mail-room.'

'Thanks, Ronnie.'

'Will you be all right on your own? Would you like me to come with you?'

'I'll be fine,' Doreen replied. 'We can't both leave everyone in the lurch – not with so many experiments coming to a head.'

'They can do without us for half a day,' said Veronica firmly. 'You look as if a puff of wind would blow you down at the minute, which is hardly surprising after the horror you've been through, and I hate the thought of you facing the ordeal of that funeral on your own. I'll sort something, never fear.'

Doreen suddenly didn't have the strength to argue. She was drained of all emotion and the tight band of pain was intensifying, with tiny sparks of light darting before her eyes. She fumbled in her handbag, found the packet of aspirin and dropped it on the floor. 'Oh dear. I'm all fingers and thumbs today,' she moaned

Veronica retrieved the packet and frowned. 'How many of these have you taken, Doreen?'

'I don't know. Four, six. I've lost count.' She massaged her temples, trying to ease the awful throb of pain that was now virtually blinding her. 'Another two won't hurt,' she breathed. 'I've got the most awful migraine.'

'You need to see the quack,' said Veronica briskly. 'Come on. I'm taking you over there now.'

'I have to get these folders to Dr Maynard,' Doreen protested.

'We'll drop them off on the way.' Veronica grasped her arm and eased her out of the chair just as the sirens began to wail. 'Damn and blast,' she hissed. 'Talk about bad timing.'

Panic overrode the pain and Doreen snatched her arm from the other woman's grip. 'I can't go into the shelter,' she gasped.

'You have to, Dor. It's their rules. Don't worry, I'll stick close.'

'No.' Doreen backed away from her and stood trembling by the filing cabinets as the sound of running feet came from the corridor outside. 'I can't, Ronnie. Really I can't.'

Veronica's reply was drowned out by the wailing siren and the thunder of planes taking off from Biggin Hill.

Doreen put her hands over her head, and she slid down the wall and curled over her knees. The noise was all-consuming, reverberating in her head and coursing through every part of her body until she vibrated with it. She couldn't bear it – couldn't bear the thought of that shelter – of the press of people – the dim lights – the smells of so many humans in such a small space where the doors were tightly locked and there could be no escape.

'The shelters are big and light and not at all overcrowded,' shouted Veronica over the noise of the last few Spitfires and Hurricanes leaving the aerodrome. 'It won't be the same, Doreen.'

She shook her head and curled tighter against the wall, her head buried beneath her hands, her nose pressed against her knees. 'Don't make me go there,' she begged. 'Please don't make me go down there.'

'All right, Doreen,' Veronica soothed. 'I'm not going to make you do anything you don't want, and I'll stay with you.' She quickly turned off the light, checked the blackout was securely fixed, and yanked the chairs away from the desk. 'All I ask is that you come with me under here until it's over. It's not much of a shelter, but it's better than nothing.'

Doreen felt the darkness creeping into her, but she crawled under the desk and huddled there as

168

Veronica dropped her walking stick and awkwardly slid in beside her. 'I'm sorry to be so feeble,' she whispered.

'Don't be daft.' Veronica lit cigarettes for both of them, the strike of the match illuminating her face and casting strange shadows beneath her eyes and cheekbones. 'We might as well break all the rules while we're at it,' she said with a smile.

Doreen gratefully took the cigarette and was shocked by how badly her hand was trembling. She had to get a grip, she thought in panic – this was ridiculous.

Yet, as the sirens' wails died down and they heard the first of the enemy bombers approaching, and the returning fire of the ack-ack guns around the fort, it took all her will power to stay beneath that desk. She felt hemmed in, enclosed in the darkness which was only alleviated by the faint glow at the end of their cigarettes. Veronica's slight body was pressing against her on one side, the sturdy panel of the desk drawers on the other. She could feel control slipping away – was taken back to the awful press in that tunnel – and found she was gasping for air.

She stubbed out the cigarette beneath her heel and forced herself to take slow, even, deep breaths. It was vital she kept control, otherwise she'd be lost. But her heart was pounding, the darkness was all-consuming and the images of that tunnel were returning.

'Hold my hand,' shouted Veronica above the noise of the dogfights overhead. 'Keep breathing, Dor. Just keep breathing.'

Doreen gripped her friend's hand as her heart

pounded against her ribs and she fought to breathe the musty air. Air raids had never bothered her before, but now the crash and crump of explosions made her flinch – the roar of heavy-bellied enemy bombers made her cringe – and the whine and scream of fighter planes engaged in deadly combat overhead seemed to accentuate the awful pain in her head. The darkness was smothering, the weight of it pressing down on her chest as she struggled to overcome the terrifying sense that she was drowning in it.

'It's all right,' shouted Veronica, putting her arm around Doreen's shoulders. 'I'm here.'

Doreen closed her eyes and prayed for the raid to be over, for this debilitating fear to ease – and for the merest glimmer of light to pierce this all-pervasive darkness.

Peggy collected the dirty dinner plates and stacked them to one side before she made a pot of tea. The blessed sirens had gone off right in the middle of the meal and although they'd got the air-raid routine off pat, it had still been chaotic.

While Harvey had howled at the sirens and Daisy had yelled fit to burst at having her meal disturbed, Cordelia had turned up the worse for wear after too many glasses of wine at Bertie's, and just as they were about to close the Anderson shelter door, Jack Smith had arrived. It was a tight squeeze – rather like playing sardines but without the fun. Thankfully, Harvey had settled down to sleep once the sirens fell silent, and Daisy had eaten her fill and was now happily drinking from her nightly bottle of milk.

Peggy looked round at the occupants of the shelter as the Spitfires, Hurricanes, Wellingtons and Lancaster bombers thundered overhead. The rather tipsy Cordelia was ensconced in her deck-chair, surrounded by pillows and being fussed over by Bertie. Jack's large frame took up a lot of space and he was squashed up between the front wall and Rita, but he didn't seem to mind as he told her about his trip to his old haunts on the motorbike. Sarah and Fran were discussing knitting patterns as they unravelled a couple of old sweaters, and Ron was fidgeting about on the bench trying to get something out of his jacket pocket as Harvey snored at his feet.

When Peggy realised that he meant to fill his pipe, she reached out to still his hand. 'Not tonight, please, Ron. There're too many of us and that thing fills the place with smoke.'

He grimaced and stuck his pipe back into his jacket pocket. 'It comes to something when a man's outnumbered by bossy women, do ye not think, Bertie?'

Bertram, who was far too polite and tactful to side with anyone, gave a rather hapless smile and busied himself by pulling the blanket more closely over Cordelia's knees. 'When one is alone, one rather misses the company of women,' he said with a gentle smile to Cordelia.

Ron grunted as Cordelia simpered and slid sideways in the deckchair. 'At least you get to escape when you want to,' Ron continued. 'To be sure, me and Harvey are stuck with them day in and day out – and there's forever a great long list of things for me to be doing.'

171

'What's got into you, Uncle Ron?' asked Fran with a frown. 'You've been grumpy for ages, and it's not like you at all.'

'Ach, that would be telling,' he said. 'Perhaps it's me shrapnel on the move, or the cold damp – or having to sit for hours in this thing when I should be out on the hills hunting.'

'Poaching, you mean,' said Peggy drily.

Ron gave a great sigh of self-pity and then reached under the bench. Having fished about for a moment, he drew out his Home Guard tin helmet. Plonking it over his disreputable cap, he folded his arms and glowered from beneath his shaggy brows.

'Why on earth are you wearing that thing?' said Peggy, trying not to laugh.

'Because I want to,' he retorted.

'You do look very silly,' giggled Rita.

'Aye, that I might. But if this roof comes down then it'll not be me with a sore head.'

'I hardly think a tin hat will stop you from getting squashed.' Sarah laughed. 'Oh, do take it off, Uncle Ron. You look so funny.'

Ron grinned back at her. 'Well at least it's made you smile,' he said as he took the offending object from his head and shoved it back under the bench. 'So it's done its job.'

Peggy regarded him with deep affection as the girls, continued to giggle and Harvey started to chase rabbits in his sleep. Ron could always be counted upon to make people smile.

She shifted the sleeping Daisy in her arms so she could drink her tea. 'I don't know what you think of us all, Jack,' she said a moment later. 'It must seem like a madhouse after being in the Army where everything is so ordered.'

'It's a home, Peggy, and that's all that matters.'

'And how are you getting on at the Crown? Gloria treating you all right, is she?' she asked carefully.

'She's a bit of a one, isn't she?' he replied with a wink and a grin. 'But I've got her measure, Peggy. A bit of flirting never hurt anyone, and if it gets me a good dinner at night, then what's the harm?' He tapped the side of his nose. 'But the bedroom door will be locked again tonight and my wallet will be under the pillow.'

Peggy laughed. 'You always were bright, Jack Smith. I'm glad that hasn't changed.'

Jack grinned at her and then eyed the other men as he reached into his pocket for a pack of rather greasy playing cards. 'Fancy a game of rummy to pass the time, you two?'

'Rather,' said Bertie heartily. 'What are the stakes?'

'A farthing a trick,' said Ron as he scrabbled in his trouser pocket and pulled out a quarter bottle of whisky. 'And this should help to liven things up.'

'I say, jolly good show,' said Bertie as he rubbed his hands together. 'Cut the cards for dealer then, Jack.'

Peggy caught Sarah's eye and they shared a grin. Life was rarely normal these days, but now and again there were moments like these that helped dispel the gloom.

At long last the sound of the aircraft fell silent

173

and the all-clear rang out. With a sob of relief, Doreen crawled quickly from under the desk and switched on the light. She didn't know how she'd managed to hold her nerves together, but she had – and even though it was clear that the events in London had affected her far more than she'd realised, at least now she knew she had the strength to combat the terrors.

'How's your head?' asked Veronica as she brushed away the dust from her skirt and picked up her walking stick.

'It's fine,' Doreen fibbed. 'A good night's sleep and I'll be as right as rain.'

Veronica regarded her sharply. 'Well, if you're sure, but I really do think you should take a couple of days off.'

Doreen was in no mood to argue, so she didn't reply. She reached for her handbag, coat and gas-mask box. 'I'll see you in the morning, Ronnie. And thanks for holding my hand through the raid. I really appreciate it.'

The door opened and Dr Maynard came in. 'There you are,' he said, running his fingers through his tousled hair. 'Have you finished those notes?'

Doreen picked up the folders and handed them to him.

He flicked through each one and then shoved them under his arm. 'Get your notebook, Doreen. The meeting's in five minutes.'

'No, Dr Maynard,' said Veronica firmly. 'Doreen will not be taking minutes of the meeting. I'll get someone else to do that.'

'I don't want someone else,' he said stubbornly,

his myopic gaze magnified by his thick lenses.

'Doreen is exhausted and grieving,' said Veronica. 'She needs to go home. I'll do the minutes.'

'Ronnie, there's no need–'

'There's every need, Doreen. If you don't rest you'll make yourself ill. Now go home, and I don't want to see you until tomorrow afternoon. Is that clear?' Before Doreen could protest, Veronica had snatched up a notebook and pencil and steered a bewildered Dr Maynard out of the office.

Doreen followed them out then headed for the side door. Veronica was a stalwart friend and she had a great deal to thank her for. In truth, the thought of taking notes at that meeting was more than she could have coped with right now.

She took a deep, restorative breath of the cold night air and looked up beyond the silver barrage balloons to the infinity of the star-studded sky. There was no sign of the fierce battles that had been waged there only minutes before, just a sense of timelessness – a feeling that although terrible things were happening down here, the heavens would never change. She found that thought comforting.

She wheeled her bicycle to the gate and wished the guard goodnight before setting off down the hill to Halstead village. The tyres hummed on the tarmac as the mudguard rattled and the wicker basket jiggled her bag and gas-mask box about. The little lamp was so dim that she hadn't bothered to switch it on, and anyway, she knew every twist of the road. She felt the cold rush of air sting her face as the bicycle raced along, and then she was riding through the trees that almost met above the lane, the starlight and pale moon dappling the way before her.

On reaching her billet, she propped the bike against the wall, quietly opened the door and tip-toed into the hall. She could hear the other girls chattering in the kitchen, but she was in no mood to join them. No doubt they would wonder at her continued absence, for she was usually very sociable, and had excitedly told them all about her planned trip to London. It was better to avoid their questions and keep herself to herself for a while until she felt stronger and more able to cope.

Once she'd gained the sanctuary of her room, she leaned against the door for a moment to catch her breath, and then kicked off her shoes and padded across the floor to the window. She would leave the curtains open tonight, she decided. There was enough light from the stars to see by, and she needed the reassurance of those vast and unchanging skies to counter the claustrophobia that still lurked within her and was so very close to breaking through again.

Doreen let her clothes drop to the floor and pulled on her soft, comforting nightdress which could never be called anything but practical. Then she stood for a moment looking down at the box of Archie's effects. She traced her fingers over the simple cardboard box, knowing what must be in there, but not yet ready to see or touch the intimate possessions that were so much a part of him and who he was.

Turning towards the bed, she pulled back the

sheet and blanket and hauled the kitbag from the ottoman. Once it was positioned to her satisfaction, she climbed in beside it and held it close so she could breathe in the last tangible scent of the man that she'd loved.

9

Peggy was absolutely thrilled to find several airgraphs from Jim in the letter box that Friday morning, and as there were two for her, she was impatient to read them. However, there was Daisy to see to and breakfast to organise first, so she suppressed her frustration and got on with her morning chores.

Fran left for her shift in theatre and Sarah headed off for her long walk over the hills to her WTC office. Rita was back in her trousers, heavy boots, First World War flying jacket and helmet: she was planning to take her father out to the race track that she'd helped to rescue from disuse. There was to be a motorcycle meet on Sunday, all proceeds going towards the building of yet another Spitfire, so she was outside fiddling with the bike to ensure it was in tip-top condition.

Having read his airgraph from Jim and stuffed it in his pocket without sharing what it said with anyone, Ron stumped off to her bedroom. He had finally decided to do something about the ill-fitting windows in there, and now he was hammering something with great vigour, much to the distress of Cordelia, who was suffering from a hangover.

'I swear he's doing that deliberately to get his own back,' she muttered. She turned off her hearing aid and opened the morning paper.

Peggy thought that was rather unfair, but didn't bother to reply as Cordelia wouldn't be able to hear her anyway. At least the windows would be mended – that was one job less to do around the house – but it was very odd that Ron hadn't let her read his letter, and she wondered what Jim had written that Ron didn't want her to see.

Stifling her curiosity, she picked up Daisy and cleaned her face before settling her into the play-pen with a collection of toys and rag books while Harvey kept guard by stretching out on the floor beside it.

Peggy sat down at the kitchen table, and to the accompaniment of hammering and the odd bit of swearing from Ron, she opened the earliest of her two airgraphs. They were minute, barely the size of a postcard, and Jim had crammed so much on the page that it was very difficult to read his tiny, cramped writing.

'Good grief,' she muttered as she read about the cross-bred three-week-old puppy Jim had taken on. 'As if he hasn't got enough to worry about.' She smiled as she read that he'd called it Patch, for that had been the name of the old Irish setter they'd had when they were first married.

She read on to discover that Jim was having a fine old time, going to the pictures and eating out at Chinese restaurants of all things. But it seemed these long days of leisure were about to come to an end, for he was leaving the following day, although he couldn't tell her where he was going.

He'd managed to sneak the puppy on board the train without having to pay full fare for it, and it sounded as if he had had great fun with the native servants and their families during the journey, for he had ended up wearing a turban. Rationing was clearly not a problem – they'd had plenty of tinned food and eggs – and he and his mates had eaten like lords in their first-class carriages.

Jim continued that he'd 'borrowed' an army issue primus stove from a chap in Signals and had set himself up as a chef, which he knew would make her laugh, but his sausage, egg and chips had proved very popular. During the journey they'd stopped off at all sorts of interesting places; at one point two of the men went missing and Jim had been sent to look for them in the grog shops of a bazaar which he'd found both fascinating and very strange.

As they changed trains and then went by truck, Jim had continued to use the primus he'd filched, and because Patch had nearly pegged out after getting fish poisoning, he'd had to feed him on boiled eggs and bully beef to get him well again. The surplus of eggs they were all eating was having an unfortunate effect on their digestive systems and sleep was accompanied by the trumpet blasts of much farting.

Jim told her he loved and missed her and that he really looked forward to her letters. He signed off SWALKxx.

Peggy blinked back the tears and reached for the

179

second airgraph. At that moment Rita began to rev her motorcycle engine and Ron shouted abuse at a stubborn something-or-other that wouldn't do what he wanted it to do, and this was followed by a volley of heavy hammering and then a loud cry of pain. She sighed and shook her head. If she'd been hoping for a bit of peace then she was in the wrong place.

The second airgraph had been written almost two weeks later even though it had been sent at the same time, and it described the hellish journey by roads that crumbled beneath the trucks' wheels and meandered up steep mountains, through jungles and across deep ravines on bamboo bridges that swayed alarmingly and didn't look at all safe. The teeming rain not only cut visibility to the length of the truck bonnet, but raised the humidity to an unbearable degree. He'd been bitten to pieces by mosquitoes, and found leeches on himself and Patch after swimming in rivers – but he'd seen elephants working on timber, tiger skins for sale in the bazaars, and had slept in wooden huts on the side of mountains surrounded by tea plantations.

He had finally arrived at the camp where he would be stationed until further notice, and his home was a basha – a bamboo hut – which he was to share with his mate Ernie. He'd managed to 'win' a tarpaulin and a pair of charpoys (beds) for them both, and had fixed himself up with chairs, torches and a couple of nice rugs so they could sit outside at night beneath the makeshift tarpaulin porch in comfort.

He didn't think much of the commanding officer, who was inclined to lecture the men without showing a modicum of common sense – and it was clear that the dislike was mutual. The motor repair shops were in a terrible state, and Jim was disgusted to find that the native mechanics were untrained and, in his opinion, basically useless and lazy. But he was sure that once all the stores had been sorted, he could begin to train them up and start work on repairing the broken-down motors. The rough terrain, the humidity, rain and heat were no friends to anything mechanical – or human – and Jim was in constant fear of getting malaria.

He sent kisses to Daisy and Cordelia, and signed off in his usual fashion.

Peggy sighed deeply and slipped both airgraphs back in their envelopes. She just hoped to goodness Jim was taking care of himself, for malaria could be a killer, and it sounded as if he'd been well and truly bitten by those mosquitoes. She'd read somewhere that the water in those foreign places wasn't fit to drink either, because people used the rivers like lavatories. She gave a shudder at the thought of those leeches, and then turned her mind to other, rather more pleasant things.

Daisy was getting bored and throwing her toys out of the playpen at Harvey, so she took her out and let her crawl and stagger about the kitchen floor while she tidied her hair, found her outdoor shoes, and took off her wrap-round pinafore. Cordelia had taken refuge from the noise in her bedroom, but Rita had stopped revving the engine and Ron's hammering had fallen silent as well, so Peggy decided that a cup of tea was in

181

order before she faced the queues at the shops.

As she waited for the kettle to boil she heard a knock at the front door and a moment later the sound of Ron's voice. He appeared in the kitchen nursing a bruised thumb, closely followed by Jack Smith. 'You must have smelled the tea,' she said after greeting him.

'Never mind the tea. Look at my thumb,' groaned Ron.

Peggy could see that it was probably very painful, so she held it under the cold tap for a while and then hunted out a couple of aspirin. 'You'll live,' she said with a soft smile.

'Ach, to be sure I will,' he grumbled. 'But 'tis awful sore, so it is, and a drop of brandy would indeed make it a whole lot better.'

Peggy raised an eyebrow. 'Honestly, Ron, you're worse than Daisy. Do you want me to kiss it better and put a plaster on it?'

'Humph. Come on, Harvey, we're off to the Anchor where a man can get real sympathy as well as a drop of brandy,' he muttered. 'And what sort of thanks do I get for all the trouble I've been through this morning?' he continued as he stomped down the cellar steps, grabbed his long poacher's coat and headed for the back door. 'Nothing, that's what, and to think that I...'

Peggy didn't hear the rest of it, for Ron's grumbling was lost in the roar of a revving motorbike engine. 'He likes a drama, does our Ron,' she said brightly to Jack. 'But he'll get over it.' She poured the tea. 'Now, before you go and see Rita, there's something I'd like to say to you.'

'She's all right, isn't she?' he asked anxiously.

'Of course she is. Although she's worried sick over that young man of hers, and has been rather upset that you haven't bothered to write much in the past three years.' She regarded him steadily and saw the colour rise in his face. 'It's not good enough, Jack,' she continued. 'Poor little Rita has had a great deal to contend with since you enlisted, and the least you could have done was write regularly and perhaps telephone occasionally.'

He shuffled his feet. 'I've been very busy,' he hedged.

'I bet you've not been too busy to go to the pub, or cinema, or attend the dances that have no doubt been laid on for the servicemen in your area.'

Peggy noted how he refused to meet her gaze and knew she'd struck home. 'I'm fully aware of how much you care for her, Jack, and of course I'm only too happy to mother her, but that doesn't mean you can just hand over all responsibility for her and go on your merry way. She needs *you*, Jack. You're her father, her only flesh and blood, and that's the most important thing – especially at times like this.'

'I'm sorry, Peg,' he said quietly. 'I just accepted that she was safe and happy with you, so I didn't worry about her.' He finally met her gaze. 'I promised her mother that I would look after her, but I've let her down, haven't I?'

'Not let her down – just not been there quite as often as you should have been.' Peggy patted his arm. 'But I'm sure you'll remember to write more often from now on.'

He nodded, his gaze drifting towards the cellar steps and the sound of the motorbike engine. 'You can be sure of that, Peggy,' he said gruffly. 'She's a good kid, and I won't let her down again, I promise.'

'I'm glad that's settled. I didn't want to spoil your leave, but I felt I had to say something.'

'And you were right to do so, Peggy. I'm just rather ashamed that it was necessary to remind me.'

'Don't take it too hard, Jack. It's not easy being a parent these days.' Peggy handed him two cups of tea. 'Why don't you take these down to drink with Rita while you both mess about with that bike? I'm off into town in a minute, so I won't see you until this evening.' She smiled up at his doleful expression. 'Cheer up, Jack,' she said brightly. 'Worse things happen at sea.'

Ron didn't head for the Anchor as he'd first intended, but walked along the twitten which ran between the back gardens of the terraces. He plodded purposefully up the steep hill as Harvey raced ahead of him, nose to the ground, tail windmilling as he followed the scents of rabbits, field mice and voles.

Ron was a bit disgruntled that Peggy hadn't seemed to take the painful injury to his thumb seriously, but he knew that fresh air and sunshine would soon put him in a better mood. The wind was cold, but the sun was low in the sky and very bright, making the dew sparkle on the grass. He continued walking until he'd reached the top of the cliffs that overlooked the town, and then stood for a moment in quiet contemplation.

Cliffehaven had been scarred by war, the familiar streets and once elegant promenade now interspersed with gaping bomb sites and the skeletons of houses, hotels and shops. The factory estate lay in the drifting shadows of barrage balloons, and ugly barbed wire and shipping traps marred the beauty of the seafront and the bay.

Ron looked down to the shingle beach which had been laid with mines right to the low-water mark, and remembered the years when he'd accompanied his father on the family fishing boat as part of Cliffehaven's large fleet. They had been the good years, when the catches were plentiful, work was readily available and there was money to spend. On his father's passing, Ron had continued the family tradition and taken over with his own sons, Jim and Frank.

He lit his pipe, dug his hands into the deep pockets of his poacher's coat and stared out across the sparkling waters of the English Channel. The First World War had intervened, but the Reilly men had survived when so many of their comrades had not, and Ron had hoped things would return to normal. But Jim had given up the fishing and turned his back on the engineering training he'd had from the Army to become a projectionist at the local cinema, and on Ron's retirement, Frank had taken over. Now they were in the midst of another war, and things would never be the same again.

Ron bit down on his pipe stem as he trudged past the hilltop gun emplacements, down the rolling slope and then along to where the chalk cliff jutted out over the tiny shingled cove of Tamarisk Bay.

He looked down to the row of five little wooden houses set on a grassy bank at the end of the rutted track which wound its way to the shore from the main road at the top of the cliffs. The end house was where Frank and Pauline had set up home to raise their family so many years before, and in the summer the tamarisk on the bank would be a rippling sea of pink fronds amid the bright yellow gorse and wild grasses. And as the different seasons passed the shingle would become a garden of rock samphire, sea campion and kale, yellow horned poppies and starry clover.

Now the houses were mostly abandoned and instead of the flowers, there were clumps of black, foul-smelling oil entangled in the flotsam and jetsam of downed aircraft and sunken ships – and the lonely beached hulk of Frank's fishing boat.

Ron regarded the boat, wondering if Frank would ever sail her again now that two of his three sons had been consigned to watery graves somewhere in the Atlantic. 'To be sure, I'd not have the heart for it,' he muttered.

He stood there for a long moment, remembering the times he'd carried those boys on his shoulders as he'd tramped the hills, and taught them how to make purse nets, to train and care for ferrets, sneak up on an unsuspecting pheasant, tickle trout, catch eels and skin rabbits. They were the days of sunshine, of hope that there would never be another war. Now Brendon was the only survivor.

Ron sighed deeply. Following his brothers' tragic deaths in 1941, Brendon had been reassigned by the Royal Naval Reserve from the minesweepers to the London docks, which could be just as dangerous as the Atlantic, and his mother Pauline clung to the desperate hope that he would come through unscathed.

Ron's gaze shifted to the line of washing that flapped in the wind. Pauline had refused Peggy's offer to come and live with them until Frank was demobbed, preferring instead to stay in the house that still resonated with the memories of happier times. He'd visited often to make sure she was coping, and although she'd worried them all at the depths of her grieving, she'd somehow found a way of dealing with it – just as everyone did in the end.

He headed away from the cliff edge towards the ruins of the old farmhouse and barns. The farmer and his family had been relocated to Scotland and the Army had requisitioned it to use as target practice for their new recruits before they'd finally abandoned it, but it still offered shelter from the elements.

Ron settled down on a fallen rafter and relit his pipe, aware that the time had come to read and fully absorb the contents of Jim's airgraph. Despite its small size, it had felt heavy in his trouser pocket – a dark reminder that the war touched them all, and that time and distance brought little comfort to already troubled hearts.

Drawing it from his pocket, he watched Harvey charge about in the pursuit of something hiding in a clump of gorse. His gaze drifted to the sweeping valley below, where the forest and fields of the Cliffe estate sprawled behind the high wire fences that had brought his poaching expeditions to an end.

He gave a sigh and let his gaze follow the country lane which meandered alongside the serried ruts of good, dark earth where spring crops were beginning to flourish, towards the distant steeple which rose above the trees and huddled roofs of the tiny hamlet where Martin and Anne had bought a cottage. They'd lived in it for less than a year before Anne left for the safety of Somerset with their baby Rose Margaret; now Martin lived with the other airmen at Cliffe aerodrome and the cottage had been rented out.

Ron knew he'd been merely putting off the moment, so he took a deep breath and drew the letter from its envelope. Jim's writing was cramped, but Ron's eyesight was good and in the bright sunlight it was easy to decipher.

Da,
I hope you're well, and that Harvey is behaving. Peg wrote and told me about your medal and I'm guessing you probably caused a scene at the Town Hall. I wish I could have been there to cheer you on. The heat and humidity here is unbearable, and we're all being eaten alive by mosquitoes. I'm one mass of bites but have so far managed to escape malaria, but Ernie's down with dysentery and it's frightening how quickly a big, strong man can be reduced to a shivering skeleton. The hospital's wicked, with bad food, lack of staff and no proper sanitation. The men are expected to lie on straw mattresses on the floor and

then virtually left there to either recover or die. It's
particularly bad for those with rot-gut as they're left
to roll about in agony in their own mess for hours. The
fact that any of them survives is a miracle, and I fear
for Ernie. On top of all that we've got some of the
deadliest snakes to contend with here, and I found one
curled up in my bed. I killed it, and now we all go on
a nightly hunt for the buggers.

We've had a bit of excitement over the last week
which I haven't told Peggy about. A large force of Jap
bombers attacked us, which resulted in numerous fires
and a lot of casualties. The ack-ack brought down two
of the blighters, and the RAF brought down seven, but
one of our fighters was shot down. Turns out the Japs
are trying to make a big push across the border, so
we're all on standby to get at them or get out. Their
soldiers are now less than forty miles away from our
HQ, and all the civilians in the town have been
evacuated. If I don't make it out of here, Da, look
after Peg and the wains for me and never let them
forget that I love you all.

Jim.

Ron's eyes misted. 'God love you, son,' he
murmured. He struck a match and the flame
caught the edge of the letter and swiftly devoured
it. As the charred fragments flew away with the
wind, Ron could only pray that the hotter winds
of India would blow mercifully on his son and
bring him home safe and unharmed.

Peggy had strapped Daisy into her pram and left
Jack and Rita to their noisy efforts with the motorbike. Cordelia had decided to keep her hearing aid

off, and was happily ensconced in her favourite chair by the kitchen fire with a new library book. She'd assured Peggy she was quite capable of preparing the vegetables for tea, and was planning to make a corned beef sandwich for her lunch.

The sun was bright but the wind was cold, so, having completed her shopping, Peggy kept up a brisk pace as she went along Camden Road and turned up into the High Street. Passing the Home and Colonial, she waved to Ted, and felt the usual pang of regret when she saw the remains of the cinema where Jim used to work. She headed on up towards the station and the humpbacked bridge.

'Hello, Stan,' she said cheerfully as she saw the portly stationmaster sitting outside the Nissen hut which now served as his ticket office. 'You're looking very well.'

He rose from his seat and tipped his hat. 'That's because I am well, Peggy,' he said with a beaming smile as he gently pinched Daisy's cheek and chucked her under the chin. 'And how are you?'

'I'm fine,' she replied. 'I got two letters from Jim today, Ron has finally fixed my window frames, and Daisy has yet to have one of her tantrums.' She eyed the straining buttons on his uniform jacket, and the plump, rosy cheeks that almost hid his eyes when he smiled. 'I see Ethel is still feeding you up, Stan,' she teased. 'I don't know how she manages on the ration.'

Stan tapped the side of his nose. 'She's got a mate who's working as a land girl on one of the farms and they've come to an arrangement,' he said quietly. 'In exchange for extra butter, eggs and cheese, Ethel does all their mending and

190

goes over once a week to clean their billet.'

'Good for her,' said Peggy without rancour. 'Well, I'd better be off. I want to catch Ivy when she comes off her shift.'

'Before you go,' he said quickly, 'there's a bit of news that isn't public knowledge yet.'

Peggy was immediately intrigued, for she loved a bit of gossip. 'Don't tell me you and Ethel are thinking of getting hitched, Stan. She's still got a husband somewhere, you know.'

He waved his hand impatiently. 'No, no, Peggy. It's Ethel's Ruby. She and Mike have got engaged.'

'Oh, Stan, that's wonderful news. When's the wedding?'

His ruddy face became gloomy. 'There's the rub, Peg. What with him being Canadian, it's going to involve an enormous amount of paperwork to get permission from his commanding officer – and from the Home Office. So it might take a while.' His expression brightened. 'But there's to be a party soon, and Ruby's already got your name at the top of the invitation list.'

Peggy loved it when romance was in the air – especially when it involved someone like little Ruby and her young Canadian soldier. 'Give her my love and congratulations, Stan,' she said happily. 'And tell her to come and visit. We haven't seen enough of her or of Ethel since they went to live in the bungalow.'

'I'll do that, Peg.' He pulled out his pocket watch and checked the time. 'The eleven o'clock is due any minute, I'd better get on.'

Peggy's step was light as she pushed the pram up the steep hill towards the dairy and the factory estate. Ruby had come to live at Beach View when she'd escaped her brute of a husband back in Bow. Since his death, she'd found work and a comfortable home here in Cliffehaven with her mother Ethel, and had fallen in love with Mike Taylor, who'd been blinded in one eye during the disastrous raid on Dieppe. There had been a time when Ruby had feared he'd be released from the Army and sent back to Canada, but the powers that be decided he'd be useful working here in admin, so things had worked out very well for both of them.

The sun suddenly seemed brighter and the wind less chill as Peggy tramped up the hill in a glow of happiness. Everything would be just perfect if Ethel could get free of her bully of a second husband and make an honest man out of Stan, for he'd been a widower for too long, and a man as kind-hearted as him deserved to have someone lovely to share his golden years.

Peggy reached the factory gates and kept a sharp eye out for Ivy as the men and women poured out after their night shift. They'd been working since eleven the night before, so it was hardly surprising that they were all in a hurry to get home.

She spotted Ivy amongst a group of other girls and took a moment to watch her. Ivy was small and as thin as a sparrow. Her unruly brown hair was partially covered by a headscarf knotted above her forehead, and she wore filthy dungarees that looked several sizes too big, heavy boots, a check shirt and a coat which had obviously been made from a tartan blanket. She looked tired and her little face was yellow-tinged and grubby, but there was still an energy about her, even after the long hours she'd just put in.

'Hello, Peggy,' she called as she came through the gate. 'What are you doing up 'ere?' She stepped out of reach as Peggy went to hug her. 'I wouldn't,' she warned. 'I'm covered in muck and bits of bullet, and you'll get your lovely coat all dirty.'

Peggy smiled fondly at her. 'Speaking of coats, I like yours. Did you make it?'

Ivy's dimples flashed as she grinned. 'With a lot of help from me mate. Doris had thrown it out and left it by the bin, so I thought I'd make use of it.' Her dark brown eyes were bright with mischief. 'So, Peggy, what brings you all the way up 'ere? You're not applyin' for a job, are you?'

Peggy laughed. 'I've got quite enough to do already without trying to hold down a job. No, I've come to ask if you'd like to move into Beach View.'

The brown eyes widened. 'Really? You mean it?'

'I wouldn't have asked if I didn't.'

'Oh, Peggy, that would be blindin'. It's not the same now Mary's gone, and I know she's your sister and all, but Doris is a worse pain in the backside than ever.'

'In that case you'd better move in straight away,' said Peggy, biting down on a giggle.

'What? Today?' Ivy breathed.

'No time like the present,' Peggy said firmly. 'Come on, let's face Doris together and get you packed and out of there.'

'Blimey, you don't 'alf get a move on when you

make yer mind up about somethin', don't cha?' Ivy said happily as they headed down the hill. 'I were only thinking the other day about calling in to see if you 'ad a place spare.'

'You should have done,' said Peggy. 'I've always told you my door is open, Ivy.'

'Well, yeah, but that were when Mary were 'ere.'

Peggy stopped walking and regarded the girl with some surprise. 'What difference would that have made?'

Ivy shrugged. 'Well, she were posh, weren't she? Like you.'

Peggy roared with laughter. 'Oh, Ivy, you are a caution. I'm about as posh as a tin kettle – and if you think it makes a ha'p'orth of difference to me if you were born in Bow or Chelsea, then you really don't know me at all.'

Ivy grinned. 'Sorry, Peggy. It's living with Doris – she never stops reminding me of my "place", as she calls it.'

'It's all nonsense,' retorted Peggy, 'and I'll have none of that in my home, believe you me.'

They continued walking down the High Street and then slowed their pace as they turned into the tree-lined road which edged Havelock Gardens. The houses were detached and hidden behind high brick walls and trees, each with a garage and neat front garden, their rear windows overlooking the promenade and the sea. Havelock Road was considered to be the posh part of Cliffehaven, which was why Doris had insisted upon living there when she'd married Ted all those years ago. However, despite its grandeur, it hadn't escaped the attention of the Luftwaffe, for two of the houses had now been reduced to rubble.

'Before we go in and face Doris, there is something I need to ask you, Ivy,' said Peggy as they reached the imposing gateway. She saw the girl frown and hurried to reassure her. 'It's nothing serious, but would you mind if you shared with Rita?'

The grubby urchin face lit up in a beaming smile as the dimples danced in her cheeks. 'Blimey, Peggy, that's like asking if I wanted a bowl of ice cream. Rita's a real diamond. 'Course I don't mind sharing with 'er.'

Peggy laughed and began to push the pram over the shingled driveway. 'I thought as much.' She reached the front door and waited for Ivy to slot in her key. Plucking Daisy out of the pram, she balanced her on her hip and followed the girl into the hallway. 'Doris? Doris, it's me, Peggy,' she called.

'What on earth are *you* doing here?' said Doris rudely as she emerged from her drawing room. Before Peggy could answer, her gaze fell on Ivy. 'Take those boots off immediately,' she ordered. 'You've been told at least a hundred times, but still you persist in disobeying me.'

Ivy grimaced and muttered under her breath as she unlaced the boots and then kicked them off into an untidy heap on the doormat.

'It's nice to see you too, Doris,' said Peggy with some asperity. 'And I'm here because I thought it only polite to tell you that Ivy will be coming to live with me from now on.' She turned to Ivy, who was hovering nervously beside her. 'Go and pack your things, dear. I'll wait for you down here.'

'You will stay where you are,' snapped Doris. She turned her glare on her sister. 'You can't just come into my home and start throwing your weight about. I will not stand for it, do you hear?'

Peggy shifted Daisy onto her other hip. 'I don't see why I shouldn't. You do it all the time at mine.' She took a couple of steps towards Doris. 'Come on, Doris,' she coaxed. 'Loosen your corsets and be nice for once.'

'Don't be vulgar.'

Peggy eyed her thoughtfully. 'What objections do you actually have against Ivy coming to live with me?'

Doris lifted her chin and looked coldly down her nose. 'The people at the billeting office have charged me with her care. It is them I answer to, not you.'

'Then it is them she and I will go to and fill in a formal complaint about the way she's been treated here,' retorted Peggy, riled by her sister's attitude.

Doris went pale beneath the carefully applied make-up. 'You wouldn't dare,' she breathed.

'Wouldn't I?' Peggy's gaze remained steady. 'You've made it plain since the day she arrived that you don't want her here. So why make a fuss? Afraid you won't be able to get someone to cook and clean for you and the snooty Caroline? Worried about having to teach someone else how to iron tablecloths and napkins to your high standards?'

'Servants are impossible to find nowadays,' said Doris. 'I thought the girl would be only too pleased to help out by way of thanks for having such a comfortable billet.'

Peggy gave a sharp, derisive laugh. 'That excuse might wash with the billeting people, but I know you too well, Doris. Ever since you lost your cook and the girl who used to do the rough work, you've been looking for replacements. Well, that's an end to it. She's coming to live with me.'

'But that would mean having a room free again, and going through all the ghastly rigmarole of finding someone halfway decent to fill it. Caroline is very particular, you know, and she won't be happy about this.'

'I'm sure she'll get over it,' said Peggy tartly. She turned to Ivy, who was unsuccessfully trying to stifle her giggles. 'Go and pack, dear, while I sort out Daisy and have a sit-down.'

'It's really not convenient,' blustered Doris as Peggy headed for the drawing room. 'I'm due to go to luncheon in half an hour, and Lady Chumley is most particular about timekeeping.'

Peggy sat down on the very edge of the couch, which had been beautifully upholstered in pale blue and cream silk. 'So, you've been accepted into the coven again, have you?' she murmured as she divested Daisy of her bonnet and mittens and shoved them in her coat pocket. 'Personally, I think you were better off without them. They never were real friends, you know.'

She put Daisy down on the luxuriously thick Turkish carpet. 'Don't let me hold you up, Doris,' she said cheerfully. 'I'll make sure everything's locked up when we leave, and Ivy can put her key on the hall table.'

Doris didn't budge, but watched like a hawk as Daisy began to totter and crawl about the room. 'I hope her hands are clean,' she said sharply as the toddler pulled herself up the edge of the couch to grasp the perfectly plumped cushion.

'I washed them before we came out.'

'Oh, no!' gasped Doris. 'She's dribbling on my upholstery.'

Peggy quickly plucked Daisy away from the cushion that she was attempting to chew. Doris's house had never been child-friendly, even when Anthony had been a baby. She wrinkled her nose at the sour smell emanating from Daisy's nappy. 'I need to change her,' she muttered.

'Then use the downstairs cloakroom,' said Doris with a shudder. 'I can't possibly allow you to do that in my drawing room.'

Peggy was stifling her giggles as she carried Daisy out to the cloakroom, and once she was all clean and dry, she used the scented soap to wash her hands. Spotting a small bottle of very expensive perfume on the windowsill, she even dared to dab some on her wrists and behind her ears. She might not have been given a warm welcome or even offered a cup of tea, but at least she'd had a tiny touch of the luxury her sister took for granted.

'Are you almost done, Ivy?' she called up the stairs.

'Finished!' Ivy appeared on the landing with two battered suitcases. She grinned impishly as she came running down the stairs, still in her work dungarees and grubby shirt, her rug coat over her arm. 'I didn't realise how much stuff I 'ad.'

'Most of it is fit only for the rag-and-bone man,' sniffed Doris.

'Well, you'd know all about that, wouldn't you?' retorted Ivy as she shoved her feet back into her boots. 'After all, you've been through my stuff often enough.'

Peggy was appalled. 'You go through her things?'

There was a flush of colour in Doris's cheeks. 'Only to check she's not hiding food up there. I don't want to encourage mice.' She held out her hand to Ivy. 'My key,' she said imperiously.

Ivy pulled it out of her dungaree pocket and placed it delicately on Doris's open palm. 'Thanks ever so,' she said. 'I hope you and Caroline find someone more to yer likin' and that you'll all be very happy together.'

'There's no need for that sort of sarcasm,' hissed Doris.

Ivy picked up her cases and turned her back on her. 'Right, ready when you are, Peggy. Let's get out of 'ere, shall we?'

10

Doreen had finally fallen into a deep sleep, drugged by exhaustion and the weight of her grief. When she opened her eyes the following morning she realised that she felt calmer and there was no vestige of that awful headache – and she couldn't remember having had any disturbing dreams.

She glanced at the clock and saw with some shock that it was past nine, but as Ronnie had said she didn't need to be in the office until this afternoon, she decided to make the most of this chance to recuperate and rest.

She lay there for a moment, her hand caressing the kitbag as she looked at the blue sky outside the window. It was going to be a fine day, and she could see the birds darting back and forth to their nests on the trees. Soon there would be fledglings, blossoms on the trees and green shoots of spring flowers pushing their way through the soil. Life went on in the endless cycle, heedless of the pain and the loss that was being suffered.

Doreen came to the conclusion that she had to keep busy and not lie about in bed thinking about things and getting maudlin. She felt stronger after her sleep, more determined, and as long as she didn't allow her mind to wander she'd get through the day somehow. She tossed back the bedclothes, rammed her feet into her slippers and pulled on her dressing gown. The others should be at work by now, and hopefully the elderly owners would have left for the Friday market they always attended.

Once she'd used the bathroom and changed into clean clothes, Doreen placed the kitbag back on the ottoman, pulled out the clothes she'd stuffed in there from her abandoned bag, and made the bed. She studiously ignored the box of Archie's treasures and sat down at the dressing table to brush out her damp hair.

Ronnie had been right, she realised, for she did

look ghastly, with shadows beneath her eyes and in the hollows of her cheeks, her skin having lost the radiance of her earlier happiness. Determined not to dwell on these changes, she carefully applied her make-up and then added a defiant dash of lipstick. As long as she kept up appearances then she could pretend she was all right and so avoid further questioning from Ronnie.

Her stomach rumbled to remind her that she'd eaten nothing since her last meal with Archie – which, she realised in horror, was over forty-eight hours ago. No wonder she'd been suffering from blinding headaches.

She went along the silent hall and into the kitchen. It was a large, old-fashioned room with a scrubbed pine table, quarry-tiled floor, huge black range and a stone sink. Pots, pans and china shared space on the dresser shelves, and an assortment of washing hung from the wooden dryer that was suspended from the ceiling.

It was the heart of the Victorian house, and in happier times, she'd enjoyed sitting in here of an evening and joining in with the other girls' gossip. In a way, it was a much larger version of the kitchen at home in Beach View, for it was shabby and warm and welcoming, even though the sunlight showed up the cobwebs and the flaking plaster.

She put the kettle on the hotplate and as she waited for it to come to the boil, she went to the huge walk-in larder to see what she could eat. Each of the girls had a shelf in the larder, and hers was sadly depleted. She'd forgotten to buy any food on her return to Halstead, and although there were a couple of eggs, half a packet of digestive biscuits and the last of her packet of tea, there was nothing really substantial for her breakfast.

Having made a pot of weak tea which she'd have to drink without milk or sugar, she picked up the packet of biscuits and went back to her bedroom. She'd have to do some shopping in the village on the way to work, and if Maynard needed her to stay late, then she could always eat supper in the Fort's canteen.

Sitting at the small table by the window, Doreen sipped her tea and ate her way through the remains of her packet of digestive biscuits. She could hear the lovely song of a thrush as well as pigeons cooing, and the sunlight had brought out the crocuses in splashes of brilliant colour. It was peaceful and quiet after the chaos of London, and she could only pray that it would help her find a way to accept what had happened and learn to cope with it.

The tea and biscuits had been a boost to her spirits, and she took her writing pad from the drawer and began to pen letters to her girls. Evelyn – or Evie, as she preferred – was eight, and Joyce was six. They'd inherited their dark hair and eyes from her side of the family, and their ability to charm from their father – not that he'd been around much. But when he was, Eddie had been entertaining and had spoilt them rotten, often taking their side when she'd tried to instil a bit of discipline into them.

The girls adored him, of course, but they had no idea of how unfaithful he'd been, or how swiftly that charm could switch off when he'd suffered too many losses at the poker tables and Doreen had refused to bail him out for the umpteenth time. She'd lost count of the occasions when he'd raided her purse of the housekeeping money – and of the lonely nights she'd spent wondering where he was and who he was with.

She set all those bad memories aside and concentrated on her letters, which she kept cheerful and light and full of silly day-to-day things which she accompanied with little cartoon sketches of the people she worked with, and the animals she saw from her bedroom window. Her children were too young for anything more serious, and she wanted them to be assured that she was well and happy and having a wonderful time here in Kent. But oh, she did miss them, and would have given anything to be able to hold them right now.

Doreen fixed stamps to the envelopes and popped them in her handbag to post on her way to the Fort. She didn't quite feel up to writing to Peggy about Archie just yet, but perhaps once the funeral was over and she was feeling less fragile, she'd telephone her instead.

Leaning back in the chair she gazed through the window, her thoughts on her childhood home and the sister she loved. She hadn't been back to Cliffehaven since before the war, and although Peggy kept her abreast of all the news, it wasn't the same as actually being there. How lovely it would be to see her again, and to meet Daisy and reacquaint herself with dear old Ron and Harvey and Cordelia – to feel the warmth and homeliness of Beach View, and be a part of her family again.

She took a deep breath and berated herself for getting wistful and soppy. It had been her choice to leave home, so there was little point in getting homesick all of a sudden. She looked at her watch, and then at the simple cardboard box that she'd left on the chest of drawers. It was almost eleven now, and although she had some washing to do before she went to the shops and then on to work, there were other, more important things to come to terms with. She hesitated momentarily and then, before she lost her nerve, took the box, sat on the ottoman and opened it.

Archie's wallet was of a worn black leather which had become moulded to the curve of his hip where it had been kept in his back pocket. She ran her fingers over it, remembering how small it had looked in his big hands. On opening it, she found the snapshot she'd sent him, her smiling, happy face looking back at her – a cruel reminder of how quickly things had changed.

A reluctant search of the wallet produced almost twenty pounds in notes, three stamps, the ticket stubs from the cinema they'd attended during his leave, the receipt for their hotel, and a hastily scribbled note of the last address he'd been given for his parents – which had turned out to be a deserted house waiting to be demolished. Poor Archie, he'd tried so hard to hide his disappointment and his worry, and now Doreen made a silent promise to him that she would do her very best to track down what had happened to them.

She set the wallet aside and picked up the watch which, heartbreakingly, was still ticking away. It was large and heavy – a real seaman's watch, with an inset chronometer, clear roman numerals and black hands. Fixed to a thick leather strap which bore the scars of age and wear, the back of the watch was inscribed,

Presented to Archibald Blake RN
on his promotion to Master Engineer
From the crew of HMS Forthright.

Doreen ran her finger over the inscription, remembering how proud and humbled he'd been to have received such an accolade from his men. She listened to the quiet tick of the second hand as it moved relentlessly around the dial, and then carefully turned the winder so it would continue to do so. It was silly really, but she felt that if the watch kept ticking, then some part of Archie would still somehow be with her.

Placing the watch on the eiderdown, she reached into the box and hesitated momentarily before lifting out his signet ring. The gold was dull and scarred, worn thin where it had been rubbed on his finger over the years. His initials were engraved on the flat round face, and she remembered him telling her that he'd had it done when he'd received his first pay packet from the Navy. He'd promised her an engagement ring on his next leave, but this was much more personal and precious, and she would wear it with pride.

She tried the ring on each finger, but it was far too large and heavy, so she took off the gold chain and crucifix she'd inherited from her grandmother and hung the ring from that. Fastening it around her neck, the ring now lay just above her heart, which was perfect.

The box now held only a brown envelope filled with the change that must have been in his trouser pockets; a packet of cigarettes with two missing, a Dunhill lighter, and a neatly folded white handkerchief. Doreen held the handkerchief to her face, but there was no scent of Archie, just the coolness of freshly laundered cotton.

She sat for a long while regarding Archie's treasures as she caressed the ring and listened to the soft tick of his watch. This was the essence of the man she loved, whose life had been cut so cruelly short. It probably wasn't worth much to anyone else, but to her it was priceless.

Galvanised by the realisation that she needed to be surrounded by his things, she quickly unpacked his kitbag. She placed his washbag and shaving kit on the top of the chest alongside the photograph he'd sent her only weeks before, and then lovingly folded his sweaters and underwear into one of the drawers. His shoes were neatly positioned next to hers at the bottom of the wardrobe, and his spare shirts and trousers were hung between her dresses.

The watch was placed on the bedside table so she could hear it ticking at night and see the dial that lit up in the dark, and his wallet was hidden away with the lighter in the drawer beneath it. She would use some of the money to buy a headstone, and a small frame for his photograph, but the rest would never be touched.

Leaving the kitbag on the ottoman, she straightened the counterpane, the tremor of grief determinedly controlled. She had to get through the coming days, weeks, perhaps even months, and letting her emotions run away with her wouldn't help. She had to forget about that tunnel and the awful way he'd died. Had to focus on work and prepare herself for the ordeal of his funeral.

'Cor, it's lovely, Peggy,' breathed Ivy as she dumped her cases and rushed to the window. 'And I can even see the sea,' she added excitedly as she stood on tiptoe and peered over the rooftops.

'It's the same old English Channel you could see from your bedroom in Havelock Road,' said Peggy drily as she picked up the cases and put them on the second single bed that she'd made up earlier with fresh linen.

Ivy giggled and her dimples flashed as she turned from the window. 'Yeah, I know that, but it looks much better from 'ere.'

Peggy laughed and gave her a hug. 'I'm glad you're so happy with the move, Ivy, but before you get carried away, I do have some rules, young lady, and I expect you and Rita to remember them now and again. The blackout has to be pulled across before you turn the light on. Don't try putting farthings in the gas meter instead of sixpenny bits – they get stuck and then I have to get the man in to mend it. You're both responsible for changing your bedding on Monday mornings and keeping the room clean and tidy. Mealtimes are flexible, because all you girls are on different shifts, but I like to have tea on the table by six because of Cordelia and Ron. If you're planning to eat out at any time, then let me know – I can't afford to cook food that won't be eaten.'

'Eat out? Chance'd be a fine thing,' said Ivy with a grimace.

'You never know,' said Peggy. 'Some chap might ask you out for a fish supper.'

'Yeah, and pigs might fly.' Ivy plucked ruefully at her oversized dungarees. 'What bloke would fancy me got up like this, I ask yer?'

Peggy smiled. 'I'm sure you scrub up just fine – and I seem to remember you were very popular with the boys at the Anchor.' She patted her shoulder. 'And if you do happen to find one you like the look of, bring him in to meet us – but remember there are no men allowed further than the bottom of the stairs.'

Ivy nodded. 'Yeah, of course.'

'Now, why don't you go and have a nice bath and I'll rustle you up a spot of lunch before you catch up on some sleep. You must be exhausted.'

Ivy drew off her blanket coat and dropped it on the floor as she began to undo the straps of her overalls. 'Yeah, I'm knackered, truth to tell, Peggy.'

Peggy eyed the discarded coat which had now been joined by the dungarees and the boots. Ivy was as bad as Rita, and she suspected that before too long, neither of them would be able to cross the floor without trampling on something.

She left her to it and went downstairs to the kitchen to find it deserted. Looking out of the window, she saw Ron and Cordelia arguing about something in the vegetable plot while Harvey was busy digging out her few surviving spring bulbs.

She banged on the window and then ran down the cellar steps. 'Stop that, Harvey,' she shouted.

'Get away from there.'

Harvey scrabbled twice more as if to prove that he wasn't the sort of dog to heed people who shouted at him, and then set about chewing on an old bone he'd unearthed.

'Oh, Harvey. Those were my last three tulips,' she wailed as she picked up the clawed remnants from the path. 'And they were on the point of sprouting, too.' She put her hands on her hips and glared at him.

Harvey was immediately contrite. He rolled onto his back amid the pile of dirt he'd shovelled onto the path, legs waving in the air, his eyes large and sorrowful.

'You are the absolute limit,' she hissed. 'And don't think you can get around me by doing that. I have no wish to see your undercarriage.'

'Now, Peggy girl, that's no way to talk to Harvey,' said Ron. 'To be sure he's just a dog and digging comes natural, so it does.'

'He's not just a dog, Ron – he's the canine version of you. And the pair of you are driving me potty.'

His wayward brows wriggled above his twinkling eyes. 'It helps to be a bit potty around here.' He looked over his shoulder at Cordelia, who was prodding the earth with one of his vegetable canes. 'Talking of which, that's the pottiest one of all.'

'Oh, Lord, what's the matter now?'

'She's interfering in me gardening, that's what,' he grumbled. 'Telling me how to plant the beans properly, and wittering on about mulch and potash and goodness knows what.'

He pulled his newspaper from his jacket pocket

and opened the door to the outside lav. 'I'm going in here for a bit of peace and quiet.'

Peggy grabbed the door before he could shut it. 'What was in Jim's airgraph?'

His gaze slid away. 'No more than was in yours, I expect.'

'Then why didn't you show it to me?'

'You had two of your own, so I knew you didn't need to see it.'

'Can I read it now?'

He patted his pockets and then shook his head. 'I must have lost it somewhere on me walk on the hills this morning,' he muttered as he attempted to wrest the door from Peggy's grip.

Peggy held firm. 'I thought you said you were going to Rosie's?'

'I changed me mind. For the love of God, Peggy Reilly, will ye not stop all this questioning and let a man be?' As Peggy's grip loosened on the door he slammed it shut and shot the bolt.

'You can't fool me, Ronan Reilly,' she said through the door. 'I know when you're hiding something, and I'll find out what it is, you can be sure of that.'

Ivy was singing to herself as she splashed in the few inches of hot water and washed away the grime of the munitions factory. She'd had a close call with that can of TNT, but that was the risk she'd accepted in return for a very good wage. It wasn't the nicest of jobs, but at least she could send her mum a decent amount each week and still have plenty left over.

She soaped the sponge with the scented bar

she'd nicked from Doris's bathroom and gave herself a long, leisurely wash before sliding down into the water to do her hair. The shampoo was Doris's as well, and although she shouldn't have done it, and Peggy would probably be cross with her for thieving, she felt she deserved something nice after all she'd gone through with the old cow.

Not wanting to dwell on her time at Doris's, Ivy rinsed out her hair under the cold tap and then clambered out of the bath. She wiped the steam from the mirror on the bathroom cabinet and regarded her reflection as she towelled her hair dry. She certainly looked and felt better, and she knew that once she'd had some food, she'd sleep like a baby.

Returning to the bedroom, she pulled on some fresh clothes and surveyed her surroundings. The furniture was a bit shabby and battered, the rug was worn thin, and the varnish on the floorboards needed stripping and refreshing, but the two iron bedsteads looked comfortable, with thick mattresses, crisp sheets, soft blankets and plump eiderdowns.

Rita's things were scattered about the place, her family photographs displayed on the narrow shelf above the gas fire and brushes and combs laid out on the dressing table.

The room was larger than the one she'd shared with Mary, the bay window letting in lots of light, and although the place was a little shabby, it was far removed from the tenement room she'd shared with her parents and siblings back in Hackney – the atmosphere a world away from the austere and forbidding one of Havelock Road. This was a real home, warm and welcoming and safe, and Ivy felt a wave of deep affection for Peggy Reilly, knowing that at last she'd found someone she could trust to care for her.

Doreen's basket was loaded with her shopping, slowing her down as she cycled up the hill to the Fort. She swung off the bike when she reached the sentry box, showed her ID papers and then crossed the quadrangle to the cycle racks. Lifting out her shopping, she gathered up her handbag and gas-mask box and hurried into her office to find Veronica sitting at her desk.

'You look much better today,' she said as she turned from the typewriter. 'How did you sleep?'

'Very well.' Doreen put her shopping bag in the bottom drawer of the filing cabinet and took off her jacket and headscarf. She shook out her hair and shot her friend a determined smile. 'I'm going to the canteen for lunch. Want to join me?'

'Why not? I've been slogging my way through Maynard's indecipherable writing all morning and I'm on the point of being cross-eyed with it all.' She reached for her walking stick and gas-mask box. 'Are you sure you feel up to working, Dor?'

Doreen nodded. 'Absolutely,' she said firmly.

'Well, if you do find it a bit much you must tell me,' Veronica insisted. 'And by the way, I've managed to get cover for us both next week, so I'll be coming with you to Bow.'

Doreen's smile faltered momentarily at the thought of Archie's funeral, and her tightly controlled emotions threatened to slip, but she held on to them determinedly. 'Thanks, Ronnie. I really do appreciate that.'

'Come on then, let's see what delights the canteen has on offer today – though I bet it's vegetable stew again, or something pretending to be cottage pie.'

11

It was Saturday morning and Jack Smith's few days of leave had come to an end. Peggy could tell how despondent Rita was about this, and had offered to go with her to the station to see him off. Rita had declined the offer with her usual stoicism, but Peggy could see that she was finding it very hard to keep her emotions under control.

Peggy waited until the girl had left the house to meet her father for breakfast at the Crown, and then gauged the length of time she would need to walk to the station. For all Rita's protests, Peggy knew she would need company and she wanted to be there for her when the train pulled out.

As time moved on, Peggy pulled on her coat and hat and left Daisy in the care of Ron and Cordelia, with firm instructions to Ron not to take her into the hills on one of his poaching trips. He'd done it before, and the idea that he could have been arrested with her baby in tow had made her go cold.

It wasn't long before she saw Rita and Jack

walking arm in arm up the High Street and held back until they'd crossed the humpbacked bridge and were out of sight. The train was already in the station, for she could see the smoke billowing from its funnel, and hear the panting of the engine. Peggy looked down from the bridge and saw the two embrace, and then Jack was climbing aboard and Stan was poised to blow his whistle and wave his flag.

Peggy hurried past the Nissen hut and arrived on the platform just as the train slowly began to pull away. With a reassuring glance at a clearly concerned Stan, who'd made it his business to watch over the girls who lived at Peggy's, she hurried along the platform.

Rita turned away as the last carriage disappeared around the bend, her little face streaked with tears, her shoulders slumped in defeat.

Peggy's heart went out to her and she silently drew her into her arms and held her as she sobbed against her shoulder. 'It's all right, Rita, dear,' she soothed. 'He'll write more often now, and he promised me he'd telephone the house the minute he arrived.'

Rita drew back finally and scrabbled for her handkerchief. 'I know, he promised me too,' she said thickly through her tears. 'It's silly of me to get so upset, isn't it? After all, he's been away for years – but seeing him again has made me realise just how much I've been missing him. And now he's gone, and I've no idea of when he'll come back.'

Peggy gave her a hug. 'It's not silly at all,' she murmured as she found a rather cleaner hand-

214

kerchief in her coat pocket and handed it over. 'Come on, Rita. Dry your eyes, and just be thankful that you've had these few days together and that he won't be posted abroad like Jim. Who knows, he could even get leave again before Christmas.'

Rita nodded and did her best to conquer her tears and compose herself. 'Thanks for coming, Auntie Peg,' she said with a watery smile. 'How would any of us manage without you, eh?'

'I'm sure you'd find a way,' Peggy said briskly. 'Now we'd better get back. I've left Daisy with Ron and Cordelia, and I dread to think what sort of mischief they've been up to.'

They said goodbye to Stan, who was itching to get to his allotment to see to his beans before he had to return for the next train, and then set off down the High Street. Turning into Camden Road, they approached the fire station and Rita drew to a halt.

'I think I'll go and check that engine, if you don't mind,' she said. 'Keeping busy will stop me thinking about Dad, and John Hicks has been on at me to service that truck for several days now.'

Peggy smiled and nodded, understanding the girl's need to keep occupied. 'I'll see you later, then.'

As Rita headed inside the fire station, Peggy hurried for home – not really concerned about Daisy being with her grandfather, but impatient to read the airgraphs from Jim that had arrived early this morning, and which she hadn't had time to read. She was hoping they'd give a clue as to what had been in Ron's, for she still hadn't been able to get him to tell her anything.

She was about to cross the road and head for the alley that would take her to the back of Beach View when she saw the unmistakable figure of her sister climbing the front steps. Her spirits plummeted. 'What on earth does she want?' she muttered as she hurried across and into the cul-de-sac. 'Doris!' she called.

Doris turned and watched her approach. She was dressed in her best tweed suit, tan felt hat and smart shoes, and looked as if she'd just stepped out of a beauty parlour – which she probably had. Doris had her hair washed and set every week, as well as getting her nails manicured.

'There is no need to shout in that vulgar way, Margaret,' she said snootily as Peggy ran up the steps. Her gaze drifted from Peggy's tousled hair, over the rather shabby jacket and skirt to the scuffed shoes. 'Good grief,' she muttered. 'How on earth can you go about looking like that? Have you no shame?'

Peggy slotted her key in the door and kept silent. Doris was not going to wind her up this morning. She led the way into the kitchen where Ron was on the floor with Daisy, showing her how to use her crayons in her colouring book, while Cordelia was doing the ironing and singing very much out of tune to the music coming from the wireless. Harvey had beaten a retreat under the table, for the floor was littered with building bricks, toys and crayons, and the wireless was very loud.

Peggy hurriedly turned the volume down and Cordelia stopped singing in mid-flow to regard Doris with little enthusiasm. 'I suppose you've

216

come to cause trouble as usual,' she muttered.

Doris sniffed in disdain as she regarded the scene. She turned to Peggy. 'I'll wait for you in the dining room,' she said. 'Put the kettle on, will you?'

Peggy raised her eyebrows and exchanged a knowing look with Ron as Doris sailed out of the kitchen and across the hall. 'What did her last servant die of?' she asked no one in particular as she picked up the teapot from the table and discovered it was still hot.

Daisy laughed and blew a raspberry as she clapped her hands, and Peggy gave her a smile and a kiss, noting that more crayon seemed to be on Daisy than on the pages of her book. She put cups and saucers on a tray alongside the teapot and milk jug, and went into the dining room.

'Your house is as disorderly as the people who live in it,' said Doris, who was sitting in an arm-chair smoking a cigarette. She'd removed her gloves and set her handbag on the floor by her beautifully shod feet, but her hat and jacket remained in place. 'And this room is positively arctic,' she added with a delicate shiver. 'How can you possibly entertain in here?'

'I don't,' said Peggy as she shed her coat and then poured the tea. 'What do you want, Doris? Only I've got a hundred and one things to do today.'

'Ivy has to come back to Havelock Road,' Doris said baldly.

Peggy was taken aback. 'Don't be ridiculous,' she said. 'You've made it all too plain that you don't want her there.'

'That is not the point,' Doris said with a hint of exasperation.

Peggy sipped her tea, which was a bit stewed, and regarded her sister over the lip of the cup. 'Then what is?'

'The billeting people are insisting I have someone to occupy my spare room until Caroline's friend can get down here, which probably won't be for another week or so. She has an important posting in London, and is waiting to be transferred by the MOD.'

'So you want Ivy to come back for a couple of weeks so you can chuck her out again? I don't think so, Doris. Ivy isn't a train carriage to be shunted back and forth, and I will not allow it.'

'But the billeting people are threatening to send me some chit from the East End who has a baby of all things. I cannot possibly allow that. I'm sure Ivy wouldn't mind helping me out after all I've done for her.'

Peggy's eyebrows shot up. 'What exactly have you done for her, Doris – other than use her as a skivvy, go through her belongings and talk down to her?'

'I have standards, Margaret. Ivy needed to be educated in the right way of doing things. Caroline, on the other hand, is a delightful girl with lovely manners and a very good private education – and when her friend comes down Ivy can come back here.'

'Ivy's not going anywhere and that's final.' Peggy put down her cup and saucer and stood up. 'Now, if that's all you came for, we're finished here. You know the way out.'

218

'There's no need to be like that,' snapped Doris.

'Doris, there's every need,' Peggy replied wearily. 'There are thousands of people who are in need of a roof over their head, and although you might find it inconvenient to have people staying with you, it really is none of my concern.'

'You could discuss my proposition with Ivy,' Doris said stubbornly. 'And let the girl decide for herself.'

'I can tell you what she'd say without doing that. I'm sorry, Doris, but you can't expect everyone to fall into line with you just because you've been inconvenienced.'

'I might have known I'd get no help from you,' Doris muttered, stubbing out her cigarette and pulling on her gloves. 'There are times, Margaret, in which I despair for this family. You and Doreen have always been deliberately awkward, and seem to take pleasure in thwarting me at every turn. I really don't understand why you should be like this when I've been so generous to you both over the years.'

'We're grateful for your generosity, Doris. Hand-me-down clothes and shoes are always welcome here, and I'm aware that you're sending regular postal orders to little Evie and Joyce, for which I'm sure Doreen is most thankful. But you persist in calling me Margaret even though you know I hate it, and do nothing but run my family down and turn up your nose at my home. And when Doreen was going through that awful divorce from Eddie, you weren't at all sympathetic or helpful.'

'I might have known you'd defend Doreen,'

said Doris with a sniff. 'You always did stick together.'

'That's how sisters should be, Doris. Now, if you're quite finished, I have better things to do than stand here arguing with you.'

'I know about the pig.' Doris's eyes were challenging.

'What pig?' Caught on the hop by the swift change in topic, Peggy became flustered.

'The one being slaughtered tomorrow. I'm sure the authorities would be interested in the part your father-in-law plays in helping to conceal such a blatant breaking of the law.'

Peggy stared at her older sister in shock. 'I don't know what you're talking about, but I certainly don't like your tone, Doris. If you've got something to say, then I suggest you get on with it.'

'I'm not a greedy woman, but a fair portion of that pork would be welcome recompense for keeping quiet.'

'That's blackmail,' snapped Peggy in utter fury.

'Call it what you like, Margaret. But if I don't get any, then I shall have no option but to inform the authorities. Lady Chumley is most particular about stamping out the black market.' Doris picked up her handbag and swept out of the room.

As the front door slammed behind her, Peggy bunched her fists and growled with fury and frustration. Doris was the absolute limit, and she wouldn't put it past her to contact the authorities – anonymously, of course – and get poor Ron and his friends into trouble. But if the price of her silence was a bit of pork, then she'd have to pay it.

She stomped into the kitchen, where Ron was attempting to get Daisy's face clean while Cordelia placed the final freshly ironed shirt on a hanger and hooked it above the door to the cellar steps.

'I see by your expression that Doris has been her usual sweet self,' said Ron. 'What's she done now to upset you, Peggy?'

Peggy told them as she smoked furiously on a cigarette. 'We'll have to give it to her, Ron,' she said finally.

'Then I hope it chokes her,' he muttered, setting Daisy onto the floor. 'Mean-minded, that's what she is, and little Ivy is best off out of there.'

'My thoughts exactly.' Peggy began to gather up the colouring books and crayons. 'But you're not to say a word to Ivy. It wouldn't be fair on her.'

Cordelia plumped down into a kitchen chair. 'I wouldn't be at all surprised if the whole thing wasn't just a means to an end,' she said thoughtfully. As Peggy frowned, she continued, 'We all know that Doris doesn't really want Ivy there, and I doubt very much if the billeting people would place a girl and her baby with her. They know Doris too well. I suspect she just saw a chance to get her hands on some of our pork.'

'Aye, you could be right,' rumbled Ron. 'Though how she heard about it is a mystery. There's only four of us in Alf's syndicate, and none of us would give her the time of day, much less tell her about that pig.'

Peggy bit her lip, distressed that her sister would go to such lengths. 'It does make a horrible sort of sense,' she murmured fretfully. 'But I never thought she'd stoop that low.'

'War does funny things to people,' said Cordelia darkly. 'I shouldn't waste time worrying about her if I were you.'

Peggy knew she was right, but even so, it wasn't pleasant to realise that your sister was capable of being so conniving and ruthless.

Ron took himself off on some mysterious mission with Harvey, passing Ivy on the cellar steps. She greeted him cheerfully, yet as she entered the kitchen it was clear that she'd noticed the tense atmosphere, for her smile faded and she looked suddenly wary. 'Is everything all right?' she asked with a frown.

'There's nothing to worry about, dear,' said Peggy quickly. 'I've just had a bit of a run-in with Doris, that's all.' She waved away the girl's concern. 'She winds me up until I want to scream, but that's the way it's always been.' She got up from the table to boil the kettle so she could freshen the tea in the pot. 'How was your shift?'

'The same as always.' Ivy sat down at the kitchen table, smiled at Cordelia and made a fuss of Daisy, who was standing rather unsteadily against her leg. 'I was hoping to finish early and meet Rita at the station to give 'er some moral support, but the supervisor wouldn't let me. Was she very upset?'

Peggy nodded. 'It was to be expected, Ivy. But I went there for the same reason and she seemed fairly accepting of the situation by the time we reached the fire station.' She poured the boiling water over the remains of the stewed tea and gave it a vigorous stir. 'She'll be feeling a bit lost for a while, though, so it's good that you're sharing the room. There's nothing like having a friend to confide in at times like these.'

Peggy poured the tea and handed over the two letters that had come for Ivy that morning. 'Why don't you take the tea upstairs so you can read your letters in peace?' She lifted Daisy from the girl's lap and put her on the floor. 'Are you hungry, Ivy?'

She shook her head. 'Once I knew I wouldn't catch Rita I stayed on and 'ad something in the canteen.' She picked up her letters along with the cup of tea. 'I'm off nights on Monday, so if Rita's up for it, we could go to the dance at the drill hall. That should 'elp cheer her up a bit. I'll see you all later when I've 'ad a bit of a kip.'

Peggy decided she'd calmed down enough to enjoy reading her own letters, so she placed a protesting Daisy in the playpen and sat down by the range fire. There was one from Anne, which was chatty and full of baby Emily and little Rose Margaret. Sally had moved into one of the empty farm cottages with her two, and Bob and Charlie were knuckling down and being a real help on the farm.

Doreen's letter had been written almost two weeks ago, and was full of her plans for her leave in London with Archie. She couldn't say anything about the work she was doing, so her letter was quite short, describing only the occasional trip to the cinema with her friend Veronica, and the lovely countryside nearby. She thanked Peggy for posting comics and colouring books to her girls, sent her love to everyone and hoped that Jim was coping out in India.

Peggy set the letter aside and opened Jim's air-graph. He was suffering from a bad stomach as well as a cold, the poor man. The heat and the teeming rain were beginning to get him down, but the work in the repair shops was satisfying and his new commanding officer seemed to be pleased with him. He mentioned that he and his pals had had to kill several very poisonous snakes they'd found in their bashas, and that he'd caught a huge lizard which he was planning to take to a cobbler to get a pair of shoes made from the skin.

Peggy shuddered at the thought and continued to read. Jim was working mainly on American vehicles like the Studebaker and Chevrolet trucks, repairing them and going out to rescue them after accidents and breakdowns. He described one incident where a Studebaker had gone midstream into a raging river, and he'd had to wade in, fighting against the torrent of water to reach it with tow ropes. As he and his Indian helper struggled to attach the ropes they were threatened by tree trunks and telegraph poles hurtling down the swollen river at them. He'd managed more by luck than judgement to avoid being hit, but he did lose his swimming trunks during the effort, and had been forced to climb out of the water stark naked, which all his mates found hilarious.

His second airgraph told her he was still suffering from a bad stomach although his cold was a bit better – but at least he didn't have malaria like so many of his mates. He wrote that he was thinking of her every day, and that it would feel really odd not to be with her on their wedding anniversary next week, but that, like him, she had to stay positive. He then went on to describe a series of dances he'd been invited to where there were English nurses. The sight of the fair hair and blue eyes had made him horribly homesick, and there was hardly an hour when he wasn't thinking about her and the rest of his family.

Peggy felt a stab of jealousy at the thought of Jim cavorting about at some dance with pretty nurses, but all she could do was hope that he remembered he was a married man with children and grandchildren – not England's answer to Errol Flynn. She gave a sigh, for she'd married a handsome man who was the most shocking flirt, with a bucketful of charm and all blarney and twinkling eyes every time he was within a few yards of a pretty girl.

She snapped out of it, realising it would do no good to think like that. She had to trust Jim to remain faithful – and if he wasn't, then she didn't want to know about it.

She finished reading the letter and tucked it away safely before reaching for a pen to write one back. Having done so, she dressed Daisy and put her in the pram, collected Cordelia's library books and pulled on her hat and coat. She would go to the post office and send Jim a telegram wishing him a happy anniversary – although what would be happy about spending it hundreds of miles apart, she didn't know.

Doreen had managed to get through the long afternoon by concentrating on her work and not giving herself time to think. She returned to her billet very late, relieved that the others were already in bed and therefore could be avoided.

Locking the bedroom door behind her after she'd put away her shopping and used the bathroom, she didn't put on the light, but walked across to the window. The moon was bright in the star-studded sky – a perfect night for an enemy raid. She felt a shiver of apprehension as she looked out at the gilded lawn and the deep shadows beneath the trees. The RAF heavy bombing campaign was having repercussions and it seemed there was always tension in the air – waiting for the sirens, waiting to see if their area was the chosen target for the night.

She turned from the window and prepared for bed, the luminous glow from the dial of Archie's watch a small comfort in these dark hours. Climbing into bed, she held the ring to her lips and stared out at the moonlit garden, afraid to close her eyes in case those terrifying images came to taunt her. If there was a raid then she would be forced to join the others in the Anderson shelter at the bottom of the garden – and she knew it would take all her courage to do so, for it would be cramped and claustrophobic with so many crammed inside, and once the door was shut she'd be in utter terror.

'You have to pull yourself together, Doreen,' she muttered. 'If you go on like this you'll end up in the loony bin.'

She turned over and gazed at the luminous watch dial and forced herself to think about Archie and all the memories they'd collected over their four-year courtship. And as the watch ticked and her heartbeat returned to a steadier pace she remembered his kiss and the touch of his hand, and the way his eyes lit up when he smiled. The tears of heartbreak welled up and soaked the pillow as it sank in that she would never experience those wondrous moments again.

12

Ron left the house very early that Sunday morning, for it was a long way to the smallholding where they'd kept the pig, and it had been agreed between the three of them that it wouldn't be wise to travel in Alf's van, which was emblazoned with his butcher shop sign. There were too many nosy parkers in Cliffehaven, and someone had already tipped the wink to Doris, so it was better if they all made their own way there.

He tramped through the back streets towards the factory estate and then bypassed the dairy and headed west. It was a steep climb which took him north of the ruins of the lunatic asylum and he envied Harvey his energy as he galloped on ahead, leaving him way behind and out of breath.

He finally made it to the top, his lungs wheezing like a pair of old fire bellows, and took a moment to get his breath back. Cliffehaven sprawled beneath an ethereal mist which shrouded the horizon and lay glittering over the rooftops, revealing only the tips of the remaining church spires and the crowns of the tallest trees. It was a pretty view, and he admired it for a while as Harvey chased things in the long grass, and then turned his back on it and plodded onwards.

The smallholding was deep within a fold of the hills and set apart from the tiny hamlet of Villiers Cross that nestled in the next valley. It consisted of a ramshackle wooden cottage and a series of dilapidated sheds, all surrounded by row upon row of neatly planted vegetable crops. There was a chicken coop, and a few ducks puttered about in a small pond, while cats of all colours wandered about or lay supine on the warm brick path that ran between the cottage and the sheds.

Ron knew from past visits that these sheds were mostly used as a dumping ground for old farm machinery, bits of unwanted furniture and Alf's car, which had been put on blocks for the duration. However, behind the largest shed, through a concealed door, was a small, windowless extension which housed a vast iron bathtub and a sturdy, much-scarred butcher's block.

He began to descend the steep decline, following the ancient track which had been carved into the landscape by the monks who'd built the tiny abbey in Villiers Cross and who'd come this way over the centuries to take their grain to the mill which had once stood proudly overlooking the coastline. The abbey was deserted now and the windmill was long gone, but Ron could remember seeing the rotting building and broken sails as a boy of seventeen, for even then he'd been drawn to walking alone in the hills.

There was a ribbon of smoke coming from the cottage chimney and steam was rising from the shed. As Ron came closer, he could see the old

228

man sitting on the bench outside the front door, busily sharpening his knives. Fred White – or 'Chalky,' as everyone called him – was retired now, but in his day he'd been a master butcher and had taught his young apprentice, Alf, everything he knew.

Harvey shot down the hill, tail wagging in delight at the sight of his old friend. The cats scattered with a chorus of loud hissing, the fur on their backs bristling with fury as Harvey squirmed and yipped with pleasure at the fuss Chalky was making of him.

Ron waved and shouted hello as he descended the final few yards and then plonked himself down on the bench. 'To be sure 'tis a good day fer it, Chalky,' he said, lifting his face to a shaft of early sunlight. He sniffed the air as another fragrant cloud of steam drifted out from the barn. 'It smells like our pig's already having his bath.'

Chalky nodded, his snow-white hair ruffling in the light breeze, his blue eyes bright in his weathered face. 'Killed it at dawn. Stan's keeping watch over it to make sure it doesn't boil for too long.' He grinned to reveal a set of magnificent false teeth. 'We'll be giving it a good shave before long.'

Ron filled his pipe as Chalky returned to sharpening his wicked-looking knives, reminding Ron of the years he'd spent gutting fish. Harvey went to investigate the one cat which had decided to stand its ground and swear at him, ginger fur bristling, tail fluffed out to three times its usual size. Ron watched the performance, knowing that Harvey only wanted to play, but would end up

229

the loser if he got any closer. Sure enough, he couldn't resist – the ginger tom's paw whipped out and a set of needle-sharp claws flashed across Harvey's nose.

With a yelp of pain Harvey decided retreat was preferable to valour and came to slump at Ron's feet, feeling very sorry for himself.

The tom stood squarely and defiantly on the path for a moment as if to emphasise its victory and then sat down and began to lick its bottom.

Ron stroked Harvey's head and ears, noting the beads of blood on his dog's nose. 'Ach, ye stupid beast,' he said softly. 'You know that always happens.'

Stan came out of the shed, his shirt and trousers covered in a long white apron, his ruddy face beaded with sweat. 'The pig's done. I've taken it out. Where's Alf?'

Chalky tipped his chin towards the hill. 'On his way,' he rumbled. 'I'll put the kettle on for a brew before we get stuck in. The wife's over at her sister's, but she's left a tin of currant buns which will go down with the tea quite nicely.'

Stan sat next to Ron and they both watched as Alf made his way carefully down the steep slope. Alf was a big man who didn't get much exercise, and he was clearly finding the trek a bit of a struggle. He arrived red-faced and panting, and when he virtually collapsed onto the old wooden bench it groaned and creaked in protest. 'Whew. That's one heck of a walk.'

Ron and Stan grinned. 'You should do it more often and get some of that weight off your belly,' teased Ron. 'Riding about in that van all day does

230

you no favours.'

'Yeah, I know,' he replied, mopping his scarlet face with a large handkerchief. 'The missus is always complaining that I make the bed dip so much she spends half the night clinging onto the edge so she doesn't roll into the middle.'

Chalky brought the mugs of tea and plate of fruit buns out on a tin tray, along with a bowl of biscuit and bacon bone for Harvey to chew on. The four old friends slurped their tea and munched their way through the buns as the sun rose a little higher in the sky and the air was filled with birdsong. Ron, Alf and Stan were well past retirement age now, but they'd met as young men and enlisted together back in 1914. They'd survived the Somme and the struggle to knuckle down to ordinary life again afterwards; now they were finding a sense of rejuvenation as they did their bit to keep the home fires burning while the next generation had to fight yet another war.

As the talk petered out, Ron decided it was time to tell them about Doris. He reddened at their disgust, feeling guilty that he could be even remotely related to such a grasping, conniving woman.

'She'll get her pork, all right,' growled Chalky. 'But it won't be what she's expecting.' He got to his feet and collected his knives. 'Come on, let's get this beast shaved and butchered.'

They left the barn door open so the fresh air could clear the steam and give them some extra light. The pig was thoroughly shaved until every bristle and patch of colour was erased. The trotters and head were chopped off and set to one side, then Alf used a blow-torch to singe off the last of the bristles before Chalky began to carefully and expertly gut it. It wasn't long before there were neatly butchered joints, fillets, chops and shanks lined up on the block and the men stood back to admire their handiwork, their mouths watering at the thought of the feast they would have tonight.

Stan and Chalky divided up the bounty and wrapped each portion in newspaper. As Alf and Stan packed theirs away in rucksacks, Ron tucked his into the inside pockets of his long poacher's coat. He hated the thought he'd have to give Doris even the smallest of the chops, but knew he had no alternative if she was to be kept from informing the authorities.

Chalky lifted up the pig's head and trotters, wrapped them in newspaper and stuffed them into a small hessian bag that had once contained chicken feed. 'This is for Doris,' he said gruffly as he handed it to Ron. 'I reckon she should have been more precise when she asked for pork, but she can't say we didn't oblige.'

Ron grinned at the thought of Doris's expression when she unwrapped it. 'That's grand, so it is, Chalky. But I'm guessing she won't be best pleased, and could still carry out her threat.'

'Not when she'll have to explain where she got this lot from in the first place,' muttered Alf as he cleaned the knives. 'Either way, we won't be able to do this here again. Doris has got a loose tongue, and if she knows about it, you can be sure others will.'

Stan was scrubbing down the butcher's block, his ruddy face creased in thought. 'If we could get the next one over to my Ethel's, then we could carve it up there. Mind you, she won't stand you bringing a live pig into the house. Very neat and tidy is my Ethel.'

'Can you trust her to keep her mouth shut, Stan?' asked Chalky.

'Aye. She knows the consequences if she doesn't, and her and little Ruby love a bit of pork.'

'I'll think on it,' said Chalky.

Stan gave the block one last swipe of the damp cloth. 'Right, I'm off then. See you all next Friday at the Anchor and be prepared to be thoroughly beaten at dominoes.'

The other three laughed and he went off with a cheerful wave, his rucksack lying heavy against his broad back. Alf shook hands with Chalky, hefted his own rucksack over his shoulders and set off along a different winding track which would eventually lead him to within a few yards of his house on the northern borders of Cliffehaven.

Ron felt the weight of the meat in his coat pockets as he hefted the hessian bag over his shoulder. 'Thanks, Chalky. I owe you one.'

'In that case, perhaps you'd like to help me with something?'

'If I can.' Ron frowned as Chalky bustled into the main barn and ducked behind a rusting tractor to emerge a moment later carrying something. 'What've you got there?'

'Something I can really do without,' he muttered as he held up a tiny kitten with a withered back leg. 'I've found homes for the others but this one's the runt, and the mother's rejected it. If you don't take it I'll have to put it down, 'cos it won't survive like that and I haven't got the time to tend to it properly.'

Ron dropped the sack as the tiny kitten was thrust towards his chest. 'I don't know, Chalky, me old friend. Harvey will probably try to lick it to death, and Peggy will go mad. You know what she was like when Monty was dumped on us.'

'I know all that, Ron, but I have too many cats already, and no time to care for this wee one.'

Harvey whined in confusion as Ron looked down at the tiny black kitten, which looked back at him with wide blue eyes. His heart melted, and although he knew it would get him into trouble with Peggy, he simply couldn't abandon the poor wee creature. He cleared his throat and carefully tucked it into the inside pocket of his coat so it lay close to his heart and perhaps would be soothed by the beat of it. 'Aye, well, I suppose Peggy won't really mind.'

He took his leave of Chalky and began the long climb back up the hill, aware of the kitten moving restlessly in his coat pocket, and Harvey eyeing him in puzzlement. Peggy would have his guts for garters and no mistake, but she was as soft as he was and he had little doubt that she'd fall in love with it the moment she saw it.

He watched as Harvey went charging off and wondered how long it would be before he realised he would have to share his status as the family pet.

Cliffehaven was still quiet on this early Sunday morning, and Ron plodded contentedly down the steep, winding track that would take him to what had once been the recreation ground at the back of Havelock Gardens. When he reached the boundary of the field, he spotted a couple of keen gardeners tending the vegetable allotment that had replaced the football pitch, and two young members of the Home Guard busily stacking fresh sandbags at the entrance to the large community shelter that lay beneath the old cricket pavilion and changing rooms.

He kept to the shadows of the trees as he quickly skirted the area and then ducked into the small park, now bereft of iron railings and rose beds. The pond looked murky and had been abandoned by the birds which had once swum there, and the rose bushes and flower beds had been sacrificed to grow yet more vegetables – but spring bulbs were sprouting, heralding warmer days, and Ron's spirits rose with every step.

He emerged from the park and headed towards the big house near the end of the cul-de-sac that was Havelock Road. The kitten had stopped moving about in his pocket and he quickly checked to make sure it was all right. It was sleeping peacefully, curled up into a fluffy ball.

Ron tramped across the gravel drive and gave the doorknocker a series of good hard raps, then eased the hessian bag from his shoulder and waited.

'Who is it?' called Doris from the other side of the door.

'It's me. With your pork,' he shouted back.

There was much rattling of chains and the turning of keys and the door opened a fraction. Doris's hair was in curlers, there was some shiny cream on her face and she was clearly still in her nightclothes. 'There's no need to tell everyone in the neighbourhood,' she hissed. 'And what time of morning do you call this anyway, disturbing people on a Sunday?'

Ron made a show of looking at his watch. 'It's half past eight.'

'Give me the pork and go away,' she ordered, reaching an arm through the narrow gap.

Ron held the hessian bag just out of her reach. 'Don't you want to check it first?'

Doris shuddered as blood seeped from the sack and spotted her pristine doorstep. 'I'm sure it'll be fine,' she said, waving her hand impatiently.

'Well, I'm thinking you might like to take a wee peek – just to make sure that I'm not cheating you in any way,' he said, now thoroughly enjoying himself.

'Oh, very well,' she snapped. She opened the door wider to reveal a pink dressing gown and fluffy slippers. She snatched the bag from him and held it away from her as she opened it and looked inside. 'It could be anything in there,' she said crossly as she tried to undo the parcels of meat with one hand.

'Here, let me help you.' He reached in and swiftly unwrapped the head and trotters and held them up. 'There,' he said proudly. 'Five lovely bits of pork, just for you, Doris.'

Doris went quite pale beneath her face cream. 'Trotters?' she managed as she clutched her dressing gown to her throat. 'A pig's head? What am I supposed to do with those?'

'You can roast the head – the brains are quite a

delicacy – and the trotters can be stewed or boiled down for brawn.'

'But I've invited Lady Chumley to Sunday luncheon and I can't possibly serve her a roasted pig's head,' she gasped. 'I was expecting a proper joint, and perhaps a couple of nice chops.'

Ron raised his brows and feigned surprise. 'Were you? Well, you should have said.'

Her eyes narrowed and her expression was stormy. 'You've done this deliberately,' she rasped.

'The price of your silence was a share of the pig,' he said flatly. 'I've kept my side of the bargain, and if you can't appreciate that, then there's nothing I can do about it. Enjoy your lunch, Doris.' He tipped her a wink and strolled away as the front door slammed behind him.

He was grinning widely as he and Harvey walked down Havelock Road and headed for home. 'To be sure I'd give anything to see the look on Lady Chump Chop's face when she's presented with that head for her lunch. But I'm thinking I'll be paying for that wee bit of mischief before long.'

Harvey sneezed and cocked his leg up a lamp-post.

Peggy was sharing the bath with Daisy so she could save water, and they were having a high old time chasing a plastic duck around and making bubbles out of the shampoo. She'd heard Ron leaving the house very early and the thought of roast pork for lunch was making Peggy's mouth water. It had been an age since anything had been roasted in this house – in fact, the last time had been Christmas, and that had been a rather scrawny chicken.

The water was getting a bit cold now and so she clambered out of the bath and gathered up Daisy, who was as slippery as an eel, and wrapped her in a towel. Rubbing her dry, she quickly dressed her before she caught a chill. The bathroom might be full of steam but it was very cold in here, and there had been ice on the inside of the window when she'd first come in earlier this morning.

With Daisy dressed for the day, Peggy pulled on her own clothes and brushed her teeth before cleaning the bath and basin and carrying the damp towels to the airing cupboard on the landing. Cordelia was downstairs reading the newspaper that arrived along with the milk come rain, shine, air raid or calm, but the girls were asleep, and soon Ivy would come home from her shift to catch up on her sleep before she had to go out again tonight.

Peggy sighed as she carried Daisy downstairs. The night shifts must be awfully hard to cope with, what with trying to stay awake when they should be sleeping and vice versa. At least tonight would be Ivy's last one for a while and she could get back to living life more normally again.

'They're taking a long time to kill that pig,' said Cordelia as she put the newspaper aside. 'I hope he'll get back in time for us to be able to have that roast for lunch.'

'It's a long walk to Chalky's place, Cordelia. And don't forget, he has to stop off and give Doris her share.'

'Utterly disgraceful,' said Cordelia with a sniff.

'That woman has no shame.'

Peggy let Daisy stumble about with her wheeled wooden horse as she put the kettle on the hob and spooned a few fresh tea leaves into her brown teapot. 'I'm afraid Doris thinks only of herself,' she murmured, 'and at the moment I feel enough shame for both of us.'

'Well, you shouldn't,' said Cordelia sternly. 'You're not your sister's keeper.' She rustled the newspaper impatiently and folded it over. 'Talking of sisters,' she continued, 'didn't you say that Doreen was in London at the beginning of the week?'

Peggy frowned. 'Yes. Why?'

'Well, there's a bit in the paper here about some accident in the East End.'

'What sort of accident?'

Cordelia handed her the newspaper. 'It actually says very little, and I'm sure that if Doreen was anywhere near it she would have telephoned to reassure you that she was all right. But I seem to remember that her sailor came from around that way.'

Peggy read the few short lines that had been put at the bottom of the page. It told her nothing much, only that several people had died in an accident in the East End, and that there would be an inquest and inquiry later in the year.

'The paper certainly doesn't classify it as very important or they would have given it more coverage,' she said as she handed it back. 'It's sad that people died, but then there have been so many deaths these past four years, I suppose the journalists thought we didn't need to hear about any more.'

'That's cheerful talk on a lovely Sunday morning,' said Ron as he stomped up the cellar steps with Harvey at his heels.

Peggy grinned back at him in delight as Harvey licked Daisy's face and let her half-strangle him in a hug. 'What did we get?' she asked breathlessly.

'A bit of belly to roll into joints, a lovely chunk of shoulder and leg and four whole chops with a tiny bit of liver to go with them.' He began to pull the bloody parcels from his pockets and laid them out on the draining board.

Peggy quickly popped Daisy in her playpen and joined Cordelia at the sink to unwrap the parcels and coo over the lovely, glistening, fatty meat.

'My mouth's watering already,' said Peggy. 'Shall we have a bit of that belly rolled over some of my homemade stuffing? The crackling should be marvellous once we've scored and salted it. And I can use some of the fat to roast the potatoes and carrots to go with it.' She turned from the sink, kissed his bristled cheek and beamed up at him. 'Thank you, Ron. You're an absolute star.'

'What did you have to give Doris out of our share?' demanded Cordelia.

'Well now, there's a funny thing,' murmured Ron with a twinkle in his eye. 'We decided she might like the trotters and the pig's head.'

'No,' Peggy gasped in glee and burst out laughing. 'I bet she didn't like that at all.'

'I'm thinking she was a wee bit put out,' Ron chortled. 'She'd invited Lady Chump Chop to join her and Caroline for a roast Sunday dinner.'

Peggy had tears of laughter rolling down her face as she collapsed into a kitchen chair, holding her sides. 'Oh, Ron,' she gasped. 'The image that conjures up is too funny. I can just see them all looking utterly po-faced as they're forced to stare at that pig's head in the middle of Doris's dining table.'

Cordelia was giggling so hard she too had to sit down. 'My word, Ron,' she finally spluttered. 'That was a brilliant way to get your own back.'

'Aye, well, it wasn't actually my idea,' he confessed. 'It was Chalky's. He always was a clever wee man.' He carefully took off his coat and reached into the inside pocket. 'And I'm hoping you'll be thinking that his other idea is just as clever.'

Peggy was still giggling as she looked up at him. 'What was that, then, Ron?'

He gently eased the sleepy kitten out of his pocket and placed it against her heart so she had no option but to cup it in her hands. 'The poor wee thing was abandoned by its mother,' he said smoothly, 'and Chalky thought we might be the best people to look after it.'

Peggy held the tiny, furry creature which weighed so very little, and looked down into a pair of beautiful blue eyes. The kitten was as black as night, with a pink nose and tiny pink paws, the right back leg cruelly thin and withered. How could she not be instantly in love with it? 'Oh, Ron,' she said. 'The poor little mite's absolutely adorable.'

'That's settled then,' he said as he dumped his coat on a nearby chair and reached for the sharpest kitchen knife to prepare part of the belly for rolling and roasting and score the skin.

'It's very sweet,' murmured Cordelia as she gently ran her finger over the tiny black head. 'But haven't you got enough to contend with without looking after a crippled kitten? Besides, Harvey might eat it.'

'Harvey likes cats,' Ron said over his shoulder.

Harvey whined and tried to clamber onto Peggy's lap so he could sniff the new arrival. The tiny creature hissed and struggled in her hands and Peggy was terrified she might drop it right into Harvey's jaws.

'Leave them be, Peg,' said Ron. 'Animals have their own way of getting to know one another. They'll soon sort out who's boss.'

Peggy was certain that the kitten would either get chewed or trampled by Harvey, who was now eagerly trying to lick it. 'Get down, Harvey. Sit and stay,' she ordered.

Harvey sat with his tongue lolling and his ears pricked, his amber gaze fixed eagerly on the ball of fluff that was now staring at him rather imperiously from Peggy's lap. He'd obviously learned nothing from this morning's run-in with the tom, for his endless curiosity got the better of him and he simply couldn't resist giving the kitten just one more sniff.

A tiny paw shot out and a set of claws batted his nose twice in quick succession.

Harvey backed away and whined, his gaze sorrowful as his head drooped and he sloped off to the safety of the rug in front of the range. With a snort of disgust he stretched full length, his

242

back to everyone, one paw placed protectively over his poor battered nose.

Before Peggy could stop it, the little creature scooted down her leg and softly landed on the floor. It eyed Harvey for a moment and then, dragging its back leg, stalked across the room, traversed the mound of Harvey's ribcage and, after turning in a tight circle several times, settled down between his paws and started to purr.

Harvey lifted his head and looked back at them all, the realisation in his sorrowful eyes that he was now at the mercy of a tiny tyrant who seemed determined to usurp his place at Beach View and make his life a misery.

'Well, I never,' breathed Cordelia.

'Oh, poor Harvey,' said Peggy through her giggles.

'He'll be fine, so he will,' said Ron. 'They'll come to their own arrangement, you'll see.'

Peggy watched as Harvey rested his head back down onto the rug and gave a sigh of defeat. But she noticed that he didn't seem to mind that the kitten had now shifted so that it was snuggled against his belly. As the kitten purred contentedly and Harvey began to snore she realised Ron was right – as always.

'We have to find a name for it,' she said. 'What sex is it?'

'Female, so Chalky reckons.'

'We should call her Queenie then,' said Cordelia. 'She's certainly put Harvey in his place and is obviously destined to rule us all.'

Peggy laughed. 'That's perfect, Cordelia, but I get the feeling that we'll all be run ragged with yet another little soul to look after.'

'Ach, Peggy, girl. You're at your best when you've a waif or stray to care for.' Ron turned from the sink and gave her an affectionate wink.

It was late Sunday and the rest of the household were sleeping peacefully as Ivy slipped downstairs. The sweet little kitten was fast asleep at Harvey's side in front of the range, having avoided being strangled by an overexcited Daisy, and trampled on by an unwary Rita. She'd never lived with pets before, but their presence seemed to enhance the feeling of home, and she silently vowed that when she had somewhere of her own, she'd think about a cat or dog for company.

She pulled on her coat, grabbed her gas-mask box and headed out of the door. The night was cold after what had been a pleasant spring day, with the wind whipping up from a stormy sea, but the moon was bright and the sky was clear. It was a perfect bomber's moon, and Ivy suspected there might be a raid at some point, which would be a ruddy nuisance, because it interrupted work and cost her a loss of earnings.

She headed up the hill, taking the back roads up to the factory estate, her thoughts happily occupied with the plans she and Rita had made for the following evening. She'd be glad to get off the night shifts, for it left little time for any sort of fun, and she found it hard to sleep through the day, even with the blackout curtains pulled.

Her four friends were waiting for her at the gates, and after teasing the guard, which had become a bit of a ritual, they went giggling and chattering into the munitions factory alongside hundreds of others. The workforce was a mixture of women of all ages, young boys, and men who were either too old for service or suffered from some disability. But that made no difference to the cheerful atmosphere, for there was a sense of camaraderie, the knowledge that they'd get a good pay packet at the end of this shift, and the feeling that despite all the dangers, they were united in doing a job that would help England win the war.

The girls went their separate ways and the night shift began with the machines thumping away, the stink of sulphur everywhere, and someone singing a favourite dance tune to which most of them could join in. Ivy sang along happily, not really concerned that her voice sounded more like a crow than a blackbird. She glanced round and noted that most of the others seemed to be in a good mood, cracking jokes and telling stories – although there were one or two who were a bit glum, and Ivy wondered if they'd had bad news or simply weren't feeling well amid the stink of all that sulphur.

She was actually feeling quite chirpy, for her mum had written to say that the gas board had given her dad a promotion and that she was saving hard to try and get enough money together so they could come down to the seaside for a visit. Her eldest brother had written to say he'd met a very nice girl in Liverpool on his last leave and was thinking about asking her to marry him, and her sister, Edith, was madly in love with some Yank who was promising her the earth if only she'd spend the night with him.

Edith had of course turned him down flat, but from the tone of her letter, Ivy knew that she was definitely considering it. She just hoped she'd be careful. The Yanks were only here for a short while before they were posted away, and although they could charm the birds out of the trees with their white teeth and wholesome good looks, they were the same as all other men and were after only one thing. The last thing her sister needed was to end up in the club, for it would mean losing her job and having to face their father, who would rant and rave and probably chuck her out of the house.

Ivy set aside her concerns for her sister. Edith was old enough to know the score, and they'd both had the riot act read to them by their father, so she also knew the consequences if she stepped out of line. She continued to work as she sang along and swapped gossip with Dot and Freda, who were working alongside her. The shift had only just started and it would be hours until they could take a break, so it was best to keep up the chat and the singing to make the time go faster.

An hour had passed and she'd just been to get her can refilled when the siren began to wail. She dumped the can on her workbench and shot a questioning look at her two friends. 'Shall we bother, or not?' she asked.

Freda shrugged. 'It'll probably be just the usual routine, with Jerry going over us to get to poor old London – and we'll miss out on an hour's pay. I'm staying put.'

'I'm off to the shelter for a sit-down and me

sandwiches,' said Dot. 'Are you sure you wanna risk it 'ere?'

'I'll leave it a bit and see how it goes,' said Freda.

Ivy was uncertain and she looked round to see what everyone else was doing. It was quite usual to ignore the sirens, and her friend Freda was one of several who were determinedly still working, but the majority of the others were heading obediently for the two flights of iron stairs and the safety of the large underground shelter on the far side of the estate.

'Nah, I'll be all right,' she said. 'See you later, Dot.' As her friend rushed off, Ivy started on filling yet another shell with the TNT.

The sirens stopped wailing and above the thud of the machines she could hear the planes taking off from Cliffe. 'The RAF boys will soon sort out Jerry,' she shouted above the racket. 'Then we can all just get on with winning this war.'

There was a chorus of agreement from the few left behind, but despite her bravado, Ivy was beginning to have second thoughts about staying here. It would take time to get down those stairs if there was a last-minute crush, and then about another four minutes to run to the shelter over the far side of the estate.

She kept alert for the sound of Jerry bombers and continued working, glancing across at Fred, who was manning the big mixer. If someone as old as Fred had the guts to stay, then it would be a pretty poor show if she shot off like a scalded cat.

Minutes later there was a thunderous roar over-

247

head and Ivy recognised the sound of the Jerry bombers. The danger signal rang out as the crump and whoosh of incendiary bombs and flares could be heard all over the estate. Jerry was attacking them and they were sitting on a powder keg. It was time to get out before the whole place blew up.

She and the others dashed for the stairs, urging Fred to hurry up and not get left behind, but he was at least sixty-five, with a pronounced limp and terrible short-sightedness, so Freda and Ivy got hold of his arms and virtually carried him down the stairs. And then the lights went out, plunging them into utter blackness.

'Go careful, Fred, we don't want you taking a tumble.' Ivy was wishing she'd put a new battery in her torch – not that it would have done much good, she realised, for it was down in the changing room.

Fumbling in the darkness with Fred stumbling blindly between them, they slowly descended the stairs and joined the stragglers who were pouring out of the lower floor. They finally reached the bottom, but one look outside told them it was too late to try and reach the shelter. Enemy planes were circling overhead as British fighters harried them; anti-aircraft guns were thudding; search-lights flashed back and forth as tracers stitched red lines into the sky; and the air was full of smoke and phosphorus from the enemy flares as incendiary bombs shook the earth and sent a sea of flame across the factory concourse.

'The basement,' shouted Freda. 'Get down into the basement.'

Ivy and Freda had sheltered down there several times, so they quickly got Fred down the concrete steps and into the great square space that ran the length and breadth of the munitions factory. All of them were aware that there were two floors above them, each containing hundreds of tons of machinery, live shells and gallons of TNT – and if the place went up like a Roman candle, then they would too. But beggars couldn't be choosers, and they just had to pray that Jerry's aim would be off and that the factory wouldn't take a direct hit.

The heavy iron door clanged shut behind them, blotting out the bright flares and flashes from outside and muffling the sounds of bombs and bombers; but the hurricane lamps had been lit, giving them just enough light to be able to see their way to the benches which had been put around the walls.

It always struck Ivy as rather strange that they always chose the same place to sit, and she and Freda sat down on their usual bench, while Fred stretched out his legs, closed his eyes and pre-pared to have a snooze until the all-clear went. There was no sign of Mabel, or Gladys, but there were plenty of others in the basement who'd left it until the last minute.

As they settled on the bench, Ivy became aware of a strange sort of hush in the semi-darkness. It was as if they were in church, for people talked in low voices as they discussed the prospect of a long or short raid, and their worries over their homes and families. Ivy could hear the muffled thuds from outside and wondered if they were guns or bombs. It was difficult to tell, but it seemed to her

249

that there was a full-scale attack going on up there.

She leaned back against the cold stone wall, wishing she'd had time to collect her coat and the sandwiches Peggy had made for her with some of that lovely pork they'd had for lunch. She could still taste it even now and her stomach gurgled at the memory of golden roast potatoes, glistening meat and crisp, salty crackling.

Freda had moved along the bench a bit and was chatting to one of the other girls as the bangs and crumps continued to go on above them. The talk amongst those sitting in the basement grew louder, and soon there was laughter and the passing round of biscuits. To everyone's delight, an accordion struck up in the far corner and a group of men began to sing along. Ivy closed her eyes with pleasure, for although she couldn't understand a word of it, those Welsh boys could certainly sing a lovely tune.

Freda and the other girl wandered over to join the men in their sing-song, while Fred sat up and pulled a packet of sandwiches from his jacket pocket and shared them with his old pal Charlie, who acted as caretaker for the factory. Ivy shifted away from them so she could concentrate on reading a magazine someone had left behind during a previous raid.

As time passed and the guns and planes continued to rumble overhead, some chose to settle down for a bit of a sleep, while others got out packs of cards to while away the hours. It promised to be a very long night.

Ivy gave up on the magazine, it was simply too dark down here to read it properly and her eyes were starting to ache. She curled up on the bench and closed her eyes, hoping to snatch a bit of kip before she had to return to work.

The dull thud came without warning and rocked the ground beneath their feet. Bright lights stabbed the darkness for a blinding second and then there was a deep-throated rumble that made the walls tremble.

'We've been hit!'

Ivy was snapped awake by the piercing scream from the other side of the basement. She froze in terror as the rumbling noise increased and she realised that the whole building was collapsing on top of them like a monstrous pack of cards, bringing with it the hundreds of tons of machinery and liquid TNT. She opened her mouth to scream for Freda, but something heavy knocked her flying – and the world went black.

She had no idea of how long she'd been knocked out, but when she finally opened her eyes, it was a moment before she could clear the dizziness in her head and adjust her eyes to the flickering light of the last remaining hurricane lamp. But then her gaze fell on Fred and his mate who'd been sitting beside her, and the bile rose in her throat at the sheer horror of what she was looking at. The two men had been crushed to death by the girder that had come down and missed her by inches.

She'd seen lots of dead bodies during the London Blitz, but she'd never been this close before, and the sight of those broken, mangled remains of the old men she'd come to know and admire was too much. Her stomach clenched and she vomited onto the floor.

Studiously keeping her gaze from that awful sight, Ivy cleaned her mouth with the back of her hand and suddenly remembered Freda. 'Freda!' she yelled into the darkness of the other side of the basement. 'Freda, where are you?'

There was no reply and Ivy became frantic. She had to try and get to her – and to the others still trapped, for she could hear moaning and cries for help coming from all around. She tried to move, but found that although she didn't appear to have been hurt except for a massive lump on her head, her foot was caught under something and holding her fast.

Her imagination took flight as panic set in. She glanced up at the girder that was the only thing holding back the tons of rubble and machinery that she knew must now be precariously balanced above her. She wriggled her toes in the large boots and gave a trembling sigh of relief. Her foot hadn't been crushed, and her leg was still working. All she had to do was get it free.

There was no room for her to bend and untie the laces on her boot to free her foot, so she began to frantically wriggle her foot about, tugging back and forth, twisting it this way and that, always mindful of the precarious situation she was in. One false move on her part could bring the whole lot down on top of everyone. She lost track of time as she sweated and strained – and then, at long last, her foot was free.

The sweat was cold and smelled sour on her skin as she examined her surroundings more closely. She was hemmed in on all sides, and above her head was what looked like a solid wall of toppled machinery, concrete slabs and brickwork. 'One puff of wind and it's goodnight Ivy,' she muttered. 'I gotta get out of 'ere.'

She could hear people screaming for help as she carefully wriggled and twisted off the bench and inched her way to a small niche she could see in the wall that was about the size and shape of the fireplace in her bedroom at Beach View. What it was doing there, she had no idea, but she was glad of it, for it offered just a modicum of hope that it might shelter her should everything collapse above her.

'Freda!' she yelled again. 'Freda, are you all right? Where are you?'

There was no answer and Ivy bit down on a sob of terror as dread washed over her. She might have escaped being crushed, but she was entombed down here and had no idea if anyone could hear their cries. 'Help us, please,' she called out. 'Can anyone 'ear us? We're down 'ere.'

A glimmer of something caught her eye and her heart began to race as she realised that one of the fizzing, loose electric cables had sparked fire into something nearby. She watched in growing terror as the flames grew and began to inch towards her, feeding on the shattered bits of wood that lay around.

She tried to stamp it out with her boots, but each thrust made the girder shudder and she could hear the groan of the debris above her as it shifted and settled and a thick cloud of choking dust sifted down.

'Help,' she screamed. 'Help me, please!' But her cries were deadened by the sheer volume of the debris above her, and she knew it would be a miracle if someone heard her.

She cowered in the narrow niche, listening to the groans and cries of the others around her. Some of the trapped were muttering prayers, and if she'd had an ounce of faith, she might have joined in with them. But prayers wouldn't get her out of here, or put out the ever-advancing river of fire – only the rescue teams could do it. Surely, surely they'd be on their way by now?

She sat there in abject terror, almost hypnotised by that creeping river of flame. How long would it take to catch everything alight? How much longer did she have before escape became impossible? Her frantic gaze swept her surroundings in search of a better hiding place away from those flames. And then, some feet away, she saw a machine that had crashed through the roof and landed on its end to, form an arch as it leaned against another girder. It looked as if it might provide better shelter than this niche.

Ivy wriggled and twisted on the floor until she was wedged beneath the machine, but as she looked back at the bench she almost fainted. The flames had reached the place where she'd been sitting, and were now hungrily devouring the bodies of the two elderly men.

Ivy's teeth were chattering. She knew she was close to turning into a jibbering wreck, and that it would take every ounce of courage to deal with that macabre sight and try not to let it send her over the edge. She began to scream, letting out all her horror and fear as the sound pierced the darkness and rebounded off the crumbling walls.

However, the smoke from the fire was now thick and cloying, bringing her screams to a choking end as it got down her throat and stung her eyes. She coughed and spluttered and tried to crawl further into the shelter of the fallen machine, her ragged sweater held tightly over her face. But there was no escape, and every time she took a breath she could feel it seeping into her lungs and slowly smothering her.

And then she felt something cool and wet fall on her face. Thinking she must be imagining it, she blinked up at the precarious, shifting debris above her and felt it again – and then several times more. Her spirits soared as she realised it was water – clean, cold, life-giving precious water. The rescuers had arrived and were trying to put out the fire.

'Down 'ere!' she yelled, her throat raw and her eyes stinging from the smoke.

There were other, feeble cries from every corner of the basement, but Ivy was quickly distracted by the rapid change of direction of the flames, which were now starting to lick at the toes of her boots. 'Fire!' she screamed. 'There's fire down 'ere.'

She tried to kick at the flames and smother them with her other boot. But that caught too and soon her overalls were darkening and beginning to curl and crisp. 'Me legs are burning,' she yelled as she desperately tried to beat out the flames with her hands and not think of the TNT that was probably impregnated into the material. 'Help me,' she wailed, 'please 'elp me.'

She looked up as noises came from above her, and then a sudden breath of wind blew the smoke and flames into another direction. She beat the singed legs of her trousers until she was certain they were no longer alight, and then gratefully breathed in great lungfuls of fresh air as icy water poured down over her head and drenched her. The flames sizzled and died and she sobbed in relief. She was going to be all right.

Water was now collecting on the concrete floor and she shifted a bit to try and avoid it, but it was pooling beneath her, soaking her even further. 'Bloody 'ell,' she muttered, 'I escape getting crushed to death, only to get flamin' drowned.' She looked up to where the water was coming from. 'Oy!' she yelled. 'There's people down 'ere what can't swim!'

'We can hear you, love,' shouted a man from a great distance. 'Just sit tight and we'll have you out of there soon.'

Relieved and almost hysterical with happiness that someone was talking to her at long last, she shouted back, 'Hurry up then. We've been down 'ere for bleedin' hours already.'

'Is that you, Ivy?'

Ivy laughed with the sheer joy and relief of knowing Rita would make sure she wasn't about to die. 'Yeah, it's me, and I'm all right, Rita. But hurry up, mate, there's people badly injured down 'ere, and me mate Freda's in trouble.'

'We have to make it safe, Ivy, otherwise this lot will come down on top of you. Just be patient for a bit longer. We'll get you out.'

Ivy tried to be patient as she sat like a drowned rat in the filthy puddle of water, but it felt as if hours were passing as rumblings sounded overhead and the wreckage was slowly cleared to reveal a small hole.

She shielded her eyes from the bright flares of acetylene torches as metal was burnt away and sparks rained down to fizzle out in the water, trying to make out what the men and women were saying up there against the grind of winches and the revving of heavy engines.

And then a face appeared through the enlarged hole. It was grubby and smeared from sweat and soot, but there was no doubt that it belonged to Rita. 'Where are you, Ivy?' she called down as she flashed the strong beam of her torch over the wreckage in the basement.

'Down 'ere by the left wall, about ten feet from the door. There's no one alive near me, but I can 'ear others on the other side. Me mate Freda's over there somewhere. You gotta find her, Rita.'

'Let's get you out of there first. Can you climb up, Ivy?'

'Nah, there's a socking great girder in the way holding up most of what come down, and it don't look that steady. I reckon it could crash down at the drop of an 'at.'

'Stay there then, and we'll send down a rope.'

The rope swung down and Ivy caught it. Her hands were sore from beating out the flames on her dungarees, but she was damned if she was going to let a little thing like that stop her from getting out of here. She pulled on the rope and hauled herself out of her hiding place and onto the top of the machine, which began to tilt alarmingly beneath her. Gripping the rope even more tightly, she ignored the pain in her hands and shinned up it like a monkey – just as she'd once done as a kid in the local playground.

Strong hands caught her, swung her into sturdy arms and carried her away swiftly from the still smoking rubble and the blazing fire that was destroying a nearby factory. As she was gently put on her feet she found that her legs were trembling so badly she could barely stand. She swayed against her rescuer, feeling light-headed and strangely disorientated.

He held her close and steadied her, and when she felt more able to stand on her own she looked up into the sweat- and soot-smeared face of the fireman and grinned. 'Thanks, mate. I thought I was a goner there.'

'It was my pleasure, darlin',' he replied in a strong Cockney accent. 'Now you 'old tight there and 'ave a cup of char while the medics give you the once-over, and I'll see yer later.'

His smile was quite attractive, even though it was hard to tell what he looked like under all that grime, and she wondered what a young, fit-looking bloke from London was doing down here instead of being in one of the forces.

She watched him hurry back to the enormous pile of rubble where his colleagues and the men from the heavy-lifting crews were attempting to clear a safe way down into the basement. It was no wonder she hadn't been able to make herself heard, she realised, as she saw how high and deep that rubble had been. The entire building had been flattened, and it was a miracle that the whole place hadn't exploded into a million pieces, what with all those charged fuses lying about, and the live ammunition.

Her legs gave way and she slumped down on a broken chunk of masonry, suddenly feeling the pain in her hands and the exhaustion and shock of what she'd been through. A woman appeared and handed her a cup of tea while a young Red Cross nurse put soothing balm on her hands and bandaged them before she checked that her legs hadn't been too badly burnt. They were a bit red, but thankfully not blistered – she had indeed had a very lucky escape.

'You've got one heck of a lump on your head,' the nurse said as she dabbed iodine on it. 'You really ought to go to the hospital and have it checked over.'

'I'm staying 'ere,' said Ivy, her whole focus on the rescue team, willing them to hurry up and find Freda and the others who were still trapped down there.

The nurse went to treat someone else and more ambulances arrived along with another two fire crews and a fleet of army trucks. Jets of water were being played over the burning parachute factory, smoke curling like giant mushrooms into the dawn sky, as men raised their voices to give orders and the special machinery was put in place to lift away the girders.

'Thank Gawd you're all right,' breathed Dot as she came running over with Mabel and Gladys. 'You was down there for over five hours and we thought you was a goner for sure.' She gave her a hug and looked round with a frown. 'Where's Freda?'

'Still down there,' muttered Ivy.

The girls perched alongside her and they huddled together as workers from every part of the estate began to gather behind the hastily erected barricades. 'It looks like we're all out of a job,' muttered Dot. 'And it's the same for the girls at the parachute and tool factories. They ain't gunna save them neither.'

The three of them regarded the skeleton of the parachute factory and then the great mass of debris that had once been the munitions building. With a collective sigh they lit fags and anxiously waited to see if Freda had been as lucky as Ivy and survived.

The heavy-lifting crews had removed the girders and the hole had been enlarged. The firemen went down the ladders into the basement and, after an agonisingly long wait for those watching, began to bring up the wounded. Stretcher bearers swiftly transferred them to the waiting ambulances and the few walking wounded staggered to the nearest clear space and sat down, staring in bewilderment at the chaos surrounding them.

The four girls stood as one as stretchers, covered in blankets began to be lifted up and, as one, realised in horror that these were the dead. 'Freda?' Ivy covered her mouth as the tears caught in her throat.

They watched as body after body was recovered and placed with reverence in the back of the large army trucks. Ivy began to walk towards them, and was held back by the young driver. 'You don't want to see, love,' he said.

'But I need to know if Freda's one of them.'

He shook his head, his expression solemn. 'If

she's not already in an ambulance, then I'm sorry. There's been a thorough search and only the dead are left down there now.'

Ivy burst into tears and was immediately surrounded by her friends, and together they mourned the loss of a lovely friend who'd been robbed of life far too soon.

13

Doreen had been having a nightmare when the sirens started wailing, and as she reared up in bed gasping for breath she didn't see the open curtains or the early blush of dawn beyond the window, for she was still trapped in the world of macabre dreams – the darkness of the tomb in which she'd been buried alive still closing in around her, pressing hard against her chest.

She'd sat there struggling to breathe as her heart pounded and the sirens screamed, and was only dimly aware of the sound of running feet passing her door. The sweat had soaked her nightdress and was cold on her skin, and the noises beyond her bedroom seemed muffled as if they were coming from somewhere far away.

The sharp tattoo of raps on her door made her flinch and grip the sheet even harder.

'Doreen. It's a raid. You have to come to the shelter.'

She could hear the doorknob rattling as her landlady twisted it back and forth, and knew she had to get out of bed. But she was frozen and incapable of doing anything.

'Doreen.' The voice was sharper now and more commanding. 'I know you're in there. You have to come to the shelter.'

Her heart was still pounding and her head was swimming as she tried to shake off the nightmare and get herself under control. 'I'm coming,' she managed as she swung her legs out of the bed and reached for her dressing gown.

'Hurry up then, or you'll put all of us in danger.'

Doreen realised she had to get a grip and calm down so she could think more clearly. She grabbed Archie's watch and put it in her dressing-gown pocket, and then forced herself to cross the room to fetch his photograph from the chest. Her legs were trembling so badly she could barely walk, but she managed to shove her feet into her slippers, grab her gas-mask box and unlock the door.

Mrs Fletcher was standing outside, arms folded, expression grim, her metal curlers vibrating slightly with her pent-up fury. 'About time,' she snapped. 'Now get a move on.'

Galvanised into action by this unusual behaviour from her kindly landlady, Doreen quickly followed her through the kitchen and into the back garden. The sirens were still wailing, but now the full-alert danger signals were going off, so a raid was clearly imminent. She fought down the rising panic as they approached the Anderson shelter which was at the far end of the garden. It was larger than most, but once everyone was inside and the door was shut, it would feel as if she was revisiting her nightmare.

'Come along, Doreen,' said Mr Fletcher briskly. 'I have to shut the door.'

She shot a glance up at the bright moon and saw the searchlights sweeping across the dawn sky, then took a deep breath and stepped into the shelter.

Mr Fletcher slammed the door and sat down on the bench he'd built that ran round the sides of the shelter. Dressed, as always, in a brown suit, white shirt and tie, he was the very epitome of a stoic middle-class Englishman who refused to allow standards to slip, regardless of the circumstances. He pushed his round tortoiseshell glasses up his nose, took off his hat and nodded as if satisfied that all were present and correct. He was a fussy, rather pedantic little man who'd spent his working life behind a desk dealing with people's accounts. Now he'd found his niche as the bookkeeper for the local Home Guard and saw it as his duty to act as guardian for those in his household. There had been some speculation amongst Doreen and the other girls as to whether or not he actually went to bed fully dressed, for no matter what time of day or night it was, they'd never seen him in his dressing gown.

Doreen's pulse was racing, her heart thudding in her chest so hard she was amazed no one could hear it. She sat down and watched Mr Fletcher light the tilly lamp and then pour tea from a large thermos flask into tin mugs.

Doreen's hand was shaking so badly that the hot tea slopped over and scalded her, but she grimly held on to the mug with both hands and prayed that the raid would be short and she could get out of here.

The four girls who shared the billet eyed her with some curiosity, for although they knew she didn't like being in here, she was usually the one to get them all telling stories or starting a sing-song to help the time pass more quickly. Mrs Fletcher was also regarding her with some concern, and Doreen fidgeted awkwardly on the rough bench and refused to look at any of them.

'What's up, Doreen?' asked the youngest girl.

'Nothing, not really,' she replied. 'I just hate this shelter.'

The girl nodded and a conversation began between the others about the unpleasantness of shelters. But as they began to discuss the fact that anything had to be better than spending night after night in the tube stations beneath London, Doreen was besieged with images of her own experience at Bethnal Green, and the panic began to rise and swell again.

She caught Mrs Fletcher watching her and managed to dredge up a wan smile to reassure her. But the other woman's frown made it clear that she'd been unconvincing.

Mrs Fletcher squeezed past the others, making them budge along so she could sit next to Doreen. 'I realise you've been avoiding us since you got back from leave, and as this is most unlike you, I can only assume that something is bothering you, dear,' she said beneath the chatter as the sirens stopped their racket. 'Did something happen in London?'

Doreen hesitated and then reluctantly nodded.

'But I don't want to talk about it, Mrs Fletcher. Not now – and especially not in here.'

The older woman took the cup from her trembling fingers and placed it on the floor, before gently holding her hands. 'None of us like it in here,' she said. 'So you're not alone – and if you do find you want to talk about what happened, I'm always here to listen.'

Doreen nodded again, for the kind words had touched her deeply and reminded her of Peggy.

'Then we'll just sit here holding hands until it's over,' said Mrs Fletcher as her husband opened a tin box containing doorstep sandwiches and handed them round.

Doreen declined the offer of a sandwich, but was comforted by her landlady's words and the soft clasp of her hand as the enemy planes roared overhead and the Spitfires and Hurricanes rushed to intercept them. She kept her focus on those around her and slowly the panic subsided, the final shreds of the nightmare disintegrated, and she could breathe more easily again.

'It sounds as if someone else is getting all the attention tonight,' said Mr Fletcher as the distant booms and crumps penetrated the corrugated iron walls. 'Those explosions are on the coast, if I'm not mistaken.'

Doreen felt a sharp twist of alarm as she thought of Cliffehaven and Peggy. 'Where on the coast, do you think?'

He thought seriously before he answered. 'It could be anywhere between Ramsgate and Brighton,' he said. 'The sound carries across the weald here, so it can be deceptive.'

'Don't worry, dear,' said his wife as she patted Doreen's hand. 'I'm sure your family will be fine in Cliffehaven – after all, they're not really a strategic target, are they?'

Doreen bit her lip as she listened to the whine and scream of fighter planes engaged in dogfights many miles above them. Cliffehaven might not be an important target in the scheme of things, but they'd suffered a lot of damage from tip-and-runs and direct attacks over the last few years. And according to Peggy there was now a raft of factories manufacturing parts of planes, armaments and tools, and they would be prime targets for the Luftwaffe.

'You can telephone them later,' said Mrs Fletcher comfortingly. 'Just make a note of the cost and leave the money in the box.'

Doreen squeezed her hand in gratitude. Her thoughts turned to her little girls. Wales was a long way away and there had been very few enemy attacks there, even on the cities. Evie and Joyce were living in a tiny hamlet west of the Brecon Beacons, an isolated farming community that was of no strategic importance to anyone. She'd never seen the farmhouse other than in the crayon drawings they'd sent her, but Mrs Jones seemed to be a decent sort if her many letters were anything to go by. She was a mother herself, and understood how very much Doreen needed to be assured that her little ones were happy and safe.

The last of the planes roared away and half an hour later the all-clear went. Doreen breathed a sigh of relief as Mr Fletcher opened the door and light and fresh air flooded in. She stepped outside and was greeted by birdsong and the sparkle of dew on the grass, and felt restored in spirit. It was going to be a lovely day.

They trooped indoors as Mr Fletcher fussily tidied up the Anderson shelter and his wife began to prepare breakfast in the kitchen. Doreen went into her bedroom, put Archie's things back where they belonged and then sorted through her clothes to decide what to wear. It was Monday morning and she had a day of work ahead of her – a day in which she had to push aside the knowledge that tomorrow was Archie's funeral.

There was a long wait to use the bathroom and when it was finally her turn, she had a strip wash and then got dressed in a skirt, blouse and sweater and her most sensible shoes. Going into the kitchen, she found everyone was already halfway through their breakfast of toast and dried egg, for time was moving swiftly on and they were due to be at the Fort within the hour.

'May I use the telephone now?' she asked once she'd finished eating and the others had already rushed off.

'Of course, dear. Just don't be too long, you know how anxious Reggie gets.'

Indeed she did. Reginald Fletcher was obsessed with keeping the line clear in case there was an emergency, and if he'd had his way, he'd stand by the person making the call with a stopwatch.

Doreen washed up her plate and cup and went into the hall where the old-fashioned telephone hung on the wall. She turned the handle several times to get through to the local exchange, put the receiver to her ear and gave the woman Peggy's number.

'I'm sorry, caller, but there is no reply on that number. Do you wish for another?'

'Thank you, but no. I'll try again later.' Doreen replaced the receiver and frowned. It was almost nine, and Beach View was never deserted at that time of the morning.

She stood for a moment deep in thought as her uneasiness grew and she remembered Mr Fletcher saying the raid was on the coast. Had Beach View been hit? Were Peggy and the rest of them all right?

She forced down the fear and tried to think logically. If something had happened to them then the line would have been disconnected – but it hadn't, for she'd heard it ringing, and the woman at the exchange would have said if there was a fault, which could only mean that for some reason or another, Peggy and the others had gone out.

Besieged with conflicting thoughts, she went to fetch her things from her bedroom. She'd try again the minute she got to the office.

The entire household at Beach View had been disturbed by the sirens which had gone off just after midnight, and Peggy had settled with the others in her nightclothes in the shelter for yet another uncomfortable and sleepless night.

Cordelia had taken charge of Queenie, who curled snugly into the blankets over her lap; Harvey slept during the raid as always, and Ron kept Peggy and the three girls amused by showing them some card tricks he'd learned off Chalky, while Daisy slept undisturbed in her special cot.

They'd all stilled as the incendiary bombs began to drop, and flinched as the barrage of anti-aircraft guns hammered away from the cliff-tops. But it was the huge crash of an exploding bomb that made them all sit up and listen hard.

'That was the factory estate,' said Ron. He dropped the cards and reached for his cap. 'Come on, Harvey, they're going to need help up there.'

Rita was already opening the Anderson door with Fran closely behind her. When a bomb that big fell, it was all hands on deck, especially at the hospital and the fire station.

'You can't go up there, any of you,' Peggy had protested. 'The raid's still on, and if the munition factory goes then half of Cliffehaven will go with it.'

'Those wee girls are not afraid to do their duty and neither am I,' he'd rumbled. 'And don't forget that our Ivy's up there in that factory.' He'd kissed her cheek and hurried off.

Peggy had fidgeted and fretted over the next two hours, willing the raid to come to an end, and in dread for the safety of Ron and her girls. And as the raid had gone on and on, she knew she couldn't sit there any longer. With her mind made up, she'd turned to Sarah. 'Look after Daisy and Cordelia for me,' she'd ordered. 'I'm going up to make sure Ivy and the others are all right.'

Sarah had protested vehemently, but Peggy was determined, and as the enemy bombers roared overhead and the Spitfires and Hurricanes be-came embroiled in dogfights, she'd hurried back into the house and swiftly got dressed. Having decided it would take too long to walk all the way there, she'd grabbed the bicycle Jane had once used and set off.

The security at the factory estate was tighter than ever, and although she'd begged, pleaded and threatened the guards, it was to no avail, for it was deemed far too dangerous for anyone to get close. She'd been forced to wait behind the barricade for what felt like hours of suspense and frustration – seeing Ron working Harvey amongst the rubble, and Fran arriving with the medics as Rita and the fire crews battled to get things under control.

The speculation of those who'd braved the raid and were waiting with her veered from hope to despair, and when the all-clear finally rang out, their numbers were swelled by several hundred workers emerging from the estate's deep under-ground shelter.

Now it was almost nine o'clock in the morning and Peggy had finally been allowed through to get to Ivy and her friends, who were clearly in deep distress. She gathered Ivy into her arms, holding her tightly as she haltingly told her what had happened, and how she'd lost her friend Freda. Peggy had seen the survivors taken away in the ambulances, the walking wounded stumbling about in a daze, and the dead shrouded in blankets, and could only thank God that little Ivy had had such a miraculous escape.

The factory estate was now a scene of utter devastation as the last of the smoke cleared and the exhausted fire and rescue crews began to organise their gear in preparation for their return to their various headquarters. The parachute factory was a skeleton of blackened steel, the munitions factory was flattened and the tool factory was so badly damaged it would have to be demolished.

She held tightly to the sobbing Ivy as she watched Rita wearily reeling in the hose and fastening it securely to the fire engine. John Hicks was limping badly on his false leg – a sure sign that he too was at the point of collapse – and Ron was talking to one of the heavy-lifting crew, while Harvey slumped at his feet after his exhausting hunt through the rubble of the basement for any more survivors.

Close to eighty people had been killed, with only a handful of survivors left to tell the tale of this terrifying night. It was an absolute miracle that anyone had got out, Peggy thought as she acknowledged Rita's tired smile and began to steer the girls away from the scene. 'Come on, girls, you need to get home for a good breakfast and some sleep.'

The mass of onlookers at the gates parted like the Red Sea as they approached, and questions were flung at them from all sides as the newspaper reporter's camera flashed and voices rose demanding to know how many had died and if any of their friends or family were amongst them.

Peggy herded the cowering girls through the crush and hurried them down the road. They were clearly in shock, for usually they had an answer to everything and a real fighting spirit, but now they were simply young, frightened girls who needed the comfort of their own things around them and someone to make a fuss of them.

Dot, Mabel and Gladys were billeted with old Mrs Pierce in a house off the High Street, and Peggy walked them to the door, had a quiet word with Mrs Pierce and left them to her gentle ministrations. She carried on walking arm in arm with Ivy, talking quietly to her, encouraging her to tell her everything that had happened so it wouldn't fester inside her and give her nightmares.

When she heard about the tragic manner of the death of Fred and Charlie, whom she'd known since childhood, she went cold with distress and horror. Poor little Ivy had indeed witnessed more than any person ever should, and Peggy knew she would need very careful attention over the coming days if she was to get over such a thing.

They'd reached Beach View when she suddenly remembered she'd left the bicycle behind. After a momentary stab of annoyance she shrugged off her concern and took Ivy indoors. Ron would probably see it lying about and bring it home – and if he didn't, well, it was an old bike and unimportant in the light of the tragedy she'd witnessed tonight.

She went up the steps into the kitchen and gently pressed Ivy into the chair by the fire. Daisy was banging a wooden spoon against the railings of the playpen, gurgling happily as she munched on a bit of toast. But there was no sign of Cordelia or Sarah, so Peggy had to assume Sarah had gone to work and Cordelia must be upstairs getting dressed.

Having kissed Daisy and given her a hug, she left her to her banging, shrugged off her coat and fastened her wrap-round pinafore over her jumper and skirt, and then filled the kettle.

The kitten had obviously decided the shelf above the draining board was safely out of reach of Daisy's grasping fingers, and she emerged from behind the tea caddy to squeak a welcome.

Peggy lifted her down and poured a bit more milk into the saucer someone had put out for her earlier. Queenie lapped it up greedily and then sat and stared at Peggy as if waiting for something more.

Peggy's heart melted as she saw the big blue eyes and the moustache of milk beneath her pink nose. She was utterly adorable, and so she gave her a little cuddle before carrying her over to Ivy who was slumped unmoving in the fireside chair. 'Hold Queenie for a moment while I hunt about for something for her to eat,' she said.

Ivy looked down at Queenie and began to stroke her, tentatively at first, and then more firmly until the kitten was squirming with delight and purring like a miniature engine.

Peggy smiled as she hunted out some scraps of pork, and a teaspoon of porridge. It was a strange mixture, but the kitten needed fattening up, and it was all she could think of at the moment.

She turned to find that Ivy was now cuddling the little creature, her face rubbing against her fur as she softly talked about Freda and what had happened in that basement. Peggy smiled, for she was well acquainted with the healing qualities of a pet. Harvey had often been her confidant and comforter during the nights when she couldn't sleep for worry over everyone. Pets didn't talk back or try to give well-meant advice, nor did they criticise – they just knew their human was upset, and did their best to give them solace.

Cordelia came into the kitchen and took the scene in at a glance. 'Sit down, Peggy,' she ordered. 'I'll make the tea and sort out breakfast for you both.'

Peggy sat at the table and realised she was dog-tired after braving the cold and the air raid, and having to deal with so much anxiety and distress. 'Sarah got off to work all right then?' she asked.

Cordelia placed a cup of tea in front of her and nodded. 'The raid made her late, but I'm sure they'll understand,' she soothed. 'Daisy has been washed and fed, and the paper arrived about half an hour ago. I thought I heard the telephone ringing earlier, but I was upstairs getting dressed, so I can't be sure if it did or not.'

'If it did, it was probably Doris wanting to give me an earful about that pork,' sighed Peggy. She glanced across at Ivy, who'd fallen asleep by the fire with the kitten now nestled into her neck. 'We'll let her sleep,' she said softly. 'The poor child has had the most awful night.'

Cordelia sat down and listened solemnly as Peggy told her what had happened. There were tears in her eyes and she brushed them away with trembling fingers. 'I knew Charlie when he was just out of short trousers,' she said. 'A lovely lad he was too. Used to come during the school holidays and do some gardening for my father.'

Peggy patted her hand and waited for her to compose herself. 'On a practical note,' she said, 'Ivy and a great many others will be out of work now unless the other factories can take them on.'

'Perhaps that's a good thing,' said Cordelia thoughtfully as she regarded the sleeping girl and her bandaged hands. 'Ivy's a bright little girl, even if she is a bit rough round the edges, and I'm sure she could find something less dangerous to do.'

'Yes, she probably could,' Peggy agreed, 'but nothing will pay her as well.'

Cordelia was about to reply, when the telephone shrilled from the hall. Peggy dashed out to answer it before it woke Ivy. 'If that's you, Doris, then I'm hanging up,' she said without any preamble.

There was a giggle at the other end of the line. 'Well that's certainly a novel way of answering the telephone. I take it there is still a lack of sisterly love down there?'

'Doreen! Oh, Doreen, what a lovely surprise.' Peggy settled down on the hall chair for a good long gossip and dug about in her apron pocket for her cigarettes. 'Did you ring earlier?'

'Yes, and got no answer, so I was worried something might have happened to you.'

'Cordelia thought she heard it ringing, but she was upstairs,' Peggy explained. 'Everyone else was out of the house because of the raid.' She went on to tell her sister about the attack on the factory estate.

'That's awful for everyone, but I'm just relieved that you and the others are all right. We could hear the raid from here and Mr Fletcher suspected it was on the coast.'

'And how are you, Doreen?' Peggy asked

eagerly. 'How was your leave with Archie? Was it fun? Did you go to nightclubs and the theatre?'

There was a long silence at the other end and Peggy was instantly alert. 'You and Archie did go to London, didn't you?'

'Yes, and we had a wonderful time.'

Peggy heard the hitch in her voice and knew something was very wrong. 'What happened, Doreen?'

'There was an accident – a false alarm, really – and ... and ... we were caught up in it.'

Peggy shivered with apprehension. 'Was that the accident in the East End?'

'Yes. But how do you know about that?'

'There was mention of it in the paper – no details except that people died...' Realisation hit her like a hammer blow. 'Was Archie...?'

Doreen took in a shuddering breath. 'He and I... We got trapped underground and... Archie's funeral is tomorrow,' she finished on a sob.

Peggy's heart twisted at the sound of her young sister's sorrow. 'Oh, Doreen, I'm so sorry, love. I'll sort things out here and be on the first train tomorrow. You can't possibly deal with that on your own. And then you must come home to rest and recover and–'

'The funeral's in Bow, Peggy. And I won't be alone, my friend Veronica is coming with me.'

'That's very kind of her, but I still want to be with you, Doreen. Family support is important at times like this.'

'I know it is, but Ronnie has been like family to me these past few years, and I know how very difficult it will be for you to make the journey here. Stay with Daisy and the others and I promise to come down and visit when I'm feeling a bit stronger.'

Peggy gripped the receiver. 'You've promised to come before and haven't.'

There was a tremulous sigh at the other end. 'I know, and I'm sorry – but I've been moved about so much and have been so busy that...' She fell silent and Peggy heard the click of a lighter and the exhalation of cigarette smoke. 'But I do miss you, Peg, and there are times recently that I've longed to see you and home again – especially in these past few days. I'll get some leave and come down as soon as possible, I promise.'

Peggy had heard it all before and knew that something would crop up at the last minute to make her sister change her plans – but Doreen was mourning and clearly on edge, so she said nothing. 'What time's the funeral?'

'Eleven o'clock at Bow cemetery. Ronnie and I will travel up early to arrange things with the stone-mason, then after ... after, we'll catch the half-past twelve back here.'

'What about his parents? Did he manage to find them?'

'No, but Ronnie's spoken to a friend of hers who's a member of the Sally Army, and she's promised to do her best to find them. I've written a letter to his sister, but she's got small children and it's too far for her to travel, so I'm not expecting her to turn up.'

Peggy was saddened that Archie, who she'd known only through Doreen's letters, would be buried without his family around him – and sad-

277

dened too for Doreen, who would find it excruciatingly lonely standing by that graveside, even though she had a friend with her. 'I wish you'd let me come,' she said. 'I could leave this evening and stay with you so we could travel up together.'

'You are a darling, Peggy, and the very best sister anyone could have. But no, I won't hear of it.' Her tone became more brisk. 'Look, Peggy, I'm calling from the office, so I'll have to hang up now. I'll telephone tomorrow evening, I promise. Love you.'

Peggy heard the click of the receiver at the other end and the soft burr of a disconnected line. With a sigh, she replaced her own receiver and then sat there staring at nothing in particular as her thoughts whirled.

The idea of going to Halstead to be with Doreen was all well and good, but there were travel restrictions to overcome and she had poor, traumatised little Ivy to consider. And then there was Sarah, who was clearly still missing her sister, Rita, who was probably exhausted and down hearted after the night's dramas and her father having to leave – and of course Daisy and Cordelia. She couldn't take Daisy with her – funerals were no places for small children – and she couldn't leave her with Cordelia, for she simply wouldn't be able to manage.

'But Doreen's my sister,' she murmured, 'and she's always relied on me. I simply can't let her down at a time like this.' Her mind made up, she went into the kitchen in search of Ron, whose voice she'd heard a moment ago. Ron would find a solution – he always did.

Ron had made sure that Harvey had a good bowl of biscuits and scraps. Queenie had investigated the bowl and Harvey had growled at her, so she'd stalked off to go and scrape a patch in the garden to do her business. He watched her through the window, worried she might run off, but she came back again and disappeared somewhere in the basement. On his bed, no doubt, he thought wearily.

Little Ivy resembled one of Dickens's street urchins in her filthy dungarees and torn shirt and sweater, with those big boots on the end of her skinny legs and grubby bandages on her hands. But she looked peaceful sleeping there, so he made Harvey sit under the table so he wouldn't disturb her. He scratched his head and scrubbed his face with his filthy hands, then gave a vast yawn. A bath and a couple of hours' sleep would make him feel better. He'd heard the beginning of Peggy's telephone conversation, and he hoped that her spirits had been lifted by Doreen's call. He liked Doreen, for she could be fiery and funny and they hadn't seen enough of her these past four years.

As Peggy walked into the room he realised immediately that something was up. 'Peggy? What's the matter?'

'It's Doreen.' She sat down and Harvey rested his nose on her lap.

'She's all right, isn't she?' he asked in alarm.

Peggy told him about Archie and the funeral. 'She always was stubborn, but I could tell that

279

she needs home and family and time to get over his death. I have to bring her home, Ron. But I can't do that unless I go to Halstead tomorrow.'

'Aye, you're right there, Doreen can be wilful, so she can. You'll have a job persuading her, Peggy girl.'

'I can deal with Doreen,' she replied. 'It's all the others I'm concerned about.' She shot a glance at Cordelia, who was reading the newspaper, and the sleeping Ivy, before her gaze fell on Daisy.

'To be sure I'll look after them for you, Peg. 'Tis only for a day, after all, and the other girls will be here.'

'Dear Ron,' she said, 'I knew I could rely on you.'

He cleared his throat and patted her hand. 'That's what fathers-in-law are for. No need to thank me, Peg. You just get that girl home safe.'

'Doreen always was your favourite, wasn't she?'

'She's a bonny wee girl, so she is, and a grand one to have at your side when faced with Doris.' He grinned. 'To be sure there will be ructions ahead, and I'm quite looking forward to a bit of excitement.'

'I don't know that she'll be in the mood for fun and games with you,' Peggy said. 'She didn't tell me what that accident was that killed Archie, but she did let slip that she'd been trapped underground with him somewhere.'

Ron regarded her thoughtfully. 'It happened in the East End?'

Peggy nodded. 'There was a small piece about it in the paper, but no real details.' She regarded him sharply. 'Do you know something about it, Ron?'

He thought of the conversation he'd had that very morning with his friend, Ken Lowry, who was a stringer for the nationals and part-time reporter on the local rag. He'd remarked about the tragic death toll in the aftermath of the raid on the factory estate, and Ken had quietly told him about the even bigger toll at the tube station in Bethnal Green.

Ken had warned him not to say anything to anyone, for there was a news blackout on that particular tragedy – but surely Peggy had a right to know what had happened to her sister? He played for time by filling his pipe as he wondered just how much to tell her – and then came to the conclusion that Doreen was probably trauma-tised and would be unable to say very much at all, and that Peggy should be prepared for what lay ahead.

He looked across the table and realised that Peggy was tense and waiting for an answer, so in-stead of lighting his pipe, he set it aside and held her hands. 'Aye, I know something of what hap-pened, Peggy. And it's a sorry, sorry tale.'

Peggy had paled and her eyes were troubled as she looked back at him. 'Tell me, Ron.'

'I know that Doreen is grieving for Archie, the Lord love her, but it's how he died that she must be finding so very hard to bear,' he said quietly.

Peggy frowned. 'But there were no details of what happened, or where. How could you pos-sibly know how Archie died?'

Ron explained about Ken and the government order to block all news on the tragedy except for a blunt statement, and then went on to gently tell

281

her what had happened at Bethnal Green tube station.

'Dear God,' she breathed. 'She must have been petrified, trapped like that in the dark.' Tears filled her eyes and her voice wavered. 'Doreen was always terrified of the dark, especially as a child. We had to leave a candle in her room at night, even when she was fifteen or sixteen.' She stared at their interlocked fingers. 'It's a miracle she's alive with so many others killed – a miracle that she's still sane.'

'That's why you have to bring her home, Peg,' he said gruffly. 'She's experienced something that could affect her for years to come if she isn't looked after and made to talk about it and rest. I've seen it before in the trenches, when men got buried by a shell blast or a tunnel caved in. They seem all right and some can carry on as normal for months, or even years – they bury it deep and try to ignore what happened to them. Then something happens and it triggers them off, leading to all sorts of problems.'

Peggy's eyes widened. 'You mean she might go mad because of what happened?'

'Not if we look after her,' he soothed. 'She needs people she loves around her, and the time to accept what's happened so she can talk about it and get the whole experience out of her system. She's a strong-minded young woman, Peg, just as all you Dawson girls are. She'll come through this, you'll see.'

Peggy nodded. 'I'll make certain of it.'

She got up to hunt through the dresser for the train timetable, and Ron lit his pipe and went down into the garden. He had not only witnessed the aftermath of traumatic events, but had also been plagued by them himself. His experiences in the first war had taught him many things about the human mind and how it could shut down to blot out the horrors – and then, without warning, something would happen and the floodgates would open to release all the worst memories and feelings that had been lying in wait just beneath the surface.

He took a deep breath of the salty air and tried to distance himself from the images flashing through his mind. It had happened a long time ago, and the scenes were blurred and distant, but the horrors of the trenches and tunnels where he'd seen so many of his comrades die were with him still. And at night, when he least expected it, the sounds, sights and smells would sometimes thrust him awake, leaving him breathless and terrified in the darkness.

Ron scuffed his boot against a paving slab and kicked out at a dandelion that had dared to poke its head up next to his spring cabbage. He'd told no one of those episodes, and never would. But at least he knew how best to guide Doreen and Ivy through their troubles, and with that thought, he turned back into the house.

14

The spring sunshine was bright on that Tuesday morning, glinting through the bare branches of the trees surrounding Bow cemetery. Doreen stood stiffly beside Archie's grave as the vicar ended the service. She'd hardly heard a word of it, for her focus had been on that coffin which was now being slowly lowered into the ground. Her emotions were tightly reined in, but the slow, emotive sound of the Last Post almost broke her and she struggled to maintain her dignity, determined not to let Archie down.

As the last note faded and the rating lowered his bugle and saluted alongside his superior officer, Doreen felt numbed and distanced by all that was happening, as if she was merely a spectator watching herself from afar. And then she felt a soft nudge from Veronica and realised the officer was approaching.

'Our condolences, Mrs Grey,' he said as he solemnly handed her the neatly folded naval ensign and then saluted. 'Chief Engineer Blake was much respected by all. He will be sadly missed.'

Doreen nodded, unable to speak, and he seemed to understand, for he saluted again and then walked away. She remained by the graveside, dimly aware that Archie's funeral hadn't been the only one today, and that many of the victims of the Bethnal Green tragedy were being laid to rest here. And yet she'd noticed there was no government representative amongst the mourners and the rescue crews that had attended on that fateful night, and she realised the men in Westminster still wanted the whole episode hushed up.

She looked around the old cemetery where gravestones tilted and lichen smothered the Victorian table tombs and stone angels. Beyond the trees she could see the rooftops and smoking chimneys of Bow where Archie had been born, and hear the rumble of traffic on the streets where he'd played as a boy. 'At least he's come home,' she said brokenly. 'I hope he's at peace now.'

Veronica put her arm round her waist. 'I believe he is,' she said quietly.

Doreen took a shuddering breath and blinked away the tears. 'Goodbye, my love.' She placed a small posy of spring flowers on the mound of earth next to the awful pit. 'You'll always be in my heart.'

She stepped back, and with one last sorrowful look, turned away and headed for the gate. Her legs were trembling and her back ached from holding it so stiffly throughout the short service, but she was determined to remain in control at least until she'd returned to the sanctuary of her room.

Veronica seemed to understand her need for quiet contemplation as the train puffed and chugged along the rails towards Knockholt station, and Doreen stared blindly out of the window, not seeing the passing scenery, but thinking of Archie and the last precious days they'd spent together.

285

They'd made love in that big soft bed in their hotel room – sweet, tender love which had taken her to a joy she'd never experienced before. They'd walked the streets of the city hand in hand; had danced to the big bands which played in the ballrooms; had gone to the cinema and nestled in the back row as Fred and Ginger tap-danced across the screen; and had even managed to get into a matinee at the theatre. They'd filled every minute of the short time they had together, living life to the full and not thinking about tomorrow.

But tomorrow had come and dealt fate's devastating blow. Now all she had were the memories, and although they were so few in the scheme of things, that made them all the sweeter. Doreen blinked away her tears. She must cling to those memories, think only of the good things she'd shared with him, and then perhaps she could learn to cope with the darker, more disturbing images that haunted her.

'We're almost there,' said Veronica, pulling on her coat. 'Why don't you come to my billet and catch your breath for a while? I've made sure your work is covered for the rest of the day.'

Doreen dragged herself from her thoughts and looked at her friend. 'That's very kind, Ronnie, but I'd rather just go back to my place for a while.'

'It won't do you any good being on your own,' said Veronica. 'At least come back to mine for a cup of tea or something.'

Doreen shook her head, her gaze falling on the case in the luggage rack. 'I want to take that home, and you have to be at work. I'll be fine, really.'

'You say that, but you won't. You'll open that

case and see all his things and it will break your heart all over again.' Veronica took Doreen's hand. 'I know how it is, Dor,' she said softly. 'I've been there, remember?'

Doreen nodded and gripped her hand. 'Thanks, Ronnie. Thank you for everything. You've been the most marvellous friend, and I know how hard it must have been for you today.'

Veronica wordlessly gave her hand an answering squeeze and then got to her feet. Hauling the case down, she set it on the floor between them as the train began to slow and the familiar sidings of the station came into view.

'Well, I need a cup of tea and something tasty to eat,' she said firmly, picking up her walking stick. 'So I propose we go to the Honeysuckle tearooms and see what Mrs Osborne has in the way of cake or scones. My treat, Dor, and I won't take no for an answer.'

Doreen had no appetite for anything, but her friend had been so loving and kind, it seemed churlish to refuse. She buttoned up her coat and pulled on her gloves, her gaze fixed on Archie's case, which the officer had given her when they'd met at Bow station. The tears were threatening again and the tight hold she'd had on her emotions was beginning to slip. She grasped the handle and walked along the swaying corridor to stand by the door.

The train pulled in and came to a halt with a great sigh of billowing smoke and steam. Doreen released the broad leather strap to open the window, and then leaned out to turn the handle. She stepped down, helped Ronnie to negotiate the steep drop, and then began to walk through the smoke that rolled along the platform with the light wind.

As the smoke cleared she saw a small figure waiting by the ticket office – a figure that was wonderfully familiar, and very dear. She broke into a run, then dropped the case and flung her arms around her. 'Oh, Peggy,' she gasped. 'How did you know how much I needed you here today?'

Peggy held her tightly. 'Because you're my little sister and I've always known when you've needed me,' she replied hoarsely. She stood back and cupped her face. 'I'm here to take you home, Dorry.'

The use of her childhood pet name almost broke through her resolve to stay calm and in control. 'I can't. I have work and–'

'You can and you will,' Peggy said firmly. 'I haven't come all this way to just turn round and go back on my own.'

'But–'

'There are no buts about it,' said Veronica. 'I've already looked into you having two weeks' leave – on half pay, I might add – so there are no excuses.' She smiled at Peggy and introduced herself. 'I'm glad you came, Mrs Reilly. Doreen can be very stubborn at times, but she needs to get away and rest after all she's been through – and there's nothing more healing than having one's family around you, is there?'

'My thoughts exactly,' Peggy replied.

Doreen looked at both of them. 'Why do I get the feeling I don't have much choice in the matter?'

'Because you don't,' they both replied and then laughed. 'Come on, Doreen,' said Veronica, 'We'll go and have that cuppa. The next train's not for an hour.'

'I can't just up and leave,' she protested. 'What about all my things back at the billet?'

'I've already packed everything,' said Peggy. 'Your cases, as well as your bicycle, are quite safe in the left luggage.'

'But what about Mrs Fletcher? She'll need to know how long I shall be away, and the rent's due and–'

'I've had a long chat with Phyllis, and we've come to an arrangement,' said Peggy blithely. 'She fully understands the situation and has agreed to keep your room vacant for two weeks and then, if you decide to extend your leave, she'll keep it for a bit longer.'

Doreen knew when she was beaten, but she was also strangely contented to have decisions made for her. She hugged her sister and kissed her cheek. 'Thanks, Peg,' she murmured.

They'd returned to the station after their visit to the tearooms, and Veronica had seen them onto their train then stood on the platform waving until they were out of sight. Peggy settled on the seat next to Doreen, the suitcases and bicycle safely stored in the guard's wagon at the end of the train.

'Your friend Veronica seems a very nice girl,' she said as the train picked up speed.

'Ronnie's been an absolute brick this last week. I couldn't have a better friend.' Doreen fell silent and then changed the subject. 'I don't know how you managed to get round the travelling restrictions, let alone organise everything at home to get here,' she said. 'But I'm very glad you did.'

Peggy smiled. 'It was actually quite easy in the end,' she admitted. 'Ron is looking after Daisy with help from the others, and our friend Stan at the station filled out all the necessary forms so I could travel outside the twenty-mile zone.'

'Stan's still working? But he has to be well past retirement age.'

'He certainly is, just like Alf the butcher, Fred the Fish and a dozen other men who've taken up the reins while this war is on.' Her smile was warm with affection. 'Even Ron is doing his bit with the rescue services during the time he has off from the Home Guard. And of course he frequently helps out at the Anchor so he and Rosie can have some time together.'

Doreen's smile was wan. 'So, he's still courting the glamorous Rosie, is he? Any sign of a wedding yet?'

Peggy sighed. 'Sadly, no. Her husband is still alive and committed in that asylum. But they seem happy enough with the way things are for the time being – although I think Ron is getting a bit frustrated by it all.'

'She's still keeping him at arm's length, then?'

'It seems so, and I think it's a shame. They're wasting the chance to really be together, and with the way things are...'

Doreen nodded and stared beyond her sister to the far window where the fields were burgeoning with the spring crops and Land Army girls were wielding hoes to clear the weeds.

Peggy took the opportunity to study her more closely. She'd lost weight – but then so had everyone as the rationing tightened – and there were shadows of tiredness, and grief beneath her eyes. Her skin had lost its glow, and her dark, curly hair seemed dull beneath that black hat. There were also signs that Doreen was at the very end of her tether, for there was a tic in her cheek, one of her eyelids kept twitching and her hands fiddled constantly with her handbag.

Peggy's heart went out to her, for this was the little sister she adored. She'd gone through so much over the years, and this last bitter blow must have almost broken her. She took her hand and gave it a reassuring squeeze. 'We'll soon be home,' she murmured. 'And when you're rested and feeling a bit stronger, we can talk.'

Doreen shook her head. 'I don't want to talk, Peggy. It just makes everything worse.'

'Ron told me what you've been through,' Peggy said quietly, 'so we do understand how hard it will be to come to terms with.'

Doreen's eyes widened. 'How does he know? We were all told to say nothing, and there's been just a paragraph about it in the papers.'

'He has friends everywhere and one of them told him.' Peggy gripped Doreen's hand. 'He understands better than most what you must be feeling – don't forget, Dorry, he was in the trenches and the tunnels during the first shout.'

Doreen remained silent as she stared out of the window and saw the familiar countryside of rolling hills, patchwork fields and snatched glimpses of the sea. She knew that talking it over with Peggy probably would help, but at the moment she simply couldn't find the words to express the horror, and the anguish she was still experiencing.

'Do you remember I told you about that air raid on the factory estate?' At Doreen's nod, Peggy continued. 'Well, one of my girls was caught up in that. I won't go into detail now, but her experience was very much like yours, and Ron is encouraging her to talk about it. He seems to think it's better to talk it out than keep it all inside – and I have to agree with him.'

Doreen looked at her with eyes dulled by pain. 'What happened to her?'

Peggy hadn't really wanted to say too much, but realised that if her sister was ever to get over her experience then it was best to bring everything out in the open right at the start. She quietly related what Ivy had told her, and what she herself had witnessed.

Doreen's face was paler than ever as she listened, and her eyes sparkled with tears. 'Poor girl,' she murmured. 'She must have been terrified – and to see such things...'

'She's only eighteen,' said Peggy, 'but she's like you – resilient. You'll both come through this, I know you will.'

'Poor Peggy,' Doreen sighed. 'You do take on a lot, don't you?'

'It's no burden,' she said with a small shrug. 'I'm not working on a factory floor or digging for victory – or even manning guns or doing a turn on fire-watch – but in my own small way I do what I can for those I love.'

Despite everything, Doreen felt a tingle of excitement and pleasure as the tram came out of the tunnel running beneath the sheltering hills that surrounded Cliffehaven and she saw the familiar sidings and platform.

Peggy pulled the strap to open the window and leaned out. She waved and then hurried to collect her gas-mask box and handbag. 'We've got a reception committee,' she said.

'Who?' Doreen was wary, for she didn't really feel up to any fuss.

'Fred the Fish, Ron, and of course, Stan.'

Doreen frowned. 'But how did they know when we'd be coming?'

'I telephoned home from your billet. Phyllis was very accommodating.'

As they waited for the train to stop, Doreen saw the familiar stationmaster's cottage, and the not so familiar tubs and beds of flourishing vegetables lining the platform. Stan was clearly taking to heart the decree to dig for victory – but then he'd always loved gardening, and she remembered the many pleasant hours she'd spent as a youngster on his allotment.

Her thoughts turned to more practical things. 'How are we going to get everything back to Beach View?'

'That's where Fred the Fish comes in,' replied Peggy. 'He kindly agreed for us to use his van.' The train hissed steam as it rolled to a stop, and smoke curled past the window. Peggy opened the door and stepped down, and Doreen followed. As the smoke cleared she saw the three sturdy-looking men standing on the platform and recognised them instantly, but it was to Ron's open arms that she was drawn. She felt the strength of him as he held her tightly, and the rasp of his bristled chin as he kissed her cheek, and when she stepped back from the embrace, it was as if she'd never been away.

'I see you're still avoiding the barbers,' she gently chided.

He wiggled his wayward brows, his blue eyes twinkling. 'To be sure you haven't changed, you wee tease. It's good to see you, Dorry. It's been too long.'

She was hugged by Stan and Fred, who then rushed off to collect her luggage from the guard's van under Peggy's supervision. Doreen watched for a moment and then turned back to Ron. 'Where's Harvey?' she asked.

'He's under strict orders to mind the house,' he replied. 'You'll see him when you get home.'

A movement at the end of the platform caught her eye and she chuckled. 'I think we'll see him sooner than that.'

Harvey came hurtling towards them and then threw himself at Doreen, his paws on her shoulders as he tried to lick her face.

Doreen pushed him down and made a tremendous fuss of him as he squirmed in delight. 'Yes, Harvey, it's lovely to see you – and you haven't changed a bit. You're still a disobedient old thing, aren't you?' she said fondly.

'He's a heathen beast, so he is,' said Ron without rancour, 'but it beats me how he knew where we were.'

'I expect he followed the scent of Fred's fish van,' said Peggy as she pushed the bicycle towards them. 'That nose will get him into trouble one day, you mark my words.'

As the banter went back and forth Doreen felt as if she'd never been away, but when they emerged from the station she realised that a great deal had changed in the intervening years. The lovely old ticket hall was gone, as was the waiting room. There were ugly gaps between the shops and elegant buildings in the High Street, and looking up the hill to the north, she could see the sprawl of factories where once there had been green fields.

Once Harvey had been settled in the back of the van along with the bike and the cases, Fred slammed the back doors and squeezed his large frame behind the wheel. With Peggy beside him and Doreen squashed up against Ron, they waved goodbye to Stan and set off down the High Street.

Doreen could smell the fish that had been carried in this van, over the years, and it reminded her of when she'd earned pocket money by helping him to deliver it around the town every Saturday morning. She looked out of the window as they passed the rubble that had once been the Odeon cinema where Jim had worked, and the remains of Woolworths where she'd spent that pocket money. There were high stacks of sandbags in front of the Town Hall and the council buildings, and the lovely old church on the corner by Havelock Gardens had been reduced to a pile of shattered stone.

As the van turned into Camden Road she noticed other changes, for the small clothing factory had been greatly enlarged, and both the school and the block of flats next to it were nothing more than an unsightly bomb site. But the Lilac tearoom was still there, as were the hospital, the fire station, the Anchor and the short parade of shops. Childhood memories flooded back, and she saw herself skipping down the street to do the shopping for her mother, and going eagerly to school, plaits flying as she joined in with games of hopscotch.

Fred ground the gears as they came to a stop at the crossroads, and the van stuttered a bit as it went up the steep hill and finally came to a halt at the end of the narrow twitten that ran between the backs of the tall terraced houses.

'I hope Cordelia's got the kettle on,' said Peggy as Fred unloaded the bike and Ron grabbed the cases, while Harvey raced towards the back gate. 'I could murder a cuppa.'

Doreen dumped her bag and gas-mask box into the basket and wheeled the bike along the twitten, the memories coming rapidly one after the other. She'd been about ten or eleven when Peggy and Jim had taken over Beach View, and she'd walked with Ron and his old dog Rex along here on their way to the hills where he'd shown her badgers' setts and foxes' dens. Earlier memories were of her father, who would stand by the back gate smoking his pipe as he waited for her to come home from school – and of her mother at the kitchen window, always ready with a hug and something nice to eat. They were good memories, and she held them close, knowing they would help her get through the coming days.

'Are you all right, Dorry?' asked Peggy as they reached the back gate.

'Yes, I'm fine. It's good to be home.' She followed Ron and Fred down the garden path, noting the Anderson shelter, and how the lawn had been turned into a vegetable patch. The outside lav had been rebuilt and a chicken coop was now where her old swing had once stood, but the washing line still stretched across the garden, and the ugly coal bunker remained against the back wall of the house.

She left the bike beneath the tarpaulin shelter that stood under the kitchen window and then followed Peggy through the door and up the scullery steps to the kitchen. It was the same as she remembered it, slightly shabby and cluttered, but homely and warm and very welcoming.

'Hello, Dorry. It's lovely to have you home again,' said Cordelia as the men carried the cases through and up the stairs.

Doreen gave her a gentle hug, the scent of her lavender perfume so familiar and reassuring – and yet it was difficult not to feel sad at how crippled her hands were, and to realise she was smaller and more birdlike than ever. 'It's wonderful to be back, Cordelia,' she murmured. 'Are you well?'

The bright blue eyes twinkled. 'Never better now you're back in the fold. It'll be good to have someone else to sort out that old scallywag.' Cordelia glanced across as Ron came back into the kitchen and rolled her eyes. 'He's as naughty now as he ever was – a bit like his dog, really.'

Doreen smiled as Harvey collapsed with a grunt on the rug in front of the range, and then she caught sight of the little girl standing in the playpen. 'Daisy? Oh, my goodness, look at you!' She lifted the child out and gave her a hug, the sharp memories of her own little girls tugging at her heart. 'I can't believe how much she's grown since you sent that last photograph,' she said to Peggy.

'She's walking too now,' Peggy replied proudly. She turned to Fred. 'Stay and have a cuppa, Fred. You've earned it after being so kind today.'

'Thanks, Peggy, but I've got to get back to the shop.' He tipped a wink at Doreen. 'If you find yourself at a loose end, Dorry, there's always some fish to wash and prepare.'

Doreen chuckled. 'I think my days as a fishmonger's assistant are over, Fred. But I'll certainly pop in for a natter.'

Peggy made the tea and they sat round the table as Daisy tottered back and forth to show Doreen her toys. 'Where's the kitten?' she asked.

'Asleep on my bed,' rumbled Ron. 'It seems she's taken a liking to it, so she has.'

'She's about the only one who would,' said Cordelia with a shudder. 'That room of yours is nothing better than a pigsty.'

Peggy interrupted before the banter got too heated. 'I thought it was best for you to have your old room, Dorry,' she said. 'The other girls are in two of the doubles, but of course you could have one of the others if you'd prefer,' she said hastily. 'That back bedroom is a bit small.'

'No. My old room would be perfect,' Doreen said softly. 'I suppose the others are at work?'

'I don't know where Ivy is,' said Peggy, 'but the

298

others will be home for their tea in an hour or so.'

'Ivy's gone up to the factory estate to see if she can get a job,' said Ron.

'But it's far too soon,' protested Peggy, 'and her hands are still very sore.'

Ron shrugged. 'It's Ivy's choice, Peg. She's dealing with things in her own way.'

Doreen sipped her tea and let the conversation go on around her. She was bone-weary, and although these were the people she loved, she needed time to herself after the long day. She waited until there was a lull and said, 'I think I'll just go up, to sort out my things and get settled in. I'll be down again soon to help with supper.'

Peggy nodded and smiled. 'Take your time, love.'

Doreen went upstairs to the back room at the top of the house. Closing the door behind her, she leaned against it for a moment and then went to the window. She looked down at the garden and then across the rooftops to the hills. The view had hardly changed and it was comforting.

She regarded the bedroom where she'd slept for so many years. It too was just the same, the old furniture gleaming with the beeswax polish that scented the air, the faded dark stain still marking the ceiling where a gutter had leaked many years before. The eiderdown and bedspread were faded, as were the curtains – and the same rather badly executed watercolour of Cliffehaven's seafront that had been painted by one of the boarding house guests still hung above the chest of drawers.

She sat on the narrow single bed where she'd

dreamt of all the wonderful things she'd achieve once she was adult enough to leave home and strike out on her own. Her smile was wry as she watched the gulls swoop and hover over the roof-tops. She had been in such a tearing hurry to grow up and leave Cliffehaven, and had indeed achieved some of her dreams. Yet now she was older, perhaps wiser – and certainly battered by experience – she knew that none of it could have been possible without those early years of love and support.

Doreen ran her hand over the downy quilt as she let the sights, scents and sounds of home soothe her pain and repair her tattered spirits. Beach View had already begun to work its magic.

15

Ivy was feeling remarkably bright despite the nightmares that had disturbed her sleep. She dug her lightly bandaged hands into her trouser pockets and walked back down the hill from the factory estate, her gas-mask box bumping against her hip.

She'd left Beach View very early that morning in her quest to find another job, and because she'd been the first to arrive at the estate offices, and another girl had been dismissed, she'd been very fortunate to be given a post in the large hangar where aircraft parts were put together. With her sore hands cushioned by thick gloves, she'd spent the rest of the day getting stuck in to learning how to use the tools and which bits went where, and although the pay wasn't half as good as she'd been getting, it was better than nothing and kept her mind off the horrors of her entrapment. The other girls had also proved to be good company, and she'd discovered that she already knew a couple of them, having met them at various dances and pubs.

It had taken quite a bit of courage to go and look at the devastation on the far corner of the estate during her lunch break, but Ron had advised her to do it, because it was important for her to come to terms with what had happened. Yet the sight that met her was not what she'd expected, and she'd stood there dumbfounded trying to take it all in. The great piles of rubble had already been cleared, the parachute and tool factories had been demolished, and there was an army of men busily erecting the steel framework for new ones. It was as if the raid had never happened – had simply been a bad dream – and Ivy had found this more difficult to contend with than if things had been left as they were.

She'd stood for a while remembering Freda and all the others who'd died, and then turned away. Life and the effort to win this war went on regardless, but it was difficult to forget the terror she'd felt, and the sights she'd seen – and very hard to accept she would never see Freda again.

She reached the humpbacked bridge and waved to Stan, who was waiting for the next train, and then hurried down the High Street. She hadn't seen the other girls from the East End in the canteen or at the factory gates, and she wondered how they were getting on.

The tall Victorian villa was situated off the High Street in one of the terraced back streets. In many ways it was similar to Beach View, but the front garden was unkempt and the doorknocker needed a good clean – as did the windows, she noted as she rapped the knocker and waited.

The elderly woman who opened the door resembled a cottage loaf in shape. 'Hello, dear,' said Mrs Pierce. 'It's Ivy, isn't it? I'm sorry, dear, but the girls aren't here.'

'Have they found other jobs then?'

'Gladys and Mabel have got something at the uniform factory in Camden Road, but Dot's decided to go back to London.' Mrs Pierce smiled. 'I heard you were looking for a new billet,' she said. 'So you're very welcome to stay here now I've got the room.'

Ivy explained about Beach View, thanked her and walked away. It was good her friends had found work, but she was surprised Dot had thrown in the towel and gone back to the Smoke. Life wasn't half as pleasant there, and Dot had seemed very settled in Cliffehaven. It was a bit of a mystery, but she gave a mental shrug of acceptance and headed back down the hill. It was down to choice in the end, and she'd long decided she liked to be by the sea.

Instead of turning off into Camden Road she went down to the seafront and stood for a moment to enjoy the late sunshine and look at the sparkling sea. The air was so clean and fresh compared to London, and she liked the sound the waves made as they broke over the shingle and then made it rattle as they drew it back down the beach. She watched the gulls mewling and squabbling overhead, still in awe of how very large they were, and then she strolled down the promenade, hands in pockets, feeling very much at home.

She exchanged a bit of banter with the soldiers manning the anti-aircraft guns, but kept on walking, and all too soon she'd reached the end of the promenade and had to navigate the hill towards Beach View.

Ron had told her this morning that Peggy was bringing her sister back from Kent, and she wondered if they'd arrived home yet. The poor woman obviously must be in a bad way if Peggy thought it serious enough to fetch her home. Going by what Ron had said, Ivy guessed that she probably was suffering from nightmares, just like she herself was, and sudden flashing images of what she'd been through.

As she slogged up the hill, Ivy wondered if Peggy's sister would appreciate talking about what had happened to her – it had certainly helped when Ron had made her tell him about being trapped in that basement. But everyone was different, so she had to keep her gob shut for once and find out how the land lay with Doreen before she approached her about it.

She was a bit out of breath by the time she reached the alley at the back of the house, and she was still panting a bit as she went into the scullery and up the stairs. Fran was helping Peggy with the tea, Cordelia was laying the table, and the kitten was avidly watching everything from the shelf above the drainer, but there was no sign of anyone else.

'Hello, dear,' said Peggy. 'Where have you been?'

'Getting meself a job making bits of plane.' Ivy dumped her gas-mask box on a nearby chair and shrugged off her coat.

'It's a bit soon, Ivy,' Peggy fretted. 'Are you sure you're up to it?'

'I need the money,' Ivy said. 'Besides, work keeps me busy and I don't 'ave time to think about other things.' She poured herself some lukewarm tea and gulped it down. 'I'm off out with Rita tonight, so I'd better get changed.'

'By the way,' said Peggy, 'you had a visitor.'

Ivy frowned. 'What visitor?'

'A very nice young chap called Andy Rawlings.'

'I don't know no Andy Rawlings. Who is he and what did he want?'

'He's one of the fire crew who got you out of that basement, and he wanted to see if you were all right.' Peggy chuckled. 'There's no need to look so fierce, Ivy. He was just concerned, that's all, and so I told him you'd be home for tea and to call round again.'

Ivy remembered a pair of strong arms and broad shoulders, dark brown eyes in a face smeared with sweat and soot, and a Cockney accent. She felt a tingle of pleasure at the thought that he'd been worried about her, but she wasn't going to let Peggy know that.

'I don't know why he come round. He knew I were all right anyway.' She met Peggy's amused gaze and infuriatingly felt the heat rise in her face. 'What's a young bloke like that doin' messing about with fire engines when he should be in the Army or something?'

'He's profoundly deaf in one ear and the Army wouldn't take him,' said Peggy rather shortly.

'Oh.' A chastened Ivy shuffled her feet as the blush deepened. 'Well, I weren't to know that, were I?' she managed before she shot out of the room and took the stairs two at a time.

As she swung round the newel post to take the next flight she crashed straight into someone coming the other way and they had to cling to each other to stop themselves from falling over.

'Goodness me. You *are* in a rush. Where's the fire?'

Ivy giggled. 'It's not the fire – it's the fireman what's the trouble.' She looked into the amused face that was so like Peggy's and realised this must be her sister. 'Hello, I'm Ivy.'

'And I'm Doreen.' She cocked her head and regarded Ivy, the amusement still clear in her eyes. 'So, who's the fireman stirring you up, Ivy?'

'Just some bloke what reckons his chances,' she replied with a nonchalant shrug. 'Honestly, blokes are a funny lot, aren't they? They seem to think that carrying a girl out of a burning basement gives them the right to take liberties.'

Doreen smiled. 'What sort of liberties?'

'Coming round 'ere, letting Peggy get ideas. You know what she's like with 'er matchmaking – she'll 'ave us married off before the week's out.'

'Oh well, you can't have that,' said Doreen, clearly trying not to laugh. 'Goodness me, Ivy, no wonder you're in such a rush to escape.' She patted Ivy's arm. 'You'd better get changed for

305

your night out. Tea will be ready very soon.'

Ivy watched her go down the stairs. She seemed very nice, not at all like snooty Doris. And even though she was twice her age, Ivy had an inkling that they would get on very well.

She ran up the last flight and crashed into the large front bedroom on the top floor, startling Rita who was in the middle of pulling a dress over her head. 'Sorry,' she muttered. 'I'm running a bit late, but I'll be ready in time, don't you worry. I've been looking forward to tonight and no mistake.'

Rita buttoned up the cotton dress. 'Did you manage to get a job then?'

Ivy told her all about it as she stripped off her dungarees and thick shirt, then grabbed her ratty dressing gown and her washbag. 'The pay ain't as good, but they're rebuilding the munitions factory, so I expect they'll be taking people on and I'll be earning better soon enough.' She paused in the doorway, wanting to question Rita about Andy Rawlings, but then changed her mind. She'd discover for herself what he was made of, if he was interested enough to come to the house again – and if she was interested enough to want to find out more about him.

Harvey was sitting poised by the table as Queenie emerged from beneath it demanding to be fed. Ron had rolled a second piece of pork belly over stuffing for their tea, and when Peggy took out the roasting tin, the delicious smell wafted through the kitchen.

Peggy let Ron carve, and said nothing as he

dropped a few scraps down for the animals – everyone deserved a treat. She loaded each plate with golden roasted potatoes and a heap of vegetables from the garden. There was a pot of gravy to go with it, and some of the apple sauce she'd made from last year's crop which Sarah had secretly harvested from the orchard on the Cliffe estate.

Peggy made sure Ron divided the meat fairly and then gave Harvey his bowl of bonemeal and scraps to keep him occupied while they ate. She picked up Queenie and set her on the wooden drainer well away from Harvey's greedy nose, and gave her a saucer of milk and another of tinned cat food.

As the animals tucked into their meal, Rita and Ivy came into the kitchen, closely followed by Sarah and Fran, each looking very fetching in the dresses they'd made out of some old curtain material they'd found on a market stall. Rita and Ivy had pinned sparkling combs in their dark curls, Fran's Titian ringlets were held back by a green ribbon and Sarah's fair hair had been smoothed into a neat French plait.

'Well, don't you all look lovely?' said Peggy with a sigh. She glanced across at her sister and realised it wouldn't be kind to reminisce about the days when she and Jim had gone dancing in the ballroom at the end of the pier, for no doubt Doreen and Archie had gone to dances during their stay in London. 'Sit down then and eat before it gets cold,' she ordered. 'It's not often we have such a treat.'

As Peggy spooned the food into Daisy's mouth and tucked into her own meal, she wondered if

307

that nice young man would call again. She'd questioned Rita closely and discovered that he was twenty-two and single, and although he was forced to wear a hearing aid, he hadn't let his disability slow him down. According to Rita he was popular at the fire station, and John Hicks spoke very highly of him. She felt a warm glow of pleasure that he'd sought Ivy out, and rather hoped something might come of it if he'd taken the broad hint she'd given him earlier.

'Peggy Reilly, you're up to something,' muttered Ron, beneath the chatter around the table. 'It wouldn't have anything to do with a certain young fireman, would it?'

'Don't be silly, Ron,' she replied airily. 'The thought never crossed my mind.'

'Hmph. And pigs might fly,' he retorted before tucking into the pork.

Ivy and the other girls clattered down the road in their high heels on their way to the drill hall, where the town council were laying on the dance for the servicemen. Rita was hoping that Matthew would manage to get away from the aerodrome for one night, while Fran had already arranged to meet Robert there.

They arrived at the draughty old hall which was used by the Home Guard, the Guides, Scouts and the Women's Institute, but for tonight was decked out in bunting, flags and balloons. The sound of the rather good local band drifted through the ill-fitting windows and thin wooden walls, and people were standing about chatting and laughing. Matt was outside with Robert, and

Rita and Fran ran on ahead to meet them.

'It looks like we're on our own,' said Sarah, linking arms with Ivy. 'Still, there will be plenty of chaps to dance with. Some of the Yanks from Cliffe are planning to be here and I can introduce you if you like.'

Ivy grinned back at her, and they paid their six-pence at the door then stepped into a whirlwind of sound and movement. The band was playing 'Under the Spreading Chestnut Tree', and the dancers sang along as they followed the sequence of hand movements that were so much a part of the fun.

Ivy and Sarah went to the long table that had been set up as a bar, and once they'd got their glasses of beer, they shed coats, bags and gas-mask boxes and tapped their feet in time as they watched the dancers and joined in the song. The hall was full to bursting, and there were a lot of servicemen in their uniforms, both American and English – but the uniforms of the Yank soldiers were very much smarter than the baggy, un-flattering khaki of the British boys, and with their clear skin and wholesome good looks, the Americans were a magnet for the girls.

There was a rush to the bar as the song ended and then the band struck up 'The Lambeth Walk' and Ivy couldn't resist. 'Come on, Sarah. We gotta do this one.'

They left their drinks with their coats and gas-mask boxes and joined in, laughing as some of the Yanks got confused and did the wrong steps, and before long they found themselves with part-ners and the old, creaking floor groaned beneath the stamping feet as the rafters rang with the noise.

One tune was succeeded swiftly by another, and they were both whisked off their feet in a fast foxtrot, followed by a quickstep. Eventually Ivy had had enough of getting her feet trodden on and slipped off to the side to enjoy her beer and get her breath back. She sipped the warm, slightly flat beer and watched the other girls who were still dancing, glad that Sarah had seemed to shake off her gloomy mood and was enjoying herself.

'Hello, Ivy. D'you want to dance?'

She looked up at the tall, well-built, dark-eyed young man and her heart missed a beat. 'I'm sitting this one out,' she said, 'but you're welcome to stand and talk to me.'

'It's very noisy in 'ere,' he shouted above the racket. 'Can we go outside and talk? I find it easier to hear things with less background noise.' He pointed to the hearing aid in his right ear.

She didn't want to seem too keen, but Andy Rawlings scrubbed up all right and it would be rude not to go outside with him so he could hear properly. 'Yeah, all right,' she replied with studied nonchalance.

They got outside to find that other couples were quietly talking and smooching in the blackout, and feeling a bit awkward, they moved away from the hall and found a low garden wall to perch on.

'I expect Mrs Reilly told you I called in this afternoon,' he said, lighting cigarettes for them both. 'I hope you didn't mind, Ivy.'

'Course, not. Why should I?'

His grin lit up his face. 'So you ain't bothered

then if I was to ask yer out?'

Ivy giggled. 'A bit fresh, ain't yer?'

'A bloke's got to strike while the iron's 'ot, Ivy, gel. And I reckon you're a proper little smasher and no mistake.'

Ivy reddened as her pulse began to race. He was ever so handsome, and that smile of his made her go all unnecessary. 'You don't know nothing about me,' she hedged.

He chuckled. 'I know you're spiky and stubborn and brave – and that you've got dimples that flash when you smile, and dark brown eyes the colour of chocolate.'

'Blimey,' she breathed. 'You ain't 'alf got the gift of the gab. D'you use that on all the girls?'

He shook his head. 'Only on the one I'm really interested in, Ivy.' He cocked his head, his own brown eyes teasing her. 'So what about it, gel? You and me stepping out for a bit to see what 'appens next?'

'I'll think about it,' she replied, trying to keep a straight face.

He grinned back at her as the music filtered out to them. 'Don't think for too long, gel. Half the night's wasted already.'

'You ain't half got a cheek, Andy Rawlings,' she chided softly. 'But I suppose I could see me way to dancing with yer. Just to find out if yer footwork's as fancy as yer line of chat.'

He stubbed out their cigarettes and, careful of her lightly bandaged hands, helped her to her feet. 'What we waiting for then? Come on, gel.'

Ivy didn't protest as he led her back into the hall, and was soon impressed by the way he could dance the jitterbug – but when the band started playing a slow number, she felt a little awkward to be in his arms, for she only reached his midriff.

'Blimey, gel, what you doin' all the way down there?' He lifted her up until they were on a level. 'That's better. I can see what you're thinking from there.'

'Put me down, you great lump.' She laughed. 'People are staring.'

'Let 'em,' he said and gave her a broad grin. 'They're only jealous 'cos I've got the best-looking gel in the place.'

She playfully punched his shoulder. 'You ain't 'alf full of it, Andy Rawlings. D'you make it an 'abit to carry girls about?'

'Only the ones that need rescuing,' he replied as the music changed and he set her back on her feet to whirl her round in a swift quickstep.

Blimey, thought Ivy joyfully. I found a right one 'ere – but for all 'is north and south, he's lovely. And to think, he first clapped eyes on me looking like a drowned rat in me dungarees. Thank Gawd I look 'alf decent now, or 'e'd think I was a right let down.

Doreen had left the curtains and the blackout open so she could lie in bed and look at the sky. Clouds were scudding across the moon and veiling the stars, but the RAF bombers had taken off in great numbers from Cliffe some time ago, so she could only assume they were once again on a raid over Germany.

It felt strange to be back in the bed where she'd

once slept as a girl. She'd hoped that her home-coming would somehow soften and fade the memories of that tube tunnel, yet, as the girls came home and the house settled down for the night, they remained as graphic as ever. She turned on her side and in the pale green glow of Archie's watch she looked at his photograph and tried to concentrate on all the good things they'd shared.

Time passed as the watch softly ticked and the moon rose higher in the sky, and despite all her efforts, she was assaulted by flashing images of darkness, of being crushed and unable to breathe – of Archie lying in her arms, already distanced from her by death.

She felt the weight pressing on her chest, the race of her pulse and the cold sweat of fear as the sights, sounds and smells of that night sharpened. Tormented, she reared up and stared out of the window, longing for light, for an end to this torture. When it didn't come, she threw back the bedclothes, rammed her feet into her slippers and grabbed her dressing gown. She couldn't stay here, not even if she drew the curtains and turned on the light. She had to move and feel free.

The house was silent but for the usual soft groans of old timbers and gurgling pipes, and she crept down the stairs. There was no sound from Peggy's room, only the soft glow of the nightlight she kept on for Daisy seeping under the door. Doreen tiptoed across the hall and closed the kitchen door behind her. There was no sign of the animals and she assumed they were both down in the basement with Ron. Not wanting to disturb any of them, she closed the door to the scullery and then switched on the light.

She opened the door to the range fire and quietly poked it back into life, then put the kettle onto the hob. Feeling more relaxed, she silently moved around the kitchen to set the table for breakfast and tidy away Daisy's toys. She stood for a moment with one of the dolls in her hand, thinking about her own little girls – then, because it made her feel sad, she put the doll away and tidied up the jumble of things strewn across the dresser. There were letters, magazines, old newspapers, recipes, sewing and knitting patterns mixed in with bits of china, a basket of cotton reels and, strangely, a roll of bandaging and a ratty flat cap.

Once this was done she made a pot of tea and sat at the table with the warm cup in her hand, regarding the photographs on Peggy's cluttered mantelpiece. There was Jim in his uniform with a naughty gleam in his eye, and one of Cissy standing by a staff car and looking very grown-up and sophisticated in her WAAF uniform. Her gaze travelled to the lovely pictures of Anne with her baby and Rose Margaret, and then moved across to the one of Frank and Pauline with their three sons which had been taken before the war. There were separate photos of Seamus and Joseph, who'd been killed, their passing marked by black ribbons tied across the frames.

She gave a deep sigh. There was so much sadness in the world, and at every turn she was reminded of it. When would it end? When would she be able to look at photographs and not feel that terrible ache of loss?

Determinedly closing off these thoughts, she looked at the snapshots which had clearly been taken in the back garden of Beach View. She recognised Cordelia, Rita, Fran and Sarah, but the other girls must have been evacuees who'd since moved on. They looked like a happy bunch, just like the girls who were living here now. But they too had been touched by sorrow, and the terrible anxiety of not knowing what tomorrow might bring.

Doreen sipped the tea, comforted by the warmth of the fire and the soft light coming from the low-watt bulb hanging above the table. Her thoughts drifted to Ivy, who'd seemed very cheerful considering what she'd been through so recently, and she wondered if it was simply youthful resilience, or if she was merely playing the part as she herself had done over the past awful week.

Just then, as if her thoughts had conjured her up, Ivy came creeping through the kitchen door. Seeing Doreen, she hesitated. 'Sorry,' she whispered. 'I didn't know you were in 'ere. D'you want me to leave?'

'Not at all,' she whispered back. 'But shut the door. We don't want to disturb Peggy.'

Ivy closed the door carefully and then went to fetch a cup. Once she'd poured the tea, she sipped it thoughtfully. 'I couldn't sleep,' she said finally. 'Was it the same for you?'

Doreen nodded. 'Awful nightmares,' she confessed. 'And sort of flashing images of things.'

'Me too. Awful, ain't it? D'you think it will stop after a while?'

'I hope so, Ivy.' Doreen reached into her dressing-gown pocket and drew out a packet of Park Drive and Archie's lighter. She offered one to Ivy and they smoked in silence for a while, each with their own thoughts.

'Did you have a good time tonight?'

Ivy grinned. 'Yeah, it were blindin'. Danced me feet off, I did.'

'Was a certain young fireman there?'

Ivy blushed scarlet. 'Yeah, he were all right too.'

'Peggy thought you'd get on,' said Doreen with a wan smile. 'Which is why she told him where you'd be this evening.'

Ivy giggled. 'Gawd 'elp us. I might've known she couldn't leave well alone.'

'Peggy's got a soft heart and an eye for a romance. She means well, so don't be too hard on her.' Doreen regarded the young girl sitting opposite her with interest. She might only be eighteen, but there was a sense of steely strength in that skinny frame, and a determined tilt to her chin as if she saw the world around her as a challenge to be faced and vanquished.

'I understand you were billeted with my sister Doris,' she said into the silence. At Ivy's nod, she continued, 'Peggy and I often wondered if she was even related to us when we were kids. She was simply awful then, and I gather she still is.'

'She's a snooty cow,' said Ivy and then reddened. 'Sorry, but she is.'

'Yes, I know,' Doreen replied calmly. 'She and I have never got on, and I'm actually rather dreading seeing her again. She has a way of making me feel like a naughty kid to be talked down to and bossed about.'

Ivy's gaze was level and contemplative. 'I reckon you won't take no nonsense from her – not now,' she said. 'You got enough on yer plate without lettin' her get under yer skin.' She gave a trembling sigh and stubbed out her cigarette. 'I thought I were managing all right,' she confessed, 'and it were lovely tonight with the girls and Andy and all, but...'

Doreen reached across the table and stilled her agitated fingers. 'Why don't you tell me about it, Ivy?'

The brown eyes were glistening with unshed tears as she looked back at her. 'Only if you tell me what 'appened to you.'

Doreen nodded. 'That sounds fair.'

As Ivy began to relate her story, Ron moved away from the door and quietly went back down the concrete steps to his bedroom. Climbing into bed, he listened to the purring kitten and the snoring dog which were curled up beside him, and smiled contentedly. Doreen and Ivy would begin to understand and accept what had happened to them after tonight – and the healing process could begin. It was wonderful how fate often brought people together at just the right time.

16

The other girls had already left for work, and Peggy noticed that Ivy was looking quite bright this morning, despite the fact she and Doreen couldn't have gone back to bed until well past three. She handed her the tin box of sandwiches and flask of tea that she'd prepared for her lunch and smiled as the girl ran down the garden path, eager for her day's work. Ivy might be as small and skinny as a sparrow, but she was a spirited little thing. She'd come through just fine.

'And how are you after your late night, Doreen? I wasn't expecting to see you until at least lunchtime.'

'Oh, Peg, we didn't wake you, did we?'

Peggy had heard them come down and had listened momentarily at the door to find out who it was in her kitchen. Discovering it was Ivy and her sister, she'd stifled her instinct to go in and offer her support, and gone back to bed.

She grinned as she poured tea for Cordelia and began to spoon boiled egg into Daisy's mouth. 'The fourth stair up from the hall squeaks, so I always know if someone's moving about.'

'Goodness,' breathed Doreen. 'You should get Ron to fix it.'

'No fear. That squeak has been there since Mum and Dad first bought the place. They used it to alert them to any goings-on, and so do I.'

'Well, I never knew that,' said Doreen. 'To think of all the years I'd gone up and down those stairs... Still, this old place creaks all on its own, which is probably why I never noticed that stair.'

Peggy eyed her sister, who was definitely looking a bit brighter this morning, although there were signs that she'd been crying. 'Did talking to Ivy help in any way?'

Doreen put down her slice of toast and nodded. 'She's been a tremendous help, actually. Made me see that I'm not alone and that together we can share our nightmares and talk them through so they lose their power and we can see them for what they are. She understood, you see, because she's been through it.'

'Aye, 'tis always a good thing to talk,' said Ron, dropping an inedible crust of wheatmeal bread into Harvey's ever-open mouth. 'Not that I'm one for encouraging women to talk, you understand. They do too much of it, if you ask me – and it's usually all nonsense.'

He must have seen the warning glint in the eyes of the three women, for he winked and wriggled his brows. 'But talking is good when it comes to things like that, and I'm glad you've got Ivy to help you through.'

'We're helping each other,' said Doreen. 'I might be old enough to be her mother but that doesn't seem to make any difference, and last night, I do believe we became friends.' She finished her slice of toast and sipped her tea.

'Well, I'm glad of that,' said Peggy. 'Friendship is very important, especially at times like these.'

Silence fell as they all finished their breakfast

and Harvey mopped up the crumbs and bits of eggy bread from beneath Daisy's high chair. Queenie was doing her Greta Garbo act, sitting alone on the rug by the fire and studiously ignoring them all.

'You always did run a happy home, Peg,' said Doreen eventually. 'And it seems your match-making is working. Andy turned up at the dance, and although she's a bit wary of admitting it, I suspect Ivy is rather taken with him.'

'So she should be,' Peggy replied. 'They're both Londoners and single – and he is a very hand-some, pleasant young man. It's time Ivy had someone nice to take her out and show her a bit of fun.'

'Here we go again,' sighed Ron. 'For the love of God, Peggy Reilly, are you not satisfied that Rita and Fran are suited? Do you have to pair us all off?'

'She's even got romantic notions about me and Bertie,' sniffed Cordelia. 'Though what on earth she thinks I want with a man at my age, I can't imagine.'

'To take you out to lunch at the Conservative Club and dinner at the golf club, and drive you about in his car like Lady Muck,' said Ron without rancour.

'That's just being useful,' Cordelia retorted. 'It's not romance.' She eyed the three of them over her half-moon glasses. 'There's a lot of rot being talked this morning, and if it goes on much longer I shall turn my hearing aid off.'

'That won't make much difference,' muttered Ron. 'You're as deaf as a post anyway.'

'I heard that, Ronan Reilly, and I'll thank you to show some respect for your elders and betters.' Her reprimand was slightly weakened by the glint of humour in her eyes.

'Elder, certainly,' he agreed, glaring at her from beneath his brows. 'But when it comes to gardening and common sense, you're no better than anyone – certainly not me.'

'I grant you your gardening skills are adequate, but when it comes to common sense, you were obviously at the back of the queue when that gift was handed out.' Cordelia challenged him with her eyes.

'Right,' said Peggy as Ron was about to retort, 'that's enough from both of you. Honestly, Dorry, I have to put up with this every day, and it would be marvellous if we could have just one meal that doesn't end in a spat between those two.'

Doreen grinned. 'But that would spoil all their fun, Peg. You know how much they love each other really.'

Ron snorted and Cordelia sniffed as she shook out the newspaper vigorously to show that she wasn't impressed with any of them.

Peggy finished feeding Daisy and set her down on the floor, where she promptly tried to climb onto Harvey's back, shouting 'Gee gee!' Queenie shot up the curtain beneath the sink to the sanctuary of her high shelf, and after a look of disdain began to clean her whiskers.

'I wonder if anything can be done about Queenie's poor leg,' said Peggy. 'Though it doesn't seem to hamper her in any way.'

'Best to leave it alone,' said Ron. 'But I am

going to have to fork out to have her spayed. We don't want to be lumbered with every stray tom coming round and then be presented with a litter of kittens.'

'She's a bit young yet to be thinking about such things,' said Peggy. 'Though I agree it should be done.' She began to clear the table then looked round at the sound of the back door slamming. 'Who on earth is that?'

Doris appeared at the top of the stone steps, dressed to the nines in her best suit and hat, a fox fur over her shoulders, her make-up and hair immaculate as always. Unfortunately her furious expression rather marred this vision of perfection and Peggy was immediately on her guard.

'If it's about the pork, then you've only got yourself to blame,' she said to get in first.

Doris glared at her. 'Do you have the slightest idea of how *excruciating* it was to have to present that pig's head to Lady Chumley and Caroline for their Sunday luncheon? I was mortified, and no doubt it will be the talk of the town by now. I'll never be able to hold my head up in high society again.'

'Lady Chump Chop isn't high society, Doris,' said Peggy. 'She's the wife of a man who managed to make a fortune in armaments and munitions during the first war and was knighted for his efforts. She's not from the top drawer and certainly wasn't born with a silver spoon in her mouth – she just makes out she was.'

'She's a stalwart fundraiser and the patron of many charities,' snapped Doris. 'Her home is the most gracious in the town and her generosity is unimpeachable. Compared to you and the rest of the people in Cliffehaven, she's definitely "top drawer" as you so crudely put it.'

'Well, I for one am delighted to be out of her range,' Peggy retorted. 'That woman irritates me beyond belief, and the way you suck up to her is hugely embarrassing. But your high and mighty Lady Chump Chop was born plain Bertha Smith above her father's greengrocer's shop in Hastings, so she's got nothing much to crow about.'

Doris waved away this piece of information, either because she already knew it, or because she couldn't bear to think that her idol had feet of clay. 'I do wish you wouldn't call her that,' she said crossly. 'It's extremely common and not at all funny.'

'It suits her, though, with that thick, blunt face, so why not?'

Doris's lips thinned. 'At least she's made something of herself,' she snapped. 'Which is more than you and your disreputable household have done.' She glared balefully at Ron, who winked back at her and continued to fill his pipe.

'Don't start that, Doris,' Peggy warned. 'I've heard it all before, and just because your plans to show off to the silly woman didn't work out, there's no need to come round here at this time of the morning to vent your spleen.'

Doris suddenly noticed Doreen, who was sitting back in the kitchen chair, arms folded and with a wide grin on her face. 'What are *you* doing here?'

'I've come for a holiday.'

'It's about time you remembered you had a

family,' said Doris as she pulled off her gloves, used them to dust the chair and sat down with her back to Ron. 'But I suppose you've been too busy gadding about to spare a thought for any of us.'

'I've been busy working,' Doreen said flatly. 'There isn't time to gad about where I'm posted.'

Doris eyed her thoughtfully as she draped the beautiful fur over her lap. 'People don't have holidays in wartime. I suppose what you're really saying is you've been sacked. Well, it's hardly surprising, you always were a flibbertigibbet.'

Ron decided to make a hasty retreat with Harvey, and Cordelia adjusted her hearing aid so she could fully enjoy the conversation, while Peggy braced herself for fireworks.

The smile slid from Doreen's face. 'What do you mean by that exactly?'

'You left home when you were barely out of a gymslip and had more jobs than anyone I know – and probably more men than is decent to number in polite society,' Doris added with a sniff of disapproval. 'Then, to add insult to injury, you caused a scandal by getting a divorce and leaving those poor little girls without a father and a decent home.'

'You know very well why I got that divorce,' said Doreen, her voice dangerously calm. 'Eddie was a gambler and a womaniser.'

Doris looked down her nose. 'All men have their funny ways. It's a wife's duty to train her husband out of such disgraceful habits.'

'Just like you trained Ted so well that he went off with one of his shop girls?' Doreen unfolded her arms and sat up, her eyes sparkling with fury. 'If

324

you had an ounce of sense you'd mend your own ways and beg that man to take you back, Doris. He's the best thing that ever happened to you, only you're so busy social climbing and trying to outdo the neighbours, you can't see what's in front of your nose.'

'My marriage is none of your business,' said Doris haughtily. 'Put your own house in order before you start picking on mine.'

'I would, if my house hadn't been repossessed by the bailiffs to pay Eddie's gambling debts,' Doreen snapped. 'Why don't you go and mind someone else's business and leave us alone?'

'I'm not leaving until I get a decent piece of that pork,' Doris retorted, swiftly rescuing her fur from Daisy's exploring fingers.

'You're too late,' said Doreen. 'It's all gone.'

'Don't be ridiculous. It can't be.'

Doreen shrugged. 'You had your share. It's no one's fault if you didn't appreciate it. After all, you blackmailed Ron into giving it to you in the first place – which I think is despicable.'

Doris lit a cigarette and glared at her. 'What exactly *are* you doing here, Doreen?'

'I told you. I'm on leave.'

'Then why aren't you with your children?'

'Because I haven't been well and I needed to get right away for a while.'

Doris snorted. 'Nothing too trivial, I hope,' she said nastily.

'Sorry to disappoint you, Doris, but I'm recovering.' Doreen's eyes glinted dangerously.

Doris hitched the fur over her shoulder and snorted. 'A fine mother you turned out to be, I must say. Poor little mites. They've been abandoned down there in Wales, while you gallivant about here. I bet there's some man involved. There usually is,' she added spitefully.

'Just get out, Doris, before I slap that smug face of yours and shove you down those steps,' snarled Doreen.

'I can see that I've struck a chord,' she replied as she stubbed out the cigarette and stood up. 'The truth is never palatable, is it?'

Doreen pushed back from the chair and faced her. 'You want the truth, you bitch? Well here it is. You smothered Anthony and made his life a misery until he met and married Suzy and finally had the balls to cut himself off from your apron strings.'

She took a step towards Doris, who'd gone rather pale. 'And what about Ted? You made his life a misery too, didn't you? With your demands for bigger and better things so you could show off to people like poor Peggy who has to graft for every last bloody penny. And what about your complete disregard for Ted's feelings and opinions? You showed him no respect and treated him like a lackey, so it serves you right that he found comfort and fun and good honest sex with someone else – because I bet that marriage bed of yours was about as welcoming as a bloody morgue.'

Doris paled further and took another step back as Doreen once again advanced. 'There's no need–'

'There's every bloody need, Doris. You come round here with your bitchy remarks and your sniping and expect us to say nothing – but you don't like it at all when the boot's on the other foot, do you?' She gave Doris a sharp jab in the shoulder. 'Well, we don't need this sort of harassment – and we don't need you. So sling your hook and stay away.'

'Well, I never,' gasped Doris and she looked to Peggy, who was now holding Daisy on her hip. 'Are you going to let her talk to me like that, Margaret?'

'My name is Peggy, and she's only saying what the rest of us haven't been brave enough to say for years,' she said mildly. 'And it was you who started this. You can hardly blame Dorry for speaking her mind after you've been so nasty to her.'

'I'll remember this,' Doris hissed. 'And to think of all I've done for you over the years. It's utterly disgraceful that I should be treated in this vulgar fashion by my own flesh and blood.' She swept the fox fur around her neck. 'But then you were both always inclined to be common.'

'Oh, put a sock in it, Doris, and clear off,' said Doreen.

Doris hesitated and then turned on her heel, went down the steps and slammed the door behind her with such force it shook the walls.

Peggy put Daisy back on the floor and collapsed on the kitchen chair with a burst of laughter. 'Oh, Dorry,' she gasped. 'You were quite, quite magnificent. Doris didn't know what had hit her.'

'She'd have known if I'd let rip with a right hook,' Doreen fumed. 'I've been taking self-defence lessons at work and can pack quite a punch.'

'It's about time someone told her what's what,' said Cordelia, chuckling. 'I'm glad you're home, Dorry. Life is far more interesting when you're here.'

Doreen was still furious and her hand trembled as she reached for the teacup. 'I didn't mean to come out with all that – and I certainly didn't mean to be quite so heartless. But she just made me so angry it all poured out, and once started I couldn't stop.'

Peggy put her arm round her shoulders. 'Doris is tough. She'll shrug it all off like water off a duck's back – worst luck. But at least you got that out of your system. Do you feel the better for it?'

Doreen smiled. 'Yes, I do, strangely enough. It's been a long time since I've had a run-in with Doris, and I'd forgotten how liberating it can feel.'

Peggy laughed. 'It was quite like old times with you going hammer and tongs at one another. Let's freshen the pot and have another cup of tea to celebrate your homecoming, and happier times to come.'

'A glass of sherry would be more appropriate,' said Cordelia hopefully.

'It's barely past ten in the morning,' gasped Peggy. 'Besides, we haven't got any.'

'There's a bottle in my wardrobe,' Cordelia replied. 'And as it's after ten, we'll call it early elevenses – the perfect time for a drop of what you fancy.'

Ivy was feeling much more cheerful after the long talk she'd had with Doreen the night before. There had been tears, of course, and quiet confidences exchanged in the knowledge that the other really understood – and when they'd finally gone back to their beds, Ivy knew they'd both benefited from their shared experiences. The memories of what had happened to them would still linger, but they were now more capable of dealing with them, knowing that in time they would fade.

She should have been tired after so little sleep, but she was full of energy, and she wondered if her high spirits might have anything to do with Andy Rawlings. She firmly tamped down the thought, for although he was a nice bloke who seemed to know Hackney almost as well as she did, and could certainly dance and give the old chat, he was probably only trying his luck, so she shouldn't get too excited about it. Once a bloke realised you weren't the sort of girl to put it about, they soon lost interest. And yet, annoyingly, the thought that she might not see him again saddened her.

When she'd finished her shift she wandered over to the site where the new factories were slowly emerging from the ashes of the others. Sitting down on a slab of broken concrete, she drank the last of her tea from Peggy's flask and thought about what had happened to her. She'd seen some terrible sights during the London Blitz, but had never actually been caught up in something, and now, with the debris cleared away and the new buildings rapidly going up, it felt as if it had all been a bad dream.

She screwed the cup back on the flask and buried it in her gas-mask box, then brushed the dust off the seat of her dungarees and headed for the gate. Peggy would have tea on the table soon and she was rather hoping there was some of that cold pork left.

'Hello, Ivy.'

She looked round to find that Andy was looming over her with a silly grin on his face and a bunch of drooping wild flowers grasped in his large hand. Her heart did a little skip as she smiled back at him. 'What you doin' here then?'

'Come to walk you 'ome, ain't I? These are for you,' he added, thrusting the half-dead flowers at her. 'Sorry they ain't much, but it were all I could find.'

Ivy dutifully admired the poor bedraggled things – after all, it was the thought that counted. 'I am quite capable of walking back on me own, yer know. Ain't you got work to go to?'

'I just thought you might like a bit of company, gel. And no, I've finished me shift, so I wondered if you'd like to come with me and 'ave a fish supper?'

She was aware of the blush heating her cheeks. 'That's ever so nice of you, Andy. But Peggy's expecting me home for me tea.' She looked up at him and saw the disappointment in his eyes. 'But you can walk me home, if it's not out yer way, like.'

He held out his arm. 'That's the best news I've had all day,' he said cheerfully.

She looked up at him as she held onto his arm and tried to match his pace. 'You 'ad a bad shift then?'

'Just a bit boring, that's all. No fires, just cleaning the engines and doing a stocktake on the equipment.' He grinned down at her and slowed his long stride so she didn't have to trot to keep up with him. 'How were your day?'

She shrugged. 'The usual drilling and banging and lifting 'eavy things,' she replied. 'But I can't believe how quick them builders cleared everything and started again. I hardly recognised the place where those factories were.'

'It has to be done quick, Ivy. Factories like that are essential if we're going to win this war.' He eyed her quizzically. 'How you 'olding up, gel?'

'All right. I gotta get on with things, ain't I? Not much use to anyone moping about and feeling sorry for meself.'

He came to a halt in the High Street and looked down at her solemnly. 'Brave words, gel. But I know you musta been scared rotten down there.'

'Yeah, I was,' she admitted softly. 'But I'll get over it.' She looked up at him and saw the concern in his expression. 'You must see things – awful things. How do you cope?'

'We go back to the station, drink lots of tea laced with brandy and talk it out,' he replied solemnly. 'Blokes feel it too, you know, and John Hicks understands that, which is why his door is always open if we need to get things off our chest.' He broke into a smile. 'Let's talk about something else before we both get depressed. What sort of fish do you like?'

'Anything in lovely greasy batter, but not herring,' she replied and then giggled. 'But if that's all they got, I'll eat it.'

They chattered away as if they'd known each other for years rather than just a few hours, and by the time they'd reached the back gate of Beach

331

View, they were laughing uproariously over a silly situation Andy had found himself in with an enormously fat woman who'd become stuck in her bath.

'You'd better come up and say hello,' she said as they reached the scullery. 'Peggy's very particular about things like that.'

'She's all right, ain't she? You're lucky to have fallen on yer feet here.'

Ivy could hear music playing and a great deal of laughter coming from the kitchen. Puzzled, she led Andy up the steps and they both stood in the doorway and took in the sight of Ron waltzing Cordelia around the room to 'If You Were the Only Girl in the World' while Peggy swayed with Daisy in her arms, Fran played along to the tune on the violin, and Sarah danced a very odd version of the waltz with Rita, while Doreen sat chatting to Rosie, the landlady of the Anchor. The kitchen table was laden with plates of food and a lot of bottles, and the volume on the wireless had been turned right up.

'Blimey,' she breathed, seeing Cordelia clinging on to Ron for dear life as she tried to keep her footing. 'It looks like someone's hit the sherry.'

Peggy saw them and waved them in. 'We're celebrating,' she said above the noise. 'Come and join us.' She looked at them both and shot them a lopsided smile. 'There's plenty of food, so tuck in, the pair of you.'

'What you celebrating?' asked Ivy.

Peggy frowned. 'I can't remember,' she replied. 'But I think it had something to do with Dorry reading Doris the riot act.' She giggled. 'I do know we opened a bottle of Cordelia's sherry, then Ron came back with Rosie and it all went downhill from there. Join the party, you two, don't be shy.'

Ivy grinned as Peggy went rather unsteadily to a chair and plumped down with Daisy in her lap. 'They're all at least two sheets to the wind,' she muttered to Andy. 'We've got some catchin' up to do.'

Ron swayed towards them and pulled a couple of bottles of beer from the collection on the table. 'Here we are, compliments of my Rosie. Get that down you and enjoy the craic,' he ordered them. 'To be sure 'tis a grand night for it, so it is.'

Andy and Ivy exchanged beaming smiles, and once Ivy had put the poor wilting flowers into a jam jar of water, they helped themselves from the tureen of vegetable soup before tucking into the cold pork, spring salad and large chunks of bread. It might not be as intimate as a fish supper in the little chip shop with the check tablecloths and the dim lights, but it was certainly fun.

As they finished their food, Ivy noticed that everyone was looking quite dressed up, and realised she must look a complete shambles with her dirty face and tatty dungarees. She quickly whisked off the scarf she'd knotted over her hair. 'I'm just gunna get washed and changed,' she said to Andy, who was watching Rita trying to jitterbug with Rosie.

'Nah, you look lovely just the way you are.' He took her hand and pulled her to her feet. 'Come on, gel. Let's dance.'

There wasn't much room, even with the table pushed right back against the wall and the playpen relegated to the hall, but the music on the wireless was coming from the Hammersmith Palais, and was far too tempting to ignore, so she happily joined in.

It was almost ten by the time the music mellowed and one by one the others began to collect their things and head for bed. Andy slipped on his uniform jacket, picked up his hat from the dresser and smiled at a yawning Peggy. 'Thanks, Peggy. It's been a lovely evening, and that pork and soup were blindin'.'

'It was a pleasure,' she said. 'Though I think we'll all have sore heads in the morning.' She smiled as she regarded them both with twinkling eyes. 'I hope you won't leave it too long before you come again.'

'Would it be all right if I took Ivy out for a fish supper on me next night off?'

Peggy's eyes sparkled even brighter in her flushed face. 'Of course it would,' she replied with a chuckle. 'Though I think that's really up to Ivy.'

He turned back to Ivy, who was a bit embarrassed at being the centre of attention from a giggling Peggy, Rosie and Doreen. 'Come on, gel,' he said softly as he took her hand. 'You can walk me to the gate.'

She followed him down the scullery steps and through the back door into the garden, her face burning, her pulse racing so hard she felt quite light-headed.

He came to a halt halfway down the path as the tune changed on the wireless, and a mellow voice began to sing one of the songs from the new film,

Casablanca. As the lovely melody of 'The Very Thought of You' drifted out into the night, he took her into his arms and led her into a slow, shuffling dance.

'Andy,' she protested softly. 'What you think yer doing?'

'Dancing in the garden with my girl,' he said.

She buried her scarlet face in his midriff. 'Getting a bit ahead of yerself, ain'tcha?'

'There's a war on, Ivy, and as I said before, you gotta strike while the iron's 'ot.' He stopped dancing and put his finger under her chin so she had to look up at him. 'Is that all right with you, gel?' he murmured.

Ivy's heart was thudding and her stomach was doing cartwheels as she looked into those deep brown eyes. 'Yeah, Andy. It's all right, I reckon.'

The world seemed to stop spinning and she was rather hoping he might kiss her, but the breathless moment was snatched away by the sound of the sirens.

'I better go and see if they need me at the station,' he said. 'Take care of yerself, Ivy, and I'll see yer as soon as I can.'

As he raced down the path and vaulted over the gate to disappear down the alley, she smiled. 'And you take care of yourself, Andy Rawlings,' she whispered. ''cos you and me, we got unfinished business.'

17

At the first wail of the siren, Ron had hurried off with Rosie and Harvey to get to the pub so they could keep Harvey's pup, Monty, company through the raid. Rita was a bit tiddly, but she seemed to have sobered up enough as she swiftly followed them on her way to the fire station. Cordelia had to be woken from a sherry-induced sleep and was still a bit unsteady on her feet as Sarah helped her down the stairs.'

Doreen was impressed by the speed with which Peggy and the rest of the household swung into action, for within minutes of that siren going, everyone was carrying something and heading down the path to the Anderson shelter. And yet the thought of being in there slowed her steps and she hung back.

'It's all right,' said Ivy, taking her hand. 'I hate the thought of it too after the other night, but together we can get through this.'

Doreen stepped inside and sat down close to the door, her nerves jumping, the effects of the beer rapidly wearing off. It had been such a lovely, happy evening, and she was determined not to ruin it by acting like a fool. She took a deep breath when Peggy closed the door and her heart raced as they sat in the momentary darkness before the lamp was lit.

Peggy seemed to understand how uneasy

Doreen felt, for she smiled across at her and patted her knee. 'I've tried to make it homely,' she said, 'but none of us like it. Let's just hope this is a false alarm.'

'It's not the raid, or the noise,' Doreen replied. 'It's being enclosed with other people.'

'To be sure it's a terrible thing, claustrophobia,' said Fran. 'Peggy, do you happen to have a brown paper bag in that box of yours?'

'Well, yes, dear. But I've got Daisy's rusks in it.' She scrabbled about in the emergency box, pulled it out and tipped the rusks into a tin mug before shaking the bag free of crumbs. 'What on earth do you want it for?'

Fran handed it to Doreen. 'When you feel the panic coming on, take deep breaths into this. It will help, I promise.'

Doreen eyed the paper bag, not at all convinced.

'It does work,' said Sarah. 'A girl at school suffered panic attacks, but once our teacher showed her what to do, she was fine.'

Doreen felt very foolish sitting there clasping that paper bag as the planes took off from Cliffe aerodrome. She felt the squeeze of Ivy's hand to reassure her, and the tremble in her small frame, and realised that she was also finding it very hard to be shut in here. 'Let's sing a song to drown out the noise,' she said. 'What about "Little Brown Jug"?'

They sang loudly and defiantly, clapping their hands and stamping their feet to drown out the distant crumps and thuds of exploding bombs, interspersed with the rattle of the ack-ack guns and the boom of the Bofors guns that were strung all along the southern coast.

Peggy made tea on the camping stove, while Daisy sat on her rug clapping her hands, and Cordelia eventually slid lower in her deckchair and nodded off.

But then the lamp went out, plunging them into absolute darkness.

Doreen heard Ivy's gasp of fear and felt the tremor run through her body, and although she could feel the panic rising as her chest tightened and her heart began to thunder, she knew Ivy needed her help. She gripped Ivy's hand as Peggy scrabbled about in the pitch-black for the matches to relight the gas ring on the camping stove. The darkness was closing in and she could hear the sounds of those voices crying out in the tunnel – could feel the press of people, and smell the fear.

'Use the bag, Dorry,' said Fran calmly.

Doreen opened the bag, but instead of pressing it to her own mouth, she handed it to Ivy. She heard her breathing deeply, felt the tremors begin to lessen and marvelled at how simple and efficient Fran's remedy was. Then she felt Ivy pressing the bag into her hand and after only a few deep breaths, she too began to feel much calmer. The bag went back and forth between them and by the time Peggy had managed to light the gas ring, their breathing had returned to normal.

'There, see? I told you,' said Fran. 'Keep the bag and use it until you find you don't need to any more.'

'Are you both all right?' asked a concerned Peggy.

Doreen and Ivy looked at one another and smiled, for they'd come through and knew they would do so again.

It was now late March and Doreen had been home for almost two weeks. Although she was still grieving deeply for Archie, the troubling nightmares and flashing images had not been as bothersome. Her fear of dark, enclosed places still made her panic, but having seen how Ivy had begun to cope so well, she knew she had to overcome it. Now, every time the sirens went she was first in the shelter with the emergency box and blankets, and when the door was shut she endured those first few minutes of darkness determinedly until the lantern was lit. At night, she drew the curtains and blackout and used only a small nursery lamp to chase away the shadows. She was getting better, feeling stronger, and it was all down to Peggy's love and Ivy's stalwart support.

She finished reading the letters that had come from her girls, and then opened the one that looked rather official. It was actually from Veronica, who'd filched the office stationery to write to her. Work on the experiments was going well, Maynard was as impossible as ever, but the project he'd been working on was due to be tested sometime the following month. She couldn't go into detail, of course, but Doreen knew what she was talking about, and was quite excited by the thought that the bouncing bomb would be tested again – and this time at sea.

Veronica went on to say that her friend who worked for the Red Cross had finally managed to track down Archie's parents. His mother was in Wales with the rest of the family, but sadly, his father had died of a heart attack during a raid.

Doreen sighed. At least one of them had survived, and his mother would be far safer in Wales. She would write to her later and let her know how the funeral went.

Returning to Veronica's letter, she learned that her friend had been meeting a colleague of her late husband's for the occasional dinner now he was posted at Biggin Hill. He was a wing commander, very good company and rather keen to take things further, but Ronnie was having doubts, for it felt disloyal to her late husband to be stepping out with one of his closest friends.

After several pages of the current gossip going around the Fort, Veronica wrote that she'd had a long and serious conversation with the head of Admin, and it had been decided that Doreen should take an extra two weeks off. There would be some money coming to her from the emergency fund, and Mrs Fletcher was happy to keep her room until she got back, so she wasn't to worry.

Doreen finished the letter and looked over at Peggy, who was deeply immersed in her latest airgraphs from Jim. Not wanting to disturb her by asking her what she should do about this extended leave, she left the kitchen, collected her coat and headed for the seafront. She could think clearly there.

She walked down the hill and stood for a moment to look at the cliffs that towered over the pebble beach, remembering how once there had

340

been fishing boats sitting on the shingle above the high-water mark, and several wooden huts strung along the end of the promenade where the nets would be hung to dry and the catch would be cleaned and gutted and sold to the eager house-wives. Now it was fenced off with great coils of barbed wire, the shingle laid with mines and the lovely bay strung with ugly concrete shipping traps.

Doreen sighed, dug her hands in her pockets and began to walk past the wreckage of the Grand Hotel and the houses that had stood next to it. The boarding houses and private hotels had either been boarded up and abandoned, or requisitioned by the council or the Army to house men or evacuees. The white paint was peeling on the balconies, rust was beginning to set in on the metal window frames, and the gardens where holiday-makers had once sat under umbrellas were now just plots of weeds and long grass.

Everything changed, but somehow it was still the same. The essence of Cliffehaven remained in the stalwart spirit of the people who lived here, the common goal of winning this war bringing them even more closely together. Despite the destruction, the shortages and the air raids, brave little Cliffehaven survived to fight another day.

Doreen raised her face to the sun as the salty breeze blew in from the sea and ruffled her curls. The familiar cries of the scavenging gulls, the splash of waves on pebbles and the scent of the sea had helped to heal some of the hurt these past two weeks, for they'd reminded her that life was too precious to be wasted on regrets for what

341

might have been. She and Archie had experienced something very special, and although he was gone, she could feel him beside her every step of the way. And because of that, she would find the strength to live the life that she'd been granted, and live it to the full.

She carried on walking along the promenade, feeling free and secure and a million miles away from her previous life. Eddie wouldn't find her here, and eventually he'd realise that his letters would never be answered, so would stop writing them and let her get on with her life.

It was a lovely morning and several others had come out to enjoy it, for there were strollers and dog walkers, women with prams and old men simply sitting on the stone benches, at peace with their pipes as they stared out to sea or shared reminiscences with their cronies. She had always planned to bring Evie and Joyce here for a holiday, but somehow there'd never been enough time or money – especially once she'd divorced Eddie. But the minute the war was over she would go and collect them from Wales and bring them home to Peggy, and let them enjoy a taste of what her own childhood had been like.

She finally reached the wooden tearoom at the end of the promenade, and seeing that it was open, she stepped inside and ordered a cup of coffee and a rock cake. It turned out to be more rock than cake, but the freshness of the sea and the exercise had given her a bit of an appetite, so she didn't waste a crumb.

As she sat there, she wondered what Doris was doing. None of them had seen her since that morning's row, and as time had gone on, Doreen had begun to feel rather ashamed at the way she'd lashed out at her. The poor woman wasn't happy, according to Peggy, for she really was on her own now Anthony was married, and Ted refused to leave his bachelor flat above the Home and Colonial. For all her posh ideas and ridiculous posturing, she had no real friends, and even her family were reluctant to have anything to do with her.

Finishing the last of the coffee, Doreen paid her bill and headed for Havelock Road. She suspected she'd be sent off with a well-deserved flea in her ear, but she couldn't rest until she'd at least tried to mend the fences between them.

The house was just as she remembered, all neat and tidy, the windows and paint gleaming, the garden planted with military precision. She took a deep breath and rapped the knocker.

'Who is it?'

'It's Doreen. I've come to apologise.'

The door slowly opened and Doris stood there looking very different from her usual perfectly groomed self. Her face was devoid of make-up, her eyes were swollen and red from crying and she was still in her dressing gown at midday.

'Oh, Doris,' she breathed as she instinctively reached out to her. 'What's happened?'

Doris eased her arm from her sister's grip. 'I don't want the neighbours to see me like this,' she said gruffly. 'You'd better come in.'

Doreen stepped into the hall, deeply concerned. Realising her sister wanted no tactile sympathy, but thankful that she'd made the effort to come

343

here this morning, Doreen followed her into the magnificently appointed drawing room where the large bay window provided a panoramic view of the sea. She unbuttoned her coat and sat down as Doris stood by the window, her fingers restlessly twisting the belt of her dressing gown.

'What is it, Doris?' she asked quietly.

'I have spent my life doing my best for everyone,' she said after a long pause. 'But it seems I am to be vilified and abandoned by those who I thought were closest to me.'

Doreen left the couch and went to stand beside her, wanting to put her arm about her, but knowing it wouldn't be welcome. 'I'm so sorry for what I said the other week, Doris,' she said earnestly. 'It wasn't kind.'

Doris took a trembling breath and dabbed at her eyes with a lace-edged handkerchief. 'No, it wasn't,' she said thickly. 'But I have had time to consider the things you said, and I realise that I might have been rather harsh with you.'

Doreen waited for the apology but it didn't come. 'But you're very upset this morning,' she said. 'And it can't be over that silly spat we had, so what has happened? Why do you feel vilified and abandoned?'

Doris turned from the window and ran her hand over the highly polished piano before perching on the edge of a nearby armchair. 'I thought long and hard about what you said, Doreen, and so yesterday I went to see Edward.'

Doreen felt a twinge of guilt, because there was little doubt that the meeting hadn't gone well. 'That must have been quite hard,' she murmured.

344

Doris dabbed her eyes again and then mangled the handkerchief between her fingers. 'He wouldn't listen to me – refused to believe that I could make things better between us. He just said he was staying where he was and that I should get a letter from his solicitor by the end of the week about a divorce.' She swallowed and blinked back her tears. 'He said he realised it might cause a scandal, but he was willing to put things into place so that I could sue him for infidelity and abandonment.'

'Oh, Doris, I'm so sorry. How awful for you.'

'And then...' She swallowed hard as the tears began to roll down her pale cheeks. 'And then I received a telephone call from Anthony. He's been posted to somewhere ghastly in the Midlands and Susan is going with him.'

'But they'll be back the minute the war's over,' Doreen soothed. 'They have their own little house, remember?'

'That's not the point,' said Doris. 'Susan is expecting a baby, and I will not be able to have anything to do with it until they do return to Cliffehaven. And even that isn't guaranteed, because Susan is already talking about them moving to London to be near her parents once the war's over.'

'I don't know what to say, Doris,' she murmured. 'Only that whatever they decide to do after the war, you'll be able to visit them and get to know your grandchild.'

'Susan doesn't like me,' snapped Doris, 'and the feeling is mutual after the way she got between me and Anthony. She calls me interfering and

345

bossy, when all I was trying to do was make their wedding a very special occasion.'

Doreen had heard all about that in Peggy's letters, and, frankly, came down on Susan's side. But she said nothing and tentatively reached out to give her sister's shoulder an encouraging squeeze. 'I'm sure things will settle down between you once the baby's born.'

Doris blew her nose and dried her eyes. 'Maybe,' she said, 'but I won't be holding my breath. That girl will make certain that I have very little say in the raising of my grandchild.'

'Perhaps it's best not to give any advice and let her muddle through on her own,' said Doreen tactfully. 'New mothers can be very tricky, but she'll calm down and realise that you can be a great help and adviser.'

'Do you really think so?'

There was so much hope in those reddened eyes and the voice was so plaintive that Doreen put her arm around her sister and held her close. 'I'm sure of it,' she fibbed. 'Anthony will want you to play a part in that baby's life, and he'll see that you're not shut out.'

Doris didn't move from the embrace, but she was stiff and obviously felt awkward with such intimacy.

Doreen released her. 'I'll go and make you a nice cup of tea.'

'I'd prefer a whisky and soda,' said Doris. 'The bottles and glasses are in that cabinet.'

Doreen opened the cabinet door and was greeted by the sight of rows of bottles of spirits as well as mixers and two soda syphons. Doris certainly wasn't feeling the pinch of rationing and she wondered where it had all come from. Again, she said nothing, poured them both fairly hefty slugs of whisky and spritzed them with soda.

'Why don't you get dressed after that and come with me for a walk on the seafront? It's a beautiful day, and I don't like to think of you being all alone until Caroline comes home.'

'Caroline doesn't live here any more,' Doris said briskly. 'She and her friend decided they'd prefer to rent a flat so they could entertain and be more private.' Her tone was bitter. 'That's the thanks I get for all the things I did to make that girl feel at home here.'

'It was probably the pig's head that did it,' said Doreen in an effort to lighten the mood and get Doris to smile.

Doris's expression was stony. 'If you persist in making light of my situation then you should go,' she snapped. 'That damned pig was the start of all my troubles.'

Doreen didn't see how the pig could have had anything to do with Ted wanting a divorce, or Anthony and Susan going to the Midlands, but kept her thoughts to herself. She drained the whisky and set the glass on the coffee table. 'What's done is done,' she said on a sigh. 'Come on, Doris. Get dressed and we'll go for that walk.'

'I have no wish to go for a walk,' she said stiffly. 'I cannot possibly be seen in public until I've visited my beautician. There is enough sniggering behind my back as it is after that disastrous luncheon with Lady Chumley.'

'Oh, dear. Have they all closed ranks again?'

'It seems I have not been invited to the annual garden party this year. Neither have I been invited to the fundraising luncheon next week.' She stood up, her pale face now flushed with fury. 'You can tell that disgusting old man Reilly that it's all his fault – and furthermore, if I hear one more whisper about illicit meat, I shall go to the police and get him locked away.'

'Doris, Doris,' she soothed. 'There's no need to vent your spleen on Ron. He's not to blame for everything that's happened to you.'

Doris's eyes were blazing now and she climbed right onto the back of her high horse. 'That man is to blame for a great many things in this town,' she snapped. 'And as you seem to side with him, then I'd like you to leave.'

'Don't start all that again,' Doreen said mildly. 'We'll only end up having a row, and all I came for was to say I was sorry for the last one.'

'Just go, Doreen. Go back to Margaret's and live in squalor with those disreputable people you seem to want to defend. I don't need you or your dubious apology.'

Doreen gritted her teeth as she grabbed her bag and gas-mask box. She would not rise to it – was determined to quell the spike of fury that was urging her to shake Doris until her teeth rattled. 'I'll see myself out,' she muttered.

Peggy had finished reading the two airgraphs from Jim, so she tucked them back in their envelopes and got on with her knitting while Daisy played on the floor with her toys. The house was quiet with everyone out, and it was rather pleasant to have a moment of peace and quiet.

'Did Jim have anything exciting to report?' asked Cordelia, closing her partially read library book with a sniff of disgust.

'Not much, really,' Peggy admitted. 'It seems he's in charge of the workshop over there and is being sent back and forth to rescue trucks and things that have broken down. He was a bit fed up, I think, because he's had bellyache for a while, and the endless rain and heat are beginning to get him down. On top of all that, his mate Ernie has gone down with malaria, so he's had to go to hospital. But Jim's been kept very busy at work, and it sounds as if he's managed to get a swim each day in the river. There's entertainment laid on most nights in the mess, but he didn't appear to be too enthusiastic about it.'

'I certainly don't envy him working in the tropics,' said Cordelia, 'and of course one has to be very careful how food is prepared and cooked in places like that. It's little wonder he's got a touch of Delhi belly.'

'He's got a stomach lined with asbestos, has my Jim,' said Peggy fondly. 'He'll get over it soon enough.'

'Well of course he's feeling rough. So would you if you'd eaten something that was off.'

Peggy didn't correct her, but picked Daisy up from the floor and cleaned her hands and face. 'It's a lovely day out there,' she said loudly over her shoulder. 'Do you fancy a walk to the shops?'

'Pansies and hops? Whatever are you talking about, dear? They don't have those in India.'

That hearing aid had to be on the blink again.

349

'I said, would you fancy going to the shops?' she shouted.

'That's a very good idea,' Cordelia replied, struggling out of the fireside chair. 'I could do with some exercise and fresh air after being cooped up indoors for so long.' She picked up her library book and added it to the stack on the dresser. 'They can go back,' she said with a wrinkle of her nose. 'Most of them are complete drivel anyway.'

Peggy bit down on a smile, for she knew Cordelia liked a bit of blood and thunder in her reading, and considered soppy romances a waste of time. She dressed Daisy in her hat, coat and gloves and strapped her into the pram. 'I'll get our coats then.'

She returned from the hall and helped Cordelia with her coat, found her gas-mask box, walking stick, handbag and hat, and then put her own coat on. 'I thought that we'd have a look in the nearby shops to see if there's anything worth having, and then, once we've been to the library, perhaps we might take a bit of a stroll by the sea.'

'I had one earlier,' grunted Cordelia as she buttoned up her coat.

'Had what?'

'A wee. Really, Peggy, I'm a little too old to be reminded to use the lavatory every five minutes.'

Peggy gave a weary sigh, steadied her as she went down the steps, and then bumped the pram down them and slammed the back door. It was going to be one of those afternoons.

Doreen took her time to stroll back along the seafront and up the hill to Beach View. She needed the opportunity to calm down after that run-in with Doris. Really, she thought, my sister is the most irritating, overbearing, deluded woman I ever met. She simply couldn't help but lash out, even though she knew she was in the wrong. Well, that's the last time I try and mend fences, Doreen thought crossly as she plodded up the steep hill. She can stew in her own juice.

She arrived back at Beach View and soon realised she had the house to herself, so she tidied up the kitchen and made a fish paste sandwich and a cup of tea for her lunch. The kitten sat expectantly at her feet as she ate the sandwich, her blue eyes watching every mouthful until Doreen felt so guilty that she put a smidgeon of the paste on her finger and offered it to her.

Queenie gave it a good sniff, then turned her back on both Doreen and the fish paste and went under the table to begin her daily ablutions.

'Fussy little thing,' said Doreen fondly. 'You're as bad as Evie. She doesn't like fish paste either – or indeed most things.' At the thought of her eldest daughter's picky eating habits, Doreen wondered how on earth she was managing on the ration.

She finished the sandwich, washed the plates that were in the sink and then wondered what to do next. It wasn't much past two and none of the girls would be back before six. She came to the conclusion that it was the perfect time to sit down and write letters to her daughters and to Archie's mother. She'd decided on her walk that if the MOD were willing to give her extra leave, then she would take it. Perhaps even use it to travel to Wales to see her girls. With her thoughts on how to arrange a travel permit and ticket, Doreen headed for the stairs so she could fetch her writing pad.

The knock on the door startled her as she was halfway up to her room, but she ran down again quickly and opened the door. Her spirits plummeted instantly when she saw who was standing on the doorstep. 'Eddie. What are you doing here?'

He took off his brown hat and smiled winningly. 'Hello, Doreen. I was rather hoping for a warmer welcome, but at least I've found you at last.'

Unimpressed, Doreen remained standing in the doorway. 'What do you want, Eddie?'

'Now, Doreen,' he coaxed, running his hand over his thick fair hair. 'Is that any way to welcome someone who's been halfway across England trying to find you?' He took a step towards her, his smile still very bright, but not quite reaching his eyes. 'Aren't you going to ask me in?'

'You can say what you've come to say right there on the doorstep,' she said firmly.

He gave a rather dramatic sigh. 'You don't make things any easier for me, do you, Doreen?'

'I don't see why I should,' she replied. 'We've been divorced for nearly four years and I haven't seen hide nor hair of you since.'

'Hardly my fault, old thing. There is a war on, you know, and I've been very busy.'

Doreen regarded him with little affection, being reminded of what had first attracted her to him when she'd been naive and stupid – and why she'd divorced him. The smile was still the same;

352

the easy-going talk was all too familiar – as was the smell of his cologne – but now she knew from hard-won experience that there was nothing behind the smile, the talk and the nice clothes, and it grated. He clearly wasn't in any of the forces, so what he'd been busy at for the past four years, she had no idea and didn't really want to know. It was probably illegal if he was running true to form.

'Let me in, Doreen,' he wheedled. 'I've come a long way to find you, and there are things we need to talk about.'

'What things?'

'The girls, really.'

Doreen felt a stab of unease. 'What about the girls?' she asked sharply.

'Let me in and I'll tell you.' The charming smile slipped and the blue eyes narrowed. 'I'm sure you don't want to hold this sort of private conversation on the doorstep.'

The unease grew as she reluctantly stood aside to let him in. 'In here,' she said, leading the way into the kitchen.

He surveyed the room with undisguised displeasure. 'Good grief, Doreen. You've certainly gone down in the world. What *is* this dump?'

Considering the fact he'd left their home to live in a succession of seedy bedsits, he had a damned cheek to denigrate her family home – which he'd refused to visit during their ill-fated marriage. 'It suits me just fine,' she said shortly. 'How did you find me, anyway?'

'I tracked you down to Kent and managed to persuade the delightful Mrs Fletcher to give me the address of where you'd gone for your holiday.' He brushed one of the kitchen chairs with his gloves, much like Doris had done, and then sat down and placed his hat carefully on the table.

Phyllis Fletcher should have kept her mouth shut, she thought furiously. But then Eddie probably put on the charm and the silly woman had fallen for it. Doreen regarded him with loathing, damned if she'd offer him tea or more than five minutes of her time. 'You said you wanted to talk about the girls, so get on with it, Eddie. I don't have all afternoon.'

'I want them to come and live with me,' he said.

'Over my dead body,' she retorted.

'Yes, well, that could be arranged, but it would be a bit dramatic and messy, don't you think?' He regarded her thoughtfully. 'You look older,' he said quietly, 'and tired. Are you not well? Is that why you're here?'

Doreen bristled, but kept her temper. 'Don't change the subject, Eddie. You are not having the girls to live with you, now or ever. They're happy and settled in Wales, and when this war is over I'll have enough money to buy a proper home for them.'

'But I can give them that now,' he said. 'You see, I'm getting married again, and Muriel has already got a well-set-up place in Buckinghamshire. The girls will be very safe there, I assure you.'

'The courts gave me custody. You can't just go against that.'

'Oh, but I can, you see. If I'm married and have a settled home, I'm fully entitled to have my children with me on a more permanent basis.'

'Never,' she hissed. 'Never in a million years.'

'The house is very nice,' he continued as if she hadn't spoken. 'It's large and rambling, with an acre of land, and positively stuffed with antiques. There's a good school nearby, and the girls can get to know Muriel's daughter, so they'll even have a playmate.'

Doreen could suddenly picture the whole scene. 'I suppose Muriel is a rich widow?'

His smile widened, showing some expensive dental work on teeth that had once been slightly crooked. 'She certainly is – and very attractive too for a woman in her forties.'

'Well, neither of you are going to get your hands on my girls,' she said flatly. 'So you'd better go back to Muriel and enjoy your new and very comfortable life.'

'Ah, well,' he said as he studied his nails. 'There's the rub, you see, Doreen. Muriel has expectations, and I'd hate to disappoint her by returning empty-handed.'

Doreen suddenly knew where this conversation had been heading since the moment it started. This was the Eddie of old – the Eddie who was always after money. She decided to play along with him.

'What sort of expectations? Most women wouldn't want to take on someone else's children unless it was all legal and above board. And I will fight you tooth and nail, Edward Grey, you can be certain of that.'

'I could make it very difficult for you to do so,' he said casually. 'After all, you're a single woman

355

now in charge of two innocent little girls, and should your reputation become tarnished in any way, then it won't look good for you in court.'

'My reputation is not and never will be tarnished,' she snapped back at him.

He raised his fair eyebrows. 'Really? But you've recently spent a whole week with some sailor in a London hotel, Doreen. I hardly think...'

His words hit her like a thunderbolt. 'How did you know about that?' she managed.

'I hired a private detective and had you followed,' he returned blithely.

Doreen bunched her fists. 'How dare you poke and pry into my private business?'

'Well, it won't stay private for very long once it gets to court.'

'You bastard,' she hissed. 'You absolute bastard.'

'Sticks and stones, Doreen. Sticks and stones,' he said airily. 'You can swear at me all you like, but that doesn't alter the fact that you're an unfit mother who sleeps with sailors.'

Doreen was so furious she couldn't speak.

'But there is a way around this dilemma,' he said quietly.

She regarded him with loathing. 'What way?'

He suddenly couldn't look her in the eye. 'If you give me a hundred pounds, then I'll forget all about taking the girls, and stay out of your hair.'

The hatred for him was so intense it knotted in her stomach and made her feel sick. 'So it *was* about money after all,' she breathed. 'It always was with you, wasn't it? It's the only thing you've ever cared about.'

'Money makes the world go round, Doreen. I

just happen to be a bit strapped for cash at the moment, and Muriel is expecting me to close a business deal and bring home the bacon, so to speak.'

'I haven't got that sort of money,' she said flatly.

'Of course you have. You're earning well with the MOD, and I wouldn't mind betting you've squirrelled away a tidy sum over the years.'

He knew her too well and she struggled to keep her expression bland. 'A hundred pounds is a fortune. Of course I don't have it.'

'Then you'd better find it before tomorrow.'

'And if I don't?'

'I shall go to Wales and see my daughters, and make sure they learn all about what you've been up to while they've been conveniently sent away. I shall also tell them about Muriel and the house, and my plans to bring them to live with me.' His smile held no warmth. 'And you know how much those girls adore me, Doreen. They'll be putty in my hands.'

She regarded him coldly, noting the familiar signs of desperation she'd got so used to during their disastrous marriage. This had never been about the children. He was in trouble and needed money to get himself out of a tight corner – probably because he was deeply in debt to someone too powerful and mean to defy.

'I never imagined you could stoop so low as to use your children as a way of blackmailing me,' she said, keeping a tight rein on the fury that was bubbling very close to the surface. 'You're an utterly despicable *rat*.'

Her loathing washed over him like water off a

duck's back. 'I'll come back for the money to-morrow morning, eleven sharp,' he said, picking up his hat and gloves.

'Not here, you won't. I'll meet you outside the Post Office in the High Street.'

He smiled as he put on his hat. 'I knew you'd see sense in the end,' he murmured and headed for the hall.

Doreen slammed the front door after him, leaned against it and then let rip with every swear word she knew. Having got that out of her system, she went back into the kitchen, lit a cigarette and tried to figure out how on earth to get that money, and more importantly, how to stop him from using the children to blackmail her again – because he would, and she had to protect them from him at all costs.

18

Ivy was enjoying her ten-minute tea break, sitting outside the canteen on one of the benches in the afternoon sun and dreaming about Andy. They'd met at every chance they could over the past two weeks, and had had the promised fish supper, gone dancing and been to the pictures, where they'd sat holding hands in the back row. He was a smashing kisser, and she felt quite gooey at the memory. He'd also never tried to take liberties, so she was beginning to trust her instincts that he was a genuinely lovely bloke and she was a very lucky girl.

She sipped her tea and wondered what they'd do tomorrow night when he was off duty. There was a dance at the Town Hall which the Americans were laying on for some of their boys who'd just got back from North Africa, which meant there'd be loads of lovely food and drink and a big band to dance to. She loved doing the jitterbug, and was getting quite good at it, but by the end of the night she was always completely knackered. Still, being that tired meant she slept like a log and didn't dream.

'Oy, Ivy. Are you with us?'

Her thoughts scattered as she felt the nudge in her ribs. Ruby Clark had very sharp elbows. 'I were having a nice dream, thanks very much,' she replied.

Ruby grinned. 'Yeah, and I bet it were about that fella of yours, and all. He's a smasher, ain't he? Mind you, he ain't as 'andsome as my Mike.'

Ivy liked Ruby and they'd palled up on their first day at the plane factory during their lunch break. Ruby came from Bow originally, but now she lived with her mum, Ethel, in a bungalow just a few hundred yards away from the estate. She'd been working in the tool factory which had suffered the same fate as the munitions one, and when they realised they also had Beach View and Peggy in common, since Ruby had stayed at Beach View before her mum had joined her in Cliffehaven, it was as if they'd been friends for years.

Ruby was engaged to her Canadian chap and wore his ring on a chain around her neck while at work. They were hoping to get married, but government red tape was proving to be a complete nightmare. Mike was good-looking, all right, but Andy was taller and much fitter – but then Ivy was rather biased.

'Are you going to the dance at the Town Hall tomorrow?' Ivy asked. 'Only I thought it might be fun if we made up a four again.'

'Yeah, sounds blindin,' but we might be a bit late, 'cos me mum's cooking a special tea.'

Ivy had met Ethel, who reminded her so much of her own mum it made her feel homesick – but she was ever so nice, it was easy to like her. 'Celebrating something?'

'Sort of.' She leaned in closer so she wouldn't be overheard by the other girls clustered on the nearby benches. 'She got a letter this morning telling her me stepdad bought it in Tunisia.'

Ivy frowned. 'You don't seem too upset about it. Funny thing to celebrate.'

Ruby's expression darkened. 'He were a mean bastard, handy with his fists and all, just like the toerag I were once married to. Good riddance to bad rubbish, is what I say. Me mum's gotta new life here, and if Stan plays his cards right now she's free, I reckon they'll be in clover.'

Ivy giggled. 'Stan's all right, ain't he?'

'Yeah,' sighed Ruby. 'He's a diamond, and I know he'll never hit her or go off with other women. Just like I know my Mike will always be faithful.'

'Andy's the same,' Ivy replied dreamily.

'Bloody hell,' muttered Fat Beryl, who'd obviously been listening in. 'You'd think you were walkin' out with Clark Gable and Errol Flynn the way you're goin' on about those two.' She gave a snort of derision.

Ivy and Ruby were immediately defensive. 'So?' said Ivy. 'At least we got fellas, unlike some I could mention.'

'Some fellas,' she sneered. 'One's only got one eye – and the other's deaf. I wouldn't fancy either of them.'

'And they wouldn't give you the time of day,' said Ruby. 'Let alone fancy you, you spotty cow.'

Beryl's face reddened beneath the awful acne. 'You take that back, Ruby Clark, before I lump yer one.'

'Yeah? You and whose army?' retorted Ruby menacingly. 'Just you remember what I done to my old man before you start on me.'

Beryl clearly did remember that Ruby had put her late and unlamented husband into hospital for several weeks by hitting him over the head with a heavy skillet. 'All right, keep yer 'air on,' she muttered.

Ruby and Ivy simmered down and exchanged knowing looks. Beryl had a huge chip on her shoulder because she was fat, spotty and un-popular. She had a gob bigger than the Blackwall Tunnel and a spiteful tongue, and all the girls did their best to avoid her. Ivy pulled a magazine out of the back pocket of her dungarees and they huddled together, deliberately shutting her out.

'You might think your bloke is the bee's knees,' Beryl said, poking Ivy in the back with a hard finger. 'But I know things about him you don't.'

Ivy refused to rise to the bait and continued to

look at the pictures in the magazine.

'You can't trust any man,' Beryl continued slyly. 'They're only after one thing and if you don't put out, they're off.'

Ivy and Ruby exchanged glances. Beryl was clearly on the wind-up and best ignored.

'You need to keep yer eyes open, Ivy. That fella of yours ain't all he appears to be.'

Unable to resist, Ivy bunched her fists and turned to face her. 'What you mean by that?'

'I mean he can't be trusted, gel. That's what.'

Ivy saw the sly look in her eyes and the nasty smirk on her lips, knew Beryl was trying to get the rise out of her, and that she'd succeeded. 'You don't know nothing of the sort,' she snapped. 'Just because you ain't got a bloke don't give you the right to slag off mine.'

Beryl's eyes were gleeful as she shrugged the comment off. 'I'm better off on me own without 'aving some toerag two-timing me,' she replied.

'Put a sock in it, Beryl. My Andy ain't a two-timer. He ain't got the chance, anyway, 'cos we're together every minute we're both free from work.'

'Oh, is that right?' Her smile was cunning. 'So he were working last night, then?'

Ivy didn't like the look of that smirk or the feeling she was getting that perhaps Beryl *did* know something. But she masked it by lifting her chin and challenging her with a glare. 'He's been on night shift all week – though what it's got to do with you, I don't know.'

'I don't care one way or the other,' Beryl replied. 'But if he were working last night, as he told you, what were he doing tucked up nice and cosy in the Crown with some blonde piece?'

Ivy felt a dart of fear as she saw the triumph in the other girl's eyes. 'It weren't him,' she snapped. 'You got it wrong.'

Beryl's expression was one of a cat who'd eaten the cream. 'If you say so. But I know what I saw.'

Ivy just about held on to her fear and her temper. 'You're just trying to wind me up 'cos you can't stand to see other people happy,' she retorted.

'It don't matter to me one way or the other what he's been up to,' Beryl said with a smirk. 'But you'll soon find out I were right.'

The klaxon went to warn them they had to return to work. Ivy gathered up her things, furious that Beryl had managed to get under her skin, and worried sick that perhaps she *had* been too taken with him to see what was under her very nose.

'Don't let her get to you,' advised Ruby as they walked into the huge hangar. 'She's just jealous and likes stirring up trouble. Your Andy's a good bloke and I'm sure that was all just a pack of lies.'

'But what if it's true? I don't think I could take that, Ruby.'

'Then tell him what Beryl said and ask him straight out.' Ruby stopped by the huge racks of tools and pulled out a large drill. 'Better to know, Ivy. But I reckon you'll both end up laughing about it. Andy wouldn't do that to you, I just know he wouldn't.' She squeezed Ivy's hand and went off to her own work area.

Ruby's words had been a small comfort, but the seeds of doubt that Beryl had sown so liberally

363

were beginning to flourish, and try as hard as she might, Ivy couldn't dismiss them. She returned to fixing large metal studs firmly into the fuselage, her thoughts skittering over what she should do.

Ask him and maybe have to face an unpleasant truth – or don't ask him and always be suspicious? Either way, things would never be the same again. There might very well be a perfectly reasonable explanation as to why he was at the Crown with another girl – but at the moment she couldn't think of a single one that didn't point to the fact that he'd been lying to her.

Doreen had paced the kitchen for some time after Eddie had left, her thoughts chasing one another as she tried desperately to think how she could get that much money together. She knew exactly how much she had in her Post Office account, and it wasn't nearly enough – and even if she did manage to scrape up the rest, there was no guarantee that Eddie would keep his word and stay out of their lives.

As the clock ticked away on the mantelpiece she realised she'd have to hurry to get to the Post Office before it closed. She ran upstairs to her bedroom and opened her underwear drawer. There beneath the slips, bras, vests and cami-knickers were the savings books she'd guarded so jealously over the years. One for her, and one each for the girls.

She slumped down on the bed and flicked through them, her heart heavy at the thought that she would have to take money out of all of them if she was to raise anything close to the amount Eddie was demanding. But she felt quite sick to think that all her hard-earned savings were to be handed over to the deceitful, conniving and utterly untrustworthy Edward Grey – who would no doubt just hand it over to some thug he was in debt to.

Her stomach clenched and the bile was bitter in her throat. She just made it to the toilet on the lower landing before she was very sick. She flushed it away, closed the lid and slumped down. The sweat was cold on her skin, making her shiver as the knots in her stomach began to ease, but she still felt queasy and as if she'd put been through the wringer.

Once she'd got her breath back and felt more able to move about, she checked the time and stumbled into the bathroom to wash her face and clean her teeth. Catching sight of her reflection in the mirror, she grimaced. She looked dreadful – her hair was lank, her face was pale and drawn and there were shadows under her eyes. It was quite shocking that being confronted by Eddie for less than half an hour could reduce her to this.

Angry that she'd let him get to her in this way, she returned to her room and picked up the savings books. There was no alternative but to pay him, but even if she emptied all three accounts, there would still be a shortfall.

Her gaze drifted to the bedside drawer where the last of Archie's money lay in his wallet. She wouldn't touch that – couldn't bear to endure the shame she'd feel if she gave Eddie even one of those pound notes. Besides, there were only five in there after she'd paid for the headstone.

'He'll just have to be satisfied with what I've got in mine,' she muttered as she threw the children's books back into the drawer and slammed it shut.

Running down the stairs, thankful that no one was there to witness her utter despair, she pulled on her coat, snatched up her handbag and the wretched gas-mask box she was sick of carting about, and headed for the back door. Not wanting to bump into the others who might be on their way home in Camden Road, she took the back streets that wound through the houses on the hill and eventually opened out into the High Street.

There was a queue at the Post Office and she tried to be patient, but it was very frustrating when one of the tellers closed his window and disappeared into the back, for it meant the wait would now be even longer. With a sigh of exasperation, she let the chatter go on around her and silently urged the elderly woman manning the solitary counter to get a ruddy move on. This was hard enough without having to prolong the agony.

It was finally her turn, and she pushed the savings book under the grille along with her identity card. 'I want to close the account,' she said.

'That's a great deal of money,' the woman said, eyeing the total. 'I don't know if we have the funds to do that today.'

Doreen gritted her teeth. 'But I need it today,' she said. 'Surely you keep enough for things like this?'

'There is a war on, Mrs Grey,' she said solemnly. 'And for security reasons we are advised not to keep too much cash on the premises. Also, it is pension day, and that's where most of it has gone.'

Doreen was aware of the growing restlessness in the queue behind her. 'Then how much *can* you give me?'

The woman opened the drawer beneath her desk and began to flick through the notes. 'I can let you have forty.' She peered at her through the screen. 'Are you sure you need quite so much, Mrs Grey? The government has, quite rightly, urged us all to save, and a sum like this–'

'It's my money,' said Doreen firmly. 'And I have a perfect right to take as much as I want.'

The expression hardened with disapproval. 'Then you'll have to come back tomorrow for the rest.'

Doreen nodded impatiently and shuffled from one foot to the other as the woman took an age to count out each of the forty notes, and then double-check. As they were grudgingly pushed beneath the grille, she scooped them up and stuffed them in her purse while her book was carefully written in and stamped. 'Will I be able to have the rest first thing tomorrow?'

'Lunchtime would be best. Friday's pay day, and *most* people are only too keen to add to their National Savings Accounts and Government Bonds.'

Doreen heard the condemnation as she took her passbook and identity card. Her face was burning as she walked past the gawping queue and left the Post Office. She felt humiliated and tearful, but most of all, she simmered with anger. Eddie had put her in an impossible position. She dared not call his bluff, because she wouldn't put it past him

367

to go to Wales and drip poison in Evie and Joyce's ears – but paying him meant that her plans to go and see them would have to be shelved. As for her dreams of buying a little house after the war, they were ashes.

Peggy had returned to find Beach View deserted, and she'd wondered where Doreen had gone. She'd been doing a lot of walking lately, which seemed to have made her feel better, so she had to assume she was up on the hills with Ron. It was something they'd done together before Doreen had left home for the bright lights of London, and as her leave was due to end soon, she probably wanted to recapture those moments of freedom before she returned to her office.

Cordelia was very tired after their long walk, and they hadn't made it down to the seafront because Peggy realised she couldn't possibly manage that hill. She helped her off with her things and settled her into the fireside chair, where she promptly fell asleep. Peggy smiled with deep affection and left her to it.

Queenie meowed and wound herself round her legs, so she gave her a spoonful of cat food and refreshed her water bowl. The kitten purred as she ate, and once she'd finished, she allowed Peggy to give her a bit of a cuddle before she got bored and struggled out of her arms to return to her perch on the shelf.

Peggy pulled on her wrap-round pinafore and began to prepare the chops for everyone's tea. There weren't really enough to go round, even though Fran was on lates and would eat at the hospital, so she sliced off some of the leg meat into a fillet and coated everything in a mixture of egg and breadcrumbs. She still had a nice pot of pig fat to roast potatoes in, and there was a lovely cabbage in the larder alongside a few very early carrots.

She'd prepared everything and had just sat down for a cup of tea and a fag when Doreen came up the cellar steps. One look told her that her sister had not been walking the hills, but was in a furious bate about something.

'Sit down before you explode, Doreen,' she said mildly. 'Then, once you've got your breath back, you can tell me what's eating you.'

Doreen shrugged off her coat and dumped everything on a nearby chair. She sat down and eased her feet out of her shoes. 'Is it that obvious?'

Peggy pushed the cup of tea towards her. 'I'm afraid it is. Want to talk about it?'

Doreen's gaze slid away and she concentrated on sipping her tea as Ron came through the back door and stumped up the stairs with Harvey at his heels.

Peggy gave Ron some tea as well, then as Harvey collapsed wearily on the hearthrug, she sat back down again. 'Doreen was just about to tell me what's eating her,' she said with a warning look to keep his trap shut.

'Oh, aye? So who's been upsetting you then, Dorry?' he asked around his pipe stem.

'It was my own fault,' she said. 'I went to see Doris to apologise.'

Ron's eyebrows shot up and Peggy gasped.

'Whatever for?' she asked. 'She was appallingly rude and deserved everything she got.' Peggy eyed her younger sister, surprised to see her so out of sorts. Run-ins with Doris usually enlivened her. 'It would have been better to let her stew in her own juice,' she said dismissively.

'That's what I thought for a while, but I felt guilty, Peggy. And now I feel even worse.'

Peggy frowned as Ron snorted. 'Why?'

As Doreen described how shocked she'd been at their sister's appearance, then told them about Ted's determination to have a divorce, the de-camping of Caroline, and Anthony's imminent move to the Midlands with Suzy, Peggy felt slightly more sympathetic towards Doris. As awful as she could be, Doris genuinely regretted the break-up of her marriage and, of course, adored Anthony.

'That must be hard for her to take,' she said, 'but life must go on, and Doris has to learn that she can't possibly keep tabs on poor Anthony for the rest of his life.'

'I know. But the fact that Suzy's expecting has really put the tin lid on it.'

Peggy brightened immediately. 'Suzy's expecting? Oh, how wonderful. She and Anthony must be thrilled.' She glanced over to the dresser and the pile of knitting patterns, her mind already working on what she could make to give her before she left.

'I don't think Doris feels quite that way,' said Doreen. 'She seems determined to believe that Suzy won't let her have anything to do with the baby – and as they'll be in the Midlands until at least the end of the war, she won't get a chance to see it either.'

'Oh, dear,' sighed Peggy. 'Poor old Doris. Life has been unkind to her, hasn't it?' She stubbed out her cigarette in the Guinness ashtray Ron had filched from the Fishermen's Club. 'But then she made a rod for her own back, the way she insisted on trying to take over their wedding plans, and making it clear that she felt Suzy had come between her and her only son.'

Doreen nodded. 'I got the impression from what she said that she still feels that way.'

'Then more fool her,' rumbled Ron as he pushed away from the table. 'That wee Suzy has been the making of that boy. Mark my words, your sister is bringing a whole heap of trouble on her head if she keeps up that sort of thinking.' He clenched the pipe between his teeth and went down the steps to his room.

Doreen drained the cup of tea and changed the subject. 'By the way, Peggy, my leave has been extended for another fortnight.'

'But that's marvellous. Will you be going to see the girls?'

'I did think I would, but having looked into the travel arrangements, it seems I'll need endless permits to travel all that way, which could take time to come through – and the few trains that go there are unreliable and often cancelled. So I'll just have to make do by writing lots of letters.'

Peggy noted the sadness in her, reached across and took her hand. 'I'm so sorry, Doreen. This damned war has a great deal to answer for, split-ting up families and bringing so much heartache to everyone.'

'Yes,' she murmured. 'Still, there's not much any of us can do about that except just keep on going.' She straightened in the chair. 'I feel a bit of a fraud staying here, to be honest, Peg. I'm much better now, so I'll probably return to Halstead in a few days anyway. There's a lot of work going on there and they'll need me.'

'Stay a while longer, Doreen,' Peggy pleaded. 'It's been so lovely to have you home.'

Doreen returned the pressure on her fingers and then collected up her things. 'We'll see,' she murmured before she left the kitchen.

Peggy sat at the table for a while after she'd left. The spat with Doris couldn't possibly have upset her that much, she reasoned. Something else was clearly worrying Doreen, and Peggy meant to get to the bottom of it.

She finished her cup of tea and began to set the table. The thought that dear little Suzy was expecting thrilled her. She and Anthony made a lovely couple and deserved to be happy. Peggy just hoped that they'd call in before they left, for she hadn't seen much of either of them since their wedding.

Rita came flying up the steps into the kitchen and dragged off her coat to reveal a pretty woollen dress and cardigan. 'I'm sorry, Peggy, but I'm running late and will eat at the fire station tonight. I forgot I was on night duty, what with all the excitement of having Matt to myself all day.'

Peggy smiled as the girl dashed into the hall and thudded up the stairs. Rita never did anything slowly, and she suspected that the room she shared with Ivy now resembled a jumble sale – and a very untidy one at that.

Smiling indulgently, she put the vegetables on to boil and slid the tray of crusted pork into the oven. There would be an extra helping for Ron now – and why not? He'd certainly earned it.

She was humming quietly as Sarah came home and was almost knocked flying by a hurtling Rita. 'I can't stop, Auntie Peg,' Rita said as she pulled on her uniform jacket. 'But will you tell Ivy I've got something important to tell her?'

'Oh, yes. And what's that?'

'It's nothing for you to worry about, really it isn't. It'll keep until morning.' With that she was out of the door, her heavy boots clumping on the garden path as she ran towards the gate.

Peggy's curiosity was piqued, but, she reasoned, it was probably nothing as Rita had said. Those two girls were as thick as thieves, and she was sure that if it was anything serious, Rita would have confided in her, rush or no rush.

Ivy knew very well that Peggy had sharp eyes and could tell if something was wrong in an instant, so she determinedly plastered a smile on her face as she climbed the steps into the kitchen. 'Hello,' she said brightly. 'That smells lovely. I'm so hungry I could eat a horse.'

'It's pork chop and roast spuds,' said Peggy, giving her a hug. 'Have you had a good day?'

Ivy took off her blanket coat and kicked off her boots. 'The same as always. Me and Ruby had one of the other girls to sort out, but the rest of the day was like usual.'

There had been an incident a few days ago in which Ivy had tussled with another girl over something and nothing. She was a bit of a scrapper, was her Ivy, but for all that, Peggy couldn't help but be fond of her. 'I hope you haven't been fighting again, Ivy,' she said, trying to look stern. 'The last time you nearly got the sack.'

'It weren't my fault. She started it. Weren't my fault today either – and no, I didn't pull her hair or try to scratch her eyes out, even though I really wanted to.' She gave Peggy her cheekiest grin to fend off any further questions, for she didn't want to tell her the reason behind the falling-out with Beryl. 'Is Rita home yet?'

'She shot in and shot out again. Forgot she was on nights after a day out with Matt. She said to tell you she's got something important she wants to talk to you about.'

Ivy stiffened and her pulse began to thunder in her ears. 'What were that then?' she asked, as casually as she could.

'She didn't say. I expect it's about cancelling her ticket for the dance tomorrow night. She obviously won't be able to go now she's on nights.'

'Yeah, probably.' Ivy picked up her boots and coat. 'I'll go and 'ave a wash and get changed,' she said. 'I'm meetin' Ruby for a drink later.' She was doing nothing of the sort, but Peggy didn't need to know what she was actually planning.

'That's nice. I'm so glad you've become friends. Ruby's a sweet girl, and I rather miss not having her around.'

Ivy nodded. 'I suppose you 'eard about her stepdad?' Peggy obviously hadn't, for she frowned.

'Well, he's dead. So Ruby's hoping Ethel and Stan will finally make it legal.' She flashed her dimples. 'After all,' she added, 'they've almost been living together for a while now.'

'That would be wonderful,' sighed Peggy. 'Stan's been a widower for too long and Ethel needs to have a man like him in her life after what she went through with that other toerag.' She gave a little chuckle of happiness. 'It's lovely to get so much good news in one day.'

Ivy listened as Peggy told her about Suzy's coming baby and Doreen's extended leave. She let her ramble on, only taking in enough to keep track of the one-sided conversation as her thoughts skittered over what Rita might have to tell her – and her plans for tonight.

'Ivy? Ivy, you haven't been listening to a word I've said.'

Startled, Ivy looked back at Peggy and then quickly looked away again. 'Course I have,' she replied.

'Ivy, is something troubling you, dear? You don't look quite the ticket, if you don't mind me saying so.'

'Nah, I'm fine,' she said brightly. 'It's just been a long day, that's all.' She clutched her boots and coat to her chest, aware that Peggy was watching her closely – clearly suspicious that something wasn't right – and she hurried upstairs to avoid any further questions. She needed to prepare for the evening, but she really wasn't looking forward to it at all.

Ivy helped wash the dishes after the lovely meal,

and then spent some time helping Cordelia with her tangle of knitting. Eventually, realising she couldn't put her plans off any longer, she pulled on her coat and left the house.

The blackout meant that it was quite tricky to negotiate the potholes and cracks in the pavement, and to avoid the lampposts which suddenly seemed to loom in front of her. There wasn't even a moon tonight to guide her, and so it took a while to reach the fire station, which was at the bottom of Camden Road. The large building appeared to be in darkness, but she knew that behind those blackout curtains Rita and the others would be tending their engines and preparing for any emergency that might arise.

Her heart was thudding as she crept along the broad expanse of forecourt to the pale bead of light coming through the keyhole in the big double doors. It was a small hole and the view of the main area was restricted, but as she watched, she began to count the men and women who walked past. She knew from Rita that there were eight full-time firemen in each watch, the volunteers and part-timers only coming in when they were needed. So far she'd counted seven, but there was no sign of Andy, and she wondered if perhaps he was in the upstairs office with his chief, John Hicks.

And then John appeared and gathered his crew together. 'Fireman Rawlings won't be with us again tonight,' he said. 'So I've called in Fred Sharp to keep up the numbers, and I want...'

Ivy had heard enough. She stepped back from the keyhole, her legs trembling so badly she could barely stand. Again? He wouldn't be there *again?* Just how many times had Andy not turned up for work? What the hell was he playing at? The awful realisation that Beryl's snide revelations were actually rooted in some kind of truth made her feel quite ill.

She took deep breaths of the sharp night air and then pushed away from the wall and headed for the High Street, the anger and hurt lending her speed. Reaching the turn-off that would take her to his billet in South Street, Ivy's mood darkened. If he was in, then she'd make him tell her why he'd lied to her – and if he wasn't, then she'd go to the Crown and see for herself just what he was up to.

She checked the numbers on the two-up, two-down terraced houses and came to a stop outside 55. The blackouts were pulled across, and she couldn't hear any noises coming from the house, but that didn't mean no one was there. She walked along the short, tiled path to the front door and rapped the knocker, her heart thudding as she waited.

The door opened and a middle-aged woman appeared in a floral, wrap-round pinafore and tatty slippers. 'Yes, love?' she asked.

'Is Andy in?'

'Sorry, ducks, you just missed him. He's gone for a drink at the Crown.'

Ivy's mouth was dry and she had to swallow before she could reply. 'Was he with anyone?' she asked, hating herself for sounding so feeble.

'Someone did call for him earlier, but I was in the kitchen so I didn't see who it was.' The faded blue eyes regarded her with some kindliness. 'I expect it was just one of his friends from the fire station,' she said gently.

'Thanks,' Ivy muttered. She hurried back down the path and broke into a run as she headed back towards the High Street and the Crown.

There were knots of servicemen and women standing on the pavement outside the pub door, drinking, smoking and generally making a lot of noise. Ivy could hear someone crashing out a tune on a piano and a raucous sing-song going on inside, and as she pushed through the door she was met by a wall of noise and a blast of fag smoke and spilled beer. The place was positively heaving.

The atmosphere was very similar to the boozer in Hackney where she'd spent many hours as a kid, sitting on the doorstep with a bottle of pop and a few chips waiting for her parents to take her home, and on any other night she would have joined in with the fun. But now her whole focus was on finding Andy.

She weaved through the tightly packed saloon bar, ignoring the banter from the men and slapping away fingers that tried to pinch or fondle her backside as her gaze darted over the faces and round the bodies to see if he was there. A few tables were set with benches at the far end, but still she couldn't see him, and she began to wonder if she should just go home and confront him tomorrow. After all, if he was with a mate from the fire station, she'd look pretty daft. And yet the fact that he'd lied to her about being at work rankled, and she needed to hear his explanation.

'Hello, Ivy.'

Ruby was at her shoulder, and her doleful expression didn't augur well. 'What you doing 'ere, mate?' Ivy asked.

'The same as you, I expect,' said Ruby. 'Thought I'd come and 'ave a butcher's to check whether Andy's here.'

'Well he ain't at work, that's for sure.' Ivy quickly told Ruby what she'd been up to. 'But he ain't here neither,' she said. 'Must'a gone to a different boozer.'

Ruby took her hand and held it tight, her expression sorrowful. 'No, love, he's here all right – and he ain't alone, neither.'

Ivy felt her heart miss a beat. 'Who's he with?' she managed.

'I'm sorry, mate, but you'd better come and see fer yourself,' Ruby said quietly below the surrounding racket. 'They're in the lounge bar.'

'He's with a woman, ain't he?'

Ruby didn't reply but kept tight hold of Ivy's hand, and they began to push and shove their way through the melee by the bar. They reached the narrow corridor leading into the more salubrious lounge. The wall dividing the lounge from the rest of the downstairs was half-panelled in dark wood and topped with thick stained glass, and Ivy looked away, suddenly reluctant to have her worst fears confirmed.

'Over there,' said Ruby as she pointed. 'By the fireplace.'

Ivy hesitated momentarily and then looked through the thick swirl of glass, saw them immediately and turned away without a word. Holding back the tears and the hurt, she pushed and elbowed her way through the chaos of the other bar and wrestled to get past the heavy door and out to the pavement. She'd been so sure of him – had begun to trust him – but he was nothing more than a rat-faced cheat.

'It's all right, mate, I'm 'ere,' soothed Ruby as she put her arms round her. 'You 'ave a good cry and get him outta your system.'

'He ain't worth crying for,' Ivy rasped, struggling to keep her tears at bay. She eased herself from Ruby's embrace. 'Lying, two-timing pig. He's lucky I didn't storm in there and tip that beer all over his flaming 'ead.'

'I was a bit surprised you didn't,' said Ruby with a chuckle. 'If it were me, I'd 'ave upended the bloody table over the pair of them.'

Ivy knew her friend was only trying to cheer her up, but her heart was so heavy she doubted she'd ever smile again. 'At least I know now,' she murmured. 'But I did think he 'ad better taste than that.'

'Yeah, she were a bit of a tart, weren't she? All that bleached hair and red lipstick.' Ruby shuddered. 'You're well out of it, gel.'

Ivy didn't feel well out of it. Her emotions were jumbled and conflicting: hurt and heartsore one minute, furious and vengeful the next. 'Thanks, Ruby, you've been a real mate, but I wanna go home now.'

'Not like that, you're not. Peggy will know immediately that you're upset, and unless you want to go through it all again, I reckon we ought to go back to mine until you feel a bit better.'

Ivy realised this was good advice, so she nodded and they turned away from the Crown and headed off, arm in arm.

19

Peggy stirred hot water in with the mash for the chickens and handed the bowl to Ron, then tidied up the mess Daisy had made of her breakfast, cleaned her face and hands and set her on the floor. There was something going on in this house, and she was determined to find out what it was before the day was out.

She sat down at the table and watched Daisy pushing her wheeled horse about while Cordelia read her newspaper and Ron clattered about in the chicken coop outside. Ivy had called from a telephone box last night to say she was staying at Ruby's and not to worry because she'd borrow Ruby's spare working boots and overalls for the morning. There had been something in her voice that had alerted Peggy, but when she'd asked if everything was all right, the girl had quickly replied that of course it was and hung up.

Peggy sipped her tea, her fretfulness now centred on Dorry. She'd been pale when she'd first come down for breakfast, had eaten very little and said almost nothing before she'd gone back up to her room. Ron had noticed, too, for she'd caught him watching Doreen and seen the concern in his eyes.

Peggy scrubbed her face with her hands and

gave a deep sigh. She had to be at the Town Hall later this morning to do her stint with the WVS, and there was a great pile of washing to get through first. She finished her tea and went down into the basement to light the boiler and start sorting through the laundry. It might not be Monday, but the washing stacked up during the week, what with all the work clothes and Daisy's nappies, and she liked to be clear of it before the weekend. But she hated wash days, especially when she hadn't had much sleep and there were so many things to fret over.

The hot water gushed into the large stone sink and she added the soap powder, swirling it around with a wooden stick to get the lumps out. The whites could be left to soak for a while until the water cooled enough to put her hands in, so she exited the steamy atmosphere of the scullery and went outside to talk to Ron.

'There's something the matter with Dorry,' she said without preamble. 'And with Ivy. I don't suppose you know anything about it, do you?'

Ron shook his head and eased his back as the chickens pecked away at the mash, and Harvey stretched out on the sun-warmed garden path to watch them. 'Ivy's probably had a falling-out with her fireman,' he said. 'You know what girls are like at that age.'

'Only too well,' Peggy replied, remembering how Cissy used to fall in and out of love at the drop of a hat. 'I hope that's all it is. But I get the feeling something far more serious is troubling Dorry, and that it has nothing to do with our dear sister.'

'Why don't you ask her?' His blue eyes regarded her steadily from beneath his wayward brows.

'I tried that. She denies anything's wrong. I can hardly force her to tell me, can I?'

Ron smiled and patted her shoulder. 'You can't take everyone's troubles on those narrow shoulders, Peggy girl. Dorry and Ivy are both old enough to solve their own problems. Leave them be, is my advice. Things will sort themselves out – they always do.'

She watched as he whistled up Harvey and clumped down the path in his wellingtons to go and fetch Monty from the Anchor and take them for their walk. He was right, as always, but it was frustrating to be kept in the dark. With a sigh of acceptance, she turned back into the house and got on with her washing.

Doreen was feeling sick with nerves and thoroughly out of sorts as she sat on the bed and looked out of the window. It was now almost ten o'clock and soon she'd have to leave and meet Eddie. He wouldn't be at all happy that she couldn't give him the full amount of money he'd demanded, but perhaps there was another way to get him off her back.

She opened the leather case in which she kept her few pieces of good jewellery and plucked out the engagement ring he'd given her all those years ago. It had been pawned several times during their marriage, but she'd managed to redeem it, planning one day to give it to Evie when she turned eighteen. The small ruby was surrounded by diamonds on a gold band worn thin by wear –

although it hadn't been on her finger for more than four years.

The wedding ring was a simple, thin gold band that she still wore because it was expected of a woman who had children. It had once been too tight, but now it slipped easily from her finger. She held the two rings up to the light. They had to be worth something, surely?

Doreen carefully placed the rings in the envelope that already held the forty pounds. Dropping it into a side pocket of her handbag, she applied her make-up and brushed out her freshly washed hair, knowing that if she looked better, she'd feel more confident when it came to facing him.

She paused as she fastened her clean blouse and caressed Archie's signet ring, which lay with her grandmother's crucifix between her breasts. It was the only ring she needed now. Doing up the last button, she pulled on the neat jacket she wore to the office, smoothed down her pleated skirt and picked up her handbag. She'd seen Ron go off earlier with Harvey and his pup Monty, and watched as Peggy had wheeled the pram down the alley on her way to the Town Hall. With the others either sleeping after their night shifts or at work, there wasn't much chance of bumping into anyone and having to explain where she was going.

She went downstairs, and without first going into the kitchen to say goodbye to Cordelia, she let herself quietly out of the front door and hurried away. The Post Office would be open now, and as long as she could collect the rest of the money and hand it over, she wouldn't have to hang about. She needed to get Eddie out of Cliffehaven and out of her life as swiftly as possible.

There was no sign of him as she joined the inevitable queue, but she knew he'd arrive promptly at eleven, for he was never late when it came to collecting money. The queue edged forward and finally she reached the counter. It was a man behind it this time. 'I want to take out the balance and close the account,' she said firmly.

He scrutinised her identity card and then opened the book. 'Thirty pounds, three shilling and tuppence halfpenny,' he said. He opened the drawer and began to count out the money. 'Treating yourself to something nice?' he asked as he set it aside and stamped the passbook.

'Not particularly nice,' she replied, 'but certainly something necessary.'

He looked a bit confused by her answer but wisely made no further comment. He closed the book and tucked it away before pushing the identity card and money beneath the grille.

Doreen took the money and card and left the counter. Sitting on a chair at the front of the Post Office, she put every last halfpenny in the envelope and stuck down the flap. It was blood money as far as she was concerned, and the resentment at having to hand it over was as bitter as bile. Tucking her identity card back into her purse, she looked out of the window and saw him leaning nonchalantly against a nearby lamppost as he smoked a cigarette and ogled the passing women. The loathing made her want to throw up again, but she fought down the urge and went out to meet him.

'That's all I have,' she said as she handed the envelope over. 'Now go away and stay away.'

He tossed the cigarette away and opened the envelope. Frowning, he flicked through the notes and then plucked out the rings. 'There's only seventy-odd quid there. I told you I needed a hundred.' He fished out the rings. 'And what am I supposed to do with these?'

'They'll make up the shortfall,' she said briskly.

'Ha! Is that what you think? They're not worth a light.'

Doreen felt a cold shiver run over her spine. 'But that's a ruby and diamond, and they're both gold.'

'You're not very observant, are you, Doreen?' he said nastily. 'The wedding ring might be gold, but the ruby and diamonds are paste, the ring itself just cheap yellow-metal.' He thrust them into her hand. 'Keep them. They're no use to me.'

She clasped the rings and looked at him in bewilderment. 'But the last time I had to pawn them the stones were real enough,' she managed.

'That was before I had a copy made and sold the original.'

'But how ... when did you do that?' Her voice was tremulous as she stared back at him.

'Just before they repossessed the house.' He looked again at the money in the envelope. 'You're still thirty quid short, Doreen. So what are you going to do about it?'

'I can't do anything,' she said. 'I have nothing of any value, and that's all my savings. If you don't believe me, go into the Post Office and ask the man behind the counter.'

He regarded her as he slipped the envelope into his jacket pocket. 'What's that round your neck?'

She instinctively put a protective hand to her throat. 'Just the chain and crucifix I inherited from my grandmother. The only value they have is sentimental.'

'I seem to remember they were eighteen carat gold,' he replied, and his hand whipped out to snatch the chain and rip it from her neck.

'No!' she cried out in distress. 'No, Eddie, you can't have that!'

He pushed her away as he dangled the chain from his fingers and greedily eyed Archie's signet ring. He felt the weight of it and grinned. 'Now that's more like it,' he said, slipping it free of the chain and dropping it into his pocket. 'Here, you can have the other rubbish.'

Doreen was in tears as he dropped the broken chain and little crucifix at her feet. 'Please, Eddie, don't take that ring. I'll get the money somehow, I promise,' she sobbed.

Eddie's smile was smug as he patted his pocket. 'I haven't got time to hang about here waiting for something that's never going to materialise. I've got a train to catch. See you around, Doreen.' He mockingly tipped his hat at her and then strode away towards the station.

'Are you all right, ma'am?'

Doreen's tears blinded her as she looked up from scrabbling on the ground for her chain and crucifix and let the young GI help her up. 'I'm fine, but thank you.'

'Was that guy bothering you, ma'am?' His

387

expression was deeply concerned.

'No more than usual,' she muttered, trying desperately to stem her tears. 'I'm all right, really.'

'Well you don't look all right to me, ma'am,' he persisted. 'I think we should call the cops.'

'No, please don't do that. It was just a domestic set-to, and I'm fine, really I am.' She brushed past him and started to run. She didn't know where she was going, knew only that she needed to find somewhere that was quiet and private so she could give in to the tears and the anguish of losing Archie's precious ring.

Havelock Gardens were quiet at this time of day, and Doreen staggered along the cinder path until she reached the old rose arbour that was almost hidden in the far western corner. She'd often come here to play as a child because she loved the peacefulness and the smell of the roses, and now she slumped down on the bench, buried her face in her hands and wept for all that she'd lost.

Ivy and Ruby came out of the factory together, studiously avoiding Fat Beryl, who'd been smirking at them ever since she'd come on to her shift. They didn't rise to her loud and nasty comments, but just kept on walking.

'What you gunna do about tonight?' asked Ruby as they headed for the gate.

'I dunno, but I won't be going to the dance, that's for sure,' Ivy said gloomily.

'Then why don't you come to ours for yer tea? Mum did ask you last night, and there's plenty of it.'

Ivy had been mulling the invitation over for most of the day. 'Are you sure she don't mind? Only I already spent the night once, and she might be getting fed up with me.'

'Don't be daft. Mum likes 'aving you around, and it'll be better than you moping about at Beach View all night trying to avoid Peggy's questions.'

Ivy gave a wan smile. 'Yeah, I reckon it would. Thanks, Ruby. You're a real pal.'

'Right, well go off and get changed and be back at ours as soon as you can. And bring yer night things and stuff for tomorrow. The bed's already been made, so you might as well stay another night and then we can have our day off together.'

Ivy hugged her friend and felt slightly lighter in spirit as she headed down the hill. She was still hurt and bewildered by Andy's deceit, and the last thing she wanted to do now was walk past the fire station in case he was there. She took the long back route and emerged on the main road that led up from the seafront, then quickly walked down the alleyway.

Peggy and Cordelia were in the kitchen and tea was on the go. 'I'm sorry, Auntie Peg, but Ruby and her mum have asked me to go to theirs for tea,' Ivy said breathlessly on her way to the hall. 'I'll be staying the night again as well, so don't worry about me.'

Peggy's reply was indistinct as she took the stairs two at a time and went into the bedroom. Rita wasn't there, but that was all right. She knew the truth about Andy Rawlings now and didn't need to hear it again from Rita.

She stepped over the discarded clothes on the floor and then sat on the unmade bed to take off her borrowed boots and socks before she stripped off Ruby's shirt and dungarees. It would have been better if she could have washed them before she gave them back, but there wasn't time, so she bundled them into a string bag she managed to unearth from the jumble at the bottom of the wardrobe. She'd do them tomorrow, at Ruby's.

She had a quick strip wash, brushed out her hair and changed into a pair of nice slacks she'd bought at a local jumble sale and topped them off with a blouse and hand-knitted sweater her mum had sent her last week. A dash of face powder, a swish of mascara and a swipe of lipstick, then she bundled her nightclothes and wash bag in with her borrowed work clothes. She was ready.

'Can't stop,' she said as she raced through the kitchen. 'I'm already late. See you sometime tomorrow.'

Peggy stood in the doorway and watched Ivy run down the alleyway and disappear from view. 'I don't know what's got into everyone today,' she muttered as she went back up the steps to the kitchen.

'What it is to be young,' sighed Cordelia. 'Dashing here and dashing there, so busy and full of energy. It quite tires me out.'

'Mmm,' said Peggy, who interpreted all this charging round as subterfuge to hide things from her. 'There's too much of it about for my liking,' she said darkly.

Cordelia smiled and fiddled with her hearing

aid. 'At least we got this fixed yesterday,' she said. 'So it's not all bad.'

Peggy looked at the clock, wondering where Dorry and Ron had got to. It wasn't like either of them to be out this late without telling her. She called up to Sarah and Fran that tea was almost ready and checked on the pork and dumpling stew. The dumplings didn't look very appetising because they were a muddy sort of brown from the wheatmeal flour and therefore probably full of inedible bits that would get stuck in her teeth. But it would be rich and filling and set them up for the night, and that was all that really mattered.

Queenie came in from the garden and demanded to be fed, so Peggy saw to that, and then started to drain the vegetables. As Sarah and Fran came down to help, she looked at the clock again and frowned. Where on earth had Ron and Dorry got to?

Doreen had lost track of time in Havelock Gardens. The tears had flowed, releasing all the anguish she'd stored up since losing Archie in that terrifying tunnel, and she'd found that although she was utterly drained, she did feel better for it.

She sat there in the peace and quiet, listening to the birds in the trees and the mewling gulls, her gaze travelling over the lines of vegetables that had replaced the lovely rose garden she remembered from her youth. There was early blossom in the trees and a few tulips and daffodils had managed to survive the transformation into an allotment, so not all was lost.

391

As the sun slowly moved across the sky, she left the garden and began to walk towards the winding tracks that led up the steep hill to where the old windmill used to be. She wasn't really wearing the appropriate shoes or clothing, but she didn't care. She just needed to be alone, to lick her wounds and restore the resolve that had seen her through the toughest times before.

It was mid-afternoon by the time she reached the top of the hill. The windmill was gone now, and there were only a few broken bits of stone and metal scraps to mark the place that had once been a popular local landmark. She sat on a tussock of grass and looked out over the town and towards the sea, remembering how her parents had brought her and her sisters up here for picnics.

Her father had never quite managed to fly a kite, but her mother had made daisy chains for them all, and they'd gone on treasure hunts in the ruins, learning the names of all the wild flowers and the creatures that lived up here. Later, when she was growing fast and becoming restless, Ron would bring her up here and talk about the old days when the monks would come from their abbey to have their wheat milled. They were good memories, ones that were worth storing so that when she felt like this, she could bring them out like a wonderful picture book and once again be that little girl.

She finally looked at her watch and realised with shock that it was almost five, and Peggy would be wondering where on earth she'd got to. She dug her handkerchief out of her handbag and used her compact mirror to help her see to clean her face. The morning's careful application of make-up had been a waste of time, she realised, for her tears had washed it all away.

She was about to get to her feet when Harvey came tearing over the brow of the hill with short barks of delight. 'Hello, boy,' she said, making a fuss of him. 'What are you doing here on your own? Where's Ron?'

'I'm here,' he panted, appearing over the brow.

'This isn't your usual walk, is it?' she said as he plumped down beside her and tried to catch his breath.

'Too steep, so it is. But I've been trying to find you for half the day and this was the last place on my list.'

'But why were you looking for me?' She felt a pang of alarm. 'Nothing's happened back at Beach View, has it?'

'No, no, nothing like that,' he said, reaching for his pipe. 'But I'm thinking 'tis you that has experienced trouble today.'

She looked back at him as his bright blue eyes held her. 'I don't know what you mean,' she stammered.

'Ach, Dorry, you always were a stubborn wee girl. Always ready to fight your own battles and not ask for help.' He lowered his voice and reached for her hand. 'But sometimes it's better to share your troubles, Dorry, for they don't seem so bad when they're out in the open.'

She realised there was little point in continuing to pretend she didn't know what he was talking about. 'How did you find out?' she asked quietly.

'Well now, there's the thing.' He sat up and lit

393

his pipe, and when he had a good fug going, he stared out towards the sea where the setting sun had almost reached the horizon. 'I knew something was very wrong when I saw that scoundrel you'd been married to walking past the Anchor. Quite a swagger he had too, with his hands in his pockets, looking very pleased with himself.'

He grimaced and puffed on his pipe. 'I would have challenged him then and there, but I was intrigued to know what he'd been up to. It was clear he'd been to the house, and I knew you were there alone, for I'd seen you return from your walk earlier.'

'Nothing much gets past you, does it, Ron?' she said fondly.

'Not a lot,' he said with a wink and a waggle of his eyebrows.

'So what did you do?'

'I waited for a while to see what you would do, for I had a fair idea you wouldn't stay long in the house once he'd left. I followed you to the Post Office and stood in the queue until I heard what you had to say to the woman behind the counter.'

'But I had no idea you were following me,' she gasped in surprise. 'How come I didn't see you when I left the house?'

'I was hiding in the shadows of that bomb site on the corner.' He looked at her from beneath his brows. 'You should have come to me, Dorry. I'd have sorted him out for you before it went as far as it did.'

'Dear Ron,' she murmured. 'I know you would have. But he's really not worth the trouble it would have got you into.'

Ron smoked his pipe and said nothing for a few minutes. 'I realised after that conversation you had with Peggy you weren't going to say anything to either of us, so I followed you again this morning,' he said eventually. His jaw tightened. 'Unfortunately I was too far away to be able to help when he snatched that necklace off you, but then that Yank stepped in, so, realising you would be all right for a bit, I carried on with the second part of my plan.'

Doreen regarded him with great affection and amusement. 'You do love plans, don't you, Ron?'

'Once a soldier always a soldier,' he replied gruffly. 'You can't do anything without having a proper plan of action.'

'I hope you didn't get the police involved,' she said sharply. 'Or challenge him in any way. He's too cunning and quick with his fists and I'd hate to see you get hurt.'

He chuckled. 'Do I look hurt? To be sure, Dorry, I might be an old man with a touch of snow on the roof, but I could snap that rat like a twig if I wanted to and walk away without a scratch. But there are better ways to get revenge.'

She was alert now, and intrigued. 'How?' she breathed.

'Let's just say that a young acquaintance of mine is very gifted when it comes to relieving people of things in their pockets, and replacing them with other things.'

'You know a pickpocket?' she gasped.

He tapped the side of his nose. 'I know people from all walks of life, Dorry. And believe me, they all have their uses.' He reached into the pocket of his scruffy tweed jacket and pressed the envelope into her hand. 'I believe this is yours.'

She burst into tears as she opened the envelope and saw Archie's ring. 'But the minute he realises what's happened he'll be back here again,' she sobbed. 'Oh, Ron, I can't thank you enough, but you've only made things worse.'

'There, there, girl, don't be fretting. To be sure I knew that, which is why I got Stan to ring through to the police in London.'

'The police?' she whispered.

'Aye, the police,' he said firmly. 'A man with counterfeit notes stuffed in his pocket is always of great interest to the police.'

'Counterfeit? But won't he notice?'

Ron shook his head. 'They're very good unless you take particular notice of the serial numbers. They're all the same, you see.'

Doreen tipped back her head and laughed, and Ron joined in as Harvey barked his approval. 'Oh, Ron, you're priceless,' she stuttered. 'Absolutely priceless.' She flung her arms round him and gave him a smacking kiss on the cheek. 'And I love you very much, you old scallywag,' she murmured against his hairy ear.

Ron tried not to look flattered, but the colour rising in his face was testament to it. 'Come on, wee girl, away with all this nonsense. Let's get home before Peggy sends out a search party. It'll be dark soon, and those shoes are not really the best thing for walking these hills.'

Doreen was still laughing as they went arm in arm down the hill with Harvey rushing ahead of them. She was blessed to have Ron and Peggy;

396

blessed to have been reunited with Archie's ring – and certainly blessed to have her two lovely little girls. And now she also had both the money and the time to go and see them.

20

Peggy wasn't quite sure whether to laugh or cry as Ron and Doreen told her about Edward Grey, but she was relieved that both of them had come through unscathed – even if Ron's methods had been highly suspect.

'I always said you were a rogue and a scoundrel,' chortled Cordelia. 'But of course there are times when that sort of behaviour is acceptable.' She smiled at Doreen. 'Let's hope he spends a nice long time at His Majesty's pleasure before he's sent off to some army camp. I'm just amazed he managed to avoid call-up in the first place.'

'He probably got a dodgy certificate from some even dodgier doctor,' said Doreen, polishing off the last of her stew. 'His gambling means he knows a lot of unsavoury people.'

'A bit like our Ron here,' said Cordelia with a twinkle in her eye.

Peggy was just clearing the dishes when there was a rap at the front door. 'I'll go. It's probably that blessed woman from the WI who keeps badgering me to join their knitting circle.'

But when she opened the door it was to find Andy Rawlings on her doorstep. 'Hello, dear,' she

397

said. 'I thought you were meeting Ivy at the dance tonight?'

'I've been waiting for 'er for over an hour,' he said fretfully. 'Isn't she 'ere?'

Peggy thought fast. 'No, she's not, dear. I'm sorry.'

He looked so crestfallen that her soft heart relented. 'Have you two had a falling-out?' she asked.

'Not to my knowledge. Everything was fine the last time we met up, and we've been planning this night since last week and I thought she were lookin' forward to it.'

'Well, I'm sorry, Andy. But something's been up with Ivy recently. Perhaps she just didn't feel like going dancing?'

'What d'you mean, something's up with her?'

'She never said, but I know girls, and she was definitely upset over something – especially yesterday.' She looked up at him and saw that he was still very miserable. 'She had a bit of a set to with one of the other girls at the factory yesterday. I don't know what it was about, but it might have had something to do with her being out of sorts.'

He thought about this, and then his frown cleared. 'Do you know where she is, Mrs Reilly? Only I've got a horrible feeling I know what all this is about, and I need to talk to 'er.'

'What have you been up to, Andrew Rawlings?' she asked sternly, folding her arms.

'Nothing. I ain't been up to nothing, but...' He fell silent, shuffled his feet and chewed on his thumbnail for a bit, and then told her everything.

'Well, I'm not surprised she's upset,' she said sharply. 'You should have told her straight out.' She regarded his hangdog expression and gave a sigh of frustration. 'Really, you young people don't have the sense you were born with,' she said crossly. 'Get yourself up to Ruby's and tell her straight, or you'll have me to deal with.'

'Yes, Mrs Reilly. Right away, Mrs Reilly.' He turned on the steps and got halfway down before he turned back to her again. 'Where does Ruby live, Mrs Reilly?'

Peggy gave him the address in Mafeking Terrace and shook her head as he went charging down the road. 'The Lord help us,' she murmured. 'Men can be so dense at times.'

'Who was that?' asked Cordelia.

'Just someone for Ivy.'

'Oh. I was rather hoping it might be Bertie. He hasn't called for a while now, and I miss his company.'

'I'm sure he'll be in touch soon enough,' Peggy said consolingly. 'He's probably been playing more golf now the weather's improved, and finds he's too tired at the end of the day to go visiting.'

'No stamina, that's his problem,' muttered Cordelia. 'Men were different in my day. They could hunt in the morning, play golf in the afternoon and dance the night away.'

'Not when they're as old as Bertie Double-Barrelled,' rumbled Ron around his pipe stem.

'He's younger than me,' Cordelia protested.

'Exactly,' he retorted.

Peggy lit a cigarette and exchanged a knowing look with Doreen. Life at Beach View was back to normal – if one could describe such goings-on as normal.

Ivy and Ruby were doing the washing-up so that Ethel could put her feet up and enjoy her glass of gin while Mike and Stan went into the other room to warm up the wireless and get the fire going so they could all be cosy.

'That were a lovely tea,' said Ivy as she dried the plates and carefully stacked them in the cupboard. 'I'm full to bursting.'

'Yeah, Mum knows how to cook all right now she's got something proper to deal with. It was all scrag end and leftover veg from the market back in Bow.' Ruby finished the last few bits of cutlery and dried her hands. 'What about your mum?'

'She does all right too, but like yours, there were never much to get fancy with.' Ivy dried another plate and gave a deep sigh. 'I wonder if Andy went to the dance with that girl?'

'You gotta stop worrying about it, Ivy, or you'll go mad.' Ruby took the tea towel away from her and unfastened the apron round her waist. 'Come on, let's have a drop of Mum's gin and listen to *ITMA* on the wireless. It's me favourite.'

They went into the front room to find Ethel happily ensconced in her favourite armchair, fag in the corner of her mouth, glass of gin in her hand. Stan was comfortably settled in the matching chair and Mike was on the couch beneath the big bay window. Ruby poured two hefty slugs of gin into some glasses and they sat down next to Mike just as Tommy Handley announced, 'It's That Man Again' to a thunder of applause from the studio audience.

The loud knock on the door annoyed them all, and with a great sigh, Stan got up to see who was interrupting his favourite comedy programme. There was a murmur of voices and then he came back into the room. 'It's for you, Ivy,' he said as he plumped back into his chair.

'Who is it?'

'That young fellow of yours. You can't leave him standing out there, so take him into the kitchen.'

'He's got nothing to say that I wanna hear,' Ivy said, folding her arms. 'Tell 'im to sling 'is hook.'

'Tell him yourself, Ivy,' he said mildly. 'I'm not a messenger boy.'

Ivy reddened and apologised, then stomped into the hall. Andy was standing on the doorstep looking very sorry for himself – as he jolly well should. 'I don't wanna see you, Andy, so go away.'

'But there's something I gotta tell yer, Ivy.'

'I ain't interested in anything you got to say,' she snapped. She went to close the door on him, but a size twelve boot was suddenly blocking it. 'Get yer foot outta there, or I'll have Stan and Mike come and make you,' she threatened.

'I ain't moving it until you've heard me out, Ivy Tucker. I know what you think, and you got it all wrong.'

She whipped the door back again and glared at him. 'Oh yeah? So telling me lies about being on duty is all right then, is it?'

'I can explain that,' he said urgently.

'What about the blonde piece I saw you with last night? How do you explain that?' she stormed.

'I can explain all of it if only you'd calm down

and give me a chance,' he said in exasperation.

Ivy felt a twinge of hope, but she wasn't about to fall for any old flannel. 'That weren't the first time you was seen at the Crown with her, neither,' she said flatly. 'So, go on then. Explain that away.'

'Ivy,' he sighed. 'Can we do this indoors? It's brass monkeys out 'ere.'

'You'll stay where you are and lump it,' she retorted. 'Now get on with what you gotta say before I get bored and shut this door.'

'I didn't lie to you about being on night shift,' he said hurriedly. 'I just didn't tell you I had to take a couple of shifts off.'

Ivy regarded him stonily.

He cleared his throat. 'There was a family crisis, and I was needed to help.'

'Oh, yeah? I suppose the next thing you're gunna say is that that blonde tart is your sister. Well, pull the other one, mate, because from where I was standin' that wasn't brotherly love you were show-in' her.'

'Ivy, will you shut up and listen to me?' he shouted.

She flinched at his loud voice and took a step back. He was big and angry, and she didn't like the way he was looming over her.

'Is everything all right out here?' said Stan from the front room doorway.

Andy let out a long sigh and relaxed. 'It's fine, Stan. I just need Ivy to shut her gob for five minutes and hear me out.'

'Best of luck on that one,' said Stan with a know-ing smile, and went back into the front room and closed the door.

'Gloria Stevens who owns the Crown is my dad's sister,' Andy said before Ivy could open her mouth. 'Her son were killed in the Far East, and the "blonde tart" as you so delicately put it, is his young widow.'

A chastened Ivy could only stare at him.

'Betty come down the other day and of course were in pieces. She's got two kids, her house in Stepney has been flattened in a raid, and both her parents were killed in the Blitz,' he rattled on. 'She's at her wits' end. So she come to stay with Gloria, and I've been trying to 'elp find a place for her and the kids so she can settle here more permanent like. Gloria was happy to put them up in the pub, but Betty didn't want 'er kids to hear all the noise and the language and such.' He took a breath finally, and reddened. 'Auntie Glo can get a bit boisterous with so many men about,' he finished.

'Poor girl,' Ivy breathed. 'I'm so sorry, Andy. But Fat Beryl said ... and I saw ... and...'

'You put two and two together and come up with eight.' His expression was grim. 'I thought you trusted me, Ivy, like I trust you. I'm hurt to know you thinks so little of me.'

'I'm sorry, Andy. I did trust you, honest. But when I saw you last night...'

'I tried to get to see you at work, but they wouldn't let me through the gates, so I asked Rita to tell you what was 'appening. Didn't she give you the message?'

'Peggy said she had something to tell me, but we've been like ships passing in the night and never got to talk about anything.' She looked up at

403

him through her tears. 'I'm ever so sorry, Andy.'

'You soppy little mare,' he murmured as he looked down at her, his expression softening. He reached out and cupped his large hand over her cheek and slowly drew her towards him. 'Oh, Ivy,' he sighed. 'What am I going to do about you, gel?'

She blinked away her tears and raised her face to him. 'Kiss and make up?' she said hopefully.

He swept her into his arms and kissed her so thoroughly that her head was swimming by the time he'd put her back on her feet. 'Can I come in now?' he asked. 'It's flamin' freezing out 'ere.'

She took his hand and led him along the narrow hall to the dining room, where they could close the door on the world and make up for all the silly misunderstandings so they could begin again.

It had taken five days to get all the travel permits in place for her trip to Wales, and tonight would be Doreen's last at Beach View until the end of the war. She'd sent a telegram to Mrs Fletcher to tell her she could let out her room, for she wouldn't be returning to Fort Halstead. There would be work in Wales once she'd relocated to a larger community than the hamlet where her children now lived. She'd miss Veronica and the excitement of developing that bouncing bomb and all the other new munitions, but her priorities had changed now and there were more important things to concentrate on.

As she slowly walked along Camden Road in a daze of happiness, she knew that this small seaside town was where she really belonged, and that one day she would achieve her dream and buy a house right here, close to Peggy and Ron and the family that she loved. This was her home, and she knew she would return with her children to make a settled life for them all by the sea, just as Archie had envisioned.

She walked up the hill and along the twitten to the back gate of Beach View. Pausing, she looked up at the window, knowing that behind it was a warm, welcoming kitchen, the true heart of her family home, made special by Peggy's love and care.

Doreen experienced an overwhelming sense of joy as she softly placed her hand on her stomach and lifted her gaze to the sky.

'Our child will be my sweetest memory of you, Archie,' she whispered. 'Watch over us, my darling, and know that I'll always love you.'

Dear Reader

I hope you enjoyed reading *Sweet Memories of You,* and although it is quite a sad story, I think it has been lightened by the antics of Ron and Harvey who continue to thwart Peggy and cause chaos at every turn. I was delighted to be able to pass Ron's bravery award onto Harvey as the Dickin medal had yet to be established, indeed the first one was given to a carrier pigeon at the end of 1943. We sometimes forget that many animals gave their lives during both the World Wars so that we humans could survive – and their work and bravery is ongoing as our world continues to be divided by conflict.

As I write the series, I'm aware of all the stories that still have to be told, and of the characters I have mentioned but never fully explored. Doreen was one such character, and as Peggy's younger sister, it was time to tell her tale. The Atlantic convoys braved mountainous seas, U-boats and aerial attacks and far too many brave men lost their lives bringing vital supplies to our shores, and although Archie survived that onslaught, he was no match for the lethal crush on those stairs leading down to the unfinished tube station. It is Doreen's stoicism which pulls her through, and of course the love and warmth of Peggy and her family home which helps to heal her.

I hope you continue to enjoy the *Beach View Boarding House* series, and I welcome you to join me as the Reilly family and their evacuees continue to battle against the odds towards victory. In the next book, we'll be following the story of Wren, April Wilton as she overcomes prejudice, pain and disgrace and learns the true meaning of love.

Ellie x

History notes

Bethnal Green tube station was still unfinished in March 1943, and as it was so deep underground, it was used by the East Enders as an air-raid shelter. It was large enough to accommodate two thousand people, and the council erected hundreds of bunk beds, a lending library and even a hall for putting on entertainment.

The local councillors were very concerned that the entranceway was too narrow for the number of people who used it as a shelter, and repeatedly applied to the government to have it enlarged. All requests were refused. The stairs had no central railings and were not marked, so it was difficult to see anything in the dim light of a single 25-watt bulb which had been partially painted black to comply with the blackout ruling.

The full horror of the disaster at Bethnal Green tube station on 3 March 1943 was deliberately kept from the general public, and the survivors were warned not to talk about it, since the government decided it could be used as propaganda by the enemy and would be bad for British morale. A total of 173 people died on that late evening, including 62 children.

The day after the disaster the council erected central handrails, the entrance was widened and the edge of each step was painted white. There were several investigations into what had happened, but the Official Secrets Act meant that none of the details were available to the public until very recently.

A small memorial plaque was placed by the entrance to the tube station in the 1990s, and in 2007 a project was set up to build a lasting and more fitting memorial to the civilians who died that night. Work began on the Stairway to Heaven Memorial in 2012, which, through determined fundraising, is now almost completed.

If you would like to donate to this very deserving commemoration, then log onto Stairway to Heaven Memorial Trust at www.stairwaytoheavenmemorial.org and click on the donate button.

A Map of Cliffehaven

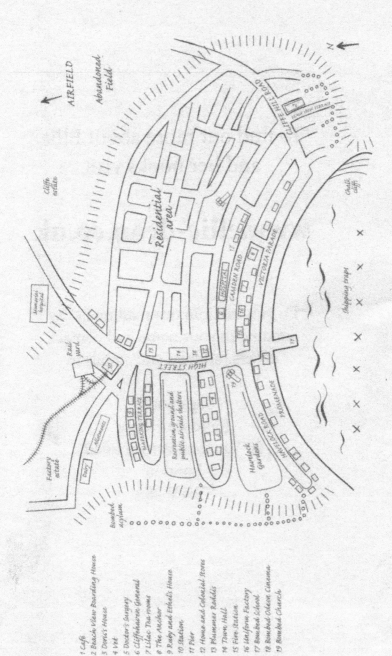

AIRFIELD

Abandoned Field

Cliffe estate

CLIFFE HILL ROAD

BEACH VIEW TERRACE

Residential area

Chalk cliffs

Shipping traps

HOSPITAL

CAMDEN ROAD

VICTORIA PARADE

Municipal hospital

Rail yard

Factory estate

Dairy

Allotments

MAFEKING TERRACE

HIGH STREET

Recreation ground and public air-raid shelter

Havelock Gardens

PROMENADE

HAVELOCK ROAD

Bombed asylum

1 Café
2 Beach View Boarding House
3 Doris's House
4 Vet
5 Doctor's surgery
6 Cliffehaven general
7 Lilac Tea-rooms
8 The Anchor
9 Ruby and Ethel's House
10 Station
11 Pier
12 Home and Colonial Stores
13 Plummer Raddis
14 Town Hall
15 Fire Station
16 Uniform Factory
17 Bombed School
18 Bombed Odeon Cinema
19 Bombed Church

This Large Print Book for the partially sighted, who cannot read normal print, is published under the auspices of

THE ULVERSCROFT FOUNDATION